PAM WEAVER

THE RUNAWAY ORPHANS

Published by AVON
A division of HarperCollins*Publishers*
1 London Bridge Street
London SE1 9GF

www.harpercollins.co.uk

HarperCollins*Publishers*
1st Floor, Watermarque Building, Ringsend Road
Dublin 4, Ireland

A Paperback Original 2022
1

First published in Great Britain by HarperCollins*Publishers* 2022

ISBN: 978-0-00-836623-0

Typeset in Sabon LT Std by Palimpsest Book Production Limited, Falkirk, Stirlingshire

Printed and bound in the UK using 100% renewable electricity at CPI Group (UK) Ltd

MIX
Paper from
responsible sources
FSC™ C007454

www.fsc.org

This book is produced from independently certified FSC™ paper
to ensure responsible forest management.

For more information visit: www.harpercollins.co.uk/green

This book is dedicated to the boys (and girls) in blue who still put their lives on the line to keep this country safe. I should also like to give a particular mention to one special member of the Royal Air Force, Anton, the man who has made my daughter very happy.

CHAPTER 1

Amy

The minute Amy heard his key turn in the front door her heart started beating faster. She lay very still listening to muffled voices in the hall. He said something to Mrs Scott, probably something like, 'Are the girls all right?' Her reply was short. 'Fine, no problems.'

He thanked her and after a short pause, probably while he helped Mrs Scott into her coat, she heard him say, 'Thank you,' and the door clicked shut.

Amy knew then that there were no other adults in the house.

She was already beginning to tremble. How long before he came up the stairs? How long before he came into her room? How long before . . .?

She whimpered and held her breath. It was hard to hear over the thudding of her own blood in her ears. When she'd calmed a little and he still hadn't come, she heard him moving around downstairs. Getting himself a whiskey, perhaps? He sometimes smelled of whiskey when he leaned

1

over her. She hated that smell. Oh please don't let him smell of whiskey tonight.

It seemed like an age before she heard his footstep on the stairs. He went to her sister's room first. Lillian must be asleep because she didn't say anything, not even when the door squeaked as he pulled it firmly shut.

Amy stared at the knob on her own bedroom door. It began to slowly turn, the light from the hallway flooding over the rosebud wallpaper. Horrible, horrible rosebud wallpaper. How could she have been so deceived?

When Meryl left home, Amy had been so excited when he'd suggested that she move into her older sister's room.

'You can choose new wallpaper,' he'd said. 'This is your room now. Your very own bedroom.'

She remembered how she'd pored over the wallpaper books until she'd found the perfect design. Pretty pink rosebuds draped over small wooden trellises. She'd wondered if he would let her have it. It was so different from the one her older sister, Meryl, had chosen when she'd been in this room.

'We'll put it up together,' he'd said, and she'd hugged him delightedly.

Until now, Amy had never really wondered why Meryl had gone. One day she was there and the next she wasn't. She hadn't come home from school and Daddy had said she had got a 'live-in' situation and wouldn't be coming back. Amy was a bit peeved that she hadn't even said goodbye. It was a bit odd because Meryl and Daddy had been so close. Amy could see how sad he was and she'd wanted to make him happy again. Maybe, he'd suggested when the room was almost done, maybe Amy would be his special little girl now? She'd agreed of course, and he'd given her a kiss, but it wasn't the usual sort of kiss and she didn't like it.

As his head came round the door, she pulled the sheet up to her face. Her stomach was in knots and she could hardly breathe. She felt sick. She knew what was coming.

'Hello, sweetheart. Daddy's home. Now where's my special kiss?'

CHAPTER 2

Norah

Worthing, Christmas Day, 1938

> *'And if you care to hear "The Swanee River"*
> *Played in ragtime*
> *Come on and hear*
> *Come on and hear*
> *Alexander's Ragtime Band . . .'*

Humming to the music on the radio, Norah Kirkwood slid the roasting pan back into the oven and closed the door with her hip.

The kitchen door squeaked open. 'Can I do anything to help?'

Norah switched off the radio and turned to grin as her younger sister Rene walked in. 'Nearly finished,' she said, 'but you can help me dish up, if you like.'

Rene took an apron from the hook on the back of the door and came towards her. 'Smells good.'

She was a pretty girl, twenty-two, mousy blonde and with

a cheeky smile. On the other hand, Norah, almost four years her senior, had dark hair and a mass of curls, the envy of both her sister and Elsie, their mother.

Norah speared the carrots in a pan on the top of the stove. 'They're done,' she said, leaning back so that Rene could take the pan to the sink and drain it. 'What are they all doing in there?'

'The usual,' said Rene, hot steam billowing around her as she tipped the carrots into a colander. 'Dad's looking at yesterday's paper, Jim is cracking the nuts and Mum is listening to all Mrs Kirkwood's woes.'

Norah grimaced. 'Oh dear, poor Mum.'

'Honestly, sis,' Rene said, 'I don't know how you put up with her.'

'Neither do I,' Norah quipped as she heaved the chicken out of the roasting pan and laid it on the carving plate. 'I must be a ruddy saint.'

As her sister laughed, Norah glanced across to the window. Two woodpigeons were shouldering each other off the bird table in the garden. Silly things. There was plenty there for all, but there they were squabbling over a few seeds while their companion on the ground underneath the table was gobbling up everything in sight. Norah smiled. How she loved it here; a bit of the country in the middle of the town. She and her husband, Jim, came to Worthing when they got married in 1933 and they'd lived in The Lilacs ever since. It came with a long garden which, in Victorian times, had been converted into a market garden. She planned to continue the work and perhaps expand. The gardening was enjoyable but it didn't yield enough to be a commercial concern. The space was quite simply too small to give them both a good living, so while

Norah carried on with the market garden, Jim stayed in the police force.

Rene still lived with their parents and worked in London where their father was a bus driver. Ambitious, she had just been promoted to senior salesgirl in a department store, but never one to rest on her laurels, she was also taking night classes in shorthand and typing.

Norah set about making the gravy in the empty roasting tin now resting on the hob, while Rene dished up the home-grown Brussels sprouts and cabbage.

They worked together in silence for the next few minutes. Norah put the roast potatoes onto a serving dish and placed the chicken at the head of the table for Jim to carve while Rene arranged the vegetable dishes before she went to call the rest of the family to the table. Norah smiled to herself as she heard the family coming. She loved this time of year.

She had taken over the Christmas celebrations from her mother the year she got married and it never varied. Pete Carson, her dad, would drive all the way down from London early on Christmas morning with Mum and Rene in the car and a boot full of presents. This year he had brought their dog, Max, as well. 'Mrs Reynolds next door says she'll feed the budgie,' Dad had said as they arrived. 'The bird is quite happy on his own but I can't leave the dog all day.'

Rene always complained about the early start but Dad said that with the Christmas rush over, the traffic was a lot less on the day and he preferred it that way. As she watched her family assemble around the kitchen table, Norah wondered if this would be the last Christmas they would share. Times were uncertain. Prime Minister Neville Chamberlain had come back in September with the Munich Agreement, but despite the piece of paper on which the British people conceded that the German-speaking Sudetenland was now part of Germany, talk of war hadn't gone away. If anything, her occasional work with the Women's Voluntary Service of the Air Raid Precaution, now known as the WVS, had convinced her that the government was saying one thing while preparing for quite another.

'This looks good enough to eat,' said Dad as he lowered himself onto a chair. Nobody laughed. They'd heard the same joke every Christmas for years.

'Can I do anything, dear?' said Elsie as her daughter filled the gravy boat and lobbed the dirty roasting pan into the sink.

'It's all in hand, Mum,' said Rene. 'You sit down next to Dad and enjoy yourself.'

Norah's husband, Jim, came into the room with Mrs Kirkwood on his arm. 'Here we are, Mother,' he said cheerfully. 'You sit here.'

Norah's mother-in-law looked around disapprovingly and sniffed. 'I can't sit with my back to the window,' she declared. 'The draught will play havoc with my rheumatism.'

'The window isn't even open,' Rene pointed out.

'I don't mind moving,' Elsie said.

Rene pursed her lips as her mother moved to the other side of the table and Mrs Kirkwood – with a great deal of huffing and puffing – sat in the vacant chair.

Jim came over to the stove to collect the plates from the rack above the hob where they were keeping warm. It was a real treat to have him home for most of the day. He usually had to be on duty on Christmas Day, but this year he had been lucky enough to be given the evening shift. That meant he didn't have to go to the station until six o'clock. He bent to kiss Norah's cheek. 'Thanks, love. Looks like you've done us proud.' Taking the plates to the head of the table he began to carve the golden chicken. Max, who had been curled up on the mat in front of the fire, came to the table and looked up at him with a hopeful expression.

'Max, go to your bed,' Dad said sharply.

The dog slunk miserably away and lay on a blanket they had put by the door.

'Not too much for me, dear,' said Mrs Kirkwood. 'I've the appetite of a bird.'

For the next few minutes everyone occupied themselves with filling their plates. It was followed by a silence as they savoured their first few mouthfuls.

'This is delicious.'

'The chicken is lovely and tender.'

'Really? My bit is gristly.'

'Shall I give you another slice, Mother?'

Mrs Kirkwood put her hand up. 'It's all right, James. I'm not one to make a fuss.' As she lowered her head towards her plate again, Rene rolled her eyes and pulled a face, Norah and her mother struggled not to giggle. Jim gave his mother another slice of chicken anyway.

'Oh, I forgot me Brussels sprouts,' said Dad. 'Pass me the dish, would you, love?'

'I hear you've joined the WVS,' said Elsie, passing the dish.

'I haven't actually joined,' said Norah. 'I just help out occasionally. It's a bit difficult to commit myself to anything more permanent as there's always so much to do, but when I can go I quite enjoy it.'

When she wasn't working in the garden, Norah was making preserves. Her kitchen dresser positively groaned with jars of jam; strawberry, raspberry, plum and blackcurrant. And if she wasn't making jams, it was chutney and pickles; marrow, beetroot, pickled red cabbage, onions and cucumbers, the list went on and on.

'Do you get a uniform?' Rene asked.

Norah chuckled and made her eyes go bigger. 'Oh I do, I do.'

'What's it like?' asked Rene.

The dog sneaked his way back under the table.

'Actually, not too bad as uniforms go,' said Norah. 'At least I'll be nice and warm in winter. It's a green tweed jacket and skirt with a red blouse. They've just issued a badge to go on the jacket, but I haven't got round to sewing mine on yet.'

'I'm sure you'll look very smart, dear,' said Elsie.

'And what exactly does the WVS do?' asked Pete, sneaking the dog a bit of chicken skin.

'Apparently we'll be doing all sorts,' said Norah. 'Right now, I've been paired up with a girl called Penny Draycot and as soon as Christmas is over, we have to go all around Worthing to collect the names of anyone who would be willing to give children from London a home.'

Elsie looked puzzled. 'What, adopt them?'

'No, Mum,' said Norah, 'but if we do go to war, they reckon Hitler will bomb London first, so the plan is to move all the children to places of safety before it happens.'

'But there won't be a war,' Mrs Kirkwood said crossly. 'Mr Chamberlain said so.'

'Let's hope he's right, Mrs Kirkwood,' said Pete, 'but I'm not so sure myself.'

Mrs Kirkwood harrumphed.

'If there is a war,' said Rene, 'I shall join one of the women's services.'

'Oh,' said Norah, 'which one?'

'Well, I did fancy the ATS but I like the WAAF uniform best.'

'Only a woman would think of something like that,' Jim said with a chuckle.

'Quite right, too,' said Rene, feigning indignation. 'I don't want to walk around looking like some old frump, do I?' She rubbed her last piece of potato around her plate to use up the rest of the gravy. 'The men look pretty dishy, too.'

Mrs Kirkwood tutted her disapproval. 'It's not right; young unmarried women mixing with all those men,' she said. 'Just asking for trouble.'

'I can't think why,' Rene said, looking wide-eyed and innocent.

'You know very well what I mean,' Mrs Kirkwood went on. 'All that temptation.'

Rene looked around the table. 'And what temptation would that be, Mrs Kirkwood?'

'That's enough, love,' said Elsie. 'Take no notice, Mrs Kirkwood. She knows perfectly well what you mean.'

'More cabbage, anyone?' said Norah. 'And there's still some roast potatoes left.'

'Well,' said Mrs Kirkwood, 'perhaps just one more potato.'

Everyone else shook their heads. 'I need to leave a bit of room for Mum's Christmas pudding,' said Rene. 'Christmas wouldn't be Christmas without that.'

Elsie looked down and blushed modestly.

When Mrs Kirkwood had finished, the two sisters cleared the table and then Rene put the plates out while Norah turned the home-made Christmas pudding out of the basin. Lovely and dark and smelling wonderful, it brought back memories of Christmases past when they were children.

Jim, who had gone into the sitting room, came back with the brandy bottle. Norah poured some over the pudding, struck a match and carried the pudding covered in a blue flame to the table. Everybody – except Mrs Kirkwood – clapped.

Norah began dishing it out.

'A small piece for me,' said Mrs Kirkwood. Rene bent to pick up her fallen napkin as she repeated, 'I have the appetite of a bird.'

'Yes, like a ruddy eagle,' Rene whispered out of the corner of her mouth.

Norah nudged her and had to suck in her lips to stop herself laughing. 'Is that piece all right, Mrs Kirkwood?'

They passed the custard round and everybody tucked in.

'Superb, love,' said Pete, kissing his fingers extravagantly. 'This is the best pudding ever.'

'Delicious.'

'Maybe you should turn your hand to making your own Christmas puddings, Norah,' said Mrs Kirkwood, 'but I don't suppose you have time if you're in this WVC thing? How long are you doing it for?'

'It's WVS, Mrs Kirkwood,' said Norah, 'and I suppose that I'll do it for as long as is necessary. Like I said, it's voluntary. It's not as if I've signed up in the way Rene plans to do.'

'I should think not,' said Mrs Kirkwood. 'You have a duty to look after your husband.'

With a smile tugging at the corner of her mouth, Norah glanced at Jim. 'You're not feeling too neglected, are you, dear?'

Jim pretended to ponder the question.

'In fact,' Mrs Kirkwood continued coldly, 'I think it's time both you girls behaved like respectable women.'

11

Norah blinked in surprise. 'Excuse me . . .?'

Mrs Kirkwood arched an eyebrow as the light-hearted banter ended and an awkward atmosphere descended on the table.

'What's that supposed to mean?' Rene challenged.

'You can get off your high horse, young lady. I'm only pointing it out.'

'Nobody asked you for your opinion,' Rene snapped.

'It needs to be said,' Mrs Kirkwood continued. 'WVS indeed. Your place is in the home.'

'I think we should call a halt to this conversation now, Mother,' said Jim.

'Oh no, Jim,' said Rene, her cheeks quite pink, 'if she's got something to say, let her come out with it.'

'Rene,' Elsie said helplessly. 'It's Christmas.' She laid her hand on top of Rene's but her daughter snatched it away.

'She's done nothing else but complain ever since she got here,' Rene went on. 'We shouldn't have brought the dog, she was right next to the fire in the sitting room but she was cold, she didn't want to sit by the window out here so you had to move, everybody else's dinner was lovely and tender but her chicken was tough, and now she's picking on Norah.'

'It doesn't matter, Rene,' said Norah.

'Oh but it does,' Rene retorted. 'So, come on, Mrs High and Mighty, let's be having it.'

Mrs Kirkwood sneered. 'I might have expected an over-blown reaction like this from the likes of you,' she said. 'The only reason you're going to join the WAAF is because the air force is full of men. Man mad, that's what you are—'

'Now just a minute, Mrs Kirkwood,' Elsie interrupted.

Rene thumped the table making everything clatter. 'How

12

dare you!' And Norah immediately sprang to her sister's defence. 'That's a terrible thing to say, Mrs Kirkwood.'

'Mother . . .' Jim waded in crossly.

'Don't you "Mother" me,' Mrs Kirkwood retorted. 'You've been married for five years now, James Kirkwood, and I don't see any signs of a baby. Why is that I wonder? Probably because she spends too much time in that garden of yours, digging all those plants and things. You earn enough to keep you both, don't you? But there again, perhaps your wife is too modern for babies. Well, I can't say I'd be surprised. I don't know what the world is coming to.'

'Mother!'

But by now Mrs Kirkwood was in full flow. 'Fancy allowing her to go gadding all over the town in her green uniform, knocking on people's doors and asking them personal questions when she should be at home being a proper wife.' Her remarks had taken on a disgusted sneer. 'You should be a mother by now, my girl. A mother.'

Everyone stared at Mrs Kirkwood in horror.

'Mother, that is enough!' Jim shouted angrily.

The dog, who was lying under the table, sat up and barked. Grabbing him by the collar, Pete shooed him back to the blanket.

'No, Jim,' Norah was saying in a measured voice. 'Let's clear the air, shall we?' Her hands were shaking and it was obvious to everyone that she was very close to tears. Her mother gave her an anxious look but Norah lifted her head and took a deep breath. 'I'll tell you why there are no babies, Mrs Kirkwood. I'll tell you even though it's none of your bloody business.'

'Darling, you don't have to,' said Jim, coming closer.

'Oh but I want to,' Norah said defiantly. She turned to

her mother-in-law. 'The reason why we don't have a baby is because I can't have any,' she said, willing herself not to break down. 'It's not Jim's fault. It's mine. I didn't ask the doctor for the medical term but there will be no babies for me. Not now, not ever.'

Mrs Kirkwood stared at her with an implacable expression.

Jim put his arm around Norah's shoulders. 'I think you owe my wife an apology, Mother.'

Mrs Kirkwood harrumphed again. 'You should have told me.'

Norah glanced up at the ceiling and took a breath. 'Well, now that that's cleared up,' she said, her voice wobbling slightly, 'who wants a cup of tea?'

'You go and sit down, love,' said Elsie, rising to her feet. 'We'll do the clearing up and make the tea.'

Her eyes were teary as Norah gave her mother a grateful smile and left the room. Jim turned to follow her.

'Give me your arm, son,' said Mrs Kirkwood, 'I don't want that dog jumping up and knocking me over.' She rose painfully from her chair and put out her hand.

Her son looked torn.

'Here, let me give you a hand, Mrs Kirkwood,' said Pete, rounding the table.

'That's quite all right, Mr Carson,' said Mrs Kirkwood, her eyes never leaving her son's face. 'You see to that damned dog. My son will help me.'

Reluctantly Jim moved himself into a position whereby his mother could take his arm. She seemed a lot slower as they made their way towards the sitting room. Behind her back, Pete shook his head and shrugged helplessly.

The layout of Jim and Norah's house was rather odd.

The kitchen was long and thin with a large pantry at one end and a bathroom at the other. The lavatory was just outside the back door. Beyond the kitchen there was a small hallway and stairs leading to the first floor. The sitting room was to the right. Facing the kitchen door was an alcove from which French doors led onto the front garden, though nobody ever used them. The only other room downstairs was a small sitting room cum study to the left of the staircase. It was also on a slightly different level. You had to go up three steps to get into it. Upstairs the layout was just as quirky. To the left was Jim and Norah's bedroom and along the wide landing to the right there were two more bedrooms, the back bedroom only accessed through the first.

As soon as his mother was in the favoured chair by the fire, Jim ignored her request for a blanket for her knees and took the stairs two at a time. Norah was sitting on the edge of their bed. Without a word, he sat beside her and put his arm around her shoulders.

'I'm sorry,' she said, through her tears. 'I've spoiled everybody's Christmas.'

'If anyone has spoiled Christmas it is my mother, and she has done that single-handed,' he said.

Norah's shoulders trembled.

'Oh, darling, I'm so sorry.'

'I know I shouldn't let her get under my skin,' she said brokenly, 'but she can be so cruel.'

'I know, I know.'

Norah blew her nose then reached for Jim's hand. 'You would have made such a good father . . .'

'Don't even think about it, darling. I've made my choice. I'd rather have you than a thousand babies.'

She looked up at him. 'You say that now but . . .'

'But nothing,' he said, wiping her tears from her cheeks with his thumbs. 'I love you, Norah, and I want to spend the rest of my life with you. This has been a bitter blow for both of us but we still have each other.'

She gave him a wan smile. 'I always imagined you playing football in the park with our son and swinging our little girl up onto your shoulders.' She choked back a sob. 'Perhaps if you'd had another wife . . .'

'One wife is quite enough for me,' he said, making a joke of it. Hugging her fiercely he added, 'Anyway, why would I want another one when I already have the best in the world?'

Downstairs in the kitchen, Elsie, Rene and Pete had set about boiling kettles, and washing the dishes, pots and pans. They worked in silence, each lost in his or her own thoughts. Pete put all the leftovers from their plates on a dish and the dog made short work of it.

Eventually Pete draped his tea towel over the top of the plate rack on the stove. 'I think I'll go and have a sit down.'

'You do that, love,' said Elsie. 'You've just got time to have a little snooze before the King's speech.'

Alone in the kitchen, Rene turned to her mother. 'Did you know about Norah and Jim, Mum?'

Elsie nodded. 'She told me when they came up in June.'

'And there's really no hope?'

Elsie shook her head. 'Apparently not,' she said. 'She was very upset about it but Jim has been wonderful.'

'Jim's a treasure,' said Rene. 'Where are they?'

'I think I heard them both going upstairs.'

'Poor Norah,' said Rene. 'She would have made a great mum.'

'She would've,' Elsie agreed.

'And she could have done without that old witch making her tell us like that,' said Rene. 'I don't know how she puts up with her; really, I don't.'

'Neither do I,' said Elsie, 'but I suppose when all is said and done, she's still Jim's mother.'

Rene blew out her cheeks. 'But why is she so bloody awful?'

'I don't know, love,' said Elsie with a sigh.

They were loading a tray with cups and saucers. When the water had boiled in the kettle, Elsie filled the tea pot. She glanced up at the clock. 'Ten to three. I hope Dad's remembered to get the wireless warmed up.'

'Mrs Kirkwood will be complaining about that next,' said Rene. 'And tell me this, Mum. Why do we have to call her Mrs bloody Kirkwood? We're all family and the old bag doesn't even let us use her Christian name.'

'Perhaps she hasn't got one,' Elsie said with a twinkle in her eye.

'She must have,' said Rene, picking up the tray. 'I saw a letter addressed to her once. It begins with a "C".'

Elsie pulled the corners of her mouth down as she held open the door for her daughter. 'Well, it can't be Cinderella, can it?' said Elsie, feeling deliciously naughty. 'The old cow.'

With the hint of a smile Rene leaned towards her as she went past and whispered confidentially in her mother's ear. 'Well said, Mum. From now on I shall always think of her as Mrs Cow-bags.'

CHAPTER 3

Amy

August, 1939

Amy was worried. These days the only topic of adult conversation was Adolf Hitler. The middle of August had seen a flurry of activity. Prime Minister Chamberlain had said the country wouldn't renege on its promise to Poland and there had been several flights between London and Berlin by British government officials to attempt to stop the country from sliding into a conflict with Germany. But that wasn't her main concern.

When she'd heard that if war with Germany was declared, all London school children would be evacuated to the country, Amy had been relieved. She didn't care where she and Lillian were sent – the further away the better – because three weeks ago, when she woke up, the sheets felt wet. Ashamed and embarrassed, she had delayed getting up until Mrs Scott came into the room to clean.

'Amy,' she'd cried. 'You're not up. Are you ill?'

Amy had burst into tears. Mrs Scott sat on the edge of her bed and put her hand gently onto Amy's hair. It took all of her strength for Amy not to flinch. It was a long time since she'd felt a genuine touch of kindness.

'I'm sorry, Mrs Scott,' she said, choking back the sobs. 'I've wet the bed.'

'Oh, my dear,' said the older woman. 'Let's have a look, shall we?'

But when she pulled back the blankets, the sheet underneath was bright red. Amy blinked and let out a panicky gasp.

'No need to worry, my dear,' Mrs Scott said quickly. 'It's your country cousins, that's all.'

Her calming voice went some way to reassuring Amy but what was she talking about? That was blood. She was bleeding. Was she going to die? And who were her country cousins?

Mrs Scott gave her a sympathetic smile. 'I never gave it a thought. What with you not having a mother to look after you, I should have told you. I'm sorry, dear.'

'Am I going to die?'

'No, my dear,' Mrs Scott said with a chuckle. 'This means you're all grown up now. This will happen every month because you've become a woman. Now, let's get you up and washed.'

'But I don't understand,' Amy said as they walked to the bathroom.

'You remember how Mrs Wandworth's dog goes into season?' said Mrs Scott. 'Well, it's the same sort of thing for girls. Your body is getting ready to have babies.'

Amy was alarmed. 'A baby! When will it come?'

Mrs Scott chuckled. 'You have to get married first,' she said. 'You can't have a baby before you're married.'

Mrs Scott ran her a bath and as Amy climbed in she said, 'You stay here while I pop to the shops and get you a towel to wear.'

The bath was relaxing but Amy kept looking at the bath

towels on the rail. Did Mrs Scott expect her to wear one of those towels? They were very bulky. How would she hide it under her clothes? How would she walk? How would it stay up? And the thought of wearing such a thing every month was a bit daunting.

Their housekeeper finally came back with a packet of something in a brown paper bag.

'These are called sanitary towels,' said Mrs Scott. She showed Amy a white padded strip with big loops on each end. 'Some people call them bunnies because the loops look like ears.'

When Amy got out of the bath, she showed her how to put one between her legs and hook the loop onto a purpose made belt which went around her waist. Amy put her knickers over the top.

'And I have to do this every month?' said Amy.

'That's right my dear. They stay for about five days.'

Amy frowned. 'Who stays?'

'Your county cousins,' said Mrs Scott with a chuckle. 'I'll tell your dad what's happened but don't mention it to your sister. She's far too young to understand.'

Amy went through the whole day feeling very grown up because Mrs Scott had said she was a woman now. When he came home, she saw the housekeeper whispering in her step-father's ear and guessed that she must have been telling him. As soon as their housekeeper was gone, her step-father glared at her and Amy could tell that he was far from pleased. 'You've spoiled everything now, Amy,' he said harshly. 'You've let me down.'

Daddy didn't come to Amy's room for the rest of that week. It was a wonderful relief until she realised that he and Lillian were becoming closer. It began with little things. Daddy started calling Lillian 'his special little poppet'. He bought her bars of chocolate and gave them to her sneakily so that Amy wouldn't see. When they sat together on the sofa, he'd tickled Lillian a lot and made her laugh. At first, Amy felt left out, rejected, abandoned; but as time went on, she felt sick to her stomach. It wasn't so long ago that he'd treated her that way, and she realised she wasn't so much jealous as confused. She knew only too well what it all added up to and her heart ached for her sister. Amy had been twelve when Daddy first came to her room, and that was frightening enough two years ago, but Lillian was only eight. Most alarming of all, just a week ago Lillian told her Daddy had promised to take her to the wallpaper shop to choose some paper to decorate her bedroom.

When talk of the evacuation began, Amy felt like it was an answer to her prayers. If she and her sister were far away in the countryside, Lillian would be safe; not only from the bombs, but also from Daddy. Most of the kids in school were apprehensive about leaving home and all that was familiar. Amy looked forward to it.

'Mrs Scott says all the children have to be at St Mary's School by eight on Saturday morning,' she told him. 'Have you signed the papers, Daddy? I have to give them in this morning.'

It was Tuesday and they were at the breakfast table. Her step-father looked up from his morning paper. 'No, I haven't signed them because you two won't be going.'

Amy frowned. 'But everybody's going.'

Her step-father shook out his paper. 'You're just about fourteen so you can go out to work,' he said coldly. 'We'll look for a live-in situation for you and Lillian will stay here with me.'

A gripping panic tightened her throat. 'But all of her school friends will be miles away.'

He carried on reading his paper. Amy chewed at her bottom lip. 'Daddy, they say the bombing in London will be very bad and Lillian will be frightened. Besides, she won't want to miss out on being with her friends.'

Her step-father turned the corner of his paper down and gave her a cold stare. 'I'm not arguing with you. Lillian. Is. Not. Going.'

Amy's eyes smarted with tears. Whenever he spoke in that tone of voice she knew he wouldn't back down. Her mind was in a whirl. They had to get away. Lillian wasn't safe. Should she tell Mrs Scott? She wasn't sure that Mrs Scott would believe her and if she didn't, and she told Daddy what Amy had said, what would happen then?

The forms had to be in by Friday. Amy couldn't even find theirs. She guessed her step-father had destroyed them.

As luck would have it, he was working early on Saturday so he left the house by seven and being Saturday, Mrs Scott didn't come in.

'We'd better get ready now.'

Lillian seemed puzzled. 'Are we being 'vacuated then?'

'Yes,' said Amy.

'But Daddy said we weren't.'

'Daddy changed his mind. He wants you to be safe from Hitler's bombs so we're going to the country.'

'Oh,' said Lillian with a whine. 'I didn't say goodbye.'

'Never mind,' said Amy. 'You can write him a letter when we get there.'

Amy helped her sister to pack a small suitcase and put a label onto her coat. After that, they walked down to the school with all the other children. Everyone was lined up and had their names checked off against a list on a clipboard. It was imperative that the teacher should never realise their names weren't on anybody's list so it was a work of art moving Lillian from one queue to another. They marched to the station in a long crocodile. There were hundreds of other children at the railway station, and a great many tearful mothers come to wave them goodbye, so keeping out of the teacher's way was a lot easier there. When the train came in, everybody decided that the carriages could accommodate eight adults or ten children. Amy watched as ten children piled into the first carriage and as soon as their teacher's back was turned, she pushed Lillian aboard the train and climbed in behind her before anyone noticed.

'You're not supposed to be in here,' said a ginger-haired girl with round glasses and pronounced teeth. 'We've already got ten.'

'I'm older than you and I'm supposed to keep an eye on you lot,' Amy said in a superior tone. She plonked her sister on her lap.

It was a nail-biting wait until they finally got going but after about twenty minutes Amy heard the guard's whistle and the train began to move. 'Shove up a bit,' she told the boy next to her and she let Lillian squeeze in beside him.

They rode in silence. What Lillian was thinking, Amy had no idea. As for Amy herself, a huge weight had been lifted from her shoulders. They were going far, far away into the countryside. Daddy would be cross, but Lillian would be safe. All she had to do now was make sure nobody knew who they were. As the countryside sped by, she had no idea where the train was going.

When they arrived at some unnamed station, everyone was herded in one direction while Amy and Lillian slipped into the Ladies'. She kept them in there for a while and when they came out, rather than join the group they had travelled with, she persuaded her sister to cross to another platform on the other side of the station to board a waiting train. It took a while before Lillian realised they were travelling without her classmates.

'Where's everybody else?'

'Oh gosh, perhaps we're on the wrong train.'

Lillian's eyes filled with tears.

'Hey,' said Amy, putting her arm around her sister. 'It's all right.'

'Are we lost?' Lillian sniffed.

'Of course not,' Amy said cheerfully. 'We'll get it all sorted out as soon as the train stops.' She paused before adding carefully, 'But don't tell anyone where we come from, will you? They might be German spies.'

Lillian's eyes grew wide.

'Don't worry,' said Amy. 'I'm here to look after you.'

Placated, her sister cuddled against her and soon nodded off in the warm carriage as the train rumbled on. While she was asleep, Amy removed Lillian's label from her coat, though she couldn't get rid of the piece of string which held it to her button. There was a sticky moment when the ticket collector came by but Amy, wide-eyed and looking a bit scared, told him their mother was in the toilet. With a broad smile, the man touched the edge of his hat and went on his way.

Her sister woke and sat up, and Amy was glad to feel

the blood start circulating in her arm again. Lillian looked around. 'Where are we?'

'Still on the train,' Amy said vaguely.

Lillian frowned. 'I know that, but where?'

'You know, I've been thinking,' said Amy. 'Now that we're far away from home, we should use the names Mummy gave us. They're so pretty and I think I should like to be called Amélie again.' Her pronunciation was almost lyrical. She gave Lillian a wistful smile.

'Daddy wouldn't like it,' Lillian said.

'Daddy's not here,' said Amélie, 'and besides, it would help to protect him from the Germans.'

Lillian frowned, puzzled. 'How?'

'Well,' said Amélie, 'Daddy does very important government business, doesn't he? If we use our old names, and we don't talk about Daddy, the Germans won't know where he is.'

Lillian sat for a moment digesting what Amélie had told her. Amélie held her breath. It was a stupid idea but with a bit of luck . . . 'You don't want Daddy to be taken prisoner, do you?'

Lillian's eyes grew wide. 'No.'

'Then, from now on, I am Amélie, and you are Linnet, just like Mummy always wanted.'

'I don't really remember Mummy anymore,' said Lillian. 'Was she very pretty?'

'Oh, yes,' said Amélie, although she sometimes struggled to recall their mother. 'She had long black hair that reached right down her back,' she said wistfully. 'And sometimes, when she and Daddy were going out, she would come into my room to kiss me goodnight and she smelled of roses and her breath was like peppermint.'

'I remember sitting on her lap and playing with her necklace,' said Lillian. 'And I remember the teddy bear she gave me at Christmas. We had a party.'

'We had lots of parties,' said Amélie. 'Everybody loved being with Mummy.'

They both smiled, each recalling their own personal memory.

'You know, she chose your name,' said Amélie.

Lillian nodded gravely. 'All right, I'll say I'm Linnet. To keep Daddy safe.'

Amélie nodded. 'Yes. To keep Daddy safe.'

Linnet relaxed and leaned against her arm again. Amélie sighed inwardly. Thank goodness she'd believed her. Now she had a real chance to keep her safe.

After that, she and Linnet spent most of the day hopping from one train to another.

CHAPTER 4

Norah

Worthing, Saturday, September 2nd, 1939

Norah Kirkwood had the strangest feeling that her life was about to change forever and it wasn't just because the clouds of war had finally gathered.

Clutching her clipboard close to her dark green uniform, Norah gave her friend Penny Draycot standing next to her a nervous smile.

'You all right?' Penny asked.

Norah nodded. 'Fine. What about you? How are the wedding plans going?'

Penny pulled a face. 'We think it'll be all right but Ted is afraid that he'll be conscripted before long.'

Penny and her fiancé planned to marry on November 4th to coincide with her twenty-first birthday but with war on the horizon their plans were looking a bit iffy.

Norah gave her a sympathetic smile. 'I'm sure it'll be fine.'

They were interrupted by a rumbling sound and the

London train came into view. Norah took a deep breath. 'This is it, then,' she said.

Penny raised a sanguine eyebrow and nodded. 'This is it.'

For the past few weeks everything had happened at breakneck speed. Throughout August, the news got worse and worse until Parliament was recalled twice. By August 29th, the Mediterranean was closed, the blackout restrictions were to be enforced and all civilian shipping was under government control.

The general consensus of opinion was that Adolf Hitler was a warmonger and that it wouldn't be long before his Nazi planes were bombing London. Even in the desperate race for peace, the country had been preparing for this moment since the beginning of January. As part of that preparation, the WVS had taken part in the national survey of households to discover suitable places for billeting children, the handicapped, the blind and the armed forces, should they need to be moved out of the capital at short notice. All through the freezing cold winter Norah and Penny had been two of the volunteers who trudged the streets of Worthing, knocking on doors and collecting information from the people who lived there. It had been a thankless task with mixed reactions. Norah often thought that if she had only written everything down, what a story she would have to tell. She recalled a worn-out-looking woman who told her she was expecting a baby in May. 'I don't see as how I can, miss,' she'd said apologetically. 'I already got six of us living here and we've only got two rooms and a kitchen.'

Another householder, who was eighty if she was a day, said, 'Oh yes, dear, I'll take somebody. If war comes again, we shall all have to do our bit, won't we.'

Not everybody was so willing. 'How much?' said a woman in a more salubrious part of the town.

'Beg pardon?'

'How much will I get to have them?'

'The government proposes that you would be entitled to claim ten and six for the first child and eight and six for each subsequent child if you take more than one.'

The woman had pulled a face. 'Won't make much out of that, will I?'

Norah had bitten her tongue in case she said something she shouldn't.

The train was slowing down.

'Right-ho everybody,' called Mr Marr, the railhead officer. 'Get to your places. Remember the quicker we get them moving the better it will be. The next train is only three-quarters of an hour behind this one.'

It was a mystery as to how they were going to get all the children safely off the train. The platform was already crowded. Billeting officers, marshals, assistants, messengers and women helpers lined the walls, each with his or her own clipboard. They had been told that the train pulling into the station now had eight hundred and fifty children from South Bermondsey on board. Norah wondered vaguely where South Bermondsey was. She knew it was somewhere in London but until this morning she'd never heard of the place. What would the children be like? She imagined they'd be crying, upset, already missing their mothers. Heavens, she didn't know a thing about children. What on earth would she say to them?

The people waiting with her to receive the evacuees were a mixed bunch. As well as the WVS, the marshals on the platform and lining the underpass were drawn from the local Rotary Club. The Worthing Air Defence Cadets had been at the station since seven this morning packing the ration packs which were to be given to every child. Each brown paper carrier bag contained enough food for the next forty-eight hours.

The train trundled to a stop.

A member of the station staff bellowed, 'Worthing, this is Worthing,' beside her, making Norah jump and a moment later the carriage doors opened and children of all shapes and sizes swarmed onto the platform with their teachers. Norah walked towards a teacher close by. 'Excuse me,' she began hesitantly, 'can I help you?'

The woman gave her a tired smile and Norah wondered how stressful her journey had been. It couldn't have been easy keeping a class full of bewildered and anxious children composed for a couple of hours on a train with nothing to amuse them.

'Could I have your name please?'

'Mrs Pike,' said the woman.

Norah wrote the name on her clipboard. 'If you would like to gather your children and follow me . . .'

'Oh, I'm not a teacher,' said the woman. 'I'm just a mother. I've come down with my Billy.' She pointed out a rather strait-laced-looking woman. 'The teacher is over there.'

Norah felt her face heat up. 'Sorry.'

'That's all right, love,' the woman said pleasantly. 'Her name is Miss Cummings.'

A few minutes later Norah was leading Miss Cummings and her class of six-year-olds down the subway and towards the Southdown buses waiting on the other side to ferry them to Broadwater.

*

With only a quick cup of tea in between trains, Norah remained on the platform all morning. At half past twelve, six hundred children from West Norwood came in and at ten past two, nine hundred and eighty-nine came from Gypsy Hill. Once again, she and her fellow volunteers made sure they received their rations and were put on the right buses. Of the last twenty children, two of them were to be billeted with Norah and Jim so they didn't get onto the bus.

'I live not far away,' she told them. 'We can walk to my house from here. It will help you stretch your legs.'

They were sisters, Ruth and Marjorie Harrison. At seven, Ruth was the oldest and her little sister was five. They were smartly turned out, though their clothes were obviously hand-me-downs. Their teacher, Miss Formby, asked Norah to make sure they were at school first thing Monday morning.

'We shall be sharing classrooms with the Worthing children,' she'd explained. 'My children will be in school in the morning, then after lunch, weather permitting, we shall be outside doing games or nature studies.'

'Which school?' asked Norah.

Miss Formby consulted her list. 'Heene Road School,' she said. 'Do you know it?'

Norah nodded and smiled. 'We live quite close. I'll make sure they're there.'

'Eight thirty,' said Miss Formby. 'We have to make the most of our time, seeing as we only have half a day.' With that their teacher hurried to the bus to join the rest of her pupils.

Ruth and her sister gave Norah bewildered smiles. Marjorie's chin was wobbly and her eyes glistened with unshed tears. 'Come along now, children,' Norah said brightly

31

as she picked up Marjorie's little suitcase. 'I'm sure you're tired but I promise you, it's not very far.'

Jim was still on duty when they arrived at home so the house was empty. Norah let the two girls in and showed them around the house, ending up in the back bedroom. There was a slightly awkward silence then Norah said, 'Perhaps you would like to put your things in the chest of drawers.' She put Marjorie's suitcase onto the bed. 'I'm going back downstairs to make us all a cup of tea. Come down when you're ready.'

She smiled encouragingly and left them to it. By the time they re-emerged, the table was laid and she had the plates under the grill to warm. As the children sat up to the table, Norah heard the familiar sound of Jim's bike being leaned against the wall under the kitchen window. The grandfather clock in the hall chimed six just as he called out and came through the door. A delicious smell of vinegar and warm paper wafted in with him.

'This is your Uncle Jim,' said Norah, giving the children a smile.

Jim handed Norah a newspaper parcel from Worley's on North Street, reputedly the best fish and chips in town.

'Blimey,' Ruth blurted out as he removed his helmet. 'He's a bleedin' rosser.'

Norah had to turn her head away in case the girls saw her smile but the awkwardness of the moment soon melted away. Jim had come home bearing two threepenny bars of Cadbury's chocolate, which made him an instant friend, although Norah said the girls would have to wait until after they'd eaten their tea before they could have them. They were very hungry and made short work of the meal. When the washing-up was done, Norah made Jim a cup of tea and the girls some cocoa and took it into the sitting room where Jim was reading them a story. She felt a tug at her heart as she saw him with a child either side of him. She mustn't think like this but there were times when life was so unfair. He would have made a wonderful father.

By seven thirty the girls were tucked up in bed and when she checked on them an hour later, they were fast asleep. She stood for a while at the half-open door watching them. The rise and fall of their chests and their little flushed cheeks made them look so vulnerable. What uncertain times they all lived in. Who would have dreamt a year ago that children would be sent far away from home and all that was familiar, to live out the war with complete strangers? How was their mother feeling? What was she doing now? Was she looking at an empty bed and wondering how they would manage without her? Norah decided she would write to their mother tonight and help the girls write a letter of their own tomorrow. She sighed. Poor little lambs. They looked so small; so innocent. Ruth had her arm around her sister's shoulder and Marjorie cuddled the one-eyed teddy bear Norah had picked up at the jumble sale. She had put it on the bed with a small suitcase and a label around his neck so that he looked a bit like them. Marjorie had loved it from the word go.

She heard a footfall behind her and turned to see Jim. Slipping his arm around her waist he nuzzled her hair and kissed her cheek. 'Don't get too fond of them, love. Remember that we've only borrowed them for a while.'

'Tickets, please.'

Amélie opened her eyes to see a man standing over her. Beside her, Linnet shifted in her seat and sat up rubbing her eyes.

The ticket collector picked up the string which had held Linnet's label and stared at Amélie. 'Are you two 'vacuees?'

Amélie didn't reply.

'Cat got your tongue?' he said tetchily.

'Are we in the country yet?' Linnet asked.

'I don't know,' said Amélie, pulling her sister closer.

The ticket collector frowned and lifting his hat, scratched his head. 'Well, you'd better get off at the next stop,' he said. 'I don't know who you was with, but they've all gone. Do you know where you were supposed to be going?'

Amélie shook her head. Linnet started to cry. 'I don't like it,' she whispered. 'I want to go home. I'm hungry.'

'Where's home?' said the ticket collector.

'London,' Linnet blurted just before Amélie gave her a hefty nudge.

'Where abouts in London, love?' said the ticket collector.

But both girls simply stared at him. 'Blimey,' he muttered. 'This'll take some sorting out.'

CHAPTER 5

Norah

Sunday was a glorious day. The children had slept well so Norah decided to have the day off and take them to the beach. Normally she wouldn't have done much in the garden on a Sunday anyway; perhaps a little watering, but that was all. After she'd cleared away the breakfast things, she set about making sandwiches for a packed lunch while they played with the rest of the toys she'd picked up at the jumble sale. Because she and Jim didn't know if they would be getting boy or girl evacuees, the trunk contained a mixture of things like dolls, cars, balls, a couple of games like snakes and ladders and ludo, a ping-pong game and a fire engine. Norah had shown Ruth and Marjorie the trunk and then left them to it.

In the kitchen, Norah made a shepherd's pie and put it in the meat safe. She planned to pop it in the oven when they got back. Jim was on duty until four o'clock so she would leave a note on the kitchen table to tell him where they were and he could meet them there. She was just about to call the girls when she heard an odd shuffling sound at the back door. When she opened it, her mother's dog, Max, bounded in.

Norah was completely flabbergasted. 'How on earth did you get here?' The dog was very excited to see her. He wagged his tail furiously and his yips and little barks brought the children into the kitchen. Max was just as delighted to see them even though they had never met before. The children were slightly overwhelmed but before long Ruth was brave enough to stroke Max's back. Marjorie hung back cautiously. A couple of minutes later, Rene walked through the door with a budgie cage in her hand.

'Rene?'

'Sorry, sis,' said Rene, as she put the budgie down and the two of them embraced. 'I was supposed to send you a telegram to say we were coming but the queue outside the post office was terrible.'

Norah turned her head towards the door. 'Are Mum and Dad here, too?'

Rene shook her head. 'They decided to stay at home but they were afraid the dog might get hurt and the bird won't cope with loud noises so they wanted you to look after them,' said Rene. 'It won't be for long. They reckon the war will be over by Christmas anyway.'

'It's no trouble,' said Norah. She turned to the girls. 'And they'll be company for my new friends.' She smiled. 'Rene, this is Ruth and Marjorie. Girls, this is Auntie Rene. She's *my* little sister.'

Rene held out her hand and Ruth gave it a shake. Marjorie hid behind her sister.

'We're on our way to the beach,' said Norah. 'Would you like to come, too?'

'I can't stay long,' her sister cautioned. 'I've got to be

back to work first thing. I had planned to come down yesterday but I couldn't get a ticket for love nor money.'

'Because the train was crowded with evacuees?' said Norah.

Rene gave her a nod.

'Let me make a few more sandwiches,' said Norah.

'Where shall I put the budgie?' said Rene. 'The back room?'

'Put him in the sitting room for now,' said Norah. 'I'll give you some newspaper to put under the cage first. I don't want budgie mess on the table.'

'Right-ho,' said Rene, grabbing the cage again. 'Come on, girls. You can help me.'

'Does it talk?' said Ruth, following her into the sitting room.

'He does,' said Rene, 'but not much. Maybe you could teach him something new.'

Their voices faded as Rene closed the door.

The walk to the beach was a fair trek but everyone was excited so they soon got there. The children didn't have bathing costumes but along with their towels, Norah had brought along an extra pair of knickers. It was a lovely day. They parked themselves at the end of Heene Road and Norah sat on the stones until Rene walked to the pier and got them two deckchairs.

'Are Mum and Dad worried about the bombing?' Norah asked as they made themselves comfortable.

'A bit, I suppose,' said Rene. 'We all are. You wouldn't recognise the place now. We've got sandbags and Anderson shelters going up everywhere.'

'What about the business? Will that be affected?'

Elsie Carson ran a domestic staff agency. In return for a small fee, she would find her clients reliable, trustworthy cleaning women. Over the years she had built up quite a reputation and her workers were very much sought after.

'If anything, it's started to pick up,' said Rene. 'Some families are moving to the country and Mum's been busy finding them girls who are willing to go with them.'

Norah grinned. 'I suppose that's one way of staying safe.'

'Mum says it'll all change when the girls start joining up.'

'Everything's changing,' said Norah. 'They've already dug underground air raid shelters in Steyne Gardens, and I've done the blackout curtains at last. You wouldn't believe the queue in Woolworth's for curtain rings.'

'I think a lot of people were hoping this wouldn't happen,' said Rene. Max bounded towards her. 'No! Down boy. You're all wet.' The dog shook itself and Norah squealed as her legs were dotted with sea water. Max barked happily and ran back towards the sea again.

'You said Mum was worried about the dog in the bombing.'

'It's not just that,' said Rene. 'Everybody else is having their pets put down. The queue outside the vet's goes right round the block.'

Norah gasped. 'Why?'

'Because they think as soon as Hitler sends his war planes, he'll aim for London and it won't be long before the place is full of wounded and starving animals. Mr Kendal says it's better to have them put to sleep.'

'Who's Mr Kendal?'

'Mum's new next-door neighbour. He's an RSPCA officer.'

'Bit drastic, isn't it?' said Norah. 'I love you so much, pussy, that I'm having you put to sleep.'

Rene shrugged. 'That's about the size of it,' she said. 'Anyway, Mum couldn't bear to do it so she asked me to bring the pets down here.'

'Well, tell her not to worry,' said Norah. 'I'll keep them as long as she wants.'

'Thanks, love. That'll be a load off her mind. She's sent me with some tins of Chappie and bird seed and there's some money in the card I left on the kitchen table.'

'What about you, Rene. Are you scared?'

'I'd be a liar if I said I wasn't,' said Rene, 'but like I told you at Christmas, I shall join one of the services.'

Norah looked stricken. 'Oh, Rene.'

'I'll be fine,' said Rene. She chuckled. 'Somebody's got to give Mrs Cow-bags something to gossip about.'

After the hectic planning and organisation of the day before, Sunday had been relatively quiet at the police station. Eight thousand evacuee children had been counted in and resettled in all parts of the town and in the villages beyond. While not responsible for the event, Worthing Police had to keep a weather eye on things. Jim and his fellow officers kept a low profile but were on hand in case of trouble. Everything went smoothly, as it turned out, but there was still plenty of paperwork to be sent to head office.

Halfway through the morning, Stan Martin from Worthing Railway Station turned up with two girls. Having told them to 'sit on the chairs by the wall and be quiet', he approached the desk sergeant with an anxious frown.

''Ello, Stan,' said Sergeant Plumb. 'What can I do for you?'

The story Stan had to tell was surprising. At ten minutes to midnight, the girls had been put off the Littlehampton train with no tickets and no idea where they were going. Stan's wife, Lily, had put them up for the night, but with four children of their own in a two up, two down in Ann Street, there was no possibility of them staying.

Sergeant Plumb leaned over his desk to take a better look at them. 'Are they English?' he whispered in a confidential manner.

'The ticket collector who found them reckons they're from London.'

Sergeant Plumb frowned. 'If they *come* from London, what the hell were they doing on the Littlehampton train going back?'

Stan shrugged. 'Search me. I reckon them's evacuees. I just took them to the town hall but it's closed. It's Sunday,' he added unnecessarily.

Sergeant Plumb drew himself to his full height. 'I suppose we'd better handle it then.'

Stan turned to go.

'Have they eaten?' Sergeant Plumb called after him.

'My Lily gave them some bread and jam this morning,' said Stan. 'Didn't have much else.'

Stan pushed the door.

'Hang on a minute, Stan,' the sergeant said irritably. 'What about their names? And if they're evacuees, where did they come from?'

'Your guess is as good as mine,' said Stan. 'The station master told me to bring 'em here and that's what I've done.'

'But you bear some responsibility,' grumbled the sergeant.

'The railway deals with lost luggage not lost kids,' Stan retorted and with that he was gone.

40

Sergeant Plumb lifted the top of the desk and walked towards them. 'Now then,' he began, speaking as if he was addressing two very small children, 'which one of you two girlies is going to tell me your names?'

After a brief discussion with the station inspector, Amélie and Linnet spent the rest of the day in the police canteen. Being a Sunday, it was empty apart from the odd constable who came to sit at one of the tables to eat his sandwiches, which was when Jim first laid eyes on them. They were huddled together under the notice board. Nobody spoke to them. He knew that elsewhere in the building the inspector was doing his best to find a place for them, but with all the evacuees in the town, everywhere was full up. Jim's heart went out to them. They were only kids. What could have happened and how come nobody had reported them missing? They had no identification although the younger one, who looked about seven or eight, still had the string which must have been attached to a label, hanging from the button of her coat. Although their hair was untidy, they were both well dressed in quality coats and highly polished shoes. The younger girl seemed scared but the older girl had a defiant look about her.

Having first raided the lost property box, Jim went over to make friends. Putting down a couple of pens and some paper, he invited them to do some drawing. As they relaxed, he produced some tired-looking toffees from his pocket. The younger girl took one straight away, the older girl hanging back, but when Jim opened his bag of sandwiches, they all shared. When they'd eaten, he opened a pack of cards that had also been in the lost property box, and they played Snap until it was time for him to report for duty again.

Poor little sods, he thought to himself as he said his goodbyes, but at least he'd left them with a smile on their faces.

Rene said her goodbyes at four thirty, soon after Jim arrived to join them on the beach. The two sisters gave each other a long hug, realising it would most likely be a long time before they saw each other again.

'Tell Mum not to worry about Max and Joey,' said Norah.

'I will,' said Rene, giving Jim a hug. 'Now I must go or I'll miss the train.'

'Write to us,' Norah called. She turned back to check on the children.

'The kids seem to be enjoying themselves,' said Jim. 'How long have you been here?'

'All afternoon,' said Norah. She smiled. 'I'm not sure that they'd even seen the sea before.'

'Don't suppose they had,' Jim agreed.

'How was your day?'

Her husband stretched luxuriantly. 'On the whole, pretty good. They've offered me three downward chevrons to put on my uniform.'

Norah took in an excited breath. 'You got the sergeant job? Will you take it?'

'I already have. I'd be a fool not to,' said Jim. 'I've no desire to run around shooting the enemy whether they're German or not and besides, I love my job. Somebody's got to stay behind and keep the King's peace.'

Norah leaned over and squeezed his forearm. 'Well done, darling.'

Jim looked down at the small bag at her feet. 'Got any food in that bag?'

42

Norah pulled a face. 'Only a squashed egg sandwich and half an apple.'

Her husband's eyes lit up. 'Sounds as good as a bean-feast.'

They left the beach at five. Jim put Marjorie on the saddle of his bike and Ruth held Norah's hand. They were both worn out but they'd had a lovely day. As they trudged back home Norah wondered if they would manage to stay awake long enough to eat their tea. The dog padded along beside them. He was worn out, too.

Norah decided she would write the children's mother another note tonight and post the letter first thing in the morning, along with the pictures her daughters had drawn for her. They didn't seem to be missing her at all but of course she wouldn't mention that in her letter.

As they rounded the corner into Clifton Road, Norah was puzzled to see someone sitting on the low wall outside their home. As they drew nearer, her heart sank as her mother-in-law rose to her feet.

'Where the devil have you been?' she said in an angry raucous voice. 'I've been sat on this wall waiting for ages.'

'I'm sorry, Mrs Kirkwood. I didn't know you were coming.'

Jim's mother proffered her cheek for Norah to kiss. 'I decided that if Hitler was going to blow us all to kingdom come, I may as well be with my family.' She pointed to an array of bags in front of the door. 'Bring them in, James,' she demanded, 'and put them upstairs in the back bedroom. I'll sleep in there.'

Norah bristled. How dare she? What right had she to just walk in on them like this, uninvited. 'I'm afraid you can't,' she said, willing herself to keep calm. The last thing she wanted was a row in front of two vulnerable children. 'Ruth and Marjorie are sleeping in that room.'

'Well, move them somewhere else,' said Mrs Kirkwood.

By now they were inside. Norah bent to the oven to put in the shepherd's pie.

'And send that mutt outside,' Mrs Kirkwood demanded. 'You shouldn't have animals in the kitchen.'

Norah rolled her eyes. 'Can you put your mother's things in the study room downstairs, love?' she asked Jim.

'But that room is awfully small,' Mrs Kirkwood complained. 'And you get all the noise from the road.'

'I can't help that,' Norah said flatly. 'I didn't know you were coming.' Then, using a much softer tone, she said, 'Listen, girls, go in the bathroom for a wash and then you can go upstairs and change into your night things. After that you can come downstairs for your tea. All right?'

Jim disappeared with Mrs Kirkwood's bags, taking the dog with him.

Tutting angrily his mother flopped into a chair. 'Who are they anyway?'

'Evacuees,' said Norah. 'They came yesterday.'

Her mother-in-law pulled a face. 'I wouldn't fancy taking kids like that in. You don't know anything about them. They could have all sorts.'

Norah made no comment. The girls came out of the bathroom and ran upstairs.

'I don't think I can stay here with people like that in the house.'

'It's up to you. I'm not sending them back,' said Norah.

'But they could pass on anything,' Mrs Kirkwood insisted. 'I mean they might have lice, or nits or impetigo or some such. Can't you get someone else to take them in?'

44

'No, I can't,' Norah snapped, 'and I'll thank you to keep your voice down.'

The two women glared at each other.

'Well I'll go to the foot of our stairs,' Mrs Kirkwood said in a wobbly voice as if she was about to cry. 'I never expected you to speak to your own husband's mother like that.'

'Look, Mrs Kirkwood,' Norah said firmly. 'You can stay if you like but I won't be told what to do in my own house. Jim—'

'James,' Mrs Kirkwood interrupted.

'Jim and I,' Norah began again stiffly, 'decided to give those two little girls a home from home until this damned war is over and I'm not going back on my word.'

'And you've got that mangy dog here, too,' said Mrs Kirkwood. She leaned back in her chair, a look of abject despair on her face.

Jim came into the room. 'I've put your bags on the bed, Mother,' he said cheerfully, and turning to his wife he added, 'I've put the budgie in the hallway for now.'

'Budgie?' Mrs Kirkwood cried.

'My mother's,' said Norah, putting the cutlery onto the table. 'And before you say anything, the budgie is staying as well.'

'Do you want me to help you unpack, Mother?' Jim asked. It was obvious that he'd sensed the tension between the two women.

'Perhaps later, son,' said Mrs Kirkwood, her voice small and pathetic. She sighed. 'I was hoping for a warm welcome and a cup of tea but I can see there's fat chance of that.' She rose to her feet painfully and shuffled from the room

Their mealtime was a bit of a struggle. Ruth and Marjorie

45

battled so hard to keep their eyes open that Norah decided to forego the fruit and jelly she had prepared for pudding. She was just about to take the girls upstairs to bed when the doorbell rang.

When Jim opened the door they never used, PC Clark stood on the step with the two girls he'd seen earlier at the station.

'Hello, you two,' said Jim with a smile.

The girls returned his smile. Behind him, puzzled, Norah frowned.

'Sergeant Plumb said to bring them here,' said Clark without preamble.

'But surely . . .' Jim began.

'We've spent all day trying to find them somewhere,' said the constable, clearly not wanting Jim to talk him out of it. 'Nobody will take responsibility because it's Sunday, or they don't go to the same school, or one's too old or the other's too young.' He pushed the smaller girl through the door. 'In the end, the inspector reckoned your Norah would take them in.'

Jim's face broke into another smile as the younger girl stepped forward and hugged his legs.

'Of course we will,' said Norah. 'Come in, dear, come in.'

At her invitation, the older girl stepped over the threshold.

'Don't know what to call the older girl,' said Clark. 'She won't say, but the little-en's got a funny name. Linnet.'

CHAPTER 6

Amélie

The two girls had been made welcome and almost as soon as they came into the house, they were sitting at the tea table. The policeman said, 'Call me Uncle Jim,' and a much older woman already sitting at the table said she was called Mrs Kirkwood. The lady who had welcomed them in was called Auntie Norah and she dished up some shepherd's pie. After eating nothing but bread and jam and sandwiches since they'd left home, it smelled absolutely delicious. The older woman was a bit grumpy but under the table, a dog sat on Amélie's foot. He seemed very friendly so every now and then she reached down and fondled his ear.

Auntie Norah explained that the other girls who were already in their nighties were very tired because they had spent the afternoon on the beach. Amélie guessed that wherever they were, she and Linnet must be near the sea. All the station signs had already been taken down in case of a German invasion and although someone usually called out the name of the station when the train stopped, Amélie had only just woken up so she hadn't heard it. She hadn't a clue where they were.

There wasn't a lot of conversation at the table although Ruth was quite chatty. She said she enjoyed running and that she was awfully good at netball. Marjorie told them she liked drawing. They had come from Gypsy Hill in London, but Amélie had no idea where that was.

'Linnet,' said Auntie Norah. 'That's a very pretty name.'

'It's French,' said Linnet, 'and it means bird.'

Ruth and Marjorie giggled.

'Are you French then?' asked Norah.

'My mummy was,' said Linnet. Amélie gave her sister a nudge and the two girls fell silent.

'So, tell us about yourselves,' said Norah, trying to resurrect the conversation.

Linnet glanced first at Amélie and when her older sister nodded she told them about her new bike and that she enjoyed singing. Amélie said she liked playing netball, too.

'In the morning,' said Auntie Norah, 'I shall take you girls to the primary school just up the road.'

'She looks far too old for a junior school,' Mrs Kirkwood interrupted. She jerked her head towards Amélie.

'How old are you, dear?' Auntie Norah asked.

'I'm nine and Amélie is fourteen,' Linnet piped up. 'And Meryl . . .' Her voice faded as her sister gave her another quick nudge.

Mrs Kirkwood tut-tutted. 'If you're fourteen, they never should have allowed you to be evacuated,' she announced. 'You're old enough to go out to work.'

Amélie felt her face heating up. For a minute she was terrified that they were going to send her back.

'You won't get any money for her,' Mrs Kirkwood went on in ringing tones. 'The government only pay the billeting allowance up to school leaving age and that's fourteen.'

'All right, Mother,' said Uncle Jim. 'You've made your point. I'm sure Norah will get it all sorted in the morning.' He smiled at Amélie. 'So where do you come from, love?'

Amélie stared down at her plate. What if she told him and he put a call through to the police station? If that happened, the pair of them would end up going back on the next available train. No, she couldn't tell him or Linnet would be in danger once again, so she pretended not to hear.

When the meal was over, Amélie got up and offered to help Auntie Norah wash the dishes. Uncle Jim carried Marjorie upstairs and it looked as if she would be asleep before her head hit the pillow. Ruth managed to go upstairs by herself but by the time Norah bent to kiss her forehead, she was almost asleep as well.

They tiptoed from the bedroom and stood together on the landing.

'How long does Mother plan to stay?' said Jim.

Norah shrugged.

'I'm sorry, love.'

Norah smiled bravely and reached up to kiss his cheek. 'We'll manage.'

Norah got some sheets out of the trunk that stood on the landing and made up the bed in the other bedroom.

'I'm going to put you and your sister together,' she told Amélie when she came back downstairs. Amélie had washed up the dishes and put them, clean, back on the kitchen table.

'I didn't know where they belonged,' she apologised.

'That's all right,' said Auntie Norah. 'It was very kind of you to wash them up. Thank you.'

Their bed had been hastily made but it was very comfortable. Amélie and Linnet had been put in the bedroom beside the other evacuees at the back of the house. The two rooms were very close together, in fact Auntie Norah explained that Ruth and Marjorie had to walk through Amélie and Linnet's room to get to theirs. Ruth and Marjorie had gone straight to sleep.

Once they were between the sheets, Auntie Norah bent to kiss Linnet's forehead. 'Goodnight, sweetheart. See you in the morning.' She regarded Amélie from Linnet's side of the bed and decided she was too grown up for a goodnight kiss. 'Try not to worry about missing your school friends,' she said gently. 'We'll do our best to sort it tomorrow.'

Amélie gave her a nod.

Auntie Norah smiled as she pulled the door slightly closed. 'Goodnight then, girls. Sleep tight.'

There was a light on in the hallway so they weren't in the dark.

'Are we going to stay here, Amélie?' Linnet's whisper was small.

'I think so.'

'Auntie Norah seems very nice, doesn't she?'

'Yes,' Amélie whispered, 'but you really must be careful about what you say.'

'Do you think she might be in with the Germans?'

'I don't know,' said Amélie. 'That's the trouble with spies. You never know who's one and who isn't. That's why you must remember not to say too much about where we live.'

Linnet moved closer to her sister. 'What about Daddy? Can I tell them about him?'

'Especially not Daddy,' said Amélie. She lifted her arm and Linnet laid her head on her chest. 'Remember what I told you? Daddy's work is very important so we have to keep him secret.'

Linnet yawned. 'I'll try,' she murmured sleepily.

'It's very important,' Amélie repeated but judging by her steady breathing, her sister was already asleep.

Amélie stared up at the ceiling. The house was quiet although she could hear music coming from downstairs. Auntie Norah must have a gramophone or a wireless in the sitting room.

She turned over and pulled the bedclothes across her shoulders as a delicious warm sleepy feeling curled itself around her. It was such a relief to finally have a place to stay and shepherd's pie had never tasted so good.

'Could I have a word with the head mistress?'

Norah had just walked all four girls to Heene Road School and as they stood in the playground waiting to go in, Norah took the opportunity to speak to one of the teachers. She was ushered inside and asked to wait on a chair outside the head mistress's office.

Breakfast had been a tad awkward. Ruth and Marjorie were chatty enough but Linnet and her sister were very quiet. Amélie wasn't a rude girl. She had obviously been brought up to mind her manners but she said very little. Norah was beginning to feel a little uneasy about her.

'I shall be nine next birthday,' Linnet had chirped. 'My daddy said he'd take me horse riding and I'm going to have my bedroom decorated. I chose the wallpaper myself.'

Amélie almost nudged her off her chair. Ruth and Marjorie stared in awe.

'That will be nice,' said Norah. 'What does your daddy do?'

'He's a—' Linnet began.

'A builder,' Amélie interrupted.

But judging by the surprised expression on Linnet's face, Norah could tell at once that it wasn't true. It was all very puzzling.

'Hey-up, Norah, what are you doing here?' She looked up to see Ivan Steele the school caretaker. For years he had been a regular customer of Norah's, buying spring plants from the market garden every year and stopping at the house for a cup of tea at the same time. A widower now, his wife had died just after Christmas and Ivan had moved into a much smaller place.

'Hello, Mr Steele,' she said. 'I've just brought my evacuees to the school. How are you?'

The old chap sighed. 'Not so dusty since my Ada went,' he said sadly, 'but I get by.'

'Pop in sometime,' she said. 'I've always got the kettle on.'

She watched him walk on down the corridor and her heart went out to him. His shoes looked down at heel and the collar of his shirt could do with a change. He wasn't looking after himself properly, that was for sure.

'Mrs Kirkwood, isn't it?' said a voice and Norah looked up to see that the head mistress, Miss Roberts, had opened her office door. 'I remember you from the Harvest Festival when you helped us to decorate the school hall so beautifully. I'm not sure I ever did thank you properly.'

Norah smiled shyly. 'No need,' she said as she went inside.

'What can I do for you?' said Miss Roberts, indicating that Norah should sit down.

Norah explained as much as she could about Linnet and her sister. 'From what I can gather they have probably come from London but it's hard to tell. Neither of them had a label on their coat and the older girl doesn't want to tell us where they're from.'

Miss Roberts pulled a face. 'How odd. Have you any idea why?'

'None at all,' said Norah, 'but they seem to be polite, well-brought-up girls.'

Miss Roberts nodded sagely. 'Leave it to me, Mrs Kirkwood. I shall endeavour to find out who they are and how they ended up here in Worthing before the day is out.'

Norah rose to her feet. 'I'm not really sure what to do with Amélie. She's already fourteen so, by rights, she doesn't have to be at school. I shall have to talk to the billeting officer about it.'

Miss Roberts looked thoughtful. 'I wonder if she would like to give us a hand with the smaller children. We do seem to have a lot of little ones and their teacher, Miss Formby, is quite new to the job and rather overwhelmed.'

'Well, Amélie seems to be a capable girl,' said Norah. 'And if she's here, it would free me up to get this mess sorted out.'

Miss Roberts put her hand on Norah's shoulder. 'Then that's what we'll do, Mrs Kirkwood.'

Norah decided to go straight round to the council offices in the new town hall. Frustratingly, it took ages to find the man in charge of London evacuees. Norah was passed from one department to another until she banged her fist on the front desk and demanded to speak to the chief billeting officer. After a further ten-minute wait a man with a florid complexion came puffing along the corridor. He pushed a folder under his armpit and held out a podgy hand.

'Cuthbert Collins,' he said, giving her a rather sweaty and limp handshake. 'I think it better if we talk in the interview room.'

He led her to a small room hardly much bigger than a cupboard and offered her a seat in a canvas-covered chair. 'Now, what's this all about?'

Norah explained the chain of events.

'Well, you never should have taken them in, Mrs Kirkwood,' he said crossly after she'd finished. 'They're not part of our allocation and if we take in all and sundry it's going to cause chaos and confusion.'

'It's all very well saying that, Mr Collins,' said Norah, trying to be reasonable, 'but it was half past six on a Sunday evening and the poor girls were dead on their feet.'

'All the same . . .' Mr Collins began again.

'I could hardly turn them away, now could I?'

'As I explained to the policeman on the telephone . . .' he began again.

'You mean you already know about them?' Norah gasped.

'I advised them to take the girls to the children's home in Bulkington Avenue,' Mr Collins retorted stiffly.

'It was full up,' Norah said through gritted teeth.

Mr Collins began shuffling through the wodge of papers in his folder. 'All the children allocated to this area arrived on the Saturday morning and early afternoon trains,' he went on. 'I fail to understand why the police brought them to you in the first place.'

'Perhaps because my husband and I seem to be the only people caught up in this sorry charade who haven't lost sight of the fact that two children had nowhere to go.'

As his face went a delicate shade of red, Mr Collins glared at her. 'Procedures are procedures, Mrs Kirkwood.'

Norah took a deep breath and struggled not to lose her temper. How ridiculous he was being. Why the inquest? Why go over what couldn't be changed? Surely all that mattered was getting Amélie and Linnet registered now that they were here in Worthing. Norah opened her mouth but Mr Collins interrupted. 'As I have already intimated, they have no business being here.'

'Fine,' Norah snapped. 'So what do you suggest I do about it?'

Mr Collins's nostrils flared. 'I have no idea,' he said. 'You don't even have a surname for them.'

'Oh for goodness' sake!' Norah said crossly. 'This is ridiculous. We're just going round and round in circles.'

Mr Collins glared. 'Ruth and Marjorie Harrison are registered as being at your address,' he said doggedly, 'but until I know the surname of the other two girls and where they've come from, they are your responsibility.'

Norah rolled her eyes. 'What would you do if I put them out on the street?' she said. She had no intention of doing anything of the sort, but she was determined to make the silly man see sense.

'Then I would have no hesitation in reporting you for child neglect,' he said, gathering his papers and rising to his feet. 'Good afternoon, Mrs Kirkwood.'

Outside the town hall again, Norah stood for a moment wondering what to do. It was clear the 'jobsworth' wasn't going to budge but she couldn't just leave it. Two girls were hopelessly lost and unaccounted for, and their parents would most likely be demented with worry. True, it was a mystery why Amélie refused to give any details about their identity, but that didn't alter the fact that they were vulnerable children.

The town hall was only a stone's throw from the police station. A few minutes later she wandered in.

'Hello, Norah, love,' said the desk sergeant. 'What can I do for you?'

'I need to report some missing children,' she began, 'and when I've done that, I should like to speak to my Jim.'

It didn't take long to explain everything and once it was logged, Norah was escorted to the police canteen. The woman working there gave her a cup of tea and Norah sat hugging it as she waited for her husband.

How long would the war last? They said it would all be over by Christmas, but her mum had told her that they'd said the same thing at the beginning of the last war and that went on for four years! What if they had to look after the girls for a long time? She would need identity cards and ration books. She was sure Jim would do whatever she asked, but that wasn't the point.

The canteen grew noisier. It was getting close to dinner time and some of the men were taking their lunch hour. Norah couldn't help noticing the tables were still full of crockery from the breakfast shift and after watching several policemen piling the plates onto one of two tables to make room for their meals, she began to stack the dirty plates more tidily.

'Thanks, love,' said the harassed-looking woman behind the counter. She was busy dishing up and clearly rushed off her feet.

'Can I give you a hand?' Norah asked. The woman looked sceptical until she added, 'I'm Norah Kirkwood, PC, no, Sergeant Kirkwood's wife.'

The woman's face broke into a smile. 'Oh, I'd be ever so

grateful,' she said. 'I've got two people called up, one off sick and only the washer-upper out the back.'

For the next quarter of an hour, Norah collected the used plates and took them into the kitchen before she returned to the canteen to wipe down the tables.

'Norah?' Jim had a puzzled expression on his face as he came into the canteen. Norah grinned and slid into the chair opposite her cup of almost cold tea.

It didn't take long to explain why she was there and what she was doing. Jim held her hand over the table. 'You're a star,' he said proudly.

Norah blushed. 'I'm only doing what anyone else would do.'

As she'd predicted, Jim wouldn't hear of sending the children anywhere else.

'It's going to cost us a bit,' Norah cautioned. 'I'll have to buy them some clothes. They don't have much and if we don't know where they come from, I can't even write and ask their mother to send some on.'

'We'll manage,' said Jim.

Norah looked thoughtful. 'Amélie looks as if she's too old for school,' she went on. 'She might be able to pay her way.'

'No hurry,' said Jim. 'One step at a time, eh?' He turned to the woman behind the counter dishing up. 'Got any spare stew for my Norah, Ma?' he asked.

''Course I have,' said Ma and pointing at Norah she added, 'Your missus wouldn't like a job, would she? I could do with a new waitress.'

Norah glanced meaningfully at Jim. 'I'll give you another hand in a minute,' she said slowly, 'but I don't think I have the time to take it on permanently.'

'Shame,' said Ma.

'But if you would consider training up a young girl,' Norah began cautiously, 'I might know someone who was up for it.'

Ma slapped a full spoon of stew onto a plate.

'I don't know her very well,' Norah explained. 'She's an evacuee but she's well spoken, polite and seems sensible enough.'

'If she comes recommended by you, love,' she said, 'she's got the job.'

CHAPTER 7

Amélie

The past few days had been a bit like sitting on a roller-coaster. Amélie's first day began at the primary school where she helped Miss Formby with the little ones. They used the classroom in the morning, and in the afternoon they went on a nature trail to the beach. It was there that Amélie finally discovered that they were in a place called Worthing, which was on the south coast of England. It was a delightful surprise but she was also a bit shocked. It probably meant that they'd got on a train heading north and somehow or other during the changes they'd made, they'd ended up back down south again. What an unmitigated disaster it would have been had she and Linnet stayed on the train because they would have ended up back where they'd started!

The beach was deserted but that wouldn't last long. 'I am told that some troops are on their way. When they arrive, they'll be putting barbed wire and sea defences all along the coast, so we'd better make the most of it while we can,' the head mistress had told Miss Formby.

The beach turned out to be pebbles but when the tide

went out, there was a reasonable stretch of sand dotted with rock pools. The children were charged with finding different types of seaweed and small creatures left behind by the receding water. Their enthusiasm and excitement meant that the afternoon passed by very quickly.

Back at the house, Auntie Norah was in the garden digging up some potatoes and carrots. Linnet had never seen vegetables in situ before and Amélie had only seen them once. She felt a little pang in her chest when she recalled spending the day at Mrs Scott's home where they grew potatoes. She couldn't remember why she had been sent there but it was a long time ago and she didn't remember Linnet being with her, but she did remember playing with Vera, Mrs Scott's daughter.

Back indoors, Linnet wanted to play schools with Marjorie but Ruth had some *School Friend* comics to read. Amélie elected to help Auntie Norah in the kitchen. There was a heart-stopping moment when Uncle Jim came in from work, Amélie turning her head sharply and taking in a startled breath as he called out a cheery hello.

'Are you all right?' Auntie Norah asked anxiously as Amélie swayed slightly. 'You've gone quite pale.'

'Yes, thank you,' said Amélie, recovering herself. 'He made me jump, that's all.' Auntie Norah chuckled to herself as she put the new potatoes Amélie had just washed into a saucepan, and the moment passed. Amélie turned her attention to chopping the carrots but her heart was still racing.

'No, dear,' Auntie Norah said gently, adjusting Amélie's hold on the knife, 'do them like this. I don't want you cutting your finger.'

They laid the table together then Auntie Norah told Amélie to call the other children to the table. Linnet and

Marjorie were still playing schools in Marjorie's bedroom while Ruth still lay on her bed, reading her comics.

'Time for tea,' said Amélie. She stepped back to let the others go first then grabbed her sister's arm and pulled her back. While the other girls were racing down the stairs, she whispered in Linnet's ear. 'Remember that Uncle Jim is a policeman. Don't talk about Daddy.'

When they came downstairs, Mrs Kirkwood was shuffling out of her room. 'Nobody bothered to tell me it was tea time,' she grumbled. 'It was only when I heard that herd of elephants thundering down the stairs that I realised it was time to eat.'

'I was just about to call you, Mother,' said Uncle Jim. He had changed out of his uniform and was wearing the same things he'd had on when Amélie and Linnet had arrived last night. He winked at them as his mother sailed past.

Everyone sat in their usual places and Auntie Norah dished up. Their meal – potato, carrots and sausages – was delicious, probably because after an afternoon outside and a long walk home, Amélie was starving.

'So, what did you do at school today?' Uncle Jim asked.

Marjorie shrugged.

Her sister pulled a face. 'Nothing.'

'We went to the beach,' said Linnet.

'Went to the beach?' Mrs Kirkwood said scornfully. 'Heavens above. That would never have happened in my day. When I went to school we all had to work, not spend the day enjoying ourselves.'

'We weren't enjoying ourselves,' Ruth retorted. 'We had to find seaweed and shells and I found a crab.'

'Why did the lobster blush?' said Linnet. Amélie gave her

a nudge as everybody turned their attention towards her. Linnet ignored it. 'Because the sea weed,' she chortled.

The grown-ups smiled and the children giggled. Mrs Kirkwood screwed up her nose in disgust and tutted noisily.

For afters, they all tucked into tinned peaches and custard.

It was later that evening when the younger girls were in bed that Auntie Norah and Uncle Jim asked Amélie if they could 'have a word'. Immediately, Amélie felt tense and worried. Was she going to get told off because of Linnet's stupid joke? She'd got it out of a Christmas cracker anyway. While Auntie Norah and Uncle Jim made themselves comfortable in the sitting room, Amélie chewed her bottom lip anxiously. Auntie Norah and Uncle Jim were very nice but how could she tell them what she'd done and how she and Linnet had ended up here? She'd be sent home in disgrace straight away.

'Amélie, we were wondering if you would like to have a job,' Auntie Norah began. 'You are old enough to leave school and I happen to know there's a job going in the police canteen.'

A job? She hadn't expected that. Amélie hesitated. What sort of a job? This was the last thing she had expected and certainly a far cry from the life she was used to.

'Uncle Jim will keep an eye on you,' Auntie Norah went on. 'You'll get a guinea a week and I think if you give me ten shillings for your keep, you can save the rest.'

Amélie blinked in surprise. Well! This was certainly a turn up for the books. 'I can't cook,' she said faintly.

Auntie Norah smiled. 'Oh, you wouldn't be expected to cook,' she said. 'They want someone to collect the dishes and keep the canteen tidy. It's not hard work. I'm sure you could manage.'

Amélie took in her breath. A new start. She and Linnet could stay here and make a new life together. A life without Daddy. Doing the dishes was easy enough. She'd learned to do that when she'd stayed with Mrs Scott that time. It was fun.

'All right,' she said cautiously. 'I'd like that.'

'We would have to make it all above board,' said Uncle Jim. 'You'd be on the station payroll so we need to tell them your surname.'

Amélie's spirit plummeted. Was this some sort of trick? Just another way of finding out who she was? She was just about to say she'd changed her mind when Uncle Jim added, 'Osborne, isn't it?'

Amélie frowned. 'How . . .?' she began.

'Linnet told her teacher,' Auntie Norah said. 'That's right, isn't it?'

Amélie looked down at her shoes and nodded glumly.

'So, shall I take you there tomorrow?' Auntie Norah said. 'I've got to take some runner beans to a customer so it's on my way and Ma says you can start first thing.'

'Ma?'

'The lady in charge of the police canteen,' Uncle Jim said with a chuckle. He glanced at his wife. 'D'you know what? It's only just occurred to me that I don't even know her proper name. Everybody calls her Ma.'

'Are you all right?' Linnet said. She and Amélie were snuggled together in bed and although she hadn't meant to, she had just woken her sister up again. It had happened a couple of times, probably because in her half-sleep state, she'd panicked when she'd realised someone else was in the bed with her. For one horrifying moment she had thought Daddy was back until she remembered it was only Linnet. Tonight

63

she'd had a bad dream and she'd woken with a loud gasp as if she couldn't breathe. Linnet was staring anxiously at her through the gloom.

'I'm fine,' said Amélie. 'I'm sorry. I didn't mean to wake you.'

'I don't like Mrs Kirkwood,' Linnet said in a loud whisper.

'Shh,' Amélie whispered. 'Walls have ears.' She smiled to herself as her sister lifted her head from the pillow to check. 'You have to be careful not to upset people.'

'But it's true,' Linnet protested. 'She's always picking on me. I hate her.'

'It's not just you,' said Amélie. 'She's not very nice to Auntie Norah either. Remember tea time?'

It grew quiet as they both recalled Mrs Kirkwood's cutting remarks, which had permeated the evening. 'For heaven's sake, Norah, this gravy is lumpy . . . You should learn to control that blessed dog, Norah. Make him come out from under that table . . . No, no, you stupid woman. I told you I don't want custard . . .'

'What did she say that made you decide you didn't like her?'

'She told me off when she went to her room,' said Linnet. 'She said I was an idiot but I was only sitting on the other side of the curtain. Ruth said there was a hedgehog in the garden and I was looking out for it.'

'I think she was cross because we have to keep the curtains drawn all the time now,' Amélie reminded her. 'We mustn't let any of the light show outside or the Germans might see us.'

But Linnet wouldn't be placated. 'It's rude to say idiot.'

'Yes, it is,' Amélie conceded, 'but she only wanted you to understand how important it is.'

There was a pause then Linnet said, 'Why do we have to stay here, Amélie? When can we go home?'

Amélie sucked in her lips. She wanted to say never, ever, but she knew that would only upset Linnet even more. 'Not yet,' she said quietly as she reached for her sister's hand under the bedclothes and gave it a squeeze. 'Soon.'

Once the other girls and Linnet were in school, Auntie Norah took Amélie on the bus to the police station. She had explained to the girls at the breakfast table that she was going to take some vegetables to an old neighbour of hers who had moved.

'I suppose that means I shall be all alone in the house again,' grumbled her mother-in-law.

'I'm sorry, Mrs Kirkwood,' Norah said brightly. 'It can't be helped. I go to see Mabel every Tuesday.'

Mrs Kirkwood scowled.

Amélie had dressed carefully and even asked Uncle Jim if she could use his polish for her shoes. Her hair was neatly tied back and she'd made sure her nails were clean. She was about as ready as she could be but she was very nervous all the same.

Ma turned out to be a plump-looking woman with grey hair and a large mole just above her top lip. She had small piggy eyes but it seemed that nothing got past her. Her manner was rather brusque but she wasn't an unfair woman. Hard working herself, she expected the best of everyone and made sure she got it. Amélie was to wipe down the tables, tidy the condiments and collect the empty dishes to take to the kitchen where an older woman called Susan was doing the washing-up.

'Use this cloth for the tables,' Ma explained. 'Pile the

dishes onto the trolley like this. Scrape away any leftovers into the white bucket. We don't waste anything here. That's for the pig man.'

Amélie did her best to hide her surprise. Pig man? She hadn't a clue who he was. She'd never even heard of one. There were so many things to get used to, like having to go outside to the toilet at Auntie Norah's; the bathroom being off the kitchen instead of upstairs; only having a kettle full of water for a wash in the morning; being treated like a grown-up; the relationship between Auntie Norah and Uncle Jim . . . It was all so different from being at home.

Ma did the cooking and until the first dinners were dished up, Amélie was expected to help prepare the vegetables in the kitchen. 'I'll show you what to do when the time comes,' said Ma.

At four o'clock, the end of the day, Amélie had to put the chairs onto the tables and sweep the floor.

The people who ate in the canteen were mostly men. The only women were a couple of WPCs and the station matron who looked after women prisoners, particularly at night. Ma ruled the canteen with an iron rod.

On her third day, as she bent over a table to pick up a dirty plate, a policeman on the next table fondled Amélie's bottom. As she squealed in shocked surprise, Amélie accidentally knocked the plate to the floor and it smashed. She froze.

The policeman thought it very funny. Ma didn't.

'That's enough of that, PC Weller,' she snapped. 'You can help her pick up those pieces and say you're sorry.'

Amélie's heart was racing. She closed her eyes and tried her best to stay calm. This wasn't Daddy. He couldn't do to her what Daddy did. She was in a room full of people.

'The hell I will,' said PC Weller. 'She shouldn't be so bloody clumsy.'

Amélie took a deep breath. 'It's all right, Ma,' she said. 'I'll do it.' She knelt down and began to pick up the broken pieces but it was difficult. Her hands were trembling.

Ma put down the ladle she was using to serve up the meals and came around the other side of the counter. The canteen had suddenly become very quiet. As she reached his table, she put her hand out to remove his plate of food but PC Weller was too quick for her. He hung on to the plate as if his life depended on it as the pair of them eyeballed each other.

'It's hard enough to get decent staff in this canteen, sunshine,' Ma said coldly. 'I can do without the likes of you overstepping the mark. Don't come in here again until you have apologised.'

'Why the hell should I apologise?' Weller scoffed.

'Because I said so,' said Ma levelly.

'Can I help it if the silly tart fumbled the plate?' Weller protested innocently. Raising his hands in mock surprise, he looked around for male support but everybody busied themselves with their food.

Every eye was on him as Ma turned on her heel and walked back to the counter. Amélie, the pieces all collected onto another plate, rose to her feet and made her way back to the kitchen with as much dignity as she could muster. Weller watched her go with a look of satisfaction on his face. 'Anyway, who does she think she is?' he asked his fellow officers. 'The ruddy Queen of Sheba?'

Ma ignored his outburst and addressing the inspector who was first in the queue she said, 'Sorry to keep you waiting, love. What can I get you?'

Nobody moved. Weller looked slightly puzzled but picking up his knife and fork and turning his attention back to his plate, he suddenly lost his appetite. The contents of the overflowing ashtray sat in the middle of his meal.

*

London Evening Standard
Friday, September 15th, 1939

Have you seen this girl?

Concern is growing for an evacuee child last seen on September 1st. Nine-year-old Lillian Ffox-Webster has not been seen since the morning when she was spotted on the platform at Euston Station where the pupils of St Mary Magdalene School were being evacuated to Kettering, Northampton. By the time they reached their destination, it was noted that Lillian was missing. Lillian is 4ft 2inches with light blonde hair worn short. She was dressed in a brown gabardine mackintosh and brown sandals.

Anyone with any information is urged to contact Kettering Police, the British Transport Police Euston or the Met from any high street police box.

CHAPTER 8

Norah

When she got back from shopping in town the next day, Norah was startled to see Penny Draycot sitting on the wall outside her house. As she came closer, she could see that her friend's eyes were red and puffy. Penny had been crying.

'Whatever's happened?'

'It's Ted,' said Penny, her tears beginning to flow again. 'He's got his call-up papers.'

'Oh, Penny, I'm so sorry. How disappointing for you.'

'The thing is, Norah, I don't know what to do.'

'Come on inside,' said Norah, slipping her arm around her friend's shoulders, 'and I'll put the kettle on.'

They let the dog out into the garden and Penny sat at the kitchen table while Norah made a pot of tea. As she listened to Penny's stifled sobs, she was getting quite worried. This had to be something more than simply Ted's call up. Penny was always smart and well turned out but today her hair was a mess and she looked as if she'd done two rounds with the British welterweight boxing champion Jake Kilrain. Norah opened the cake tin and put a slice of fruit cake on

69

a plate. 'I'll just take a cuppa and this cake into my mother-in-law and then she won't come out and disturb us,' she said in hushed tones.

A few minutes later, Norah rejoined her friend. 'So, you think you'll have to postpone the wedding?' she said, by now second guessing the real reason why Penny was so distraught.

Penny nodded miserably.

'But it's not the end of the world,' Norah said comfortingly. 'You can arrange it for another time. I'm sure they'll give him leave.'

'You don't understand,' Penny said, her voice muffled by her handkerchief. 'I simply have to be married. I can't wait.' Her friend took a deep breath. 'I'm pregnant.'

For a second, Norah was lost for words. 'Are you sure?'

Penny nodded. 'Oh, I know I should have been patient, but I love him so much and he wanted me so badly . . .'

'You don't have to justify yourself to me,' said Norah, rubbing Penny's hand.

'But what am I going to do?' Penny whimpered. 'If we don't get married, my dad will go nuts. He might even kick me out and then everyone will know.'

'Everyone will know what?' Mrs Kirkwood's sharp voice made the pair of them jump. Penny looked around, startled, before turning her back on their intruder and sniffing into her handkerchief once more.

Norah frowned crossly. 'Did you want something?' she said coldly.

'There's no sugar in my tea,' the older woman complained.

Norah rose to her feet and handed her the sugar bowl from the kitchen dresser. Mrs Kirkwood hovered as if waiting to be included in the conversation.

'Anything else?' said Norah.

Reluctantly, her mother-in-law shuffled away. Penny went to say something but Norah held her hand up until they heard the door to her room close. Norah got up and shut the kitchen door.

'Now,' she said. 'When does Ted have to report for duty?'

'October the fifth,' Penny said miserably. 'Everything was arranged for November the fourth. That's my birthday.'

'Your dad is quite happy for you to marry Ted? I mean, he's not likely to raise an objection if you're not quite twenty-one?'

'Oh no,' said Penny blowing her nose. 'He and Ted get on really well.'

Norah consulted the kitchen calendar. 'Can you two get over to the church today? If you ask for the banns to be read this Sunday, you've just got time to get three in before Saturday September the thirtieth.'

Penny's jaw dropped. 'You mean we could still be married before he has to go?'

'I think so,' said Norah. 'And if you explain that Ted is about to join the army, I'm sure the vicar will be only too pleased to help.'

The small ray of hope in Penny's eyes quickly dimmed. 'But we'll never get the use of the church hall at such short notice.'

Norah shook her head, frustrated. She was right. St Matthew's in Tarring Road, which had been booked for Penny and Ted's wedding, was ideal but its hall was also popular with fund raisers and everybody was trying to 'do their bit' for their favourite charities before the Germans came.

Norah looked around. 'Why not have the wedding break-fast here?' she said. 'It won't be as nice as the church hall but we can squeeze quite a few in and if it's a nice day, it might be warm enough to go in the garden.'

'Are you sure?'

'Of course,' said Norah, brushing away the enormity of what she was suggesting.

'Oh, Norah, thank you,' said Penny, her face transformed by a wide smile. 'I knew you'd know what to do. Thank you, thank you.'

They both laughed. 'You'd better ask your mum if she can help with some sandwiches,' Norah went on, 'and I can always ask around for a few cakes.'

They looked up as the kitchen door slowly opened. Mrs Kirkwood was coming back.

'Nosy old bat,' Penny whispered.

'Well, you'd better get going,' Norah said in a low voice. 'You've got a lot to do.'

'Sorry to interrupt,' Mrs Kirkwood began.

'That's all right,' Norah said cheerfully. 'Penny was just leaving.'

A couple of days later, Ivan Steele knocked on the kitchen window. Norah was busy doing some washing and Mrs Kirkwood was in her room. 'Come in, come in,' she called.

He came into the kitchen and snatched his cap from his head, revealing his jagged ear. Norah had no idea how he'd come to damage his ear but it must have been painful at the time. 'Have you got five minutes, Norah, love?'

'Of course I have,' said Norah, wiping her hands on her apron. 'Fancy a cuppa?'

He nodded and she indicated that he should sit down. 'Got myself in a spot of bother,' he said gloomily.

'Oh, why's that?'

'I entered a competition,' he said, shaking his head, 'and I won.'

Norah chuckled. 'You won? So why the long face?'

'It's a yard of manure,' said Ivan.

Norah couldn't help herself. She laughed aloud. There was a sound by the door and Mrs Kirkwood came into the kitchen. Ivan jumped to his feet.

'Mrs Kirkwood,' said Norah, introducing them to each other, 'this is Mr Steele. He's the caretaker at Heene Road School. Mrs Kirkwood is my mother-in-law.'

The two older people nodded to each other.

'Ivan.'

'Mrs Kirkwood.'

'You know each other?'

'Oh yes,' said Mrs Kirkwood stiffly. 'We were at school together.'

The atmosphere between them was cool so Norah guessed that they hadn't exactly been best friends. She reached for another cup and saucer. 'Mr Steele has just been telling me he's won a yard of best mature as a prize.'

'So?' said Mrs Kirkwood, sitting down. 'Why the long face?'

'I live in two rooms on the first floor,' said Ivan.

Although looking after so many people and the animals meant extra work for her, Norah welcomed the break from the usual routine. Since the evacuation, she and Penny had visited at least forty or fifty houses in the town to check on both the householders and the children. Thankfully, there were few problems. Apart from the odd grumble about the paperwork being slow, most of the complaints had been about the lack of blankets. The government had promised they would be sent to the town before the end of August but they still hadn't materialised. The women of Worthing had begged or borrowed blankets and counterpanes from their neighbours with the promise to return them as soon as possible but with the cooler evenings becoming more frequent, people's patience was growing thin. Fortunately, a large consignment of army issue blankets had come in on Wednesday and with the help of the Boy Scouts most of them had been distributed.

'How are the wedding plans going?' Norah had asked Penny during a lunch break.

'Quite well. I have the last fitting for my dress tomorrow.'

The following Saturday, Norah and the children were off on an outing. Jim and the other lads in the police station had had a whip-round and organised a trip to Devil's Dyke for evacuees. They'd hired two coaches.

Norah put the last of the sandwiches into the bag and did up the straps. Getting ready for the day ahead of them had been a bit of a marathon but she was sure it would be worth it. She filled the flask with tea and remembered to put a couple of spoons of sugar in a brown paper bag for Jim as he liked sugar in his tea.

The children were very excited. She could hear them running up and down the stairs, whooping with delight. Amélie had given herself the job of feeding the budgie, which had been left in the alcove by the door nobody used. Mrs Kirkwood kept well away from it and complained bitterly whenever the budgie squawked, but everybody else thought Joey was an affectionate bird. He even said a few words, which meant that Norah had the joy of hearing her dad's voice ringing out in the house every now and then although the dog wasn't so happy. Every time Joey cried, 'Max, go in your bed,' the poor animal slunk onto his blanket with his tail between his legs.

Of course Mrs Kirkwood did nothing to help but Amélie had turned out to be a real gem. She was thoughtful, too. One day she gave Norah a small bunch of wildflowers with a note attached to the stems. *Thank you, Auntie Norah. Love Amélie and Linnet. XX.* It had brought a tear to Norah's eye. Amélie could also be relied upon to peel the potatoes, albeit with a lot of the potato itself cut off with the skin, or cut up a cabbage ready for tea when she got home from the canteen, and most nights she helped with the washing-up as well. Many's the time Norah had thought to herself, 'what a lucky mother to have such a lovely daughter', and she wondered why Amélie was so reluctant to talk about her family. She would clam up whenever Norah raised the subject, but as time went by Linnet let a few things slip. At the end of their first week in Worthing, Norah had sat all four of them at the kitchen table with a pencil and paper to write a letter to their mothers. Ruth and Marjorie began scribbling away but Linnet said, 'My mummy is dead.'

Norah had been deeply shocked. 'Oh, I'm so sorry,' she'd begun, but resisting the urge to question the child further, she added, 'couldn't you write to your daddy instead?' Linnet had beamed and begun her letter but Amélie had deliberately put her pencil down and stared into space. Norah felt uneasy when, ten minutes later, Amélie got up and left the table. Something was troubling that girl . . . but what was it?

'How do you spell Audley,' Linnet whispered to Marjorie.

Marjorie shrugged and when Linnet saw Norah looking she put her hand across her mouth.

'A-u-d-l-e-y,' Norah said but Linnet didn't write it down.

'Is that where you live?' Norah asked, but Linnet shook her head and Norah noticed her crossing out a word on the envelope.

Ruth and Marjorie posted their letter and drawings the following Monday, on their way to school, but Linnet's stayed on the mantelpiece. Why had she stopped writing her address? It was all very puzzling but Norah promised the little girl that she would give it to her daddy as soon as she could.

Ruth and Marjorie's mother had written to thank her for looking after her girls and asking to come to see them. Norah had answered by return of post telling her she was welcome at any time but she'd also mentioned their forthcoming outing. She smiled to herself. The girls had no idea that Mrs Harrison was coming on the train and would meet them at Devil's Dyke. It would be a wonderful surprise.

The dog began to bark and the girls' delighted squeals told Norah they had found his ball. Sure enough, the next sound she heard was the ball bouncing down the stairs.

'For heaven's sake!' came Mrs Kirkwood's angry voice. 'Will you be quiet.'

'Come along, girls,' Norah called. 'We'd better get to the end of the road or we're going to miss the coach.'

'Thank the Lord for that,' Mrs Kirkwood said right behind her. 'All that racket is giving me a headache.'

'Well, now you can look forward to a nice peaceful day,' Norah said pleasantly. 'We won't be back until late. I've left you some sandwiches in the meat safe. Help yourself to drinks.' And having checked that everybody had been to the toilet, she picked up the lunch bag and they set off.

Norah and her brood met the coach on the Tarring Road. Jim was already on board. He and Norah sat together surrounded by the noisy chatter of children, some of whom hadn't seen each other for three weeks.

'Whose flippin' idea was this?' Jim asked good-naturedly as somebody in the seat behind elbowed him in the head.

Norah chuckled and gave him a peck on his cheek. 'I can't imagine. Some idiot with half a brain, I suppose.'

It didn't take long to get to Devil's Dyke. Five miles north of Brighton it was a wide area of open countryside with steep inclines and plenty of space. In Victorian times it had been a kind of pleasure park with children's carnival rides, its own railway connection, a small zoo and a cable car ride over the deepest dip. The railway line which ran from Aldrington closed in 1938, so now the only way to get there was by bus, car or coach. There was a hotel on the hill and a small kiosk that sold ice creams. On hot, sunny days in summer there were donkey rides and an enclosure with a few goats and small animals to pet. Talk of war and the onset of autumn meant that all of that was gone except for the kiosk.

As the coach pulled up at the bus stop, a woman in a light blue coat waved. Marjorie leapt to her feet. 'Mummy,' she cried. 'That's my mummy.'

Just as Norah predicted, Ruth and Marjorie were overjoyed and it brought a lump to Norah's throat when she saw them fall into their mother's open arms.

The day turned out to be a very happy one with no mishaps at all. They began by walking along a pathway to reach the top of the hill and while the adults created a picnic area, the children rolled down the steep hill to the sound of laughter. The children threw handfuls of new mown hay, their delight at being in such a large open space apparent for all to see.

77

When it was time to eat, Norah invited Mrs Harrison to sit on her blanket. Amélie and Linnet came to join Ruth and Marjorie and Norah couldn't help noticing that Mrs Harrison seemed to be staring at Linnet quite a lot.

'I can't thank you enough, Mrs Kirkwood,' she said as Norah offered her some tea from the flask. 'My girls look the picture of health.'

'Oh, Norah, please,' said Norah, 'and they've honestly been no trouble at all. I've enjoyed having them.'

'I've been thinking about taking them back,' said Mrs Harrison. 'The place is so quiet without them and I miss them so much.'

Norah did her best to hide her disappointment. 'Well, they are welcome to stay as long as you want.'

'Nothing's happened, you see,' Mrs Harrison went on. 'We've had no bombing at all and I keep thinking maybe it won't be so bad after all.'

Norah offered Mrs Harrison an egg sandwich but she had come with her own. Her girls sat close to their mother and shared her lunch. It was obvious by the way she kept fussing over them that she was enjoying herself. After their meal and about an hour's rest, everybody collected their things and strolled towards the Devil's Dyke hotel.

By the time they got there, the pub was just opening so Jim and the other men trooped inside for a beer while the women queued up by the kiosk for ice creams. When it came to Norah's turn, Mrs Harrison insisted that she pay, waving Norah's hand away as she reached into her purse. 'No, no, it's the least I can do.'

The children sat long enough to eat their Lyon's Maid wafer brick and then they all decided to take turns in rolling down the hill again.

Jim came out of the bar with a gin and it for Norah and a small sherry for Mrs Harrison. 'Half an hour,' he called to the children, 'and then we'll be off home.'

Norah closed her eyes and sat facing the early evening sun. She stretched luxuriantly. 'It's been a perfect day. I hope you enjoyed yourself, Mrs Harrison.'

When there was no answer, she opened her eyes again to see that Mrs Harrison was staring towards the children.

'Mrs Harrison?'

'Umm? Oh, yes, thank you. I've had a grand time.'

Norah followed her gaze. 'Is something wrong?'

Mrs Harrison shook her head. 'Not really,' she said, 'but I have a feeling I've seen that girl before.'

'Who, Linnet?'

Mrs Harrison frowned. 'Yes.' She paused. 'Linnet is a fairly unusual name. What's her surname?'

'Osborne,' said Norah, 'and Amélie is her sister.' Norah was puzzled now but it was too late to open out their conversation. The bus was trundling towards them.

Mrs Harrison rose to her feet. 'My mistake,' she said. 'It can't be the girl I'm thinking about. Different surname.' She called her girls and the three of them hugged each other. 'Mummy has to go now,' she said, 'but I shall come and see you again.'

Marjorie began to cry.

'Now, now,' Mrs Harrison said soothingly, 'you mustn't cry. I want you to be a good girl for Auntie Norah.' She kissed them fiercely and while Norah took Marjorie in her arms, their mother handed Ruth three rolled copies of *School Friend* and hurried to the bus stop.

CHAPTER 9

Norah

'I do wish you would get rid of that bloody bird,' Mrs Kirkwood said as Norah buttered the bread at the kitchen table.

'Well, I can't,' said Norah, 'and I don't want to.' She was beginning to feel more than slightly irritated by her mother-in-law who seemed to take delight in being awkward.

'You'll have the neighbours complaining before long,' Mrs Kirkwood continued. 'It screeches all the time.'

Norah pursed her lips and said nothing. She didn't believe for one moment that was true but just to be on the safe side she would have a word with next door. Speaking for herself, Norah was glad Joey was here. He certainly brightened the place up. The girls always made a great deal of fuss of him and Joey lapped up the attention. He loved being talked to and having his head rubbed between the bars of his cage and as soon as they came home from school, the girls ran into the sitting room to see him.

'*The girls really enjoy talking to Joey,*' Norah wrote in

her weekly letter to her mother, '*and he loves their company. His feathers are fine.*' According to her parents, if a budgie got bored, it would start pulling out its feathers but thankfully, so far, Joey had been well occupied!

The morning had been hectic. Today was Penny and Ted's wedding day. They were to marry in St Matthew's church at two this afternoon and Norah was making sandwiches like they'd gone out of fashion. Already everybody had to carry an identity card with them whenever they went out, and there was talk of food rationing coming into effect next month, but at the moment she could still lay her hands on whatever she wanted. She and Amélie had already made a loaf of egg sandwiches, half a loaf of salmon and shrimp paste, a loaf of grated cheese and tomato, and since her next-door neighbour had popped round with a tin of salmon left over from last Christmas, they were making some salmon and cucumber sandwiches with the other half of the loaf.

Because everything was taking place at such short notice, the wedding party would only number twenty-five, but thanks to friends and neighbours, the kitchen dresser already groaned with cakes including twelve fairy cakes, twenty-four jam tarts, rock buns and a chocolate sponge. Last night, the bride's father and brother brought two cases of beer and some sherry, which had been left on the cold pantry floor until it was needed. Penny's Uncle Fred would be here shortly with a tray of finger rolls, some sausage rolls, and ingredients for a fruit punch, and the wedding cake was already in the cupboard under the stairs with the door firmly shut to keep the dog out.

Norah blew out her cheeks and arched her back. 'There,' she said with a satisfied smile, 'I think we're done.'

Amélie collected the cheese grater and the empty butter dish and took it to the sink. She glanced up at the clock. 'Shall I get the girls ready?'

'Would you, Amélie?' said Norah. 'That would be such a help. I'm desperate for a good wash and it'll take at least a quarter of an hour to walk to St Matthew's.'

'Hello,' called a sing-song voice and they both looked up to see a middle-aged man with a tray of food outside the kitchen window.

'That must be Penny's Uncle Fred,' said Norah. 'Come in,' she said, gesturing him inside.

He was followed to the door by the postman bringing a couple of letters. No time to read them now, Norah shoved the letters beside the picture of her parents on the kitchen dresser and turned her attention to finding somewhere to put the finger rolls and the stuff for the fruit punch. At this rate, she'd be lucky to get to the church at all!

Of course, everything went like clockwork. The bride, only five minutes late, looked radiant. Her dress was white satin with puff sleeves and had a sweetheart neckline. She wore long white gloves up to the elbow and she carried a bouquet of autumnal flowers. When Norah complimented her Penny had chuckled.

'Mum's feet went so bloomin' fast on the treadle machine to get it finished, I honestly thought she'd take off,' she said and they both laughed.

As Norah hugged her friend and wished her good luck, Penny whispered in her ear, 'You've been a real pal. I couldn't have done it without you.'

Norah blushed. 'Get away with you,' she said. 'I only did what anyone else would do.'

'You did more than that,' Penny insisted. 'I owe you one, Norah.'

Norah gave her a playful pat on her arm. 'Don't be daft.'

The party went on for most of the evening. The weather was kind and although the women had to wear cardigans by the time seven o'clock came round, they stayed outside. Jim and a couple of the men dragged the piano to the doorway and he played all the old tunes while the bride and groom danced on the grass and everybody else sang. Neighbours gathered outside the fence and the beer flowed. When the booze ran out, the Richard Cobden pub was only just up the road. The children ran around the garden and played hide and seek, stole more sandwiches than they were meant to have and stuffed themselves silly with cake. Most surprising of all, Mrs Kirkwood parked herself on a chair just outside the door. Every time Norah glanced at her she was surrounded by people either getting her a drink or a piece of cake or simply chatting to her. She had never seen her mother-in-law smiling this much before and surprise, surprise, she even managed a dance or two.

The next morning, after breakfast, Mrs Kirkwood seemed to be hobbling more than usual. 'Bring me a bowl of water and help me do me feet, would you, Norah? My corns are killing me.'

'I can't stop yet, I'm afraid,' said Norah. The kitchen was in uproar. 'I'll do it for you later.'

As Mrs Kirkwood shuffled back to her room Amélie said, 'I'll do it for her if you like, Auntie Norah.'

Norah was only too glad. She gave Amélie the enamel bowl from the bathroom and filled it with warm water. 'Put a couple of tablespoons of bicarb of soda in that,' she said. 'It'll help to soak off the hard skin.'

A few minutes later, Amélie was in Mrs Kirkwood's room. She put the bowl down and helped her take off her slippers. Her big toes were twisted towards the others and two large corns covered the second and third toe on her left foot.

'Did you enjoy yourself yesterday?' Mrs Kirkwood asked as Amélie gently swished the water over the old lady's feet.

'Oh yes,' said Amélie.

'And what about your job in the canteen? Are you getting on all right?'

Amélie told her all about the formidable Ma and how she ruled the canteen with a rod of iron. 'She's been very kind to me though,' Amélie added.

'I never had the chance to go out to work,' Mrs Kirkwood said wistfully. 'Back in my day young ladies were only expected to get married.'

As they chatted amiably, Amélie learned a lot about Norah's mother-in-law. Surprisingly, she wasn't as old as Amélie had imagined; only fifty-eight. She had married Uncle Jim's father when she was twenty-one and they'd lived in a small, terraced house in East Worthing.

'What happened to Uncle Jim's father?' Amélie asked.

'He died,' Mrs Kirkwood said abruptly.

'Will you be going back to your house?' Amélie asked.

Mrs Kirkwood shook her head. She leaned forward confidentially. 'I may be an old grouch but I like your company.' And they both chuckled. 'I imagine this is a very different life from what you're used to.'

'It is a bit,' Amélie agreed, 'but I like it here.'

'I get the feeling you come from somewhere posh.'

Amélie said nothing.

'You remind me of myself when I was young,' Mrs Kirkwood mused.

Amélie looked up and they shared a shy smile.

Mrs Kirkwood put a gnarled hand over Amélie's. 'If you ever need help or a bit of advice, you know where to come.'

Once the old lady had soaked her feet, Amélie knelt in front of Mrs Kirkwood and put her foot on the towel on her lap. She was very gentle as she cut the nails and rubbed away the dead skin. Then she tackled the painful corn with a pumice stone.

'You look as if you're enjoying yourself,' said the old woman.

'I like helping people,' said Amélie. 'My moth—' She stopped.

'Yes?' said Mrs Kirkwood. 'You were saying?'

Amélie shook her head. 'It was nothing. Just a memory.'

When she had dried in-between her toes, Mrs Kirkwood allowed Amélie to apply cream to her feet and legs.

'How does that feel?' Amélie said pleasantly when she had finished.

'Lovely,' said Mrs Kirkwood. 'You are a kind girl.'

Back in the kitchen, Norah had done most of the clearing up. 'How did you get on?'

'Fine,' said Amélie, tipping the dirty water down the sink. 'We had a lovely chat.'

Behind her back Norah gave her a slightly bemused smile.

After such a hectic day the day before, nobody felt like doing much so they had a quiet Sunday. The girls drew pictures and coloured them in; Uncle Jim dozed in the sitting room; Mrs Kirkwood listened to the radio and Amélie watched Auntie Norah as she sat at the treadle sewing machine. She had a rather ordinary light brown jumper; plain, with a polo neck and deep ribbing at the waist. Amélie marvelled at her skill as Auntie Norah cut the polo neck off and then cut the jumper about two inches above the deep ribbing at the waist, making it a lot shorter. Norah cut right up the front of the jumper and then she sewed tartan bias binding all around the raw edges.

'Have you ever done any sewing?' Norah asked.

Amélie shook her head. 'We made a tray cloth at school but that was embroidery.'

'I bet your mum liked that,' said Auntie Norah.

Amélie said nothing. Norah felt a little uncomfortable for having mentioned the girl's mother.

The pockets for the cardigan were made from the ribbing from the bottom of the sweater and after she'd put bias binding around the edges, Norah fixed them to the front.

'Can you look in my button box and find me two buttons to match,' she asked Amélie as she sewed the pockets at a slight angle.

Amélie chose two red buttons which matched the red in the tartan. Norah made two loops out of the binding to do up the buttons and in no time at all, she had created a very pretty cardigan.

'Here,' she said when she'd finished, 'try it on.'

Amélie slipped her own cardigan off and put it on. It fitted beautifully and the colour suited her.

'Any chance of a cup of tea in here?' Uncle Jim called from the sitting room. 'My throat is as dry as the Sahara desert.'

Auntie Norah stood to her feet and Amélie went to take the cardigan off.

'No, no. It's yours,' said Norah, putting her hand gently on Amélie's shoulders. The girl looked almost moved to tears.

They packed up the sewing things and Amélie helped her lay the tea table. Norah came out of the pantry with an assortment of tins. 'Just leftovers today,' she said brightly.

Everybody came to the table eagerly because it was a chance to enjoy a few exotic tastes from yesterday's feast all over again. Nobody minded that the sandwiches were a bit soggy when there was the promise of another chocolate fairy cake or a piece of lemon tart.

'How are your feet?' Norah asked Mrs Kirkwood.

'Better,' she said in a non-committal tone.

Behind her back, Norah raised an eyebrow and pulled a sympathetic face but Amélie didn't seem to mind. Coming from Mrs Kirkwood, even that was high praise indeed.

The younger girls were ready for bed a lot earlier that evening and once they were safely tucked up, Norah invited Amélie to join the grown-ups in a game of cards. Uncle Jim brought three bottles of milk stout to the table and Norah made Amélie a cup of Ovaltine. Then they taught her how to play whist.

With Mrs Kirkwood as her partner, Amélie did her best and although she and Mrs Kirkwood didn't win, they enjoyed their evening.

'Well, Norah,' Uncle Jim said at last as he looked at the clock, 'I think we'd all better toddle up the wooden hill.'

As she said her goodnights, Amélie felt she had never been so happy. Even Mrs Kirkwood was smiling. Norah went into the kitchen to clear up and as soon as he'd taken the dog out for a walk, Jim came to help.

As she put the tea towel over the top of the grill to dry, Jim slipped his arms around Norah's waist. 'Happy?'

Norah leaned against him and smiled. 'Oh, Jim, I do like having them here and Amélie is like a daughter.'

Jim nodded. 'She's a lovely girl. And,' he added incredulously, 'look what she's done to Mother.'

Norah turned to face him and they both laughed. Jim kissed her hungrily. 'Darling.'

They kissed again and this time Jim's hand slid down her back until it reached her bottom. He pushed himself gently against her and Norah moaned with pleasure. 'Come on,' he whispered. 'Let's go to bed.'

The plates she had just dried needed to go in the kitchen dresser cupboard so as Jim left the room, Norah picked them up to put them away. It was then that she saw the letters the postman had brought yesterday. Heavens above, she'd forgotten all about them. Norah stacked the plates and took the two envelopes down. One was obviously a bill. The other was handwritten with a London postmark. Norah opened it quickly.

Dear Mrs Kirkwood,

I hope you don't mind but my husband and I have decided we should like to have our children back home. Nothing seems to be happening here and quite a few of our friends have already collected their children. Harold and I feel that even if the bombs come, we would sooner be all together as a family. With this in mind, I should like to come to collect them next Saturday. We are very grateful for all that you have done for Ruth and Marjorie and we could never repay your kindness.

Norah lowered herself into a chair as a wave of disappointment flooded over her. It was over. Taking her handkerchief from her apron pocket she dabbed her eyes to read the rest of Mrs Harrison's letter.

Further to our conversation about Amélie and Linnet, I have enclosed the newspaper cutting I told you about. The name is different but I think you will agree that Lillian bears a striking resemblance to Linnet.
   Yours sincerely
   Gwen Harrison

Norah pulled open the envelope again and in the corner she found a newspaper cutting. When she opened it out, she took in her breath noisily as her dreams of keeping her surrogate family suddenly evaporated.

CHAPTER 10

Norah

With all thought of love-making gone, Norah and Jim talked far into the night. The newspaper cutting had thrown up so many questions; so many anomalies.

'I knew she was keeping something from us,' said Norah, 'but I kidded myself it was just because she liked being here with us and didn't want us to send her back.'

'It's obviously more than that,' said Jim. He looked more carefully at the cutting. 'This only mentions a girl called Lillian. If they were together, why no mention of the older sister?'

'Are they actually sisters?' Norah said. They stared at each other in alarm.

'You're not suggesting Amélie kidnapped Linnet, are you?' asked Jim.

Norah shrugged.

'No.' Jim shook his head thoughtfully. 'If Linnet was a lot younger, that might be the case but she's old enough to speak up for herself.'

'I suppose so,' Norah said cautiously.

'And she's not scared of Amélie or anything, is she,' said Jim.

Norah relaxed. 'You're right. But why all the secrecy? And why the name change?'

Jim looked at the cutting once again. 'It certainly looks like Linnet. The uniform is the same and the girl in the picture has got the same smile.'

'That *is* Linnet,' said Norah firmly.

'This cutting is nearly two weeks old,' Jim went on. 'This girl in the picture may have been found by now. In fact, she probably has.' He was relaxing. 'Surely it would have been in the national papers if she was still missing. Front page of the *Daily Chronicle* or the *Mirror*.'

'So what shall we do?'

Jim thought for a minute then said, 'Nothing. And don't say anything or let on to the girls. We don't want them running off to God knows where before we can find out if this does have anything to do with them. I'll talk to someone at the station.'

'Good idea,' Norah conceded.

Jim leaned over her to switch off the light. 'Try not to worry, love,' he said into the darkness. 'We'll soon get it sorted.'

Norah bit back her tears. 'I can't believe Amélie is a bad girl.'

Jim's hand sought hers under the sheet and he squeezed her fingers. 'Neither can I, love.'

There was a short silence then Norah said, 'If they all go back, I shall miss them dreadfully.'

'I know, love,' said Jim. They lay quietly for a few moments and then Jim said, 'Perhaps it's time to think about adopting a kiddie of our own.'

Norah took in her breath. 'But I got the impression you weren't too keen on the idea.'

'I wasn't while there was still a chance that we . . .' His voice trailed. 'You still want one though, don't you, Norah?'

She turned towards him. 'Having the girls has made me so happy, Jim. I hate the thought of being on our own again.'

'Then let's do it.'

'Don't do it just for my sake, Jim.'

'I'm not,' he said. 'Truth to tell, I've loved having them here as well. The house won't be the same without Ruth and Marjorie and if Amélie and Linnet go as well . . .' His voice trailed.

'Do you think we'd be accepted, Jim?'

'I don't see why not,' he said. 'There are plenty of unwanted babies out there and we could offer one a good home.'

'Oh, Jim.'

They lay still for a while until Jim rolled towards her and Norah lifted her nightie.

The days which followed were filled with the usual hectic routine of breakfast, school, selling the last of the garden produce, tidying up and clearing the ground ready for winter, carefully storing the crop of carrots, beetroot and parsnips in layers in specially made sand boxes, pickling the shallots for Christmas, making marrow chutney, picking the children up from school and letting them play in the park or giving them something to do at home if it was wet, tea time, bath and bed.

After school, the younger girls picked up the windfall apples, ready for Norah to make apple pie, while Amélie helped Mrs Kirkwood sort the best of the fruit and wrap them individually in clean newspaper before putting them carefully in an old drawer.

'Make sure they're not touching,' Mrs Kirkwood cautioned. 'One rotten apple can spoil the whole lot.'

Life was never dull.

Norah had added a dachshund to their ever-growing menagerie. She'd spotted the poor little creature in town while she was doing her shopping. It yelped in pain as a man lashed out with his foot and as the dog ran away someone called out, 'Bloody German dog.' Norah immediately rushed to rescue the animal. She put it in her bicycle basket and by the time she got it home, she and Sausage were best friends. Max eyed him curiously but after a few cautious moments, they began to play. When Jim came home, he raised his eyebrows as Norah said in a superior tone, 'You've always said yourself that it's not good for a dog to be on its own,' and he'd laughed.

On Saturday, she made sure Ruth and Marjorie looked their best for their mother. She was arriving on the eleven o'clock train and Norah had invited Mrs Harrison to have a spot of lunch before they went back. Considering that they had just tipped into October, the weather was fantastic. Norah set up the table in the garden.

She and the girls set off at ten forty-five for the station. Amélie was in the canteen and Linnet stayed behind with Mrs Kirkwood and the pets. Ruth and Marjorie skipped all the way. Norah bought them all a platform ticket and the girls were excited to get it clipped by the ticket inspector. They didn't have long to wait before Mrs Harrison's train trundled alongside the platform.

'There she is!' cried Ruth as the carriage door opened

and the girls hurled themselves into their mother's arms. The four of them walked back to the house and while Mrs Harrison was dragged upstairs to see the girls' room, Norah put the kettle on. She heard a shuffle behind her.

'Coming into the garden to join us, Mrs Kirkwood?' said Norah, her back still turned.

Her mother-in-law sniffed. 'I suppose so,' she said grudgingly.

Norah put an extra cup and saucer on the tray. 'Was Linnet all right?'

'She played with that stupid Hitler dog,' Mrs Kirkwood said. 'Really, Norah, I don't know why you brought it home. We're supposed to be fighting the Germans not taking care of them.'

'For heaven's sake,' Norah retorted. 'The poor animal isn't responsible for the war so let's stop going on about it, shall we? It's only a dog.'

But Mrs Kirkwood wanted the last word. 'Horrid thing,' she said tetchily.

It was pleasant sitting outside. The sun still had warmth and there was a gentle breeze. The girls took turns to push each other on the rope swing Jim had created on the bough of the old apple tree as the three women sat at the table. Max barked excitedly but Sausage seemed rather nervous of their feet so he lay under the safety of Norah's chair.

'Anything much happening in London?' Norah asked.

'Not really.' Mrs Harrison shook her head. 'It's been five weeks since war was declared and apart from the sandbags piled up everywhere life goes on much the same.'

'They say the RAF have been flying over Germany dropping leaflets,' said Norah. 'I keep hoping that Hitler will pull back and we'll have peace after all.'

Mrs Kirkwood harrumphed. A fly landed on her shoe and she bent to wave it away.

'What did you think of that newspaper cutting?' Mrs Harrison asked.

Norah's eyes widened as she gave her a warning shake of the head.

Mrs Kirkwood sat back up. 'What newspaper cutting?'

'There was a story in the *Telegraph*,' Mrs Harrison said fluidly.

Norah stared at her helplessly, her mind in a panic. Oh, don't tell her about Linnet, she thought. Jim said to keep it under wraps. She looked around the garden desperately. Where was Linnet, anyway? 'More tea, Mrs Harrison?'

'One of our pilots, a young lad, came back from dropping leaflets a couple of hours earlier than he should have done,' Mrs Harrison went on. 'Apparently he hadn't opened the bundle but dropped the whole thing intact.'

Relieved, Norah laughed. She lifted the tea pot again.

'Stupid boy,' said Mrs Kirkwood. 'He could have killed someone dropping a heavy parcel from that height.'

A smiling Mrs Harrison shook her hand. 'No, no more tea for me, thank you, Mrs Kirkwood.'

They made small talk for a while until Norah packed everything back onto the tray and rose to her feet. 'I'll get the sandwiches.'

'Let me give you a hand,' said Mrs Harrison, getting up.

Alone in the kitchen, Norah grasped Mrs Harrison's arm. 'Thank you so much for not saying anything,' she whispered.

'That's all right,' said Mrs Harrison. 'I guessed you didn't want your mother-in-law to know.'

'My husband says to keep it quiet until he's found out

about it. He's going to talk to one of the other inspectors, you see.'

Mrs Harrison nodded. 'Very sensible idea.'

Norah handed her a tray of sandwiches covered with a damp tea towel. 'We think you may be right, but it's all very strange.'

'I can quite see that,' said Mrs Harrison. She headed for the door but paused in the doorway. 'I would be grateful to know what you find out. I'm just as curious as you are.'

'Of course,' said Norah. 'And I should like to know how you and the girls are getting on. We've loved having them here and remember, if it does get too bad in London, they are always welcome to come back to Worthing.'

Mrs Harrison was clearly moved. 'Thank you, Mrs Kirkwood. You are very kind.'

'Norah,' said Norah.

'Gwen,' said Mrs Harrison.

Chief Inspector Reece stared down at the cutting on his desk before leaning back in his chair. 'And you think this is the same girl?'

'I don't know, sir, but she looks very like her.'

Jim had told him everything. Amélie's reluctance to talk about their family, the strangeness of their arrival in Worthing and the few things that Linnet had let drop. 'When my wife asked them to write a letter home, she told us their mother was dead,' he went on. As he spoke, something else crossed Jim's mind. 'She did write to her father,' he continued thoughtfully. 'Norah has left the letter on the mantelpiece until she can find out his address.'

'I suggest you open it,' said Inspector Reece. He stroked his chin. 'Have you any idea where they came from?'

Jim shook his head. 'PC Clark brought them to us. It was late, you see, and everybody knows what a soft heart my Norah has. He was simply anxious to find them a bed for the night.'

Inspector Reece lifted the phone on his desk. 'Send PC Clark in. We'll see what Clark can remember,' the inspector continued as he turned back to Jim. 'Worst come to the worst, you'll have to bring the girls in here for questioning.'

Jim raised his hand. 'I don't think Norah would be too happy with that, sir.'

'Can't help that,' said Reece. 'We've got to know who they are.'

'They're only little girls, sir,' said Jim. He was beginning to wonder if he'd made a mistake. He'd always thought of Inspector Reece as a reasonable man but he was going at this like a bull in a china shop.

There was a knock at the door and PC Clark walked in. 'You asked for me, sir?'

Inspector Reece filled him in.

PC Clark consulted his pocket book. 'Sergeant Plumb instructed me to go to the children's home in Bulkington Avenue at eleven fifteen a.m. where . . .'

'All right, all right man,' Inspector Reece snapped. 'You're not in a bloody court now. Just tell us the bare facts. When you spoke to them did either of the girls say where they'd come from?'

'No, sir.'

'What train did they get off?'

'The London bound, sir.'

The inspector looked puzzled. 'The train was on its way *to* London?'

'Yes, sir.'

'So where had they come from?'

'Nobody knew,' said PC Clark, thumbing pages. 'Apparently the station master rang down the line and somebody saw them getting on the train at Brockenhurst but the tiddler said they'd come from London.'

Inspector Reece frowned. 'Is it possible that they came from London and were trying to get back there?' he asked Jim.

Jim shrugged.

Inspector Reece turned his attention back to Clark. 'I want you to keep mum about this, Clark. The older girl works in the canteen but nothing of this conversation goes outside these four walls. Do I make myself clear?'

'Yes, sir,' said Clark, snapping to attention.

Inspector Reece waved him away. As soon as the door closed he looked at Jim. 'First, I want you to look at that letter. In the meantime, I shall make some enquiries with my colleagues in London and Brockenhurst. All right, Jim?'

'Yes, sir, thank you, sir,' said Jim.

Outside in the corridor, Jim took a deep breath. How peculiar. What was young Amélie up to?

CHAPTER 11

Norah

'*I'm in!*' Rene's letter bubbled over with excitement and as Norah lowered herself into a chair to read it, she chuckled. '*At the end of November, I've got to report for three weeks training at No.2 WAAF Depot Innsworth, Gloucester,*' Rene continued. '*Blimey, sis, I don't even know where that is. Mum says it's in the Cotswolds between Wales and Oxford but I'm none the wiser. Apparently, it's only just opened but I'm not allowed to say any more. I don't think I'll get to Worthing for Christmas this year. I shall miss you all like crazy but I'm looking forward to doing something worthwhile. Tell Mrs Cow-bags that I'm going to be with a thousand men. Ha, ha, that'll get her going. I bet your evacuees are having a wonderful time. I'm sure you're being a great mum to them. Love to Jim and tell him to hurry up and get ol' Hitler behind bars – but not before I've had a good time. Love you loads, Rene.*'

Back from her four-day honeymoon in Littlehampton, Penny Draycot, now Mrs Ted Andrews, looked radiantly happy.

She'd turned up at The Lilacs with a bunch of flowers picked from her mother's garden. Mrs Kirkwood had let her in and she'd sat in the kitchen waiting for Norah to come home.

'Penny!' cried Norah as she walked in the door. 'How long have you been here?'

'Not long.'

'Didn't my mother-in-law make you a cup of tea?'

'She was on her way out,' said Penny. She handed Norah the flowers. 'The last of the summer roses and a few Michaelmas daisies just to say thank you.'

Norah was thrilled. 'They're beautiful. Let me put them in water but first I'll put the kettle on.' She had just finished delivering the last of the much-needed blankets for the evacuees.

'Norah, you're a real pal for what you did for Ted and me.'

'It was nothing,' said Norah.

'Oh, but it was,' said Penny. 'If you hadn't stepped in to help us, I'd be in a right pickle by now. Thanks to you, I had my wedding day and a little honeymoon.'

'So tell me all about it,' Norah said as she scooped the tea leaves into the pot. 'Did you have a nice time?'

'Lovely,' said Penny. 'We took a room near Littlehampton seafront. The landlady was awfully nice.'

'And the weather's been kind,' Norah remarked.

Penny sighed. 'We walked along the beach every day and on Monday we took the bus into Chichester.'

'And has he reported for duty now?'

Penny's eyes became teary. 'He went last Thursday. Oh, Norah. He won't get any leave for ages and ages.'

Norah pushed a cup of tea in front of her and at the same time she reached out to squeeze Penny's hand. 'It'll soon come around.'

Penny sniffed into her handkerchief. 'Yes, in six weeks,' she said bitterly.

The two friends sipped their teas. 'So what will you do now?' Norah asked.

'I'm still at Mum's,' said Penny, 'but I'm so bored. I haven't even got anything to read. All the magazines have been stopped. The newsagent says you have to order them individually now. Do you think they'd let me come back to the WVS for a bit?'

'I think that would be grand,' said Norah. She smiled. 'They could certainly do with you. I can't give them much time. There's so much to do in the market garden at the moment. A couple of the girls have left. Rebecca Kent has joined the WRENs and Sarah Barnes has gone back to Scotland. She reckons it'll be safer up there.'

Outside, they heard Max barking excitedly and Sausage came running from the sitting room and out through the back door to join him.

'That must be Linnet coming home from school,' said Norah.

Penny frowned. 'Only Linnet? But you had four of them at school.'

'Ruth and Marjorie have gone back with their mother,' said Norah. 'They went last Saturday and Amélie is at work.'

'Funny names,' Penny remarked.

'Their mother was French.'

'Poor you,' said Penny, her hand on her gently rounded tummy. 'Shame you and Jim couldn't have children.'

'We might soon,' Norah said brightly.

Penny took in a breath. 'You're not . . .?'

'No, no.' Norah chuckled.

They were interrupted as Linnet burst through the kitchen

101

door. 'Auntie Norah, can I join the Brownies? Brown Owl came to school today and she says they've got va-canties . . .' Linnet took a deep breath. 'And she says it only thruppence a week and they do some really exciting things and you don't have to have the uniform straight away and my friend Doreen is joining, so can I join the Brownies, please, Auntie Norah, please?'

'Slow down,' Norah laughed. 'Of course you can join. We'll talk about it later. Now go up and change out of your school things and then you can come and help me dig up some potatoes for tea.'

As the sound of her thundering footsteps running up the stairs receded, Penny said, 'You were telling me about a baby?'

'Oh yes,' said Norah, barely able to conceal her own excitement. 'Jim has agreed in principle to adopt one.'

'That's wonderful news,' said Penny, although her tone was a little flat. 'What will you have, a boy or a girl?'

'We haven't got that far yet,' said Norah. 'When it comes down to it, I'm not sure how he'll welcome the idea of medical examinations and being interviewed by the Welfare Office, but just the thought of having a child of my own one day is enough for me now.'

'Then I'm pleased for you,' said Penny, 'although I have to say that Ted would never want to bring up another man's baby.'

Norah was mildly irritated by her unnecessary remark but she picked up their cups and turned towards the sink rather than say so.

'When will you get it?'

'We have to go through a lot of formalities first,' Norah said stiffly. 'Now, if you'll excuse me, Penny, I have to get the tea.'

'Yes of course,' said Penny, rising to her feet and pulling on her coat. 'Sorry if I upset you. I didn't mean it. I am pleased for you both, really I am.'

They heard Linnet thundering downstairs again. Norah gave her friend a thin smile. 'So it looks as if I'll be seeing you back in uniform before long.'

'If I can get the darned thing on over my bump,' Penny said with a chuckle.

As Jim walked into his office, Inspector Reece turned to the WPC who was putting some files into the filing cabinet. 'That'll be all, constable.'

'But I haven't quite finished, sir.'

'Leave them on the top and come back later.'

The WPC did as she was told but not before she had shot Jim a look of irritation and disapproval. He gave her an apologetic smile as he held the door open for her and she swept past.

'Sit down, Jim,' said the inspector. When he'd finished writing something, he enclosed the page into a folder and pushed it to one side. Then he leaned back in his chair and regarded Jim thoughtfully. 'It seems that you have stumbled across a bit of an embarrassment.'

Jim frowned, puzzled.

'Your evacuees are the children of some big-wig in London.'

'What?'

'Not to put too fine a point upon it,' the inspector went on, 'their father works with Neville Chamberlain. He's some sort of secretary in the War Office.'

'Good God.'

'Quite,' said the inspector.

Jim frowned crossly. 'If he's that sort of bloke, how come he didn't bother to even look for his kids?'

'He thought they had both gone to their aunt's,' said the inspector. 'He says he wasn't too worried until a few days later and he hadn't heard from them.'

Jim scoffed. 'Some father.'

'Step-father,' said the inspector. 'Apparently he doesn't get on too well with the aunt so he waited for *her* to contact *him*. But of course she didn't, so in the end he decided to eat a bit of humble pie and ring her.'

'And that's when he realised the children were missing,' said Jim.

'That's about the size of it.'

Jim shook his head. 'I don't buy it, sir. There's something weird about all this.'

'You might be right, Jim, but there's nothing we can do. Word has come down from on high not to pursue the matter and he's coming to collect them at the weekend.'

'And everybody is happy with that? Have they investigated him? Doesn't anybody in the Met think it's odd?'

'He's a responsible civil servant. Not a member of the government but as good as,' said Inspector Reece. 'If the powers-that-be think he's kosher, we have no reason to question it.'

'So when he comes, I just hand them over?'

The inspector nodded. 'That's right.'

Jim gestured towards the folder on Inspector Reece's desk. 'Has that got something to do with it?' he asked. 'Because if it does, I should like you to put down how sceptical I am about this step-father, and the fact that I don't like the idea of doing what I'm being asked to do.'

'Don't worry, Jim. I'll make sure they know.'

'I'd like it put in writing, sir.'

The inspector looked uneasy. 'There's nothing wrong. The chap is obviously a bit of a berk, that's all.'

'I'd still like it in writing, sir,' Jim insisted.

Inspector Reece was losing patience. 'For God's sake, Jim, if I put something down here in black and white and it all goes tits up, it could come back to bite you on the bottom. It could damage your career, man.'

'I'll take that risk, sir.' Jim paused. 'If you don't mind.'

Inspector Reece let out a long sigh. 'All right, but don't say I didn't warn you.'

Norah was upset when he told her. 'Saturday? So soon?'

Jim nodded. They were strolling around the block with the dogs; taking them for a walk on their own. Linnet was playing with Norah's old dolls house, which Jim had carried down from the loft. Although dusty and needing a wash, everything was as it should be. Amélie was reading to Mrs Kirkwood. Jim's mother enjoyed a good book but her eyesight wasn't what it used to be. Right now, they were partway through *South Riding* by Winifred Holtby.

'Linnet will be more excited than Amélie,' said Norah. She already had a heavy feeling in her chest. She didn't want the girls to go. Didn't their father realise it was safer for them to stay down here and away from the bombing when it came?

'Inspector Reece thinks we shouldn't tell them he's coming,' said Jim.

'Why ever not?'

'In case Amélie does something stupid.'

'Like run off again, do you mean?'

Jim nodded. 'He and Ffox-Webster have been talking on

the phone and they've agreed that the girls should have a nice surprise when he turns up.'

'Ffox-Webster?'

'Their step-father,' said Jim.

'Jim, I'm sure there's something wrong about all this,' she said.

'I absolutely agree with you, darling,' he said, 'but we have no proof and if Amélie won't talk, there's nothing I can do about it.'

'Oh, Jim.'

'I know,' he said. 'Darling, they are not our children. We have to let them go.'

She slipped her arm through his. 'I know, but it's so hard. Especially when I have this feeling deep in my stomach that something is not quite right.'

They walked on in silence. Eventually Jim said, 'Remember what we talked about a few nights ago? Let's get the ball rolling.'

She looked up at him. 'Really? But I don't know where to start. What do we do? Who do we talk to?'

'Haven't a clue,' he said with a chuckle.

Norah's brain was working overtime. Mrs Kirkwood? Penny? Mr Dobbs the billeting officer? All at once it came to her.

'I could have a chat with the doctor.'

Doctor Chisholm was sympathetic. 'Adoption?' he said. 'Well, I'm sure you and your husband would be ideal material, but it won't happen overnight. There are a few formalities to go through.'

Norah nodded. She was aware that as far as adoption went, things were changing. Up until a few years ago, the regulations had been both haphazard and lax. Horror stories of babies being sold for as much as one hundred pounds, no questions asked, had been reported in the newspapers, so earlier in the year, the Adoption of Children (Regulation) Act 1939 had taken up a lot of parliamentary time.

'I would be happy to recommend you,' Doctor Chisholm continued, 'but it's not up to me. You will have to be interviewed and someone will come round to see if your home is suitable.'

'I understand,' said Norah.

'They may also ask for references.'

'That's fine,' said Norah.

'Jim is quite happy with that, too?' said Doctor Chisholm. 'A lot of men resent the intrusion into their privacy.'

'This was Jim's suggestion,' Norah said proudly.

Doctor Chisholm relaxed and smiled. 'Good, good. Now, first things first. I want both of you to come in for a thorough examination. We must make sure you are physically fit in every way. After that, I'll contact the adoption society I work with and we'll take it from there.'

'Yes,' Norah said breathlessly. 'Thank you, doctor.'

Doctor Chisholm pulled out his diary. 'Next Tuesday; will that suit?'

CHAPTER 12

Norah

It was about eleven o'clock when the dogs' frantic barking heralded the arrival of a big black car pulling up outside the house. Norah knew nothing about cars but even she could see that this one, with its forward-leaning winged 'B' Bentley emblem on the top of the bonnet, was expensive. The bodywork was a deep blue and the lamps and horns on the front shone so brightly it looked as if it had just come out of the showrooms.

When a smartly dressed chauffeur stepped out, Norah was slightly surprised. She hadn't expected that! The chauffeur's appearance was marred by a livid poppy-coloured birthmark all down the left side of his face. Norah watched as he went round the side of the car and opened the back passenger door. The passenger, who was wearing a beautifully tailored pinstripe suit, got out and looked up and down the street. He appeared to be nodding to someone in a trilby hat, waiting by the Odd Fellows Hall a hundred yards away. Norah was distracted by the rustle of a dress and Mrs Kirkwood appeared beside her. 'Is this him?'

Mrs Kirkwood was tight-lipped but that was hardly surprising. When she and Jim had told her that the girls step-father was coming to fetch them, she had been openly hostile but she had reluctantly agreed not to tell them he was on his way. Now she and Norah watched as the male passenger reached into the back seat of the Bentley to take out a huge bunch of flowers and a small bag. In the meantime, the chauffeur had opened the enormous boot to take out a large wicker basket.

The man with the bouquet brushed the side of his head with his hand to smooth his hair, admired his reflection in the wing mirror and waited.

'Cocky bugger,' Mrs Kirkwood muttered. 'What's he waiting for?'

The man with the trilby hat pulled low over his eyes walked past and the two men appeared to exchange something. Neither of them spoke, but as the man hurried away, he was tucking something into his inside coat pocket. Norah frowned to herself. How odd.

At the gate, the chauffeur shouted at the barking dogs to 'clear off', as his passenger swept past him and headed for the front door. The two women hurried to their places; Mrs Kirkwood in the chair by the sitting room door where she had a ringside seat and Norah to the double doors at the front of the house. In fact, she opened the door before Amélie's step-father actually rang the bell.

'Mrs Kirkwood?' he said in a plummy voice as he held out his hand for her to shake. 'Jago Ffox-Webster. I'm Lillian's father.'

Max and Sausage bounced at his legs. With a nervous smile Norah invited them in while attempting to leave the excited dogs out in the garden. Joey swayed on his perch and called out 'Hello'.

109

Mr Ffox-Webster smiled. 'A budgerigar,' he said. 'Very homely.'

'It's my mother's,' she said. 'My parents live in London. When war was declared, despite the dire warnings from her vet and the local animal charities, she was reluctant to have him put down.'

'Quite right, too,' said Ffox-Webster. 'I know that many of my colleagues regret their decision to have their dogs put to sleep. It was a panic reaction and as it turns out, quite unnecessary.'

He offered her the flowers and as she took them he said, 'Can Hedges put this hamper into your kitchen?'

Norah caught her breath. 'Oh, really, you shouldn't have.'

'My dear Mrs Kirkwood, it's the least I can do.'

Norah showed Hedges the way to the kitchen and much to her consternation, Ffox-Webster followed. As Hedges placed the basket onto the kitchen table, Ffox-Webster looked at his watch. 'I shall be about half an hour,' he said and turning to Norah he added, 'Can you tell Lillian I'm here?'

'Linnet . . . I mean, Lillian, isn't here,' Norah said apologetically. 'And Amélie is still doing the breakfast shift at—'

'Oh, so she's reverted back to her French roots again,' Ffox-Webster interrupted.

Norah frowned. 'She told us that was her name. What do you call her then?'

'Amy,' said Ffox-Webster, 'and what's this about a shift?'

Mrs Kirkwood was watching them by the kitchen door. For some reason best known to herself, she was glaring stony-faced at the chauffeur.

'She has a little job in the police canteen,' said Norah. She could feel herself blushing. 'She'll be home just after twelve and Lillian has gone to a Brownie meeting. She should be back around the same time. My husband is picking her up.'

'Better make that an hour and a half then, Hedges,' Ffox-Webster said to the chauffeur, a small flicker of disappointment on his face. Norah suddenly felt horribly guilty that the girls weren't here to greet him.

The chauffeur left the room, only pausing long enough to nod a greeting towards Mrs Kirkwood on the way out. She didn't respond. As he opened the door again, the dogs bounded back in.

'Can I offer you a cup of tea, sir?' said Norah.

'That would be wonderful, Mrs Kirkwood,' he said, making himself comfortable on one of the kitchen chairs. 'I'm absolutely parched.'

Norah busied herself with the kettle and then slid the hamper to one side so that she could put the cups on a tray. 'I've never had a hamper before.'

'It's just a small gift to thank you for all that you've done. I do hope you enjoy it.'

'You're very generous, sir,' she said. It looked huge and she'd already noticed the Fortnum and Mason emblem on the side.

'Thank God you took the girls in,' he said as he unbuttoned his jacket. 'I dread to think what could have happened to them, although Amy is a very sensible girl. By the way, the Metropolitan Police never told me the whole story. How did you come by them?'

Norah introduced her mother-in-law but Mrs Kirkwood refused to shake his hand. Norah felt uncomfortable but there was nothing she could do. She knew her mother-in-law would miss the girls, particularly Amélie, but it was only right that they be with their step-father. As Mrs Kirkwood turned her head away, Norah gave Jago Ffox-Webster a wan smile and then started to explain everything.

'Amazing,' Ffox-Webster said. 'I am lucky that they were found by someone like you . . . er, the both of you.'

'We have enjoyed having them here,' said Norah, reaching under the sink for a vase. 'These flowers are beautiful. I shall arrange them later.' She paused as she tore at the paper wrapping. Constance Spry, no less. 'I'm sorry that we didn't tell the girls that you were coming,' she added. 'We thought it would be a lovely surprise to find you waiting for them.'

'That's quite all right, Mrs Kirkwood. Please, it's of no consequence.'

'I shall miss them.'

'So shall I,' said Mrs Kirkwood. 'My eyes aren't what they used to be and Amélie reads to me every evening.'

He nodded in a rather distracted way. 'I'm glad she's been of use.'

'Would you care to come into the sitting room?' said Norah, picking up the tray of tea things. 'It's more comfortable in there.'

He took the tray from her and the two of them followed her into the sitting room where they all sat down. Ffox-Webster propped the small bag he was carrying against his chair.

'You should know that I'm taking Lillian straight to her new school,' he said, indicating the bag. 'Her uniform is in there and I'd be grateful if she could put it on before we go.'

'Yes, yes of course.'

'She's not going back home with you then?' said Mrs Kirkwood. Her voice was harsh, disapproving.

112

'Best to start as you mean to go on, isn't it, and London is no place for little ones at the moment,' he said. 'She'll be much safer in Surrey.'

'You might be right there,' Mrs Kirkwood muttered.

Norah was dying to say something but it was hardly her place. Poor little girl. After all this time, he could at least have given her a weekend at home with him. 'How do you like your tea, Mr Ffox-Webster?'

'Milk and one sugar,' he said with a convivial smile. 'This is a lovely, cosy room.'

Norah poured the tea. 'Lillian wrote you some letters but I couldn't post them because I didn't have your address.'

As she handed him the cup, his expression softened. 'I understand your husband is a police officer.'

'Yes, he's just been promoted to sergeant,' Norah said proudly.

'Do you have a job, Mr Ffox-Webster?' Mrs Kirkwood asked. Her tone was still sharp.

Ffox-Webster languidly took a silver cigarette case from his jacket pocket. 'Do you mind?' he asked Norah and when she shook her head, he opened it and offered her one but she declined. Mrs Kirkwood, who had never smoked in her life, was a little more canny. 'I'll save it for later,' she said as she helped herself to two.

'You must forgive me, ladies, but I can't discuss my occupation,' he said, lighting his cigarette with a gold cigarette lighter. 'It's all a bit hush-hush I'm afraid. Suffice to say that we have spent the past year preparing an underground suite of rooms where the Prime Minister and his cabinet would be safe should war be declared. Of course, now that we are at war with Germany you can rest assured that somewhere in London, your government is protected from

113

aerial bombardment and my employers can get on with the business of winning.' He brushed a little cigarette ash from his leg. 'I'm ashamed to admit that my duties for my country have allowed me to neglect my duties as a father. I feel absolutely terrible that my daughters resorted to all this subterfuge. It was all done without my knowledge, you understand, and as I've already said, I can only thank God that they ended up with someone like you.' He leaned forward and squeezed the bridge of his nose. 'The whole thing has been an absolute nightmare.'

Norah suddenly felt embarrassed and uncomfortable. Had she misjudged this man? 'Please don't upset yourself, sir. Everything is fine.'

He sat back in his chair. 'Were they terribly upset when they came to you?'

'Of cour—' Norah began.

'Not really,' Mrs Kirkwood chipped in quickly.

Norah shifted awkwardly in her seat. 'Like I said, Lillian wrote you several letters.' She paused. 'I'll go and get them now.'

She hurried back to the kitchen and grabbed the letters from the dresser. Hopefully he wouldn't notice that they had already been steamed open and read by her and Jim. She felt a bit guilty about that now. There was nothing useful in them anyway.

As she came back into the sitting room he was saying, '. . . But sadly there was nothing else they could do.'

Mrs Kirkwood looked up as Norah came back into the room. 'Mr Ffox-Webster was telling me that his wife died of TB in Switzerland.'

'Oh, I am sorry,' said Norah.

He shook his head sadly. Norah handed him the letters

and he tore one open clumsily. They waited a moment or two until he had read it. 'It seems she has been very happy here,' he said, looking up with a smile. 'Did Amy . . .?'

'I'm afraid she didn't want to write,' said Norah. 'We tried to encourage her but she never did get around to it.'

Norah saw a flicker of irritation in his face. 'Amy has always been strong-willed . . . rebellious.'

Mrs Kirkwood frowned in surprise. 'Rebellious? I've always found her to be a delightful girl.'

Mr Ffox-Webster looked up sharply. 'Perhaps rebellious is too strong a word,' he admitted with a careful smile. 'Let's say she knows her own mind.' He tore open another letter and began to read that one. 'Ah, sweet,' he said, reaching for the third. 'I know you should never have favourites with your children, but Lillian and I have a special relationship. Poor Amy struggles a little with that.'

Mrs Kirkwood looked sceptical.

Norah glanced at the clock. Five past twelve. Jim and Linnet would be here soon. 'If you don't mind me asking,' she said, anxious to clear up another anomaly, 'why did you change their names?'

'When I adopted them,' he said without looking up, 'as we were coming to live in England, I wanted them to have English names.'

They heard the front gate click and Mrs Kirkwood looked out of the window. The dogs rushed out of the room and barked by the door, anxious to be let out. 'Jim and Linnet . . . I mean Lillian, are here,' Mrs Kirkwood said.

Ffox-Webster rose to his feet. Lillian skipped down the path and went round the back.

'Auntie Norah,' she called at the back door. 'I'm home. Auntie Norah . . .'

'In here, dear,' Norah called. 'In the sitting room.'

They were all on tenterhooks until she came into the room so no one heard the gate go for a second time.

'Oh, Auntie Norah, we had such fun at Brownies,' Lillian was saying. 'We all have to be someone from fairy land. Brown Owl said when I become a Brownie, I can be a pixie.' She came through the door and gasped, 'Daddy, oh Daddy!' Running to his open arms, he swung her up and she covered his face with kisses.

Jim followed her into the room with a broad smile. It was obvious that Lillian was overjoyed to see her father because she began babbling again, the way she always did when she was excited. 'Amy said we had to keep you safe. She said we mustn't tell anybody about you because you were doing really important work to stop the war. I kept the secret, Daddy. Honestly, I did. I didn't tell anyone.'

'Well done, my little poppet,' her father said.

Lillian looked around the room before whispering confidentially, 'Is it safe to say something now, Daddy?'

'Yes, my darling, it's quite safe.' The two of them hugged each other again.

As Jim stepped away from the doorway, the broad smiles on Norah and Mrs Kirkwood's faces fell.

Behind him, Amy, as they must now call her, stood frozen to the spot with a look of absolute horror on her face.

CHAPTER 13

Norah

Uncle Jim slipped his arm around Amy's shoulders and tried to guide her into the room, but she stubbornly remained on the threshold. Her step-father put Lillian down and came towards her with a rather fixed smile.

'Hello, sweetheart,' he said. 'How lovely to see you again. Have you missed your daddy?'

All at once she broke free from Jim's comforting arm and charged upstairs. Everyone stared after her either puzzled, embarrassed, or simply curious.

'It's probably a bit of a shock,' said Norah, pushing past her husband. 'Let me go and have a chat with her.'

'No!' said Ffox-Webster. They all turned to stare at him. The tone of his voice had almost been a command. 'Forgive me,' he said, his attitude becoming more conciliatory. 'The thing is, I know my daughter and I think if I go up and talk to her, she'll be fine.'

'Well, if you're sure,' said Norah, uncertainly.

'It's probably only because I had Lillian in my arms when

she saw me,' he said. Leaning towards her and speaking in a low voice as he neared Norah he added, 'You'll remember I told you she gets a little jealous.'

Norah let him pass. 'Up the stairs and turn right,' she said. 'The room at the end of the passage.'

He already had his foot on the bottom stair. 'Could you help Lillian to change?' he said. 'I'd like her to be ready before Hedges gets back. We have an early afternoon appointment at the school and I prefer to be back in town before it gets dark.' He jogged up the stairs as if he owned the place.

Lillian was bewildered when Norah explained that she was to go to a new school.

'But I like it here,' she wailed, 'and I want to be a Brownie.'

'I know, darling,' Norah said kindly, 'but we have to do what your daddy says. I'm sure there'll be a Brownie pack you can join near the school.'

Lillian nodded miserably. Norah took off her Brownie uniform and reached into the bag. Her school uniform was of the best quality; a grey gym slip over a crisp white blouse. She had a maroon cardigan and a maroon and grey striped tie. To complete the ensemble, there was a pair of long grey woollen socks and some black lace-up shoes.

'My, my, aren't you the smart one,' said Jim as the new Lillian emerged. 'Don't you think she looks smart, Mother?'

'Very smart,' Mrs Kirkwood agreed dully.

Amy and her step-father came downstairs a few moments later. Amy had a case in her hand and her eyes looked rather puffy, as if she'd been crying. One of her cheeks was rather flushed.

'Your chauffeur has arrived,' said Mrs Kirkwood, looking out of the window.

Ffox-Webster smiled. 'Amy tells me she's left school,' he said.

Suddenly feeling the need to apologise Norah said, 'We felt that because she was fourteen . . .'

'Of course,' said Ffox-Webster, 'but from now on, you'll be pleased to hear that Amy will be going back to her studies.' He regarded her steadily. 'I expect her to work hard,' he continued, 'so there will be no time for letter writing I'm afraid.'

'I'll write to you, Auntie Norah,' Lillian said.

'That would be grand,' said Norah. She was struggling not to cry. Oh, she was going to miss these two lovely girls so much.

'No need to follow us out,' Ffox-Webster said curtly as Norah came with him to the door. He smiled and held out his hand for her to shake. 'Only prolongs the agony, you see.'

Norah and Jim stood in the doorway and watched the three of them head for the car. 'Goodbye,' Norah called and she waved her hand.

'Goodbye and good luck,' Jim shouted.

But the girls didn't look back.

Jim was in the pub. Everyone in the house was doing their best to put a brave face on it, but they were all devastated to lose the girls . . . including him. He knew Norah would shed a few tears. She was probably doing it right now, which was why he'd decided to walk up to the Richard Cobden. He wasn't a heartless man – far from it – but he knew Norah would want some time on her own. She'd wept in his arms as the girls left but then she'd stuffed it all inside and tried to get back to normal. That was her way of dealing

119

with things. If he'd stayed at home, she would have just bottled it all up.

'How do, Jim?' someone called from the bar. 'Fancy a game of darts?'

Jim looked up and gave the man a thin smile. 'Not tonight, Doug,' he called.

'You okay?' Doug said.

'Fine,' said Jim as he swilled his beer around the glass. 'Bit tired, that's all.'

It was a lie, of course. He wasn't tired. He was gutted. He fiddled with the beer mat. He was gutted for two reasons. Like Norah, he would miss Amélie and Linnet. Ruth and Marjorie were lovely kids but for some reason the bond with Amélie and Linnet was stronger. If he closed his eyes he could still see that look of determination on Amélie's face when they'd first met. Should he have let them go? Something still didn't feel right.

The main reason he was upset was for Norah. She was always the happy-go-lucky sort but these past few weeks she'd blossomed. She was born to be a mum. He sighed. Of course he'd never tell her that, and there was nothing he could do to change it, but every time she wept for a baby, it tore him into a million pieces.

The girls had made a huge difference to his mother as well. They didn't talk about what happened during the Great War, but he knew full well why she was the way she was. Look tough, act hard, that was her way of dealing with things. Norah was a brick putting up with her nonsense, but Amélie had brought out his mother's softer, more kindly side; something he hadn't seen in years.

The sound of laughter near the dart board brought him

120

back to the present. Putting his glass to his lips he downed the rest of his pint and stood to leave. He'd given Norah half an hour to herself. That should be enough. He had to get back. He had to be there for her.

By a stroke of good fortune, Norah's parents were coming down to see them that week. It was a welcome distraction. All three of them had been very upset about the departure of the girls and Norah had hardly slept at night. She just couldn't shake the unsettling feeling that she was missing something. Mrs Kirkwood was very quiet, too. As soon as the girls had gone, she'd shuffled into her room and shut the door. Norah called her when she'd made some sandwiches for lunch but her mother-in-law didn't appear at the table. Norah and Jim ate very little themselves and even the dogs seemed withdrawn. Joey swayed on his perch making comforting noises. It had been a sad day.

By the time Norah's parents arrived, a leg of lamb with all the trimmings was roasting nicely in the oven. Max and Joey were delighted to see her mum and dad and although Sausage had never met them before, he joined in the excitement as well.

'He looks like a pedigree,' Elsie remarked. 'Where on earth did you get him?'

Norah told her about the cruelty the little dachshund had suffered.

'It's the same all over the place,' Elsie said sadly. 'We've got two German shepherd dogs roaming around the streets where we live. Somebody must have turned them out when the war started and now they've got nowhere to go.'

'Didn't anybody tell you, love?' Norah's father, Pete,

interrupted. 'The army took them on. They're going to train them as war dogs.'

'What are war dogs?'

'You know, guarding military installations. Army depots and such.'

Elsie tutted disapprovingly. 'Well, I suppose it's better than nothing.'

'What's it like in London now, Mum?' Norah asked.

'We haven't had any bombs as yet,' said Elsie, 'but the place has changed. We've got sandbags everywhere, and brown paper strips on the windows, not to mention anti-aircraft guns on Wormwood Scrubs and barrage balloons behind all the houses.'

'How's the business?'

Elsie shook her head. 'A lot of people are leaving London and the girls are talking about joining up if the war gets going. I've plenty of staff at the moment but I think a daily woman will be like gold dust before long.'

'It'll do some of those lazy go-for-nothings good to have to clean their own places for a change,' Mrs Kirkwood said scathingly.

'The trouble is,' said Elsie, 'they don't know how to.'

Everybody gathered around the dinner table.

'Maybe you could give them classes, Mum,' Norah said with a chuckle.

'What about down here?' her father asked. 'Has the war made any difference to Worthing?'

'They're putting some flipping great concrete blocks on Splash Point,' said Norah, 'and from now on, coach trips coming into Worthing are banned.'

'I thought you said in your last letter that you had some evacuees,' said Elsie, looking around.

122

'Ruth and Marjorie went back home with their mother a couple of weeks ago,' said Norah and then she told them about Amy and Lillian.

'Will you take in anyone else?' Elsie asked.

'I would if I was asked, I suppose,' said Norah.

Her parents looked from one to the other and all at once Norah's heart soared. 'Why, were you thinking of leaving London? You could come here. We could easily make room for you both and you'd be most welcome.'

'Oh, thanks, darling, but no,' her mother said with a chuckle.

'That's a relief,' Jim joked and Norah gave him a playful nudge.

They ate Norah's roast and in the afternoon, while they all relaxed in the sitting room, she opened one of the tins of biscuits which was in the hamper Mr Ffox-Webster had brought.

'Mmm,' said Elsie, munching on a ginger nut. 'This is delicious.'

'That hamper must have cost a packet,' Mrs Kirkwood remarked.

'There's all sorts in it,' said Norah. 'Wine, a tin of short-bread, strawberry preserve; all sorts. I shall save the rest until Christmas.'

'Preserve is only a posh way of saying jam,' said Mrs Kirkwood as if she was determined not to be impressed.

'You might be right,' said Norah with a smile, 'but I shall still save them for Christmas.'

'What did you think of their father?' asked Pete.

Jim shrugged. 'Hard to make a judgement on so short a visit. Bit of a snob, I would imagine, but he seemed a decent

123

enough sort of chap. He was very grateful that we'd taken them in and Linnet was obviously very fond of him.'

'Lillian,' Norah corrected and the conversation paused.

'What did you think, Norah?'

'I don't know, Mum. I had hoped he would let the girls stay with us. They were happy here and a lot safer than being back in London.'

'But they won't be back in London, will they?' said Jim. 'He said the school was in Surrey.'

'Lillian will be in Surrey but it sounded like Amy was going back to London with him,' said Norah. 'And there's another thing, if he's working all hours that God gives in that underground office, who's going to look after her?'

'I didn't like him,' Mrs Kirkwood said, pulling a face. 'Shifty eyes, and as for the chauffeur . . .'

'Anyone fancy a bit of a walk?' said Jim, changing the subject.

'I'd love a stroll along the front,' said Elsie. 'Bit of fresh air.'

The wind was keen so they wrapped up in head scarves and wore gloves and took the dogs. Mrs Kirkwood elected to stay at home.

'She doesn't do much, does she?' Elsie remarked as she and her daughter walked away from the house. 'Is she ill?'

'No, Mum,' Norah said with a chuckle. 'Just old.'

'Not that old,' Elsie scoffed. 'What is she? Sixty, sixty-five?'

'Fifty-eight,' said Norah.

'Fifty-eight!' Elsie gasped. 'She behaves as if she were eighty. Heavens above, is she really going to sit around waiting to die for the next twenty years?'

Norah hadn't really thought about it before, but her

mother was right. Mrs Kirkwood wasn't that much older than her own mother and yet she acted as if she'd already given up on life.

'See you later, Mother,' Jim called out as he hurried to catch up with Norah and her parents. He slipped his arm through Norah's. After a while, Pete and Elsie were lagging behind.

'Are they going to put those great big things all along the seafront?' Elsie called out. They had reached Marine Parade only to find the way to the beach barred by a big concrete block.

'I think so,' said Jim, turning his head towards his in-laws. He and Norah waited for them to catch up with them. 'They're supposed to stop enemy tanks coming up the beach.'

'Never thought of it before,' said Pete, 'but then I suppose Worthing is on the front line for an invasion.'

'Hardly,' said Jim with a chuckle. 'The water offshore is much too shallow for any large incoming troop ships but that seems to have been lost on the powers-that-be.'

'Bloody war,' Elsie muttered. She turned to her daughter. 'You know what you said at the dinner table seems like a good idea.'

Norah looked puzzled. 'What was that, Mum?'

'That I should offer classes to those women who end up having to keep house for themselves. In fact, I think I'm going to ask my girls for some tips when we get back home and work something out.'

Norah chuckled. 'I think that's a brilliant idea, Mum. You go for it.'

After their stroll, it was back home for a cup of tea and a piece of Victoria sponge before Pete and Elsie said their goodbyes.

'Keep in touch,' Elsie called as she waved to Norah from the train.

'I will,' said Norah and who knows, she thought to herself, maybe the next time I see you I shall have a baby of my own.

CHAPTER 14

Norah

The run-up to Christmas 1939 turned out to be much the same as every other Christmas before. The weather was cold and damp and most days a chilly mist came off the sea. Norah had spent her time helping the ladies of the church who were making up boxes of Christmas cheer for the elderly and infirm who would be on their own. They'd managed to create a dozen or so and Norah took on the task of delivering them all. It took a while because she always accepted the offer of a cup of tea and a chat. She knew she was probably the only person they would see other than the doctor or the district nurse. After squeezing in the last visit, Norah came back home, tired and frozen to the marrow. There was no nice welcome waiting for her when she walked in the door. Jim was on duty and Mrs Kirkwood was in her room listening to the radio with the electric fire on. The dogs were curled up together on Max's blanket in the kitchen. Norah hadn't lit the fire in the sitting room. Their coal delivery was late and she was doing her best to eke out their meagre supply.

'If you're putting the kettle on,' Mrs Kirkwood called

from her room before Norah even had time to take her coat off, 'you can make me an Ovaltine.'

Gritting her teeth, Norah filled the kettle. A few weeks before, her mother-in-law had had a letter which had been readdressed from her home in Queens Street. 'It says here that if I'm not going back home, the army want to requisition my house for the duration,' she said, reading the letter out at the tea table. 'I may as well let them. It'll give me a nice little income.'

Norah had bristled. No 'would you mind if I came here for the duration?' or 'please can I stay with you?' Mrs Kirkwood had just presumed. The damned cheek of the woman. She'd already stayed with them since September and she hadn't given Norah as much as one farthing towards her keep.

'Just tell me what you want to bring back here, Mother, and I'll sort it out on Sunday,' said Jim.

Norah had busied herself with the tea pot and said nothing but her temper rose.

'You are a good boy,' said Mrs Kirkwood, using a tone of voice which was clearly a dig against Norah.

'If you're staying for the duration,' said Norah, avoiding her eye, 'I would be grateful if you could give me something for your keep.'

Mrs Kirkwood just stared at her. It was amazing how loud the clatter of the tea cups being put into their saucers became as the silence between them grew.

Jim was clearly embarrassed. 'I'm sure we can manage, love,' he'd said feebly.

But Norah had stood her ground. 'And I'm sure Mrs Kirkwood could find something out of all that rent she's going to get. I think fifteen bob a week is not unreasonable.'

128

Mrs Kirkwood almost choked on her crumpet. 'Fifteen bob? But you already have my ration book.'

'I don't think—' Jim began.

'Of course, if you would rather get all your own meals,' Norah had interrupted, 'I'm quite happy to rearrange some of my cupboards for your things and we could work out a rota system so that we can both work in the kitchen at different times. We wouldn't want to get under one another's feet, would we?'

Jim's jaw dropped but Mrs Kirkwood glared coldly at Norah. 'No need for that,' she'd said quickly. 'Ten bob a week sounds reasonable to me.'

You old skin-flint, Norah thought acidly but although she had lost out on five bob, she felt a small sense of triumph.

That Sunday, Jim had borrowed a car and taken his mother to Queens Street. She arrived back at Norah and Jim's with several suitcases. Norah had a shrewd idea that Mrs Kirkwood was waiting for her to say that she could have the two bedrooms upstairs but if she let her move in there, that would put pay to her parents and perhaps Rene coming for Christmas. Her sister might not be coming this Christmas but there was every hope that she would come next year. So Norah said nothing and everything was shoe-horned into the downstairs room. The tension between the two women grew as a result, but Norah stuck to her guns all the same.

A letter in December cheered her up no end. Pete and Elsie were coming to join them for the two days of Christmas and they would sleep in the room Ruth and Marjorie had used. Norah was excited and glad of the distraction as she still hadn't got very far with the adoption. Doctor Chisholm had been taken ill and their new doctor wasn't keen on private adoptions.

129

'You'll have to go through the official channels,' he'd told them sniffily, 'but don't expect any quick decisions.'

Norah had written to the adoption agency but so far she'd had no reply. It was both frustrating and upsetting. Everything had been eclipsed by the war but why, she thought to herself, why when there were so many children 'out there' needing good parents, did the wheels of officialdom move so slowly?

The mantelpiece of her little sitting room was crowded with Christmas cards, including one from Mrs Harrison. To Norah's great delight, Gwen Harrison had written to tell her that Ruth and Marjorie were happily settled back in their old school and sent their love. She wished Norah and her family a happy Christmas, adding that her husband had enlisted in the RAF but he would be home on leave for the New Year.

It did occur to Norah that maybe Rene, who had joined the WAAFs in November, might cross Mr Harrison's path, but then she decided that the organisation was so large it was hardly likely. Rene was coming to the end of her three weeks training at No.2 WAAF Depot Innsworth, Gloucester. For all of her enthusiasm, it hadn't been an easy time.

'*We have reveille at six flipping thirty,*' Rene wrote in her latest letter, '*and then we're on the go until ten at night. I'm worn out with PE, marching for what seems like hours, doing drills and attending lectures. I'm like a ruddy pin cushion from all the injections we have to have and I'm dreading my posting. We get no choice as to where we are sent. I can only hope I can get something exciting. I couldn't bear it if they wanted me to be a cook or an orderly.*' Norah smiled to herself. Poor Rene.

Linnet, or Lillian as they were supposed to call her, had

sent a Christmas card, too. She had enclosed a short note to tell Norah that she liked her new school and although all of her friends would be going home at the end of term, Miss Reeves and Miss Fisher (Norah guessed they were her teachers) had told her she could spend the Christmas holidays with them. When she read that, Norah had tut-tutted in disgust. So Ffox-Webster couldn't even make the effort to have his own daughter home for Christmas. There was no mention of Amy but fortunately there was an address on the reverse side of Lillian's envelope so Norah was able to send the little girl a card from her and Jim. She also made up a small parcel containing a hand-knitted hat, scarf and a matching pair of gloves, along with a small paint box from Woolworth's as a Christmas present. Although she watched for the post every day, there was no word from Amy and as she had no idea where she was, or even their home address, Norah couldn't send her anything.

When Mrs Kirkwood first came to live with them, the two women rubbed along rather awkwardly. It was only niggly things – Mrs Kirkwood said that Norah hadn't aired her washing properly or Norah hadn't remembered that her mother-in-law *always* liked her hot-water bottle halfway down the bed. Norah, for her part, was irritated that Mrs Kirkwood never said thank you and whenever she asked for a little help, her mother-in-law always had a headache, or her foot hurt, or she was just about to do something else. Now that she was living with them for the duration, Norah decided it was time to ease off a little. If she wasn't careful the woman would have her running around in circles. For that reason, she suggested that Mrs Kirkwood fill her own hot-water bottle and that she kept her own room clean and tidy. The idea didn't go down too well and things came to a head that day when Norah made herself a pot of tea and while it brewed, took a mug of Ovaltine into her mother-in-law's room.

'Here you are,' she said cheerily.

Mrs Kirkwood frowned crossly and indicating the radio added, 'Shh. I'm listening.'

When Norah took her own tea into the sitting room she was hit by a wall of heat. The dogs followed her in and flopped on the mat in front of the fire. Norah glanced into the coal scuttle. It was empty. Finding the sitting room fire consuming all their coal supply in one go was the last straw. Norah finally snapped.

She went straight back to Mrs Kirkwood's room and flung the door open.

'I've just been in the sitting room,' she said crossly. 'What is the point of having a roaring fire when nobody is in there?'

Mrs Kirkwood looked up with an irritated expression. 'I said I'm listening. It's Jimmy Hanley.'

Norah reached over and switched off the radio.

'What did you do that for?'

'You've used all the coal,' Norah snapped.

'For goodness' sake, Norah,' Mrs Kirkwood said. 'Don't be such a drama queen. You're always over-reacting.'

'Over-reacting!' Norah retorted. 'Well, I like that. You know we're low on coal and you've used a whole two days' worth on an empty room. What if my order doesn't come tomorrow? How are we going to keep warm over the weekend?'

'I'm sure you could afford to buy some out of all the money I give you for my keep,' Mrs Kirkwood retorted.

'I can't buy what's not there, Mrs Kirkwood,' she said. 'We have to be sparing and use what we have wisely.'

'What's going on?' said Jim, coming up behind her.

'Nothing,' said Norah.

Mrs Kirkwood put on a plaintive voice. 'I thought I'd get the room nice and warm for you, son,' she croaked, 'but it seems I've done wrong again.'

'I'm sure it's not as bad as that, Mother,' said Jim.

Norah was sorely tempted to hit him but instead she turned on her heel and walked away. Later, in the kitchen, he tried to put his arms around her but Norah pushed him away. 'It's bad enough having to put up with her snide remarks and her awkwardness but I draw the line at you siding with her in an argument against me.'

'I'm sure she didn't mean . . .' Jim began.

'Oh, Jim,' said Norah. 'You just don't see it, do you?'

'See what?' he said.

Norah pursed her lips and strode past him.

Jim gazed after her with a bewildered expression. 'What?' he said again.

There was little to do in the garden at this time of year. Norah had sown some broad beans but that was about it. The ground was like a rock anyway. She'd washed out some old pots and begun a general tidy-up, ready for the spring.

As news of the terrible losses of shipping began to filter through, it was obvious that every spare piece of ground would be needed if the country was to feed itself. The nation had grown comfortable relying on cheap imports from the former colonies but Hitler's U-boats were putting pay to that. Earlier in the year, before they even went to war, the government had launched the idea of Dig for Victory and it got Norah thinking.

'We should go back to the council and ask about that

bit of waste ground,' she'd told Jim. 'It seems a crying shame not to use it.'

The area of semi-waste ground at the end of their garden was a bit of a conundrum. It would have been a great asset to the business and some time ago Jim had tried to find out who owned it but nobody seemed to know. Even their solicitor drew a blank. Norah had registered her interest with the council and somebody had said they would look into it but as yet there had been no response. Although there was no sign of a glasshouse, they knew that in Victorian times there had been a nursery behind their house so they supposed that piece of ground must have been part of it. So why wasn't it on their deeds? And why had it never been used?

'If you want my opinion,' said Mrs Kirkwood, which of course Norah didn't, 'you shouldn't have drawn everybody's attention to it. If you work a piece of ground for seven years, you can claim ownership.'

CHAPTER 15

Norah

Christmas Day was a Monday and Norah's mother and father arrived on Christmas Eve.

'Probably the last time I shall drive the car,' her father said as he staggered in under the weight of the things Norah's mother had brought with her. 'I shall put it in Mrs Fielding's garage for the duration.'

'Better put it up on blocks,' Jim advised. 'Standing too long in one place will ruin the tyres.'

The evening they spent together was pleasant. Norah put the presents around the tree in the sitting room and they played cards until ten o'clock.

On Christmas Day they woke early and after breakfast walked to church. Communal prayers took on a greater resonance this year and it was hard to sing *'Peace on earth and good will to men'* without reminding themselves that such thoughts were far from Hitler's mind. As Churchill had told the country way back in November, *'we have very rough weather ahead'*. Like everyone else they put on a brave face and walked home with Christmas greetings ringing in their ears.

Norah made some tea to go with some heated mince pies and they set about opening their presents. Jim loved the watch she had bought him and the tin of biscuits and the bottle of Vat 69 went down a treat with her parents. She'd also bought her mother a delicate brooch. Elsie was so thrilled with it, she pinned it onto her dress at once. For Mrs Kirkwood, Norah had bought new slippers and she'd knitted her a warm scarf in secret. In fact, she'd sat up for hours to get it finished in time without her mother-in-law knowing. Norah received the most wonderful gifts in return. Pink Lilac scent from Rene, some Golden Glory soap from Penny, and Jim had given her a beautiful crêpe-de-chine nightdress and matching lace-edged night coat in a delicate shade of blue. Her parents had given her a Yardley's box of bath crystals and talc and Mrs Kirkwood gave her a box of three handkerchiefs.

At one o'clock they enjoyed a lovely Christmas meal. Norah had managed to get a goose from the butcher and although there was little meat on the breast, it made a nice change. They pulled crackers and wore silly paper hats trying to put all thoughts of war behind them. Rene hadn't been able to get leave and there were no children in the house so the day hadn't turned out as Norah had hoped but everybody made the most of it. At three o'clock they sat around the radio and listened to the King's speech. Because of his awkward stammer, it made difficult listening and everyone was relieved when he finally finished. He ended the broadcast with a lovely poem, something about 'the gate of the year', which drew a tear into Norah's eye.

'He did very well,' said Elsie when the speech was ended.

'Poor bugger,' said Pete. 'You can't help feeling sorry for the man.'

'They say the King and Queen are going to stay in the country,' Jim remarked. 'Apparently the Prime Minister wanted them shipped over to Canada before the fireworks start.'

Norah suggested a walk before it got dark and the dogs were delighted when everybody put on their coats. Mrs Kirkwood said she would have the kettle on when they got back.

'How are you managing with her?' Elsie asked as she and Norah walked arm in arm behind the men.

'Well, I don't like her being here,' Norah admitted, 'but what can I do?'

'Is she paying her way?'

Norah nodded. 'She is now but only under protest.'

'Oh, darling,' her mother sympathised.

'It's not that bad,' said Norah. 'We skirt around each other mostly. Anyway, I can't do much about it. She's burned her bridges. There are three army officers living in her house now.'

Elsie squeezed her daughter's arm. 'Did I tell you Dad has volunteered to do fire-watching?'

'I was thinking about volunteering for that,' said Norah. 'What exactly does it mean?'

'He has to stand on the top of some high building and watch for any fires. I suppose when the Germans bomb London it'll be helpful but at the moment he says it's a bit boring really.' Her mother smiled. 'And, of course, it means half a night without sleep.'

Norah chuckled. 'Maybe I'll give that a miss then.'

'Have you heard from the children?'

Norah told her about the Harrisons and Lillian and explained her concerns about Amy.

'If you've got the address of the school, why not visit Lillian?' her mother suggested. 'Christmas and the New Year are the perfect excuse and maybe she'll tell you her full home address in London.'

'And then I could write to Mr Ffox-Webster,' cried Norah. 'Mum, that's a brilliant idea.'

Back at home it was time to get the Christmas cake and the sherry out. Max sat close to her dad and at one point he lay across her mother's foot.

'I keep wondering whether to take him back to London with us,' said Elsie. 'So far nothing has happened and I keep wondering if it ever will.'

'It's up to you, Mum,' said Norah.

They relaxed to the sound of an orchestral concert on the radio, which was followed by a play by Dorothy L. Sayers. It was such fun listening to Lord Peter Wimsey doing his best to solve the crime in *The Footsteps That Ran* and right at the end, the BBC had cleverly included a minute or two with some light music to give the listener time to work out whodunit. They sat glued to the radio to discover that Jim was right and everyone applauded Mrs Kirkwood as she had correctly guessed where the murder weapon was hidden.

'This has been a wonderful Christmas,' Norah said as she and Jim dived under the covers in their freezing-cold bedroom.

'It has, hasn't it?' he said, pulling her into his warm embrace. 'You did us proud. Thank you.'

Norah grinned. 'You're welcome.'

'Are they taking Max and the budgie back with them tomorrow?'

'No,' said Norah.

'I'm glad,' said Jim. 'I think poor old Sausage would miss Max.'

The New Year brought mixed blessings. Rene wrote to say she had got her posting. It wasn't as exciting as she would have wished but it did make her feel quite important.

I'm not allowed to tell you too much, but at the moment I'm billeted near Manchester and I'm packing parachutes. There are twenty of us girls here and we shall be moved all over the country once our training is complete. It's jolly difficult and of course we have to remember that lives depend upon us doing a good job.

Norah and Jim also had a letter from the adoption agency calling them for an interview at the old town hall on January 19th.

The weather was bitterly cold and although they had enough coal, food was becoming a bit of an issue. There was little meat in the shops and Norah found herself paying two and two a pound for a piece of bacon which, when she'd cooked it, was so salty it was almost inedible. The next day she minced the leftovers and smothered it in a sauce that made it more palatable. At the weekend, the butcher gave them a couple of rabbits so she knew they wouldn't starve. Another time, Norah braved the arctic weather and walked along the seafront to buy from the local fishermen but even cod was two shillings a pound. It was a good job she had her mother-in-law's money or they would be in a right pickle.

Disappointingly, their appointment with the adoption agency was cancelled.

At the end of February, Penny gave birth to a baby boy. She called him Victor. Norah went along to see him as soon as her friend came home from the maternity ward. The baby stared up at her as Penny put him into her arms.

'Hello,' Norah said softly. 'Aren't you a handsome young man.' Victor waved his hand in front of his mouth and opened it as if he was hungry. 'Oh,' Norah said sympathetically, 'it's a shame his daddy can't see him.'

'We're taking him to the photographer next week,' Penny said. 'I want to make sure Ted at least has a picture of his son. He's been posted abroad as part of the British Expeditionary Force in France. Thanks to bloody old Hitler, there's no telling when he'll be home.' Her eyes became teary.

'He'll be home soon enough,' Norah said encouragingly. 'They can't keep our boys over there forever. Nothing is happening.'

She had tried to sound optimistic but the news of the war wasn't good. Although there was no fighting as such, things were hotting up in other ways. She heard someone say on the radio that one politician thought Britain's food shortage was so dire that he advocated the draining of marsh land to make it suitable for growing food, and the newspapers – such as they were, owing to the lack of paper – said the cold weather was so severe in Denmark that people could walk across the ice all the way to Sweden! Rumours began to emerge about the mass deportation of Poles to labour camps in Siberia and closer to home, HMS *Daring* was torpedoed and sunk in the Orkneys. The papers didn't say how many people died but it was obvious it must have been a lot. There were only five survivors.

The two women cooed over Victor until Penny decided

it was time to put him back in the drawer which served as his cot.

'It's only just occurred to me,' said Norah as she watched his mother tucking him up. 'He was born on February 29th. He'll only get a birthday once every four years.'

Penny nodded apologetically.

'Ah, well,' Norah quipped, 'it'll save on birthday cards.' The two women laughed.

'What about you and Jim?' Penny asked. 'How are you getting on with the adoption?'

'I'm not,' said Norah. 'The appointment was cancelled because there was no fuel and there isn't another one for ages.'

As they sat in her mother's kitchen for a cup of tea, Norah gave Penny the matinee coat and booties that she'd knitted for Victor.

'Oh,' she cried. 'They're lovely.'

Norah gave her a child's drawing as well. 'Lillian drew this when I told her you were going to have a baby, but just to be on the safe side, I've kept it until now.'

'How sweet,' said Penny, admiring it. 'Do you ever hear from the girls?'

'I've kept in touch with Mrs Harrison,' Norah said, 'and Linnet, I mean Lillian, as she's now called, sent a card at Christmas but I've never heard a word from Amy.'

'How odd,' said Penny. 'She seemed the nicest of the lot and she was devoted to Mrs Kirkwood. I wonder why she never kept in touch.'

Norah shrugged. 'I've no idea but as soon as the weather gets better, I plan to go and see Lillian then maybe I can find out.'

*

The address Lillian had put on the back of the envelope containing her card was The Wells House, Epsom. Norah set off early one Tuesday in March. She had to go up to Clapham Junction and then catch a train back down to Epsom. The journey itself would take a couple of hours.

The Wells House was outside of the town and was, from what she gathered when she asked for directions, a twenty-minute walk. As time was at a premium, she took a taxi. The house itself was rather dark and forbidding. There was a large area in the front with a small garden; it was mostly dead foliage but the odd daffodil was making a valiant effort to beautify the place. She walked to the front door and rang the bell. Eventually, a woman wearing a black dress and a white apron opened the door. Norah explained who she was.

She was ushered into a cavernous hall that had several solid oak doors along one wall. To her right was a sweeping oak staircase. She could hear the muffled sound of children's voices behind the doors. The maid asked her to sit in a chair, which stood against the dark panelling, and went to a door on the left and knocked. A rather querulous voice from inside called, 'Come in.'

The girl disappeared for a few minutes, leaving Norah alone. She wondered how Lillian must have felt when she'd arrived here. The panelled wall was beautiful but it made the hallway seem rather dark and forbidding. A little further along the corridor, a door burst open and a woman's voice said, 'Quietly,' and a long crocodile of girls, wearing the same grey uniform in which she'd dressed Lillian the day her father came, filed out of the room and walked past her. They disappeared to her left and as soon as she heard running water and flushing chains, she realised they had all been sent to the toilets.

The maid came out of the room and apologised that Norah had been kept waiting.

'Miss Reeves has someone with her at the moment,' she said. 'She asks you to wait and says she will see you as soon as possible.' Norah smiled and watched her as she hurried away.

The crocodile of girls reassembled and walked back into their classroom. A moment later another door opened and a second group of girls, slightly older than the first, came towards the toilets. All at once, Norah heard a voice cry out, 'Auntie Norah, Auntie Norah,' and Lillian stepped out of line and ran to her. Norah stood to her feet and opened her arms as Lillian flung herself into her embrace. At the same time, the door to the office opened.

'Oh, Auntie Norah, I've missed you so much. Is Uncle Jim here? And where's Sausage, have you brought Sausage?'

'Lillian,' said a voice behind them.

'Thank you for my Christmas present,' Lillian babbled on. 'All the girls in my dorm envied me when they saw my paint box. I've done lots and lots of pictures and—'

'Lillian!' said the voice, sharper this time.

Norah realised that the well-ordered crocodile had become rather ragged because a lot of the girls were staring open-mouthed at them. 'You'd better run along now, darling,' she whispered. 'I'll talk to you later.'

Reluctantly, Lillian allowed Norah to give her a gentle push back into her place and without taking her eyes from her, Lillian was sent off with the others to the toilet.

The office door opened and a man in a pinstripe suit came into the hallway, lifting his hat as he bade Miss Reeves 'good day', before heading towards the front door. Miss

Reeves turned to Norah with a fixed smile. 'Would you come this way, Mrs Kirkwood.'

The room behind her turned out to be an office. At one end, by the window, there was a large mahogany desk. On the right side of the room, a merry fire burned in the hearth beside two comfortable chairs. As Norah moved forward the door clicked behind her. Miss Reeves was a matronly woman who wore a teacher's black gown. She put out her hand for Norah to shake. 'I see you and Lillian Ffox-Webster have already seen each other.'

As Norah shook her hand, she apologised for the disruption and explained how she came to know Lillian.

'We don't usually allow visits in term time,' said Miss Reeves. Norah's face must have fallen because she added quickly, 'But seeing as how you have already met, I am happy to make an exception. She would be upset if I sent you away.'

'Thank you. You are very kind.' Although the woman was amenable, Norah felt like she was treading on eggshells.

'Of course, I shall have to tell her father you came.' The eyes had become steely.

'Of course,' said Norah. 'I quite expected that. I would have written to ask him if I could visit had I known his address but sadly we both forgot to exchange them . . .' She added with a nervous laugh, 'Although of course he knows where I live. He came to my home to collect the girls.' She was babbling now. 'It's just that when you've opened your home to someone, and you miss them when they've gone, it would be nice to know that they're well and happy.'

'As you can see, Lillian is both well and happy,' said Miss Reeves.

'And Amy?' said Norah. 'Is there any news of her?'

Miss Reeves looked blank. 'Amy?'

'Her sister,' said Norah.

'I'm afraid I've no idea about a sister, Mrs Kirkwood. In fact, I didn't know Lillian had a sister.' Miss Reeves suddenly looked awkward. 'Let me get you some tea,' she said. 'You must be parched after your long journey. Did you drive yourself?'

'I came by train,' said Norah.

Miss Reeves raised an eyebrow. Norah undid her coat and sat down as Miss Reeves rang a bell on her desk. A few moments later, the same maid in the black dress opened the office door.

'Knock first, Cecily,' Miss Reeves said sharply. 'Would you bring us some tea please and ask Miss Hunt to send Lillian Ffox-Webster to the office.'

Cecily closed the door.

'You say you've come from Worthing,' said Miss Reeves. 'It must be a little unnerving living on the coast with France only twenty miles across the water. Are things changing in Worthing?'

'More sea defences are going up,' Norah said with a slight shrug, 'and the Army Service Corps are putting gun placements along the seafront.'

The door opened again and Lillian entered. Once again, she flung herself at Norah.

'Lillian,' said Miss Reeves, 'young ladies do not behave like fish-wives.'

Lillian stood up straight. 'No, Miss Reeves. Sorry, Miss Reeves.'

It was obvious that Miss Reeves had no intention of leaving them alone so Norah made the best of it. 'How are you?'

'Very well, thank you.'

'You look very well. Sausage sends his love.'

'Who is Sausage?' Miss Reeves interjected.

'My dog,' said Norah.

Miss Reeves busied herself with some papers on her desk.

By way of comfort, Norah grasped Lillian's hand. 'I'm glad you liked the paint box.'

'It was very kind of you to send it.'

Norah's heart was breaking. She longed to give the child a hug and a kiss but she guessed that would meet with her teacher's disapproval.

Miss Reeves rose to her feet. 'Where on earth has that tea tray gone?' And with that she swept out of the room.

As soon as the door clicked shut, Norah and Lillian hugged each other. 'Are you really happy here?' Norah asked anxiously.

'It's all right.'

'Have you heard from Amy?'

Lillian shook her head miserably. 'She promised she would write to me but she never has.'

'Oh, darling. I'm sorry,' said Norah, hugging her again. 'Shall I go to see her in London?'

Lillian's eyes lit up. 'Can I come?'

'Not just yet,' Norah said carefully, 'but if you tell me your address . . .'

Lillian shrugged. 'It's near the subway.'

'What subway.'

'To the park.'

'Which park?'

Lillian shrugged again. Oh dear, this was hopeless. 'Can you remember anything else?'

Lillian shook her head and Norah could see she was fighting her tears. 'Never mind,' she said brightly.

'She took it away,' said Lillian suddenly.

'Took what away?'

'My paint box. She said I might get paint on the sheets.'

Norah bristled and at the same time the door opened again. The maid had brought the tea and Miss Reeves was following her. As soon as Cecily put the tray down, Lillian was sent back to her class.

'Thank you for coming,' she said as she bobbed Norah a curtsy.

Twenty minutes later, Norah was back outside. She had tried to get Lillian's home address from Miss Reeves but the teacher assured her she didn't have it. Norah was tempted to ask how she communicated with Lillian's father if she didn't know where he was, but at the same time she knew it was useless to argue. They had drunk tea and made polite, meaningless conversation until Norah said she had to go. On the bus back to Epsom Station, Norah wept into her handkerchief. She didn't know which was the more upsetting; seeing a feisty, bright little girl being transformed into a polite dummy or knowing that, for some obscure reason, two devoted sisters were being completely isolated from one another.

CHAPTER 16

Amy

Amy put on the sacking apron and walked down the stairs. She hated coming down to the boiler room, especially at night. The only light came from a frosted window at the top of the stairs or from the fiery furnace when she opened the trap door. Sometimes huge cockroaches jumped at her legs as she came down and the heat, once she reached the bottom of the stairs, was unbearable.

Once a week every girl had to do boiler duty. They were expected to don the apron, tip a scuttle full of coke (left ready by the handyman who had finished work earlier in the day) into the boiler itself and then sweep the loose, fallen coke back into its pile. Everywhere in the house, including the boiler room, had to be kept spotless.

Amy put on the thick leather glove left for the purpose and opened the hatch before taking a step backwards. The heat hit her like a wall. Hot and hungry flames leapt up at the opening and she heard a whooshing noise. She reached for the scuttle and heaved it up to the lip of the opening before making the gargantuan effort it took to tip the contents into the fire. The hatch was shoulder height and the first time she was sent down here, she struggled for the strength to lift the heavy scuttle. It was still difficult but over the months she had gained upper body strength and now, although still heavy, it was a lot easier than it once was.

Once the coke was inside, Amy looked around for any rubbish which had been left beside the boiler to be burned. Sometimes it was used sanitary towels wrapped up in newspaper or it might be paper rubbish from Matron's office. She glanced up to the top of the stairs to make sure no one could be watching her before she sifted through the contents of the bin. What she was looking for was a piece of virgin paper. Today she was lucky. An official letter only filled half the page. Amy folded it and tore off the bottom of the page before stuffing it into her pocket.

As soon as she'd emptied the wastepaper basket onto the fire, she closed the lid and replaced the scuttle. The glove went back on its hook and then she reached for the shovel. Refilling the scuttle took ten or twelve shovelfuls and then she rocked it back to its place next to the boiler. It only remained for her to sweep the area tidy. The broom was large and unwieldy but a few minutes later, Amy looked around to admire her handiwork.

She glanced up at the steps again, but so far she was quite alone. It was never safe to stay very long. It was scary enough being so close to the boiler, but there were occasions when the other girls took the opportunity to come down here and wreak revenge on someone. Three of them had set upon Lucy Clayton and left her with a chunk of her hair pulled out by the roots and a burn on her forearm from where she'd fallen against the hot metal. Amy was nervous for quite another reason though.

A couple of weeks ago, when she'd tipped the wastepaper basket into the flames, one envelope had sailed to the floor. When she'd picked it up she'd realised it had the address of the home on the front. She had never known exactly where she had been incarcerated before. At first it had only served as a revelation as to where she was, but after a bit more thought, it became much, much more than that. The stamp had missed being franked. It looked untouched, as if it had only just been stuck in place. The first thing she had to do was get hold of some sort of writing implement and some paper but that wouldn't be easy. Amy wasn't allowed to write home.

The day her father had come to Worthing to take Lillian to her new school, Amy wondered what would happen to her. With Lillian safely deposited, the two of them sat together in the back of the car. Her father closed the glass partition between himself and the chauffer and leaned back.

'You must know what this means,' he'd said coldly.

Amy's stomach churned and she chewed her bottom lip anxiously. She could tell by the tone of his voice that whatever he was planning for her, it wouldn't be good.

'I can't trust you, Amy,' he said. 'I thought you were really special. There was a time when we loved each other.'

'I never loved you, Daddy,' she said contemptuously. 'You blinded me for a while with your rosebud wallpaper and talk of how special I was, but after you . . . you did what you did, I never even liked you.'

He brushed some imaginary cigarette ash from his trouser leg. 'And that's why you have to go somewhere where you can't do any harm.'

Amy had frowned. 'What do you mean?'

'I've been talking to a friend of mine,' he went on, 'and

150

he has agreed that you should spend some time in a boarding school where, over time, they will help you to become a useful member of society.'

'But I don't want to go to boarding school,' she'd protested.

'Then perhaps I should go back and fetch Lillian.'

Amy froze.

'The choice is yours, my dear. Do as I say or we go back to The Wells House and you keep house for me in London while Lillian . . .' Her step-father patted her thigh. 'Well, you know what Lillian will do.'

'I hate you,' she'd said in a snarled whisper.

'Tut-tut-tut,' he'd said. 'That attitude of yours must be tamed.'

She'd turned away from him, willing herself not to cry. She mustn't give way to tears. She couldn't give him the satisfaction of knowing she was beaten. What he had planned for her wasn't fair but how could she stop him? At least with Lillian at school, he could do her no harm.

They motored for another half an hour before they turned down a long winding road. Amy hadn't a clue where she was, except that they were deep in the countryside, miles from anywhere. Eventually, they turned towards some huge iron gates bordered by a high brick wall. The chauffeur sounded the horn and a few minutes later, a man came out of the gatehouse. He examined some paperwork the chauffeur had given him and then he opened the gate. As they drove on, Amy caught a glimpse of a board by the gate; Dempster Approved School for Girls. She had turned and stared at her step-father in horror. 'Daddy?'

He had simply smiled. A satisfied smile of contempt.

Amy's heart began to thump. 'If you leave me here I shall

tell them,' she spat. 'I'll tell them you've dumped me here and why.'

'You can tell them what you like,' he'd said coldly. 'No one will believe you. You see, I've already told them what a pathological liar you are.'

'You can't do this to me!'

'But my dear Amy,' he'd said, 'I already have.'

She'd protested when they'd opened the door to make her get out, but Miss Gordon, the teacher who had come out to meet the car, was far too strong for her. With her father making broken-hearted comments and being comforted by Miss Short, the head mistress, she was hustled inside.

That first week, she'd done her best to resist them, but they gradually wore her down. The home had a very strict code of conduct and Amy soon learned, to her cost, that their answer to all acts of insubordination was corporal punishment. It was done with a rattan stick about three feet long and half an inch wide. A rap on the knuckles using the edge of the stick had her hand throbbing for half a day. Still, she tried running away once. The grounds were extensive and although she'd reached the gate, she was caught. Her punishment was eight full strokes of the cane, the maximum prescribed by law, but this time she was pinned to the caning trestle by a leather strap around her waist and the penalty was doled out in front of the whole school. Miss Gordon carried it out, savouring every moment as she brought the cane down onto her bottom, which was only protected by her thin knickers. The pain Amy felt was indescribable, but she never once cried out.

She'd taken a while to make friends with any of the other girls. At first, she'd been aloof, earning herself the nickname 'M'lady', but her stubborn and persistent tenacity won her the respect of even the most heartless girl. She shared a room with three others; Anita Partington, who had burned down her old school, Susan Smith, who had been sent to Dempster for persistent shoplifting, and Marcia Drummond, who had almost drowned another girl when she pushed her into the local duck pond. When they had asked Amy what she'd done, she merely said, 'I'm here because my step-father put me here.'

After her beating, Amy had almost reached breaking point. It finally dawned on her that there was no way of escape unless she had help and the only person who was likely to help her was Auntie Norah. Her problem was getting a message to her. The envelope and the scrap of paper was her best bet so far.

Amy had put the envelope at the back of the boiler room on a small ledge. It was safe there. The ledge was dark because it was right under the stone stairs and if someone found it, there was nothing to say it was anything to do with her. She would hide the scrap of paper alongside the envelope.

All she had to do now was to find something to write with. When they were given pens and pencils in the classroom they were counted out and counted back in after their lessons. The reason, so they were told, was because in the past girls had used pens and pencils as weapons so they had to be kept under lock and key. All writing was strictly supervised and, of course, Amy had already been told that she wasn't to communicate with anyone on the outside.

'I'm afraid not,' said Miss Gordon when Amy had asked to write to Lillian at the end of her first week. 'You are to be kept well away from all outside influences.'

'But she's only nine,' Amy had protested. 'What harm can it do?'

'Don't argue with me, Ffox-Webster,' said Miss Gordon, waving her away. 'I've told you, the answer is no.'

Amy had almost given way to tears. 'How long am I to stay here?'

'Unless you win a merit for good behaviour, you will leave here when you are nineteen,' said Miss Gordon. 'And let's face it, Ffox-Webster, you haven't exactly got off to a flying start, have you?'

Amy put the piece of paper next to the envelope and pushed both further back into the darkness. This had to work. If she got caught, she might end up with another beating, but she had to take that risk. She couldn't stay here until she was nineteen, she just couldn't. Having swept the floor clean, she put the big brush back into its place and climbed the stairs.

CHAPTER 17

Norah

Jim and Norah held hands as they made their way to the old town hall for their interview.

Things had dramatically changed in the centre of town. Reinforced concrete had been laid in front of the old town hall building and a pillbox faced the sea in case of invasion. A zebra effect had been created with white paint all along the edges of the roundabout and the bases of every lamp post had been whitened so that they could be more easily seen in the blackout. In the past few weeks, the police station had been moved as well. It was now temporarily housed in the art college in Union Place.

As Jim and Norah mounted the steps, he gave her an encouraging smile. If all went well, their lives would be changing in more ways than one. After their first interview in January had been cancelled, they had now been invited for a meeting with the county adoption agency.

They were shown into a small room, sparsely furnished but warm. A cheerful fire burned in the grate. Norah was already feeling nervous. How long would they have to wait before they could have a baby? Did they have a choice as to whether they had a girl or a boy? She chewed her bottom lip anxiously. What if they weren't accepted as prospective parents?

The door opened and a large, matronly woman entered the room. Jim began to rise to his feet but she told him to 'please sit down'. As she sat opposite them she rearranged the papers in her folder. Norah stared at her tightly permed hair. She wore a heavy tweed suit and a blue silk blouse. Her legs were as big as tree trunks and she had a round face with thin lips coated in a bright red lipstick.

'Well now,' she said with a breathy smile. 'My name is Miss Bundy.'

It suits you, Norah thought to herself.

'I have been assigned to your case,' she added pleasantly. 'I have acquired references from your superior officer, Sergeant Kirkwood, and I have references about you from your neighbours and from the WVS, Mrs Kirkwood.'

Norah held her breath.

'And I have to say that they are all excellent,' Miss Bundy went on. 'The mother of two of your evacuees has also given you a glowing reference and according to your doctor you are both healthy. In short, I would say that you are both ideal candidates to adopt.'

Norah slid to the back of her chair and relaxed. It was hard to supress a giggle. It was happening at last. She was going to have a baby!

Miss Bundy leaned across the table. 'The only other requirement is to see if your home is suitable,' she said. 'I shall need to make an appointment to come and see you and after that we are home and dry.' She smiled. 'So, when can I come?'

156

Jim didn't need to be there, she said, so Norah made an appointment for the following week.

'I have a baby in mind for you,' said Miss Bundy. 'He or she is not born yet but is due in about three weeks. The mother is a young girl; a refugee from Poland. Far too young to care for her own baby, so if you adopt him or her, it will give the mother a chance to make a new start and get on with her life.'

'Does she live in Worthing?' Norah asked. The thought that she might accidentally bump into the girl one day was a little disconcerting.

'No,' said Miss Bundy. 'And I cannot discuss her personal details with you, nor can I tell you where the child will be born, but I can assure you that we go to great lengths to make sure the whole business is conducted with the utmost secrecy. This is for your benefit as much as for the girl's.'

Norah nodded.

'When the time comes,' Miss Bundy went on, 'I shall take you to the mother and baby home myself and you should be aware that there is a three-month lapse after baby comes home before the adoption is finalised.'

'So how soon after the baby is born will we have him?' asked Jim.

'Mother looks after baby for the first six weeks of life,' she said. 'I would estimate that your son or daughter will be coming home sometime around the beginning of May.'

Norah's heart sank. May! That sounded a lifetime away. She had hoped their baby would be with them sooner than that.

'It will give you time to prepare,' Miss Bundy said encouragingly, as if she'd read Norah's mind.

*

Back out on the street, Jim gave his wife a side hug. 'Let's celebrate,' he said. 'I'm taking you out to lunch.'

'But . . .' Norah began.

'No buts,' said Jim. 'You need to build your strength up.' He put his mouth to her ear and whispered, 'You're going to have a baby, darling.'

Spring was always a busy time and Norah had already spent several back-breaking days getting the garden prepared. There were shortages in the shops and they were eating the last of the winter cabbage and the leeks, so she had to get things going. So far, she'd planted spring cabbage, carrots, parsley and broad beans. By the end of March, she was bringing on the first of her cucumbers, marrow, and tomatoes under cloches.

A week after her interview with Miss Bundy, Norah was back in the offices of the old town hall, this time to see someone from Worthing Parks and Gardens. She emerged some forty minutes later with permission to cultivate the patch of waste ground beyond her property as part of the war effort.

'I'm going to suggest that you are viewed as having a reserve occupation,' the man from the parks and gardens department told her as they parted. 'We need all the expertise we can get if we're going to feed the townspeople.'

Soon afterwards, the patch of waste ground had been created into allotments. Each one measured the traditional ten poles, which was roughly the size of a tennis court. The council had also taken part of Victoria Park and council employees were digging it up to create a brassica patch.

'There's room for six allotments,' Norah wrote to her mother, 'but I suggested that two of them could be halved.

158

A whole allotment might be too much work for an older person, or a single mother with children. The council worker was a bit sceptical, but I said it would be better to create a small plot for two people rather than one allotment that is far too large for one person to manage. How are you and Dad? And how's the home craft course going? Did you manage to get the Guide hut? Thanks for the booties you sent. They are lovely and soft and I'm sure they'll be ideal. Oh, Mum, I can't wait for my baby to come . . .'

Within three weeks most of the allotments had been taken and Norah had acquired yet another string to her bow. She was now officially the council's adviser for Clifton Road's allotment gardeners.

Too late for a tar oil wash, Norah was spraying her fruit trees with lime and sulphur in the market garden when Max gave a little bark and a familiar voice called to her from the other side of the gate. It was the caretaker from Heene Road School.

'Oh, hello, Mr Steele,' she said cheerfully. 'I don't suppose you've got another yard of manure to give away, have you?'

They both laughed at her joke. After he'd had a cup of tea with her and Mrs Kirkwood way back in the autumn, Ivan Steele had offered her his winnings and Norah had accepted it gratefully. She was glad of it then and would be even more so now. Good horse manure was hard to come by since the war. People were getting rid of their horses.

'I heard you were giving away allotments,' he said, patting Max vigorously.

'I'm not exactly giving them away,' she said apologetically. 'They actually belong to the council but they've left it to me to find tenants.'

'Any possibility of me having one?' Sausage was threading

159

himself around Ivan's legs, clearly desperate for a bit of attention as well. Ivan bent to fondle the dog's ear.

Norah chewed her bottom lip. She knew Ivan was on his own. The produce grown here was supposed to alleviate the town's food shortages. 'I'm supposed to let them go to needy families,' she said.

Ivan looked crestfallen. Norah felt rather awkward and she couldn't help noticing that his outward appearance was worse than ever. Always a smart man when his wife was alive, he now sported an untidy stubble and a shirt with an even greasier collar than she'd seen the last time. In fact, she had heard on the grapevine that they'd retired him as school caretaker. No longer up to the job, so they'd said.

'Tell you what,' she said, putting the spray gun down, 'I'll hang on to one for you and if you can find some needy cause, you can do it on their behalf. I suggest you arrange with them that you can keep enough for yourself and let them have the rest. How does that sound?'

He gave her a gummy smile. 'How long have I got?'

She shrugged. 'Two weeks?' And he lifted his cap.

There had been little time to do much in the house and after getting the tea and doing the washing-up, Norah was too exhausted to bother with housework. As she flopped into a chair, too tired even to pick up her knitting, Jim switched on the radio. While it warmed up, she turned over the three letters in her hands. One was a bill. The second was from Rene, a chatty missive full of her latest posting. Norah read and savoured every word.

You'll never guess what, I'm to be posted to a place called Ford. They tell me it's very close to Worthing. Of course

I shall have to billet on the base but if I get a twenty-four-hour pass I can come to see you. I might even be there when my nephew or niece arrives.

Norah's heart soared.

The news on the radio as it faded up wasn't good. On April the ninth, Hitler had invaded Denmark. Later in the same month he had entered Holland and now it appeared that he was on his way through Belgium. There had been a couple of moments when the British and Canadian troops had pushed back but now everything seemed lost. The Germans were advancing and there had been some fierce fighting. Norah held her breath. Jim leaned forward and put his hand to his forehead. Mrs Kirkwood sat silently shaking her head. Nobody spoke. What could they say? It probably meant that Germany would soon turn her eye towards the British Isles and who would be the first in line for an invasion? The South Coast. It was too awful to contemplate.

Norah turned over the third letter and frowned. The front of the envelope was very messy. The original address had been crossed out and her own address scribbled in pencil at the side. The letter was destined for a Miss Short but she didn't know a Miss Short. Norah lifted the unsealed flap. Apart from a few smudges inside, the envelope was completely empty.

'That's odd,' she remarked aloud.

'What's that?' asked Jim.

Mrs Kirkwood had stood to leave the room but now she hovered beside Jim's chair.

'This letter,' said Norah, handing it to her husband. 'It's addressed to a Miss Short. The old address has been crossed out and our address is written beside it.' She held it up and the two of them examined the envelope. 'Whatever made someone think a Miss Short lived here?'

'I haven't got my glasses,' said Mrs Kirkwood. 'What's the old address?'

'Dempster Approved School, Surbiton, Surrey,' Jim said with a frown. 'Do you know anyone from there, Mother?'

Mrs Kirkwood shook her head.

'Then it's just a silly mistake,' said Jim.

All at once Norah gasped. 'Wait a minute.' She jumped to her feet and when she'd left the room, they heard her running up the stairs. A couple of minutes later she burst back into the sitting room with the small note which had been attached to the bunch of wildflowers Amy had given her long ago. Putting the two pieces of paper together she gasped, 'It's from Amy. Look, the writing is just the same.'

Mrs Kirkwood took in a breath. Jim took the envelope and looked inside. 'What was in it?'

'Nothing,' said Norah. 'Either she sent it unsealed or it came undone in the post. Whichever way it was, her letter has fallen out.'

'You know what this means, don't you?' said Jim. 'She must be living at this other address.'

'But what's she doing in an Approved School?' Mrs Kirkwood wailed.

'She's most likely working there,' said Jim.

'Then why send her letter in an envelope like this?' said Norah. 'Why not write an ordinary letter with her own paper?'

Jim pushed himself back into his chair and reached for his pipe. 'Maybe she hasn't been paid yet.'

'Oh, Jim, she must have done. She's been there for months.'

'Perhaps she couldn't use her own paper,' said Mrs Kirkwood. 'Somebody could have stopped her.'

'Let's not get melodramatic, Mother.'

Norah looked at the envelope again. Jim may be right, but it didn't *feel* right. Now she was worried. Really worried. Looking at the gum on the seal it was obvious why the letter had fallen out. But why use such an old envelope? Mrs Kirkwood had a point. If this had come from Amy, perhaps she was trying to send them an urgent message. If so, what on earth could it be?

CHAPTER 18

Amy

'Five . . . six . . . and seven. Head up, spread those arms . . .'

Amy's chest felt fit to burst as Mrs Reuben's voice cut through the mist and egged her on. She hated these early morning exercises at the best of times but just lately everything was becoming an effort. There were seven of them on the lawn. They had done running on the spot, stretches by touching alternate toes and now they were doing star jumps, and all this after a run around the perimeter wall of the property. She was hot and sweaty and exhausted. For two pins she would have sat on the grass and refused to do anything more but the consequences of such a rebellion were too high. Amy was fed up with resistance. She had reached the point when it seemed stupid. The idea of the regime was to make a girl compliant and submissive, and to all intents and purposes they had won.

'Brown,' Mrs Reuben shouted, 'you're not doing it properly. Come along everybody, we'll do it all again. From the beginning one . . . two . . .'

Amy's attention turned towards the driveway. She had been

watching for the post ever since she'd managed to send her letter. After she'd stashed the envelope in the alcove it had taken another two weeks before she'd managed to find something to write with. As classroom monitor she had to empty the wastepaper basket on Fridays and to her utter joy she'd come across a piece of pencil lead. Someone had obviously been sharpening their pencil and the lead must have snapped off. It was fairly long, perhaps as much as three-quarters of an inch, so Amy sneaked it into her pocket. She'd managed to keep it until the next time she was in the boiler room and then she'd scribbled a hurried note to Auntie Norah and put it into the envelope. Hiding the letter until Sunday was the most difficult. She knew if she was caught it would mean six strokes of the rattan again, and she couldn't trust any of the other girls. If she shared her secret, someone would demand to have the pencil lead or her precious envelope for themselves.

The day she posted it, Amy was terrified of being caught. The only time they ever went outside the school walls was when they all marched in a crocodile to church. There was a post box at the side of the road but Amy still had to be careful. The teachers were at the front, the middle and the back of the crocodile so she only had one chance to post the letter and it would be doubly difficult to do it without anyone spotting her. In the end, she was lucky. A convoy of army lorries laden with troops trundled by and, of course, seeing a group of young girls meant that they leaned out of the back of the trucks wolf-whistling, shouting and blowing kisses. Miss Short, Miss Gordon and Mrs Reuben had an enormous problem keeping an orderly line of well-behaved and compliant girls and while they were chivvying everybody to keep walking and to stop waving at the soldiers, Amy had seized her chance.

Her happiness lasted about three days and then she began the anxious wait for a reply. Three days dragged on to five and then a full week but still Auntie Norah hadn't written. After ten days Amy was left with the sinking realisation that she wasn't going to write. Why should she? After all, Amy was just another evacuee. Auntie Norah probably had other girls by now. It seemed that she was doomed to stay in this dreadful place and even if she did get out, where could she go? All her dark and depressing thoughts clung to her like a suffocating wet blanket. Nobody cared about her. She was alive and well but she was just going through the motions. Nobody wanted her. She didn't know how to find Linnet and she didn't know where Meryl was either.

'Come on, come on, Ffox-Webster,' Mrs Reuben cajoled. 'Get those legs wide apart.'

Her body was already screaming to stop, so to keep going Amy fixed her eyes onto a car coming up the long driveway. She didn't recognise it and they didn't have many cars coming to the house. It pulled up outside the front and the driver's door opened. A man got out. Amy stopped jumping and took in her breath. Oh Lord, could it be . . .? Yes, yes, it was! When the passenger door opened and a woman climbed out, Amy took off. With Mrs Reuben screaming after her, 'Ffox-Webster, come back here at once,' Amy raced across the lawn shouting, 'Auntie Norah, Auntie Norah!'

As the two of them crashed into each other's arms, the front door opened and Miss Short walked briskly onto the gravel pathway. 'Ffox-Webster, get back to your class this minute,' she demanded.

Jim stepped up to her with his hand out. 'How do you do.'

Miss Short ignored his hand. 'And you are?'

166

'Sergeant Kirkwood of the Worthing Police,' said Jim. 'And this is my wife.'

When she heard the word 'police' Miss Short's expression had changed somewhat but she was still openly hostile. 'The police? What brings the police here?'

'Oh, I'm not here on official business,' Jim said pleasantly.

'I see,' Miss Short's tone was cold. 'Well, you should know that family visits are not permitted without prior arrangement. You are family, I take it?'

'No,' said Jim. 'My wife and I looked after Amy when she was evacuated.'

'In that case, Sergeant Kirkwood, I must ask you to leave.'

'We came because we had a letter addressed to a Miss Short,' said Jim.

Miss Short frowned. 'I am Miss Short. What letter?'

'Perhaps we could step inside for a moment?'

In the meantime, Amy and Norah had been hugging each other tight. 'Oh, Auntie Norah, I've been so miserable,' Amy whispered. 'I hate it here and they're going to make me stay until I'm nineteen.'

By this time Mrs Reuben had joined them. 'Ffox-Webster, go back to the group.'

Norah frowned. 'We've come a long way to see Amy. Surely a few minutes together won't hurt?'

But Mrs Reuben grasped Amy's arm firmly. 'I'm afraid it will,' she said. 'As you can see, madam, you have disrupted the whole physical exercise lesson. This is not a visiting hour.' And pulling Amy from Norah's arms, she forced her to walk back over the lawn to where the other girls were staring with open mouths.

Just before she reached the group, Amy turned her head and cried, 'Help me, Auntie Norah. Please help me.'

Norah's heart broke. Jim came towards her. 'Sweetheart, Miss Short wants us to go inside,' he said gently. 'She'll explain everything then.'

Norah allowed herself to be led indoors but she kept turning her head in Amy's direction. After a moment or two Amy and the other girls continued their exercise.

Miss Short took them into what was obviously her office, a dark and cluttered room, its walls lined with fading photographs. Norah guessed they must be previous pupils. She and Jim were invited to sit down on one side of the desk. Miss Short rang the bell and when a girl appeared at the door, she ordered a pot of tea for three. As she sat on the other side of the desk, Norah looked at her more closely. She was late forties or maybe fifty, painfully thin with a pinched expression. Her hair was badly in need of a new perm or at least a wash and set, and she had thick pebble glasses. As she looked at them and spoke, Miss Short held her head high and to one side as if she was peering under her spectacles.

'About this letter,' she began without preamble.

Jim laid the envelope onto the desk. Miss Short gave it her full attention but didn't pick it up. 'Is that your address?' she asked.

Jim nodded.

'I recognise the handwriting of the original address,' Miss Short continued. 'It was from the local laundry. Nothing of any consequence.' She sniffed. 'I can see what's happened here. Ffox-Webster must have taken the envelope out of my waste bin. She had no business doing that or encouraging you to come all this way. What did she say in her letter?'

'We don't know,' said Norah. 'When it arrived, the envelope was empty.'

'I see.'

Jim put a Basildon Bond writing pad and envelopes onto the desk and Norah took six tuppenny ha'penny stamps out of her handbag. 'We would be more than happy if Amy was allowed to write to us,' said Jim.

There was a knock at the door and the girl came in with a tray of tea. They waited until she had left the room again.

'I'll be mother, shall I?' said Miss Short as she began to arrange the cups. 'I'm afraid you'll have to take that home,' she said, indicating the writing pad. 'Ffox-Webster is not allowed contact with the outside world.'

Norah caught her breath. 'What sort of a place is this?' she said, horrified.

'The girls who came here are, in general terms, out of control,' said Miss Short. 'I'm sure your husband will tell you that, as this is an Approved School, Ffox-Webster has been sent here by the courts for a predetermined sentence.' She pushed a cup and saucer in front of Norah.

Norah gasped. 'But what has she done?'

'She kidnapped her sister, for a start,' said Miss Short, picking up her own cup and leaning back in her chair.

'Kidnapped!' Norah retorted. 'I don't believe that for one minute. Personally, I think they simply got lost. They strayed from their school friends and took a wrong turn.'

'I am not at liberty to discuss the case in detail,' said Miss Short, 'but I think you will find it's a lot more than that. Ffox-Webster has a reputation for chasing the boys and lewd behaviour. She has been sent here for her own protection more than anything else.'

Norah glanced at her husband. 'Are we all talking about the same girl?'

'Look, Mrs Kirkwood,' said Miss Short, leaning forward in a patronising manner, 'I'm sure you mean well but there is no more to be said. If you'll take my advice you'll go home and forget all this. For goodness' sake, the girl isn't even a relative of yours.'

'While she lived with us,' Norah said stiffly, 'Amy was a model child. She was kind and considerate, she was helpful and she worked hard. She gained a glowing reference from the police canteen where she had her first ever job and she was devoted to her sister. By the way, Lillian is very upset that Amy hasn't written to her.'

Miss Short stared at her, expressionless.

'Could you perhaps give us her father's address?' Jim said in a tone of voice designed to diffuse the situation.

'You know better than to ask me that, Sergeant,' Miss Short snapped.

'Then will you tell him that we've been here,' said Jim. 'I think you owe us that at the very least.'

'I owe you nothing,' she said, rising from her seat, 'and quite frankly, I think it best if you go now. I'm sorry you've had a wasted journey but there is no more to be said. I bid you good morning.'

She escorted them outside and as they got to the car Norah looked across the lawn, but there was no sign of Amy or any of the other girls.

Norah made one last desperate plea. 'Miss Short, will you at least let Amy write to her sister?'

'As I have already explained, Mrs Kirkwood,' Miss Short said stiffly, 'Ffox-Webster is not allowed to communicate with anyone, and I stress, *anyone* outside. It's part of her condition of punishment.'

Jim started the car and they drove off. Norah managed

to hold everything together until they reached the main road and then she burst into an angry tirade.

'What a ghastly place. How can they treat girls like that? The condescending old witch! I've never met anyone like her in my life. She's got no feeling; no compassion. When Amy was hugging me she told me they expected her to stay there until she's nineteen. Can that old bag really do that, Jim?'

'If she's been sent there by the courts, I'm afraid she can, love,' said Jim.

Norah wiped away an angry tear. 'But we can't leave her there! We just can't. Poor Amy. And poor Lillian. She's growing up thinking that Amy has let her down or that she doesn't love her anymore.' He slowed to a stop.

'Why are we stopping?' Norah asked. Her heart rose. Was he going back?

Jim leaned over to the back seat and picked up the map. 'I've forgotten which way to go,' he said. He glanced at the map and then handed it to Norah. 'I've got to turn left at the junction,' he went on. 'Tell me where to go from there.'

Disappointed, Norah stared down at the jumble of squiggly lines depicting the roads which would take them back home.

'Where to now?' asked Jim, turning left.

Norah hesitated.

With one eye on the road ahead, Jim stabbed his finger onto the page. 'There,' he said impatiently. 'Look, I've marked the route in pencil. There!'

At last Norah saw it. 'Right by the gasworks,' she said dully. 'Oh, Jim, can't we go back? We have to do something.'

Jim shook his head. 'I'm sorry, love. Like the woman said, she's not our child. We have no right to interfere. It's hard, I know, but it really is none of our business.'

*

171

Amy lay on her bed and stared at the cracks on the ceiling, her mind going over the events of the day. How pretty Auntie Norah looked in that yellow dress. She tried to recall if it had a pleated skirt but she remembered the little white belt and the tiny buttons on her bodice. Oh, Auntie Norah . . . Tears pooled in her eyes.

As soon as Auntie Norah and Uncle Jim had gone, she had been sent back up to the attic room and she was on bread and water for the rest of the week. Miss Short had been unequivocal in her condemnation of her behaviour.

'You betrayed my trust, you stole an envelope which didn't belong to you, you encouraged those people to drive for miles on a wasted journey and I'm sure when I tell him, your father will be very disappointed in you.'

Amy had simply kept her eyes on the floor and said nothing. She'd been here long enough to know that arguing only made everything worse. Miss Short had all the power and, for now, Amy was her creature.

As her feelings of helplessness increased, she let out a long sigh. The thought of staying in this hell hole for another four and a half years was beyond the pale. If the window in the attic could be opened, which it couldn't because she'd tried, she would have climbed out, and if she couldn't reach the ground by going down the drainpipe, she would have been tempted to throw herself into oblivion. But even as the thought formed in her head, she knew she wouldn't do it. She was too angry to give up. And there was still Linnet to worry about. Amy turned onto her side and curled into a ball as her eyes filled with silent tears. What should she do now that all other avenues were closed? Where could she go from here? She couldn't stop her step-father from doing to Linnet what he'd done to her and the thought of

172

it made her sick to her stomach. She suddenly recalled that when her mother had died, Mrs Scott had said, 'The poor dear is with the Lord now.' Amy squeezed her eyes shut and breathed a prayer. 'Mummy, Mummy . . . I miss you so much. Please ask God to help me. I can't do it on my own.'

CHAPTER 19

Norah

Norah was doing her best to keep busy. She had to. If she wasn't fully occupied, dark thoughts overwhelmed her.

When they'd got back home from Epsom, Norah put the kettle on for a cup of tea. She and Jim had talked for England on their journey home but they'd got nowhere. It had been exhausting and she didn't feel like saying much now.

'I'd better get the car back to Nobby Barrett,' Jim said, coming out of the toilet. 'I know he's only going to lock it up in the garage to prevent it falling into German hands if they invade, but I promised to have it back to him as soon as possible.' He kissed the top of her head. 'Try not to let it get to you, darling. We've done all we can.'

Norah nodded. 'I'll have the tea ready for when you get back.'

She walked past him to take a cup of tea into Mrs Kirkwood. There was a letter on the mat. The embossed label on the left-hand side of the envelope told her it was from the adoption agency. Norah put the tea on the hall table and tore it open. 'Jim!' she cried just as he was going out of the door. 'The baby. It's already been born.'

Jim beamed. 'That's grand,' he said, coming back.

Norah read on. *'His mother has called him Eric. You'll be pleased to know that he weighed in at a whopping eight pounds. He's healthy and he's doing well.'*

She and Jim hugged each other and Jim kissed the end of her nose. 'Better get off now, Mummy. Got to get this car back.'

'Is that you, Norah?' a sleepy Mrs Kirkwood called.

'Just a minute.'

Norah couldn't stop smiling. It was exciting and yet daunting at the same time. She couldn't wait to hold her son in her arms but as she waved Jim goodbye, the enormity of what they'd agreed to began to hit home. When he came to live with them, little Eric would be completely dependent on her and Jim. For the rest of his life, they would become the most important people in his life – his mummy and daddy. What a responsibility.

It was time to tell Mrs Kirkwood. Norah picked up the cup and saucer and knocked on her mother-in-law's door.

'Did you see Amy? How is she?' said Mrs Kirkwood, her eyes lighting up as Norah came in.

Norah told her what had happened as best she could. 'On a happier note,' she went on, 'I have something else to tell you.'

Until now, Norah had held off from telling Jim's mother that they were going to adopt a baby. It may have been because she didn't want the old lady to put a damper on things but it was more likely because Norah had a superstitious concern that something might go wrong and that it might not actually happen. As she showed her mother-in-law the letter and shared their news, Jim's mother seemed surprised. 'So when is he coming?'

'Probably at the end of May, the beginning of June,' said Norah, hardly able to believe what she was saying. 'He has to stay with his mother for the first six weeks and then he comes to us.'

'Do you know anything about his mother?'

'Only that she's Polish.'

'Polish!' exclaimed Mrs Kirkwood. 'Good heavens! How on earth are you going to understand what he's saying when he starts to talk?'

Although she was excited about the baby coming, Norah also felt awkward. Her life was so happy right now, which was more than could be said about Amy's. She and Jim had talked about what to do all the way home but there was no easy solution. She hated to admit it but Jim was right. Amy and her sister were not their responsibility and even if it did seem grossly unfair that the poor girl was incarcerated, what could they do? Norah was at a loss to understand why it had happened in the first place. True, she hadn't much liked Mr Ffox-Webster when he'd turned up. He was too forthright, too bombastic, but she supposed that was in his upbringing. Men like him, who had probably grown up with a nanny and the proverbial silver spoon in their mouths, expected everyone to do what they wanted. Now that she was thinking more rationally about it, he hadn't actually done anything wrong and he had been extremely generous with that massive hamper, hadn't he? Mrs Kirkwood had always muttered darkly about 'something not being quite right' about what had happened to the girls, but there was nothing she could put her finger on. Amy seemed wary of him but Lillian was clearly devoted to her father.

When she and Jim told his mother that they'd been to see Amy, Mrs Kirkwood had been visibly upset. 'You mean she was actually *sent* to an Approved School?' she'd gasped. 'She's not just working there?' She'd listened with growing alarm as Norah told her what had happened.

'So, you didn't actually get to talk to her?'

Norah shook her head. 'I wasn't allowed to,' she said weakly.

'You should have insisted,' said Mrs Kirkwood. 'You should have demanded it.'

Norah lowered her head with a sigh.

Mrs Kirkwood repeated the same opinion at the tea table when Jim got back from dropping off the car.

'We had no right to demand anything, Mother,' said Jim. 'She's not our child.'

Mrs Kirkwood harrumphed. 'There's something wrong with all this,' she said emphatically. 'You mark my words. As sure as eggs is eggs, that man is a bad'en. I can feel it in m'water.'

As soon as it became known that Norah oversaw the allotments on Clifton Road, plenty of people had come round to ask if they could take on one of the plots. Penny had turned up with Victor in his pram. He was bonny little lad and when Norah smiled at him, he stared up at her with dark eyes and gave her a lopsided smile.

'He's grown so quickly,' Norah cooed. She tickled the baby's tummy and he kicked his legs happily.

The two of them walked to the edge of the allotments.

'I've only got two left,' said Norah. 'I've half promised one to someone else but that small plot is still going.'

'It looks huge to me,' Penny murmured.

Norah laughed. 'It's half the size of a proper one.'

'I don't know a thing about growing vegetables,' Penny admitted. 'But Mum says it would help us no end, what with the rationing and all.'

'Anything you want to know, just ask,' said Norah as she agreed to let Penny have the last plot. 'Have you got any gardening tools?'

'I've got a fork but Paine, Manwaring and Lephard have run out of spades,' said Penny. 'Ever since they started this Dig for Victory stuff there's been a run on absolutely everything.'

'I can let you borrow a spade for now,' said Norah, pointing out where it was. 'Do you know what you want to plant?'

'Cucumber, tomatoes, potatoes . . .' Penny said with a shrug. 'I dunno, you tell me.'

'You might be a bit late for cucumbers,' said Norah. 'But I've got some leeks and lettuce you can bring on and there's some sturdy broad bean plants you can have from the shop. You might like to try growing kohlrabi. That's very tasty.'

Her friend gave her an embarrassed smile. 'The thing is, Ted's pay is a bit slow coming through so I don't have much money,' she said apologetically.

'Pay me what you can,' said Norah, 'and you can settle up later for the rest. You ought to make a start or it'll be too late for anything, but first you have to prepare the ground. I've dug it over once but it still needs a little more TLC.'

To help her out, Norah decided to spend the morning working with her friend. The weather was good so they made a start. 'Have you actually heard from Ted?'

Penny shook her head. 'I'm trying not to think about it,' she said.

'A shame he's not seen the baby,' Norah said, immediately regretting her hasty remark.

'Our next-door neighbour took a photo of the baby with his box Brownie and I sent it with my last letter,' said Penny, tugging at a stubborn weed. 'It's important to let people know you're still thinking of them, isn't it?'

Norah gave her friend a sympathetic smile as her own thoughts drifted back to Amy. The dogs sat by the pram wheels as if guarding little Victor as he slept on. Being out in the fresh air was obviously doing him the world of good and the two women worked on steadily.

Penny was delighted when Norah told her about Eric. 'Oh, it'll be lovely, both of us being mums at the same time,' she said enthusiastically. 'And when Victor and Eric are older, they can play together.'

'I'm not sure I like the name Eric,' Norah mused. 'I think I prefer something like Peter or Brian.'

'Well, he's your baby,' said Penny, 'you can call him what you like.'

Norah smiled. Yes, she was right. Peter – or Brian – was going to be *her* baby.

Penny stood up to stretch her back and her face suddenly clouded. 'Oh, Norah, I'm so scared that Ted might be in the fighting.'

Norah pushed her fork into the ground and went to her friend. 'Try not to worry,' she said, giving Penny's arm a quick squeeze, but she had sucked her mouth in and her eyes were bright with unshed tears. Norah took a deep breath. 'We've done enough for one morning,' she said gently. 'Shall I put the kettle on?'

Victor had woken up and started to grizzle so Penny nodded.

As she walked back into the house, Norah could understand Penny's concern. As part of the British Expeditionary Force, Ted was somewhere on the Continent and things weren't looking good. The papers were full of gloomy predictions ever since the Allies had arrived in Holland and Belgium. As Norah busied herself with tea cups and saucers, Penny came in to wash her hands.

'Are you making some tea, Norah?' Mrs Kirkwood called.

'Yes,' said Norah, rolling her eyes at Penny as she went back outside to see to Victor. 'Come and join us, if you like. We'll be out in the sunshine.'

Back outside again, Penny had changed the baby's nappy and picked him up to put him discreetly to her breast. Norah brought out another chair as Mrs Kirkwood came to join them. The baby watched them from his mother's lap.

'My, my,' said Mrs Kirkwood, 'hasn't he grown into a bonny boy.'

Penny smiled happily and without taking his eyes from them all, Victor caught his foot with his hand and swung it around as he suckled.

'Heard from your Ted?' Mrs Kirkwood asked as she negotiated the step by the back door. 'He's over in France, isn't he?'

Penny's smile faded as she nodded.

'I've been telling Penny to try not to worry,' said Norah, hoping that Mrs Kirkwood would leave the subject alone. She put the tray of tea onto the rickety old table outside the back door and lifting the tea pot, began to pour.

'Of course she shouldn't worry,' Mrs Kirkwood said,

plonking herself down. 'It won't be long before our boys give those Germans a bloody nose.'

Norah saw Penny's anxious glance and wished she could think of something to say to change the subject. They sat for a while, drinking their tea and soaking up the warm spring air.

'Would your mother babysit for you one evening?' Norah asked. 'Only, I was thinking perhaps you and I could go to the pictures sometime. Before Eric comes.'

'The girl is breast-feeding, Norah,' Mrs Kirkwood tutted.

Norah's face coloured.

'That doesn't matter,' said Penny, brightening up. 'I can express some milk and put it in a bottle, then Mum can feed him if she needs to.'

Mrs Kirkwood shifted in her chair and looked away, clearly embarrassed by the thought.

Norah grinned. 'Then that's settled,' she said. 'Penny, you and I are going to the pictures.'

CHAPTER 20

Norah

There was only the one full-sized allotment left. Norah had had loads of enquiries about it and she couldn't hold on to it much longer. She had given Mr Steele a couple of weeks to find a worthy cause he could couple with but it had been more than three weeks since she'd seen him. In the end, she decided she would go over to his place for a chat.

Never one to go anywhere empty-handed, Norah made a small shepherd's pie for Ivan when she did the dinner for herself, Jim and Mrs Kirkwood. Leaving Jim to dish up, she covered it with greaseproof paper and wrapped it in a towel before putting it into her bag. It wouldn't take long to bike over to Stanley Road where Mr Steele lived and it would still be nice and warm. When she got there, Norah parked her bike against the low wall and knocked on the door.

'Mr Steele?' said the woman who answered. 'He don't live here no more.'

'Oh!' said Norah. 'Then I'm sorry to have bothered you. I was so sure this was his address.'

'It used to be,' said the woman, 'but I had to let him go.'

Norah frowned. 'Let him go? Why? What do you mean?'

The woman leaned towards her and spoke in a confidential manner. She smelled of perspiration and her floral apron wasn't very clean either. Norah held her breath and leaned as far away from her as she could. 'Between you and me and the gatepost, love, he's let himself go since his wife died,' she said, 'and when he lost his job at the school, well, that was the last straw.'

Norah was shocked. 'So where is he now?'

A neighbour walked past the gate and the woman stepped back into her hallway. 'I'm sure I don't know,' she said loftily, 'but he ain't here no more.' And with that she shut the door.

As Norah turned towards the street, she became aware that the neighbour was hovering by her own gate. 'Are you looking for poor ol' Ivan?'

Norah put her bag back into the basket on her bicycle. 'Yes. Do you know where he is?'

The woman turned to walk up the path. 'Try under Broadwater Bridge,' she said, putting the key into her front door and letting herself in.

Norah stood for a moment trying to take in what she had just said. Under the bridge? There was nothing under the bridge, was there? She hardly ever went near the place. It had a reputation for drunks and seedy goings-on. She turned her bike round to go back home, but against her better judgement, Norah found herself heading towards Broadwater Bridge.

Her heart was thumping as she neared the place. It was dark and creepy and it smelled of urine but there was nobody about. That woman must have been having her on. Norah biked right through the underpass. Nothing. On the

183

other side, back out in the open there were some more allotments. It was early evening and a few people were still working there. A man came out of the gate of the perimeter fencing.

'Excuse me,' said Norah, slowing but not getting off her bike. 'Do you know where Mr Steele is? Only I was told he lives around here.'

The man shrugged and then his face lit up as if he'd had an afterthought. 'I don't know his name, but there's an old boy living in one of the railways sheds. That might be him.'

Norah hurried to the shed the man had pointed out. As she drew near, she could hear coughing coming from inside. She held her breath. Heaven's above, don't say Ivan really was living here. She put the bike against a lamp post and knocked on the shed door. It opened slowly and a tousled head peered out. 'What d'yer want?'

'Mr Steele?' Norah gasped.

He looked terrible. His face was grey and his eyes were puffy and bloodshot. When he saw who it was he staggered slightly and she reached out her hand to steady him as he began another coughing fit. 'You should see a doctor,' she said.

'I'll be all right in a minute,' he said as he struggled to catch his breath.

'I don't think so, Mr Steele,' she said firmly. 'In fact, I'm going back home to fetch my husband and we're taking you to hospital.'

She helped him back inside the shed and sat him on the low camp bed. Everywhere smelled damp but the temperature inside wasn't too bad. Most likely the sunshine of the afternoon had warmed it up, she decided, but she guessed it would drop like a stone come night. There was no sign of any heating and the shed only had a dirt floor. All his things were scattered around in piles.

'I brought you a shepherd's pie,' she said, looking round for a spoon. 'You eat it up and I'll be back as quick as I can.'

'Thank you, love,' he said breathlessly.

He took the small enamel dish from her with a trembling hand. Norah turned to go and as she reached the door she saw that his head was bowed and his shoulders trembled.

Ivan had begun to weep.

Jim and Norah were exhausted when they finally got home that night. Ivan Steele was in hospital with suspected pneumonia and because Jim said they couldn't risk leaving all of his things in the unlocked shed, in case some light-fingered opportunist came by, everything Ivan possessed was stashed in the porch downstairs.

'Who does that lot belong to?' Mrs Kirkwood said when she saw it.

She wrinkled her nose when Jim explained. 'What's that old devil been up to now?'

'How long do you think he's been living there?' Norah asked as she and Jim climbed into bed later that night.

Jim lifted the bedclothes and she snuggled in closer. 'Some time, I should think. I'm going to have a word with the station master tomorrow. It's time he pulled that dilapidated shed down. That old boy could have died in there and no one would have been any the wiser.'

'And if they had pulled it down, where would he have gone?'

Jim didn't answer. 'What I want to know is how did he end up there in the first place?' he said doggedly.

Norah told him about Ivan's landlady. 'Sour-faced old biddy,' she added. 'It looks like she gave him no choice.' Norah put her head on one side as she looked at him. 'He's got nowhere else to go, Jim.'

'Oh, Norah.' Jim sighed.

'But we can't send him back out on the streets, can we?' She paused. 'Especially if you get his shed pulled down.'

Jim grinned good-naturedly. 'If I'm not careful we'll end up with the rest of the world and his wife living with us.'

She kissed him. 'Thank you, darling.'

They lay side by side. 'There is one other thing,' she began again.

'Norah . . .' Jim pulled himself up onto his elbow and leaned over her.

'Don't worry. I don't want to invite anyone else to live here, but I would like to go to the pictures with Penny now and then. She's so miserable with Ted away and she needs cheering up.'

Jim gave her a quizzical look as he shook his head slowly. 'What am I going to do with you?'

Norah fingered the buttons on his pyjamas. 'I'm sure you'll think of something,' she whispered teasingly.

'Do you happen to have an old shoe box, Mrs Kirkwood?'

Norah had poked her head around her mother-in-law's door quite early.

'What for?'

'I thought I'd send a little present to Amy,' said Norah. 'If I had a shoe box, I could make up a parcel.'

Mrs Kirkwood grinned, suddenly coming to life. 'Good idea,' she said.

186

As it turned out, she didn't have a shoe box but one of the women on the allotments did. She brought it round that afternoon and Norah began putting a few things together. She hadn't used the talcum powder from the Yardley's box of bath crystals her mother had given her for Christmas, so that went in. The pretty scarf Jim had given her a couple of years ago was lovely but it just wasn't her colour and she had nothing to wear with it, so that went in, too. Norah had finished the jumper she had been knitting for Amy before she left so suddenly and although it took up a lot of room, she decided the girl may as well have it. Mrs Kirkwood put in a small home-made purse containing two bob and she also gave her a book. 'Amy loves reading,' she said as Norah pressed it down. 'And I'll put a stamp in the purse so she can write back.'

'She may not be allowed to,' Norah cautioned.

The two women each wrote Amy a letter and Norah added a bar of Fry's chocolate cream and a note pad with matching envelopes from Woolworth's. The parcel was wrapped in brown paper and string and Norah put sealing wax on all the knots. When it was done, Mrs Kirkwood shuffled off to her room. Norah watched her go and sighed. It was obvious that the old lady was missing Amy.

Despite Sunday being a National Day of Prayer, the news from France wasn't good. Halfway through the morning, a very tearful and frightened Penny turned up at her door and Norah invited her in to calm her down.

'I can't be left to bring up Victor on my own,' Penny said gloomily as she was leaving.

'Don't give up hope,' said Norah, even though she knew she would probably be feeling exactly the same if Jim was hundreds of miles away and fighting for his life. 'Your Ted is a really tough nut. It would take a lot to bring him down.'

Penny grimaced. 'It only takes one bullet,' she said bleakly.

As the end of the month drew closer, Norah's friend wasn't alone in her feelings of trepidation. An ominous atmosphere of dread that an invasion along the South Coast was imminent had pervaded the town. The pier was under military guard and closed to the public and every seat within a hundred yards of the Pavilion was turned upside down. If anyone wondered why, the answer came late in the afternoon when the town was shaken by a loud explosion.

'I don't know what the world's coming to,' Mrs Kirkwood said darkly. 'Now they've blown up the bloody pier.'

CHAPTER 21

Norah

Ivan Steele was released from hospital after only a couple of days. When Jim and Norah had taken him there that night, everyone had thought he was suffering from pneumonia but, thankfully, it turned out that it was nothing more than a touch of pleurisy and a bad cough.

'He doesn't seem to have insurance,' Norah told Mrs Kirkwood as they sat together in the evening. Norah was knitting another matinee jacket for the baby and her mother-in-law was reading a book. The two women had settled into an uneasy truce and Norah was glad of it. It still felt she was treading on eggshells at times but since she'd stood up to Mrs Kirkwood that one time, the woman seemed to be less prickly.

Jim was on duty and Mr Steele was in his room. Norah had decided to put him in the back bedroom upstairs and after their evening meal, he begged to be excused. Nobody minded. He looked pale and exhausted. The hospital had told him to sleep on his sore side and when Norah looked in on him half an hour ago, he was already fast asleep.

Mrs Kirkwood frowned. 'So who is going to pay for his treatment then?'

Norah shrugged. She hoped it wouldn't become her and Jim's responsibility. They needed all their savings for when the baby came.

'Have you asked him about it?'

'I didn't like to,' Norah confessed. 'I could hardly say, "you're welcome to stay but give us your money", could I?'

Mrs Kirkwood harrumphed. 'You weren't backward in coming forward when you asked me for money.'

Norah frowned crossly. 'You had already stayed several weeks with us at our expense,' she retorted. 'It's not the same.'

Mrs Kirkwood pursed her lips defiantly.

'Besides,' Norah continued in a more conciliatory tone, 'that's all water under the bridge now and I don't want to talk about it.' She saw Mrs Kirkwood open her mouth so she added quickly, 'And I don't want to argue with you either, so there's an end to it.'

They sat for a minute in stony silence, each avoiding the other's eye.

Norah had spent the past two days washing Ivan Steele's clothes and getting them ironed. Fortunately, the weather had been good so she'd got everything dried, but it had been hard work. His shirt collars had to be seen to be believed and of course, now she knew why. The poor man had nowhere to do any washing, or to wash himself, for that matter, which explained why he smelled a bit whiffy as well.

'Do you want me to have a look through his papers?' Mrs Kirkwood asked. Her tone of voice had mellowed slightly.

'Well, seeing as how you went to school together, I suppose

you have known him a lot longer than I have,' Norah said cautiously, 'and he's not in a fit state to look for himself.'

When Mrs Kirkwood sifted through Ivan's things the next morning, she was surprised to find that he had a Post Office Savings Book with ten pounds fifteen shillings in it. He also had a life insurance in his wife's name, which had never been cashed. That would have yielded one hundred pounds plus interest, which would have been more than enough for him to be able to survive for some time without a job, so why hadn't he cashed it in? There were also letters from the school, one explaining how he could collect his pension and the other thanking him for working for them for twenty years. If she hadn't known him so well it would have left her with a conundrum. The obvious questions were, why hadn't he done anything about it? Why was he living like a pauper when although he was far from a wealthy man, he could, at the very least, be having a far more comfortable life? Mrs Kirkwood released an irritated sigh. Those were the questions and it seemed that she was the only one who knew the answers.

That afternoon, the two of them were alone in the sitting room. Norah was just about to go in and see if they wanted a cup of tea when she heard Mrs Kirkwood's cold voice say, 'She never managed to teach you, then.'

Norah, her hand out to push the door open, froze.

'Who never managed to teach me what?' said Mr Steele.

'Your Ada, she never managed to teach you to read.'

Leaning back slightly, Norah could see the pair of them sitting opposite one another through the crack in the door.

Ivan shuffled his feet uncomfortably. 'It wasn't Ada's fault,' he said doggedly. 'And it wasn't fer the lack of trying.'

191

'She always did have an inflated idea of her own cap-abilities, that one,' Mrs Kirkwood said acidly. 'Is that why you lost your job?'

Outside the door, Norah put her fingers to her lips in horror.

Ivan turned his head away. 'I been doing that job for nigh on twenty-one year,' he said bitterly. 'Started the day after I was discharged from the army in 1918. Nobody ever found fault before but suddenly I'm not up to it.'

'What happened?'

'She left me a note, didn't she, the new head mistress,' he said. 'I used to take them home and my Ada would read them to me but after she went, I didn't have anyone to ask; not someone who wouldn't laugh at me, any road.' He glanced up at her. 'And now you can't wait to pass that little tit-bit on, can you, Chastity Kirkwood. You always did enjoy a good laugh at another's expense.'

'How dare you!' Mrs Kirkwood gasped. On the other side of the door Norah braced herself to go in. 'For your information, Ivan Steele, I've said nothing,' Mrs Kirkwood snapped angrily. 'I kept it to myself.'

As Norah walked in the room Mr Steele was muttering, 'That'll be a first,' while Mrs Kirkwood had grabbed her knitting bag and leapt to her feet.

'Anyone like a nice cup of tea?' Norah trilled.

The atmosphere between her two house guests remained frosty for a day or two until other events overtook everything. At the end of May everyone was glued to the radio as they listened with bated breath to what was unfolding on the other side of the Channel. France had fallen. The Germans were sweeping through the country, and the British had had

192

to pull back. They were now in full retreat. A flotilla of small boats left Littlehampton on its way to Dunkirk to be part of the rescue plan for thousands and thousands of British and French soldiers trapped on the beaches. All day long the people of Worthing heard the overhead drone of aircraft from Ford, Westhampnett and Tangmere, as the RAF flew to the same coastline to provide what protection they could from the skies against the enemy aircraft firing onto the helpless men stranded in the water.

Concerned about Ted, Norah went round to Penny's house to comfort her but it was very difficult. Although she appreciated Norah being there, no matter what she said, the poor girl couldn't be convinced that Ted would ever come back to her and their son. To add to her distress, her grief had affected her milk and the normally placid and contented Victor had become a very cross and hungry baby.

Jim was under pressure because several of the lads in the station had joined up, leaving the Worthing force very short of manpower. For those still in police uniform, their shifts were longer and of course the local rogues were having a field day.

For both Jim and Norah, the one bright light on their horizon was Eric's expected arrival. Norah was more than ready, having knitted a drawer full of baby clothes and put a coat of paint on the walls of the small bedroom. Jim wondered how she fitted everything in. His mother was settled. Ivan Steele was improving. The allotments were well under way and the market garden was doing brisk sales. Norah was, in Jim's eyes, nothing short of a ruddy marvel.

The letter came as a surprise. The fact that it was in an expensive-looking envelope made it stand out from the rest of the mail and when she tore it open, Norah was stunned.

Dear Mr and Mrs Kirkwood,

It has come to my notice that you and your husband have not only made an uninvited visit to my daughter's school, but you have also attempted to entice Lillian back to Worthing with Christmas gifts. I am also told that you have been to see Amy. A strict condition of her incarceration is that she be allowed to reflect upon her behaviour and that she must have no distractions while doing so. While I appreciate what you did for my children when they got lost during the evacuation, I must stress that Amy and Lillian are no longer your concern. I have therefore instructed the school to return the box you sent Amy and I must insist that the matter is closed.

Yours sincerely,

Jago Ffox-Webster, Under-secretary to the Secretary of State for War.

Norah's jaw dropped. She was hurt and confused but mostly she was very upset and angry. What was the man implying? Under-secretary to the Secretary of State for War? What a ridiculous title! Ffox-Webster was obviously puffed up with his own importance but how dare he imply that she and Jim had anything more than loving concern for his children.

When she showed her the letter, Mrs Kirkwood was equally upset. 'What are you going to do about it?'

Norah shook her head. 'There's nothing I can do, is there? He's perfectly within his rights, but it does seem very unfair. This letter implies that somehow or other we've been dishonest.'

She scrutinised the address but it only said 'London W1'. Perhaps she should write a letter of apology. His name was so distinctive, the post office should be able to work out where to deliver it.

But when Norah showed the letter to Jim when he came home that night, he was adamant that she shouldn't write. 'Let it go, love,' he said. 'You know your conscience is clear. There's no reason why you should go kowtowing to the likes of Ffox-Webster.'

The parcel arrived the next day. It had been opened and resealed with the contents hardly touched. It was perfectly clear that Amy hadn't even seen it. But if that wasn't upsetting enough, another letter, this time from the adoption agency, sent all Norah's hopes and dreams crashing to the floor.

Dear Mr and Mrs Kirkwood,

Following a communique and a telephone conversation with a senior secretary in the War Office, your suitability as adoptive parents has been called into question. In view of the seriousness of the situation in the country at the moment, there is little time to investigate this further so I deeply regret to have to tell you that Eric will not now be placed in your care.

Yours sincerely,

P. Bundy (Miss)

CHAPTER 22

Norah

'Norah? Norah darling.' Rene's voice sounded far away, as if she was standing at the end of a tunnel.

Norah blinked and turned around. At first, she only saw a pair of highly polished black lace-up shoes but as she slowly raised her head she saw the blue-grey of a uniform skirt. It came towards her and as Norah raised her eyes further she could see a belted jacket with its four flapped and buttoned pockets. Absurdly, the thought crossed her mind to wonder why the jacket was done up the man's way, left-over-right. Norah sighed. If only her sister were here, she thought to herself. If only Mum was here.

'Norah,' Rene said again as she walked towards the edge of the bed where Norah was sitting. 'Oh, darling, I'm so, so sorry.'

It finally registered that the person entering her bedroom really was Rene. As her sister sat on the bed beside her and put her hand on her shoulder, Norah could feel her warmth and she smelled Rene's delicate perfume of roses and vanilla.

'Eric isn't coming,' she said brokenly. 'I'm not allowed to have him.' She began to cry softly.

'I know, darling. I know.'

The bed was strewn with the baby's layette. Exquisitely knitted jackets, vests, and booties lay alongside embroidered shawls and romper-suits.

Rene looked up at Jim standing in the doorway.

'Mother's making some tea,' he said helplessly.

Rene nodded. 'We'll be down in a minute.'

Norah sat up straight and blew her nose. 'I know he wasn't mine,' she said, 'but I still feel like I've lost a baby.'

'Of course you have,' Rene said gently.

'Mrs Kirkwood says that's the way life is and I just have to pull myself together.'

Rene bristled. 'Don't listen to Mrs Cow-bags,' she said firmly. 'She's got as much sympathy as a praying mantis.'

Norah turned her head and gave her sister a wan smile. 'What are you doing here?'

'When I got Jim's telegram, I put in for forty-eight hours compassionate leave,' said Rene. 'I just told the warrant officer my sister had lost her baby.'

'Did they know I was only adopting it?'

'The trick is to be sparing with the facts, darling.'

Norah smiled again. 'Thanks for coming, Rene.'

'You're welcome.' She paused. 'Do you want to talk about it?'

'How much do you know?'

'Jim told me Ffox-Webber told you to lay off his kids and the adoption agency decided to dump you.'

'Ffox-Webster,' Norah corrected miserably. 'I get the feeling that everything is connected. He's a very powerful man.'

Rene gasped. 'What are you saying? That he found out that you were adopting a baby and somehow scuppered it?'

Norah rose to her feet and opened the top drawer of the chest of drawers. She rummaged under her undies, and taking out a letter, handed it to Rene.

'*Your suitability as adoptive parents has been called into question*,' Rene read aloud. She looked up. 'So you think this . . . "*senior secretary in the War Office*" is him.'

'Don't you?'

Rene blew out her cheeks. 'I suppose it's possible.' She looked again at the letter. 'Are you going to try to put your side of the story?'

'I was,' said Norah cautiously. 'I even made an appointment, but it's for tomorrow and Jim has to be in court in Chichester. They've caught a gang who have been stealing handbags from under the wall of the ladies' toilets and he has to be there to give evidence.' She sighed. 'I'm not sure I can face it alone.'

'You won't have to,' Rene said stoutly. 'I'm coming with you.'

When they got downstairs, Mrs Kirkwood and Ivan Steele were out. Apparently, they had heard that a train carrying troops plucked from the Dunkirk beaches was to pass through Worthing Station that afternoon so they had walked together to the gates to wave the men on.

Norah sat at the table staring into her cup.

'How are you liking Ford?' Jim asked her sister.

'It's grand,' said Rene. 'It's not fully operational yet but I think it will be a force to be reckoned with before long.'

Jim nodded. Norah didn't move.

'I'm still packing parachutes,' said Rene. She and Jim knew she was just making conversation.

Jim nodded. 'I thought Ford belonged to the navy.'

'It does,' said Rene. 'It's part of the Fleet Air Arm now but they say the RAF will be taking over soon.'

There was a noise by the back door and Mrs Kirkwood and a man came in.

'Rene, this is Ivan Steele,' said Jim. 'He's been ill so he's staying with us for a while. It turns out that he and my mother went to school together.'

'Lucky you,' said Rene. Her sarcasm was lost on Ivan as they shook hands and Rene did her best to avoid staring at his jagged ear.

'Did you see the boys?' said Jim, reaching for two more cups.

'They looked a sorry sight,' said Ivan, giving him a nod. 'Filthy dirty and looking like death warmed up.'

Mrs Kirkwood stood in the doorway with a shocked expression. 'Most of them were asleep,' she said. Norah was surprised to hear the sympathy in her voice.

It was with some relief when everybody listened to the wireless that evening and heard the announcer, Bernard Stubbs, tell the nation that over three hundred thousand men had been rescued. It was obvious that the BEF had been to hell and back but even though many were wounded, they had managed to stay cheerful.

'Imagine not being able to take your boots off for four days,' said Jim when the news-cast had finished. 'Poor sods.'

'And being bombed and shot at when you're stuck on a beach with no cover,' Rene said quietly.

The room went silent until Norah said, 'I wonder if Penny has heard from her Ted.'

'Nobody would be bothered to take name, rank and number when they got off those ships,' Mrs Kirkwood said crossly. 'They'd just want to unload them as quick as they could and get back over there to fetch some more.'

Norah jerked in surprise at the sharpness of her voice and was about to snap back when Ivan's steadying voice said, 'All right, all right, keep yer hair on, gal. She didn't mean nothing by it.' Mrs Kirkwood sat back in her chair, looking slightly embarrassed. Behind her back, Norah and Rene exchanged a look of astonishment.

The next morning, Jim set off early. 'Sorry I can't be with you today, love,' he said. 'If you change your mind and you don't want to go through with it, that's fine by me.'

'I want to go,' Norah said determinedly. 'And thank you for making sure Rene came over.'

'Oh, but . . .' Jim began.

Norah reached up and kissed his cheek. 'Don't bother to deny it, Sergeant Kirkwood,' she said firmly. 'She's told me about your telegram so I've got you banged to rights.'

Jim gave her a small grin. 'All right, I admit it; but she was only too willing to come.' He kissed her tenderly as they parted.

Norah and Rene arrived at the old town hall in good time for her appointment. This time Miss Bundy wasn't alone. As they sat down, she introduced a rather austere-looking man in a shabby grey suit as Mr Pettigrew, her supervisor. Norah guessed that they had agreed to see her in force in case she made a fuss.

Having gone over the particulars of the case, Mr Pettigrew outlined the complaint that had halted the adoption plans.

'It came to our notice,' he began, 'that you had taken in

some evacuees. One mother took her children home after only a few very short weeks, and I'm told that the other children were removed soon after that by their father. Since then, you have, quite frankly, made a nuisance of yourself by visiting his children at odd hours and sending parcels that were totally unnecessary.'

Deeply offended, Norah sat forward in her chair to address this gross misrepresentation but Mr Pettigrew interrupted her before she'd even uttered a word. 'However,' he continued, raising his hand, 'it has been suggested – from a highly eminent source, I might add – that perhaps your mental capacity might be . . . shall we say, a little unstable, rendering you incapable of coping with sudden changes. Quite understandable in the present circumstances, but that is why we have regrettably decided to think again about your application to adopt.'

Norah stared at him, horrified. Rene's eyes blazed. 'And have you bothered to check my sister's character with local people?' she demanded. 'Because I cannot believe that *anyone* in Worthing would have *anything* but praise for her. She is a stalwart of the community.' Rene's voice rose. 'She and my brother-in-law have taken in evacuees and the homeless and she is currently a co-ordinator for the Dig for Victory campaign. Are you really suggesting that a person of such high calibre could be mentally unstable?'

'That's not for me to judge, Miss Carson,' he said sniffily, 'and I would caution you to calm down or I shall terminate this interview forthwith.'

Rene sat back in her chair with a sulky expression. 'I apologise for my outburst, Mr Pettigrew, but you must understand the unfairness of the situation.'

'You say the evacuees left after a few weeks,' Norah began. 'That is true, but it wasn't because there was a problem. My husband is a police officer and several of his colleagues organised an outing to Devil's Dyke. Gwen . . . er, Mrs Harrison, the children's mother, met us there and we all enjoyed a very nice day. Mrs Harrison left them in my care once more when she went back home and the children returned with us to Worthing.'

'We have it on good authority that they then went back to London,' Miss Bundy said doggedly.

'Yes, they did,' said Norah, 'but only because their mother was missing them.'

The two officials seemed uncomfortably embarrassed.

'I can ask Mrs Harrison to write to you, if you like?' said Norah, sensing a small victory.

Mr Pettigrew shuffled some papers. 'Let us discuss what happened with Amy and Lillian,' he said sourly. 'Apparently, you kept the girls for some time without informing their father of where they were.'

'I didn't know where he lived,' Norah emphasised. 'Amy wouldn't tell me and Lillian was under the impression that their father was involved in some secret government stuff and that by not telling me where they came from, she was protecting him.'

Mr Pettigrew scoffed. 'It sounds as if you've been reading too many spy mysteries, Mrs Kirkwood.'

Norah frowned angrily. For two pins she wanted to give him a smack but a glance towards her sister reminded her to keep control of her feelings. 'As a matter of fact,' she continued, 'I moved heaven and earth to discover the whereabouts of Mr Ffox-Webster. In the end, Mrs Harrison sent me a London newspaper cutting with a picture of Lillian. Her father had declared her a missing child and was searching for her. I made contact and he came to Worthing.'

'I see,' said Mr Pettigrew.

'He seemed quite happy that the girls had been well looked after,' said Norah, relaxing a little. 'In fact, he arrived with a very expensive gift.'

'Oh, we know about that,' said Mr Pettigrew. 'And I must say that I'm surprised that you, a policeman's wife, and knowing the risks for taking bribes, should even ask for such a gift.'

Rene's jaw dropped.

'What?' Norah cried indignantly. 'But I didn't! How dare you suggest that I would do such a thing.'

Miss Bundy unscrewed her fountain pen. 'I'm afraid it doesn't alter the fact that you went uninvited to Lillian and Amy's schools, Mrs Kirkwood.'

'I went because I was concerned,' said Norah, speaking in a deliberate tone of voice. 'If you don't mind me saying so, Mr Ffox-Webster seemed a rather distant man. I knew he was very busy and that the girls had lost their mother. I just wanted to be a friendly face, that's all.'

'But Mr Ffox-Webster made it very clear that there should be no contact,' said Mr Pettigrew.

Norah sat back in her chair once more. 'Don't you think you should be asking yourself why he would want such a thing? When he came for Lillian, she was quite happy to go with him. Amy didn't want to go. I was concerned that there was something wrong.'

'But you're no childcare expert, Mrs Kirkwood,' said Mr Pettigrew. 'You're not even a mother.'

Norah almost burst into tears there and then.

'That remark was uncalled for, Mr Pettigrew,' Rene snapped.

'I was concerned for their welfare,' Norah said, her voice quavering. 'That's the only reason I kept up the contact.'

Mr Pettigrew glanced up at the big clock on the wall. 'We seem to have reached an impasse, Mrs Kirkwood,' he said. 'I am sorry if you have found this interview upsetting, but we like to give everyone a fair hearing.'

'A fair hearing,' Rene scoffed. 'That's a laugh.'

'I shall discuss the matter again with the other members of the committee,' he said, ignoring her comment, 'and we shall write to you again.' He rose to his feet and gathered his papers. 'I think we're finished here, Miss Bundy. Thank you for your time, Mrs Kirkwood, Miss Carson. I bid you good day.'

With that, Mr Pettigrew swept out of the room but Miss Bundy lingered for a minute. 'I am sorry, Mrs Kirkwood,' she said. 'I'm afraid my hands were tied.'

Norah was shaking but she managed a grateful smile. As Miss Bundy reached the door, Norah called out, 'Would you do me one favour, Miss Bundy?' The woman froze, as if expecting an angry tirade. 'Would you make a note that I think something is terribly wrong with the relationship that man has with his children? You can think what you like about me, but my only concern is to keep them safe.'

CHAPTER 23

Back out on the street, Rene slipped her arm through Norah's. 'You all right?'

Norah could only nod. Speaking would reduce her to tears and she knew it.

'Let's go to Mitchell's for a piece of cake,' said Rene. 'My treat.'

For once, Norah was grateful for the suggestion. She didn't want to go home. She couldn't bear the thought of explaining everything to Mrs Kirkwood and watching her gloat. Not yet. Mitchell's Bakery and tea shop was almost opposite the new town hall in Chapel Road. It had a reputation for good food and was popular with the townspeople. Most customers aimed for a window seat but Rene picked a table near the back and by a pillar. Here, she and Norah had a little much needed privacy in a public place. When the waitress came, she ordered tea for two and the cake stand.

'I don't understand how all this happened,' Norah said brokenly. 'I mean, what is so threatening about a visit to a school?'

'I think there can only be one explanation,' said Rene. 'You clearly stepped on Ffox-Webster's toes somehow and this is his revenge.'

'Now who's been reading too many mystery novels?' said Norah, shaking out the napkin and laying it on her lap.

The tea arrived and the two women made their choice of cake.

'Just think about it, darling,' said Rene, slicing into her piece of Worthing Wonder cake with mock cream, 'who else could have complained about you? Certainly not Mrs Harrison. It can only be Ffox-Webster.'

'I agree,' said Norah, 'but why tell them all that stuff about the present he brought me?'

'Because he's obviously a vindictive bastard,' said Rene, her mouth full of cake.

'I don't want to think ill of him,' said Norah, 'but I've always had this gut feeling there's something terribly wrong about the whole situation. Nothing I can put my finger on, but he gives me the creeps.'

Rene reached over the table and squeezed her hand. 'Is there nothing we can do? Perhaps get Mrs Harrison to write to the agency for you? I'm sure she'd do it.'

'Oh, I don't know, Rene,' she said, taking a bite of her honey cake. 'I don't want to give up on adoption but I just can't think straight right now.'

'You need time to lick your wounds,' said Rene. They ate in silence and although the cherry Madeira she'd chosen looked delicious, to Norah it tasted like sawdust. Rene said softly, 'Why not take a couple of days off and go to Mum's?'

'I can't leave Jim,' Norah protested.

'Jim will be fine,' said Rene. 'His mother can look after

him, can't she? Go on. It's the perfect time and Mum would love to see you; I know she would.'

The next day, Mrs Kirkwood had her apron on before Norah even left the house. She had been up with the lark and Jim, who normally only wanted a boiled egg, had enjoyed a fry-up breakfast before he biked off to the station. Norah looked a little less stained but she was still very pale. She declined her mother-in-law's offer of a cooked breakfast and only nibbled at a slice of toast. She had packed a small suitcase and Ivan offered to walk her to the station. Handing her the case after she'd stepped into the carriage, he lifted his cap and gave her an encouraging smile.

'You have a good time, my lovely,' he said. 'Let yer ma spoil you and put a bit of colour in yer cheeks. It'll all come right in the end.'

He could tell she didn't believe him but he reckoned that she was glad of the sentiment. He stayed on the platform and watched and waved until the train was out of sight. Back in Clifton Road a delicious smell of bacon wafted towards him as he opened the back door.

'Madam gone then?' said Mrs Kirkwood with a smile.

Ivan pulled his cap off and stared at her. 'Why do you 'ave to be like that with 'er, Chastity? That girl has shown you nothing but kindness.'

He saw her stiffen. 'I don't know what you mean,' she said in an indignant tone.

'Yes, you do,' he insisted. 'You wasn't like it when we was at school but you've been like it for years. Anybody who does you a good turn, you bite their bloomin' heads off.'

She gave him a stony glare. 'You'd better sit down for your breakfast,' she said coldly.

'My Ada used to say you was prickly because of what happened to your Cecil.'

Mrs Kirkwood stiffened. 'I don't want to talk about that.'

'Why not? It's all water under the bridge now.'

He pulled out the chair and sat as she banged down the plate in front of him. 'People have no idea what it was like,' she said crossly.

'Then tell me.' He looked up at her flushed and angry face. 'Sit here beside me and tell me.' His voice was gentle.

She hesitated for a moment but slowly her knees bent and she lowered herself into the chair. He raised his eyebrows and nodded encouragingly. 'You know what,' she began acidly, 'I've been beaten over the head every day of my life because of him. Living here has been the first time in twenty years that I haven't had someone reminding me of what he'd done.'

'I know he was had up for desertion,' Ivan said kindly. 'I guess we'll never know what made him do it, but it's not your fault, gal.'

'You wouldn't be saying that if you had my neighbours,' she added bitterly.

'Tell me what happened?' said Ivan.

'When they sent him home on leave, he was in a right old state,' she said, pulling her handkerchief from her sleeve. 'He begged me not to let him go back. He was terrified. I'd never seen a man cry as much as he did and he couldn't stop shaking. Any loud noise and he'd fling himself under the table. He was a wreck of a man, anyone could see that.' She paused then added angrily, 'Anyone except the army doctor, of course. He passed him. A1.'

'Shell shock,' said Ivan.

Mrs Kirkwood nodded. 'Only they didn't recognise it then.

208

They said he had to get a hold on himself and be a man so sent him back to the front.' She sighed. 'A week later, in the middle of the battle, he just put down his rifle and started walking.'

'And for that he was court-martialled?'

Mrs Kirkwood nodded. 'Found guilty and shot at dawn.' She dabbed the end of her nose with her handkerchief. 'When people found out, nobody would speak to me. I had dog pooh through the letter box and bricks through the window,' she began again. 'Can you understand what that was like? James was only thirteen at the time. I had to send him away to his grandparents to protect him from it all. When I went shopping people spat in my face and I had enough white feathers sent to me in the post to fill a flippin' pillowcase.'

'I'm sorry, lass,' he said, reaching for her hand but she snatched it away.

'I thought it would stop eventually but it didn't.'

'Look it's a terrible memory . . .' he began again.

'And you wonder why I'm bitter,' she snapped.

'But folks are being kind to you now, aren't they?' said Ivan. 'Look at your Norah; she's a brick. She'd never do anything to hurt you, now would she? Give her a chance, will you?'

'She'll turn on me in the end, you see if she doesn't.'

'Don't talk so daft,' said Ivan. 'Norah has shown you nothing but kindness.'

Mrs Kirkwood knew he was right but she didn't give an inch. Sitting up straight to compose herself she said, 'Eat your breakfast before it gets cold.'

'Think on,' he said, 'that girl is better than a daughter to you.'

Mrs Kirkwood stared down at her own hands. 'I keep waiting for it,' she said quietly.

'Waiting fer what?'

'The nastiness, the cutting remark. When you least expect it, that's when they do it.'

Ivan chuckled. 'You've got it all wrong, gal,' he said, 'and hell will freeze over before Norah will do that.'

Mrs Kirkwood managed a thin smile.

He smacked his lips. 'This looks good, Chastity.' Once again, she avoided his eye and her face went pink. 'What?' he said. 'What have I said now?'

'I don't like people calling me by my Christian name,' she said, getting up to fetch a plate of bread and butter she'd put on the work top. 'It's Mrs Kirkwood.'

'All right,' he said cautiously. 'Have you got a second name?'

'I don't like that either.'

'What is it?'

She slid back onto the chair opposite him and offered him the bread and butter. Ivan began tucking into his meal and it was obvious that he was enjoying every mouthful. 'She should feed you men a proper meal,' said Mrs Kirkwood. 'One boiled egg never fattened anybody up.'

'Perhaps that's the idea,' he said. Waving his knife at her he added, 'And there you goes again. Always criticising.'

Mrs Kirkwood blushed and looked away.

'Do you know what?' he said. 'I thinks it's just a habit, Chastity. You don't mean to be unkind.'

'I just told you not to use my Christian name,' she said tetchily.

'Can't do much else if that's what you'm been called,' he said, stroking the plate with a piece of bread to soak up

210

the bacon juice. 'That was champion. I enjoyed it but we'd better put something in the larder to replace it.'

Mrs Kirkwood opened her mouth to say something but when he looked up at her she had obviously changed her mind.

'So, if you don't like your Christian name and you don't like your second name,' he said, putting two spoons of sugar in his tea and stirring vigorously, 'what shall us call 'e. What name do you like?'

'I can't just change my name,' she said incredulously.

'Why not?' he demanded. 'You can call yourself what you like.'

Mrs Kirkwood thought for a moment and then said, 'I always liked the name Christine. I had a friend called Christine once.'

'Christine Andrews,' said Ivan, remembering. 'Nice girl. Always what you might call "happy-go-lucky".'

Mrs Kirkwood nodded. 'She sat next to me in primary school.'

'She went away, didn't she?'

Mrs Kirkwood sighed sadly. 'To Australia. She said she'd write but she never did.'

Ivan slurped his tea. 'All right then, Christine Kirkwood. From now on, that's what you be called.'

Mrs Kirkwood felt her cheeks flame, but all the same it sounded nice.

'You'll have to live up to her name, mind,' he said sagely. 'No more cutting remarks.'

Mrs Kirkwood grinned. 'Yes'ir,' she said, giving him a mock salute.

She poured herself another cup of tea. Ivan rubbed his ragged ear and put his cap back on.

'I saw him,' she said. 'The man what done it. He was here.'

'Who was?'

'The bloke who bit off your ear.'

Ivan frowned. 'How do you know about that?'

'That night I was waiting at the bus stop,' she said. 'I saw it happen.'

Ivan stared at her, obviously struggling to take in what she'd just said.

'I was curious,' she began again. 'Everybody was talking about the wonderful Oswald Mosley, the saviour of the country; the man who was going to put the Great back in Great Britain.' Her tone was sarcastic now. 'I wanted to see for myself so I joined the crowds outside the Pavilion that night. I was just across the street when he came down the steps.'

They were talking about October 9th, 1934, when Oswald Mosley had come to Worthing to deliver a speech in the Pavilion. A large crowd had gathered outside to heckle him and as he'd come down the steps, the crowd surged forward. Flanked by several black-shirted heavies, Mosley had lashed out at the bystanders, and a bit of pushing and shoving soon became something much uglier. One man was punched in the mouth and lost several teeth and several other people were injured in the melee that followed. The most shocking had been the injury of an old lady.

Ivan looked down at the table. 'I was trying to protect poor old Mrs Hodgkiss,' he began. 'That bastard, excuse my French, hit her over the head with his swagger stick. For God's sake, she was ninety-six!'

'I read about that in the paper,' said Mrs Kirkwood. 'What on earth was she doing there?'

'Same as you, I suppose,' said Ivan. 'Curious.'

'Anyway, I saw what happened to you,' she went on. 'That man with the birthmark. I saw him pull your head towards him and then he bit your ear.'

'Bloody hurt and all,' said Ivan, looking up. 'The police couldn't find him, you know. They told me I was making it up, that he didn't exist.'

'Oh, he exists all right,' said Mrs Kirkwood. 'And he was here. He's only his lordship's chauffeur now.'

'You what?'

'It's true, Ivan,' she went on. 'He carried the hamper into the kitchen for them. I saw him; large as life with that horrible birthmark right down the side of his face.'

He regarded her over the rim of his cup for several seconds and then deliberately changing the subject he said, 'So, what is your second name?'

She lowered her eyes. 'Beulah.'

Ivan made no comment, but when she looked up again she could see a twinkle in his eye.

'My father was very religious,' she said, picking up their dirty plates with a haughty air.

'Was he really?' Ivan teased. 'Mine was an Irish tinker.'

They made eye contact, then Ivan Steele and Christine Kirkwood began to laugh.

When Norah reached Victoria Station, Elsie Carson was waiting for her at the barrier. Norah flung herself into her mother's arms and they held each other tight. A moment or two later, Elsie broke free and said, 'Your dad's waiting outside in the car.'

Norah picked up her suitcase. 'I thought he was putting it away for the duration.'

'He did,' said Elsie, 'but this is a special occasion.'

213

It was comforting to be back home for a while. Nothing had changed and it was good to be among all the old familiar sounds and smells. The velvety darkness in the corridor and the quietness when you shut the front door and couldn't hear the street noises anymore; the squeak of your shoes on the lino; the cosy smell of Mum's kitchen; the high-pitched whistle the kettle made when it boiled; the oil cloth on the table and her mother's apron hanging on the back door. Norah felt five or eight or eleven all over again.

As they talked over a cup of tea, Elsie and Pete let their daughter take her time. She cried a little then ranted and raged. They didn't tell her to pull herself together. They didn't even advise her what to do. They gave her time to let it all out until she was calm again.

Eventually Pete said he had to go. 'I'm on the Battersea route today,' he explained. 'One o'clock start.'

Norah's mother went to the door to see him off. When she came back, Elsie said, 'Do you still want to find out about this man, what's 'is name?'

'Ffox-Webster? I don't see how I can,' said Norah, 'but I feel a huge responsibility towards Amy. Everybody tells me I shouldn't, but she asked me for help and I just know something is wrong. Jim says he can't do anything because the man hasn't committed any crime, so where do I go from here?'

'There are ways and means,' her mother said mysteriously as she rose to her feet to refill the tea pot.

Norah frowned. 'You mean hiring a private detective or something?'

Elsie chuckled. 'Nothing like that,' she said, 'but I could tell you a thing or two about the toffs around here and what they get up to.'

Norah stared at her.

'For instance,' her mother continued as she leaned forward in a confidential manner, 'I know of a certain member of the government who likes picking up young men and taking them home for the night. And there's a very famous singer who has just had a baby that isn't her old man's. Or maybe I could mention a certain wealthy person who buys ladies' knickers from jumble sales.'

Norah pulled a face. 'Ugh.'

'Quite,' said Elsie. 'Of course, I won't tell you their names, but believe me, I know a secret or two.'

'How do you know all this?'

'Who takes any notice of their daily woman?' said Elsie. 'My girls in the agency could tell you a thing or two about the people they work for as well, but I swear them to secrecy.'

'What has this got to do with Ffox-Webster?'

Elsie put her finger to her nose and patted it. 'Leave it to me, darling. If there's anything we need to know about him, I'll find out.'

'But how?' asked Norah. 'You don't work for him, do you?'

'My girls aren't the only domestics in the city. We stick together. We look out for each other and warn each other if someone is a bit dodgy, so if he's not kosher, there'll be someone willing to spill the beans.'

CHAPTER 24

Norah

Having behaved like an invalid for so long, it had come as a bit of a surprise when Mrs Kirkwood suddenly decided to 'do her bit' for the war effort. After the terrible events at Dunkirk, she told Norah, 'I've decided to join a Red Cross group. They meet in the Methodist Church in Tarring Road.'

'Good for you,' said Norah, although she was slightly surprised.

'Apparently they roll bandages and pack food parcels for poorer families,' Mrs Kirkwood continued.

'And I'm sure they appreciate it,' said Norah.

Her change of attitude seemed to have made quite a difference to the atmosphere at home. She was still a little 'buttoned up', as Norah's mother would say, but she had become far less morose and prickly.

Ivan had made a good recovery and while Norah had been in London with her mother, he had borne the brunt of the work needing to be done in the market garden and the allotments. By the time Norah returned to Worthing it was almost as if she hadn't been away.

The country was in the grip of an uneasy worry that an invasion was imminent and in the middle of the night on June 7th the Worthing air raid warning sounded for the first time. The household gathered in the hallway, having grabbed dressing gowns and slippers as the blood-curdling wail filled the night air. The dogs were terrified and Jim threw a tea towel over the budgie's cage to calm him down. There was little point in going outside because their Anderson Shelter was not yet finished so the family huddled together under the stairs.

After a few minutes, Mrs Kirkwood clutched at her chest. 'James, I'm having a heart attack.' Her breathing became rapid and laboured.

Norah was both alarmed and helpless. What should you do if someone was having a heart attack? How could they get help? No one would want to run down the road to the phone box with an air raid going on. Jim pulled a blanket over his mother's shoulders and grabbed her wrist to check her pulse.

Ivan leaned forward in his chair and patted her knee. 'Calm down, ol' gal,' he said softly. 'Breathe slowly. Do it with me. In . . . out . . . in . . . out . . . That's right. You'm going to be all right. We won't let anything happen to you. In . . . out . . .'

Over the top of Mrs Kirkwood's head, Norah glanced at her husband in disbelief as Ivan's soothing words calmed her mother-in-law down.

They stayed together until the all clear, about an hour later, and then made their weary way back to bed. Sleep eluded her for a while so Norah lay on her back staring at the ceiling. It was a daunting thought but this was probably going to be the pattern of life for a while; air raid warnings, sleepless nights, the ever-present threat of invasion and who knew what other hardships they'd have to face. Amy drifted into her thoughts. Should she risk writing to her again? No, the situation was hopeless. That old witch of a matron would be checking the post so there was no chance of anyone sneaking an envelope past her. But how could she let Amy know she wasn't forgotten? She turned over and although she couldn't see it in the blackout, she knew she was facing the baby's drawer. The pretty matinee jackets and the shawl had all been packed away in a suitcase. When she came back home from her mother's, Jim told her everything was in the loft. She was grateful to him for sparing her the pain of opening and reopening the drawer but it didn't stop the ache in her heart. She couldn't have Eric, she knew that, but would she ever be allowed to have another baby? Had this terrible business scuppered all of her chances of adoption? A renegade tear dripped off the end of her nose and Norah sighed. Why was life so unfair?

In the morning, Norah went round to see Penny. She was dying to hear any news of Ted but one look at her friend's face when she opened the front door told her that was a forlorn hope. The BEF had suffered heavy losses as well as a miraculous escape. The papers said Churchill had told the House of Commons that thirty thousand men had died. Thirty thousand! Norah could hardly think in such numbers. If, as Jim said, there were seventy thousand people living in the town, that meant the losses for BEF amounted to nearly half the town's population! Not only that, but now the country was hardly in a position to fight back. The army had had to abandon all of its tanks, ammunition, fuel, vehicles and equipment on the beaches and several British destroyers had been sunk.

Penny's mum was in the kitchen with Victor who was happily cooing in his pram. 'Can I pick him up?' Norah asked.

Her heart lurched with desire as Penny sat him on her lap and Norah breathed in his baby warmth. At four months old he was a solid little boy. He leaned back and gave her a puzzled stare before his face broke into a wide smile. Norah spoke to him softly and the two of them soon bonded as friends.

Penny put a cup of tea on the table beside her and Norah was startled to hear her say in a flat tone of voice, 'I think his father is dead.'

'Try not to give up,' Norah encouraged. 'It's only a couple of weeks since they all got back. Everything is bound to be up in the air for a while. Men were sent all over the country. He could be anywhere.'

Penny looked away miserably. 'I can't go on without him,' she said. 'It's too unbearable.'

'And if you don't,' Norah said firmly, 'what's going to happen to Victor?'

Penny pulled a face.

'Come on, love,' said Norah. 'You must think of your son. His life is just beginning.'

Penny sighed and as she glanced down at her son, Norah knew that in her heart of hearts Penny would never do anything stupid.

'Mrs Kirkwood told me the adoption fell through,' said Penny, putting her own cup of tea on the table beside Norah's. 'That must be hard for you.'

'It is,' said Norah.

'There'll be other babies,' Penny said, lowering herself onto a chair. She put her hands out and Norah gave Victor back. Penny put him in his pram and although he complained it wasn't long before he had his thumb in his mouth and was looking drowsy. The two women drank their tea.

'If the weather holds and you're not doing anything on Sunday,' said Norah, 'how do you fancy a stroll on Highdown and a picnic?' The idea had only just occurred to her, but it seemed like a good one. With doom and gloom hanging over them, they could do with a bit of cheering up. 'We'll catch the train to Goring-by-Sea Station and walk from there,' said Norah. 'You can put the pram in the guard's van.'

'Sounds great,' said Penny with a sad smile.

When Sunday came the weather was glorious. Penny's mother had decided to come, too, so Norah had persuaded Jim to tag along with the dogs as well. At the last minute, Mrs Kirkwood and Ivan asked if they could join them so with their picnic and a couple of old blankets stashed under Victor's pram the party set off at eleven.

'Pity there's no church bells,' Mrs Kirkwood remarked.

'No more until victory,' said Jim.

'We're not going to talk about the war today,' Norah said firmly. 'This is going to be a happy time.'

Penny decided to stay in the guard's van with the pram so Norah took the dog leads from Jim and joined her. Her mother had suggested that Penny leave the pram and put Victor on her lap in the carriage but she said she didn't want to leave the picnic where she couldn't see it.

'Don't be daft,' said Mrs Kirkwood, 'who's going to touch that?'

But after that business with all those handbags being taken

under the wall in the ladies' toilets, Norah could understand her friend's caution. The story had caused a newspaper sensation for its audacity and it came as a bit of a relief to hear that the women, two eighteen-year-olds, their mother and an aunt had been found guilty of their crimes – twenty-four in all – and sent to prison. One of their victims, a rather foolish eighty-four-year-old who kept everything of value in her handbag, had lost her life savings.

Everybody trooped off the train at Goring-by-Sea and they began the walk to the hill. The dogs trotted beside Jim and once they reached the bottom, much to the delight of the others, Jim took Max and Sausage off their leads. Fooling about with Norah, he carried her a few yards piggyback style. Norah squealed with laughter until her let her down.

Mrs Kirkwood wasn't used to much walking, so she was a bit puffed by the time they'd reached the shade of the big trees at the top. Halfway up, Mrs Draycot had offered her arm, which had helped, but it was obvious that she was more than grateful when they spread the blankets to sit down.

'It's good to be here again,' Mrs Kirkwood whispered happily.

'I did my courting up here,' said Mrs Draycot.

'You and me both,' said Mrs Kirkwood.

They watched some children playing in the surrounding trees, their excited squeals echoing all around. Victor slept on in his pram, Jim stretched himself out and closed his eyes while Norah and Penny talked quietly and set about making daisy chains the way they had done as children. Apart from the children, the only other sounds were the buzzing of bees, the chirruping of the crickets, and the occasional high-pitched trill of a skylark.

It was getting hotter by the minute. Norah took off her

cardigan and loosened her waist belt. Then she unlaced her shoes to pull them off and wiggle her toes. When Victor woke up and demanded to be fed, they set up the picnic. Norah had brought sandwiches, some cold chicken, and pickles. Mrs Draycot had brought some sliced ham, a large crusty loaf and the first of her allotment tomatoes. They pooled the food together and drank tea from their flasks. There was also a fruit cake Norah had baked and a Victoria sponge Penny had made only that morning.

Victor loved being on the blanket and the centre of everyone's attention but being so young, it wasn't long before he was ready to sleep again.

'Anyone fancy a walk up the hill?' Norah said, but the only one ready to take up her offer was Penny. Ivan had walked away from them to 'inspect the plumbing' in the bushes lower down the other side of the hill and Mrs Kirkwood was watching a Clouded Yellow butterfly, which had settled on her hand.

'You go, love,' said Penny's mother. 'We'll keep an eye on the baby.'

Jim, who had his back against a tree, had made himself a knotted handkerchief hat. He opened one bleary eye. 'I'll catch you up.'

Norah leaned over him and kissed his forehead. 'You stay and have a rest, you poor old man,' she teased, and he made a feeble attempt to grab her leg before she darted away laughing.

Norah and Penny walked on in silence for a while. It was so good to breathe the warm Sussex air and to feel the sun hot on their faces. Up here, on the hill, all thoughts of war had vanished. Norah bent to pick a Goat's-Beard clock and blow the tiny seed head from the stalk.

'When we were at school, we used to call this "*Jack goes to bed at noon*",' she recalled.

'That's because the flowers close up tight in the afternoon,' said Penny. She smiled at her friend. 'You never did tell me what happened when you went to see Amy.'

Norah let out a sigh before she told her the whole story. When she'd finished, Penny frowned. 'You really think that going to see her uninvited was the reason they stopped you adopting the baby?'

Norah nodded.

'But that's so unfair!' cried Penny.

'Isn't it just,' Norah said sourly.

Penny linked her arm through Norah's. 'Thanks for what you said to me the other day,' she said, giving her a squeeze. 'It really helped. I'm going to start a new job next week. The Canadian soldiers will be here soon and Uncle Fred is opening a café in Broadwater for them. He asked me if I'd like to serve at tables.'

'The Uncle Fred who brought round the sausage rolls for your wedding breakfast?'

'That's him,' said Penny. 'Mum said she'd look after Victor so I can go. I've made up my mind that I shall save all the money I can so that when Ted comes home, we can get a place of our own.' There was a pause. 'And if he doesn't . . .' she began again.

'Penny!' Norah scolded.

'No,' Penny insisted, 'if he doesn't come back, I shall have something put by for Victor, for when he's older.'

Norah beamed. 'What a brilliant idea,' she said. And it was. Penny was being far more positive, and it was so good to hear her planning for the future at last.

They decided to walk past the chalkpits and on to the

very top by the tall clump of trees. From there they could look down over Worthing and far out to sea. The day was clear so they could see Littlehampton and Portsmouth in one direction and the Seven Sisters in the other. Out to sea, the Isle of Wight was shielded by a heat haze. It was so lovely and peaceful, but the spell was broken by the drone of engines. In the distance they could just make out three planes circling one another over the sea, and the two women watched in horror. Norah cupped her hands either side of her head to get a better view. 'It's a dogfight,' she breathily.

Penny had her hand over her mouth as if any small sound she made might interrupt the pilots' concentration. It was hard for them to work out exactly what was happening but every now and then, they could hear the sharp rat-tat-tat of gunfire. After a while, one plane – the one they presumed was German – began to spiral downwards with a huge black smoke trail behind him.

'He's got the bugger,' Penny cried. 'He's got him!'

Norah was too shocked to reply. When he hit the water, they heard no sound. It was difficult to see because of the heat haze but a moment later, as the other two planes flew inland, one did a victory roll. Waving frantically, Penny jumped up and down and shouted. She couldn't wait to get back to tell everybody what they'd seen so she ran on ahead. Norah followed her with mixed feelings. While she was proud of the RAF boys and grateful for what they were doing to protect the country, the pilot who had ditched in the sea was undoubtedly dead. Yes, he was the enemy, but it seemed so sad that anyone should have to die on such a beautiful day.

CHAPTER 25

Norah

Dear Norah,

How are you? I hope this finds you both well as it leaves us. Everything goes on much the same. Some of the kids round here who were evacuated and came back are going to be sent away again. I saw a few of them waiting by the bus stop when I looked out of the window. They looked so forlorn with their little suitcases and labels on their coats. It came as such a shock to hear that Paris had surrendered. Mrs Reynolds next door says when you look on the map, it's so close, it won't be long before the Germans are marching up the Mall. I told her off. I mean, it's no good thinking like that. It only pulls you down. It's not likely that we're going to give up without one hell of a fight and we do have the Channel between us and them. Dad and I read in the paper that the King says we mustn't turn back and that's good enough for me. My domestic agency is still getting by. My girls can get as much as half a crown an hour, sometimes more in a toff's house. Ever since Dunkirk, all their regular girls are *signing up, even the married ones. Dad is still fire-watching two nights a week but so far, thank God, there hasn't been much to report. He gets a bit bored with it all. We see vapour trails in the sky so we know there are dogfights over the Thames but we've been all right. I asked around the girls about you-know-who and I have some news for you but it would take far too long to write it all down. If you could jump on the train and come to us for the day on Saturday, that would be grand. Let me know and I'll arrange everything.*

Your ever loving Mum and Dad.

When the train pulled into Victoria Station on Saturday, Elsie Carson was again waiting at the barrier. Norah hugged her tight. The station so was busy it seemed the whole world was on the move. Groups of soldiers gathered with their kitbags and a few children congregated under the big clock with their teachers. There was a shout and they were marshalled towards the platform as Norah and Elsie linked arms to walk across the concourse.

'They're saying the bombing is going to start soon,' her mother said. 'God help us then.'

'You can always come and stay with us,' said Norah.

'I shan't leave your dad,' said Elsie, and then using a more determined tone added, 'and besides, why should I leave my home? It may not be much to write home about but it's where I belong.'

Norah squeezed her mother's arm affectionately. 'I know, Mum, but the offer's there if ever you need it.'

They caught a bus to the East End.

'Why are we heading this way?' Norah asked.

'We're meeting someone,' her mother said mysteriously,

and as Norah opened her mouth again, she added, 'How's Jim?'

They got off near a side street and walked into a small working man's café crowded with bus drivers and factory workers, delivery men and some stevedore porters. One side of the café had tables in booths, with wooden partitions on either side. Elsie walked in and sat at the table right in the corner marked 'reserved'. The proprietor, a portly man with a tobacco-stained moustache, was standing behind the counter. He looked up and gave her mother a nod and as Norah made herself comfortable, he brought over two mugs of tea. 'Anyfing else, love?'

'Maybe when my friends arrive,' Elsie said with a smile. She helped herself to a spoonful of sugar and the man went back to his counter.

'Mum, what's all this about?'

'I asked around my girls,' her mother said, leaning forward and talking in a confidential voice, 'and at first no one knew the gent in question. Then Freda Green comes up trumps. She does for a lady in Kensington, a titled lady, who's very well known but she ain't got time for his nibs, see. So I says, what's he like? And she says, "If I was you, I'd keep well away from him, Els. He's poison."'

Norah frowned. 'What does that mean?'

'So, I says, who does for him then?' Elsie went on, completely ignoring Norah's question. 'But nobody knows. Then Win Andrews says she knows his daughter and that's who we're meeting today.' Her mother leaned back in her chair. 'And now that it's all out in the open, it's a right ol' can of worms I can tell you.'

Norah sipped her tea. Already her heart was beating a little faster. Clearly her mother was enjoying her bit of

227

mystery and cloak-and-dagger, but at the same time, she was more than a little worried about what she might find out. 'Please don't keep me in suspense, Mum. I've been worried sick about poor Amy and even though we've been warned off, and all that's happened since, I can't just leave it there.'

Elsie reached out and grasped her daughter's hand. 'I know, love.'

Norah looked away quickly, afraid of tears. 'I still get the feeling he had something to do with me losing the chance to adopt little Eric,' she said, staring into her cup. 'Jim says it's just coincidence and that I'm being paranoid, but the feeling doesn't go away.'

'He'll believe you when he hears what I've got to say,' her mother said stoutly. 'Norah, love, there's another daughter.'

'Oh, Mum,' said Norah, trying to be patient with her. 'Of course, there is. I told you. We went to see her in her school, remember?'

Elsie shook her head. 'And I'm telling you, there's *another* one.'

Norah's head shot up as a group of workmen called their goodbyes and opened the door of the café to leave. At the same time, three women entered.

'Co-ee,' Elsie called and waved her hand. The women headed in their direction. All three looked very different. One was about her mother's age, a cheery-looking woman with a ruddy complexion whose floral cross-over apron peeped out from under her lightweight coat. The other two were younger. One looked about twenty-four-ish. Her pale blue short-sleeved dress had three pleats on the front of its skirt and she wore quite a lot of make-up. Norah got the impression that she might be a shop girl from the beauty counter. The other girl was not quite so fashionable but she was clearly practical. Brown slacks, a short tan-coloured jacket over a lightweight blue top with the collar of a white blouse pepping out from neck. She couldn't have been any more than nineteen. Norah had never met either of them before but there was something vaguely familiar about the girl in the slacks. After shuffling along the bench seats and realising there wasn't quite enough room for all of them, the proprietor brought a chair and put it on the end of the table for the older woman. Elsie asked him to bring three more teas and a plate of sandwiches.

'You got here all right then,' Elsie said to the older woman as she put her handbag under the table.

'No problems, love. Is this your daughter?'

Elsie nodded. 'Win, this is Norah.'

Win gave her a nod. 'This is my Trixie,' she said, indicating the older of the two girls, 'and this is her friend Meryl.' She paused for effect. 'Meryl is Amy and Lillian's older sister.'

'I've made some sandwiches for your lunch,' said Mrs Kirkwood, coming out into the market garden.

Ivan had been busy all morning in the small shop, which was doing a brisk trade. He took his handkerchief out of his pocket and mopped his brow. 'It'll be good to get indoors,' he said, blowing out his cheeks. 'It's blemmin' 'ot out here.'

She watched him as he washed his hands under the tap on the outside wall of the house and soaked his handkerchief before putting it to his brow again. 'I reckon we'll be having a thunderstorm afore long.'

They kept the back door open to let in a through draught

but it was still very humid. The dogs panted as they lay on the flagstone floor near the pantry.

'I'm thinking of suggesting that your Norah has a stall on the market,' said Ivan. 'It would be a good way to shift some more produce, especially when we gets a glut.'

'She won't have time to do that!' Mrs Kirkwood exclaimed.

'I wasn't going to ask her,' said Ivan. 'I quite fancy the idea of doing it meself.'

'Oh.' She sniffed. 'By the way, you've had a letter from the insurance company,' she said, pouring them both some tea. 'They've sent you a cheque.'

Ivan picked it up and stared at the writing.

'One hundred and sixty-two pounds,' said Mrs Kirkwood, 'including interest. What with that and the pension you've got from the school, and the bit you get from the government, you should be able to live out the rest of your life quite comfortably from now on.'

'It won't last forever,' he remarked sullenly.

'If you put it into a bank account you should get some interest.'

'And how can I do that?' he said, slouching forward in his chair.

'I can help you,' she said. 'No one need ever know. Well, nobody in the family, that is.' She frowned. 'What's the matter? You don't look too happy about it.'

'I suppose it means I'll have to move on,' he said with a sigh. 'I wish I didn't have to. I likes it here.'

'Why should you have to move?' said Mrs Kirkwood. 'Norah is quite happy to have you here. She couldn't have gone to London today without you stepping in for her. Offer her some rent. She'll keep you on.'

Ivan looked up and gave her a toothless grin. 'You reckon?'

'I don't see why not,' said Mrs Kirkwood. 'And she'd like you a lot better if you put your teeth in a bit more often.'

Frowning, he pulled a face and tut-tutted as he wagged his finger. Then they both laughed.

A mountain of sandwiches appeared in front of them and the proprietor slopped three mugs of tea on the table. 'Whoops, sorry,' he said, and after mopping the spillage with his dirty tea towel, he left them to it.

Elsie passed the plate of sandwiches around and everyone took one. Norah had been shocked to realise that Amy and Lillian had an older sister but now that she had had a proper look at her, she could see the family resemblance.

Meryl made eye contact. 'Mrs Andrews – Win – has told me you looked after my sisters for a time.'

Norah nodded. 'I live in Worthing. They were evacuated just before war was declared.'

Meryl took a deep and shuddering breath.

'I'm sorry,' said Norah. 'I had no idea that they had an older sister. If I had known, I would have contacted you.'

Meryl gave a hollow laugh. 'It wouldn't have made any difference,' she said. 'He'd have seen to that.' She paused, sensing everybody's discomfort. 'Tell me about them,' she added earnestly. 'Win said you live by the sea. Did they go to the beach?'

Norah told her about Amy and Lillian's arrival, their happy times on the beach and at Devil's Dyke; how good Lillian was at her lessons and all about Amy's first job.

'But they're not with you now?' said Meryl.

Norah shook her head. 'Your father—'

'He's not my father,' Meryl interrupted angrily. 'He was

231

never my father.' Her sudden outburst surprised them all, including herself. She made her hand into a fist and put it over her mouth. 'I'm sorry. I can't talk about this in here.' She looked up with an anguished expression. 'Can I talk to you in private?' she asked. 'This is such a public place.'

'It's what you wanted, dear,' Win protested mildly.

'I know, but that was before I knew I could trust you.' She turned to Norah and gave her a wan smile. 'This is my lunch hour. I work at the Tate and Lyle factory across the road. Can I talk to you after my shift? I finish at six.'

'I had planned to catch the five o'clock train,' Norah began. 'I'm not sure.'

'You could always stay the night,' said her mother. 'We can send Jim a telegram and then Meryl could come to ours, couldn't she?'

And so it was agreed.

It was six o'clock and Ivan was taking off his boots by the back door. He'd had a busy day but he was feeling contented. There may be a war on, but for him, life was good again. Plenty to do, a nice room, good food and company whenever he wanted it; what more could a chap ask for?

'She's just sent Jim a telegram,' said Mrs Kirkwood.

His heart sank. 'Oh my God. What's happened?'

'Nothing terrible,' she said, 'but she's staying in London for tonight so Jim says he'll have a pie and chips with his mates. He's gone to join them in The Egremont as there's a boxing match on in the room upstairs. Just give me an hour and I'll get some tea on.'

Ivan tottered as he pulled his second boot off. 'No, you won't,' he said. 'Let's go out.'

She stared at him in surprise. 'Go out?'

232

'Why not?' he said. 'I'll take you for fish and chips somewhere and we could go on to the pictures if you like.'

'I don't know what's on,' she said dully.

'Look in the paper then,' he said. 'Come on, Christine. Thanks to you I've got a little money in me pocket. You've helped me get on me feet again. Let's have a little celebration.'

She hesitated.

There was a twinkle in his eye. 'I'll put me teeth in,' he promised.

CHAPTER 26

Norah

Norah watched the hands of the clock moving slowly towards seven thirty as she waited nervously in her mother's front room for Meryl and her friend Trixie to arrive. They didn't often sit in the front room. It was usually reserved for special visitors and her parents didn't get many of them. Friends and neighbours who popped in for whatever reason usually headed for the kitchen, but Elsie was insistent that the girls should be in the best of surroundings when they came.

Already the questions were reverberating around Norah's head. Why the reaction when she'd mentioned that Ffox-Webster was Meryl's father? She recalled how Amy had run away from him when he'd come to collect her. How she wished that she'd told Amy he was coming. Maybe the girl would have opened up if there was something wrong, but Ffox-Webster had wanted her to have a 'nice surprise' when he turned up unannounced. It had seemed innocent enough at the time, but now she wasn't so sure, especially when she recalled Amy's pink cheek when she came back downstairs. Had he slapped her?

When she heard the sound of the door-knocker, Norah lowered herself into one of the big armchairs. Elsie bustled into the room followed by the two girls. Meryl had changed into an attractive polka-dot knee-length frock with a Peter Pan collar. She and Norah shook hands solemnly.

'Now,' said Elsie. 'Can I get you all a sherry? Or would you prefer tea?'

There was a slightly awkward atmosphere. 'First, I need to apologise to Mrs Kirkwood,' said Meryl, turning to Norah. 'I shouldn't have snapped at you like that.'

Norah waved her hand. 'We're all on edge,' she said. 'I feel terrible that you didn't know where your sisters were. And please . . . call me Norah.'

'Perhaps if we all agreed to keep Lillian and Amy in mind while we discuss this,' said Elsie. Having sensed the tense atmosphere she was handing round sherry, rather than tea. 'It would help us not to get upset. After all, both of you are only here because you care about those girls and what's happened to them. Nobody is here to score points.'

Norah and Meryl made eye contact and nodded in agreement.

Before they got down to business, the four women sipped their sherry and made small talk about the fall of Paris and the one topic of conversation that was gripping the nation at the moment – the seemingly inevitable invasion and when it would come.

'Now,' Elsie said eventually, 'would you two prefer to talk on your own? I'm sure you both have very private things to say to each other. I think I can speak for Trixie when I say we are happy to keep any secrets but if you prefer to be on your own, we can go into the kitchen.'

'I'm quite happy for you to stay, Mum, but if Meryl prefers . . .'

'Trixie knows all my secrets,' Meryl said, glancing at her friend who gave her a shy smile. 'And quite frankly, I think I'd be at the bottom of the Thames if it weren't for her.'

Norah's eyes widened.

'I'm sure you wouldn't . . .' Trixie began.

'I was at rock bottom when I met you,' Meryl went on determinedly. 'I didn't want to live and I had nothing to live for. That man took everything away from me, including my baby.'

Norah was struck dumb.

'I think you'd better start at the beginning, love,' Trixie said gently.

Meryl took a deep breath. 'When my father died, we had money and servants but my mother had no relatives. I was nine, Amy was seven, and Lillian was only three.' She faltered so Trixie reached out and squeezed Meryl's hand.

'I'm sorry,' Meryl apologised. 'This is so hard for me.'

'Take your time,' Norah said sympathetically.

'We lived in Paris. My father had been with the British consulate but with his death we had to leave. *Le cochon* – Ffox-Webster – had been after *ma mère* for some time. She was very beautiful and, of course, she was rich.' She turned her head in disgust. 'At least that's what I thought it was all about.' She fell silent, clearly struggling to find the words.

'I had two other evacuees,' Norah said quietly. 'They wrote to their mother at the end of their first week with us. That's when Lillian told me your mother had died so she wrote a letter to her father instead.'

Meryl took another deep breath. 'After they married, we

236

moved to England. That's when he told me my mother had TB. He said not to talk to her about it but he was taking her to Switzerland for a cure. But it was too late. She died.'

The room was quiet.

'I'm so sorry,' Norah said, and Meryl gave her a sad smile.

'Was your mother French?' Norah asked.

Meryl nodded.

'I guessed as much. Amy told us her name was Amélie and Lillian was Linnet. I suppose she wanted to keep a connection with your mother.'

'Those are our names,' said Meryl. 'I was christened Mireille.' She frowned. 'I don't know why I don't revert back to my proper name.'

'It is a lovely name,' said Elsie.

Meryl looked up. 'We only changed them because *he* wanted us to.' She began to rock her body slightly. 'I was eleven when he decorated my bedroom. I was so excited. We chose the wallpaper together and he bought me a bigger bed. I had Mabel Lucie Attwell wallpaper, lace curtains and a pink powder puff chair . . .' Her voice trailed and then she added harshly, 'I bloody hate pink now.'

Norah closed her eyes. She may be naive in some respects but she knew what was coming. Was this why Amy hated Ffox-Webster, too? 'From now on,' she said stoutly, 'my husband and I shall make sure you are known as Mireille.'

Mireille lowered her eyes. 'Thank you.'

'I will, too, if you like,' said Trixie, 'although it might take me a bit of getting used to.'

Mireille smiled and continued. 'He told me it was my duty to take my mother's place.' She curled her lip. 'I wasn't to say anything. It was our little secret. He asked me if I would do this for him and I agreed. Of course, I didn't understand what it meant at the time. I thought I'd just have to make sure he had his favourite tobacco or I'd put his slippers on like she used to do before she was taken ill.'

The room had become so quiet you could have heard a pin drop.

'I was fourteen when I got pregnant,' Mireille said bitterly. 'Fourteen and he made me feel it was all my fault.'

'Oh, Mireille,' Norah whispered. 'I'm so sorry.'

Mireille tossed her head defiantly. 'He sent me away to a mother and baby home. That's where I met Trixie—' She stopped suddenly and looked stricken. 'Oh, I'm sorry. I needn't have told them that. Sorry, sorry.'

Trixie shook her head. 'It's all right,' she said. Turning to Norah and Elsie she added with a shrug of her shoulders, 'Mine was the usual thing. He was good-looking and I wanted to be his girl.' She laughed sardonically. 'He couldn't get away fast enough when I told him about the baby, but I was one of the lucky ones. I gave my baby up for adoption and Mum stood by me. I got a new start.'

'I told *le cochon* I wanted to keep my baby,' Mireille continued, 'but of course he didn't want that. I might tell someone what he'd done. It might damage his career. He's a high flyer, did you know that?' Her voice was becoming increasingly bitter. 'He's in the War Office now. "Helping to save the country from tyranny and injustice,"' she added, clearly quoting Churchill.

'Tell them how he shut you up,' Trixie prompted.

'I have a label now,' Mireille said bitterly. 'Dirty little tart, wanton, I was supposed to have climbed out of the bedroom window every night in my eagerness to be with the boys. He told everyone he'd spent nights searching for me in the back streets. He told them I had no morals, that I was nothing more than a common prostitute. Then he told me if I told them the truth, I would be within a whisker of being sent into a mental institution.'

Nobody spoke. It was difficult to listen to this and even harder to think of anything helpful to say.

'Mireille,' Norah said eventually, 'I hate to say this, but I think he may have done the same thing to Amy.'

All three of them jumped as Mireille suddenly threw her head back and howled. 'No, no, oh God no!'

Norah was pouring fresh water into the tea pot in her mother's kitchen when her father walked through the back door. He seemed surprised to see her.

'You still here, love?' he said, taking off his London Transport summer uniform jacket and hanging it on the peg. 'I thought you would be back on the train by now.' A loud wail coming from the direction of the sitting room interrupted them. Pete cast an anxious glance towards the door.

'It's all right, Dad,' said Norah. 'It would take too long to explain but Mum's got someone who's very upset in there and I'm supposed to be bringing in the comfort.' She put a small bottle of brandy beside the tea cups on the tray then kissed her father's cheek. 'Your tea is on a plate over the saucepan on the hob. Mum says there's some more gravy in the jug on the table if what she put over your dinner has dried up.'

Pete lifted the saucepan lid over his plate and smacked his lips. 'Mmm, steak and kidney pudding. Last time I had one of these pies I managed to find *two* pieces of meat.'

Norah laughed. 'Don't get too excited, Dad,' she joked, picking up the tray. 'I'll be back in a minute.'

'That's all right, love. You see to whoever it is,' said Pete with an innocent smile. 'I'll eat me tea and then I'll take a wander down to The Red Lion . . . but you needn't tell your mother for now.'

Norah grinned.

Mireille was sprawled across the sofa with Trixie and Elsie Carson doing their best to comfort her.

'I wasn't your fault, love,' Elsie was saying. 'If you were stuck in the mother and baby home, how were you to know? Besides, you were only a kid yourself.'

Norah passed the first cup of tea to Mireille. 'Shall I put a nip of brandy in it for you?'

Mireille pushed herself into a sitting position and shook her head. She looked an absolute mess and Norah's heart went out to her. Poor kid. Elsie handed her another handkerchief and Mireille blew her nose noisily. 'Did he get her pregnant, too?' she asked Norah brokenly.

'Not as far as I know,' said Norah, handing the rest of the tea round. 'I always felt Amy was worried about something but I couldn't get her to talk. You can't do anything if people won't talk.'

Mireille gulped her tea.

'Mum,' Norah said quietly. 'Dad's home and he's eating in the kitchen. Do you want me to keep him company?'

Elsie shook her head. 'Nah, leave him to it. He'll probably welcome the chance to sneak off to The Red Lion.'

Norah smiled to herself. How well they knew each other. She could hear the love in her mother's voice and after listening to Mireille, she knew she was lucky to have such parents.

Mireille put her cup back onto the tray. 'I'm sorry to have made such a fool of myself.'

'Not at all, love,' said Elsie. 'I'd feel the same.'

'The thing is,' Mireille began again. 'I want to *do* something.'

'What can we do?' asked Trixie. 'Scoundrels like that get away with . . .' She pulled herself up, 'I'm sorry. I didn't mean . . .'

'Don't apologise for my sake,' Mireille said bitterly. 'The man is a pig and that's an insult to a pig. I hate him and I want to hurt him but I can't.' She looked up at Elsie. 'You do understand, don't you?'

'Of course I do, love,' said Elsie, 'and I agree with you. If I had the chance, I'd punch his lights out.'

Trixie and Mireille nodded and everybody lowered their eyes helplessly.

'If I could say something,' Norah interrupted. She chewed at the side of her mouth. 'What you *really* need to do is to decide what you *really* want.'

'I want to help both my sisters,' Mireille said stoutly. 'And I want us to all be together.'

'I'm not sure that's possible,' said Norah. 'They're both in boarding schools.'

'I wish they were still with you,' said Mireille. Her voice had an accusing edge to it. 'Why didn't you keep them?'

'Believe me, I wanted to,' said Norah. She explained how Ffox-Webster had come to collect the girls. She told Mireille how, although Lillian was excited, Amy hadn't wanted to go. She told her about Lillian's letter and her visit to The Wells House school. Mireille listened with an expression of absolute horror as Norah explained that Dempster was an Approved School and that Amy was forbidden all contact with the outside world.

'But that's monstrous!' she cried.

241

'I think so, too,' said Norah, 'but as you can see, my hands are tied.' She took a deep breath. 'More than that,' she continued. 'He's warned us off, my hubby and me.'

Mireille's hands became fists. 'How I hate that man! How many other lives will he ruin?'

'There's one other thing,' Norah ventured. 'We all agree that he probably did the same to Amy as he did you . . .'

'So what's to stop him doing the same to Lillian?' Mireille said coldly and everybody nodded.

CHAPTER 27

Norah

They were short staffed at the police station so when Inspector Reece called Jim into his office, he thought it was to tell him that they were going to get more manpower at last.

'Sit down, sit down,' said Inspector Reece, as Jim walked through the door. 'I want to talk to you about promotion.'

Jim lowered himself into the chair.

'As you know,' the inspector continued, 'we've lost another three men to conscription, and I get the feeling that we're in for a bumpy ride as far as recruitment is concerned.'

Jim had to agree. The force had restricted the number of men who could volunteer for the armed services but that didn't mean their officers were exempt from conscription. Since Dunkirk, several of the younger Worthing officers had left the police force to join either the navy or the air force.

'We're asking some of our retired officers to return to duty,' said the inspector, 'and as you know we've advertised for young lads between fourteen and eighteen to come forward as Special Constables and War Reserve Police.'

'Yes sir,' said Jim, 'and I'm pleased to report there are four requests in the in-tray even as we speak.'

'Good, good,' Inspector Reece continued. 'You're a good officer, Jim, which is why I'm putting your name forward for fast-track promotion.'

Jim's mouth fell open. 'Why thank you, sir,' he said with a gasp, 'but if you remember, I've haven't long been promoted to sergeant.'

The inspector picked up a sheaf of papers from his desk. 'I'm trying to juggle too many balls in the air,' he said bitterly. 'Not only do we have to keep the peace and the criminals behind bars, but now we must enforce the blackout, assist rescue services, check for enemy aliens and a hundred and one other things – and now they've put finding army deserters onto our plate as well!' His voice had risen to an angry crescendo before he took a moment to compose himself again. 'I'm about to be promoted myself and I want to leave this station with a good man at the helm.'

'So you're asking me to be . . .?'

'Station Inspector,' said Inspector Reece, 'and in six months' time, when I become Chief Super, you will move up to Chief Inspector.'

A little air escaped from between Jim's lips.

'It's going to take some hard work for you to get up and running, Jim, but I have every faith in you,' Inspector Reece said firmly. 'That will be all.'

Jim's mind was whirling as he rose to his feet. 'Yes, sir, thank you, sir.'

As he turned to leave, Inspector Reece barked, 'This bloody war has few advantages Jim, but this is one of them.'

*

The train ride home gave Norah time to reflect on everything that had happened in London. The hours she had spent with Mireille had been harrowing, to say the least. The more she heard about Ffox-Webster, the worse it seemed. What frustrated them was the fact that they all felt so helpless. The attitude of police officers didn't help. Mireille had tried reporting her step-father but no one had believed her. The tall tale Ffox-Webster had spun around her had done its worst and after the baby was born, the poor girl had been left to pick up the pieces of her life by herself.

'If you want to make a completely new start,' Norah had told her, 'you are welcome to come to Worthing. I'm sure my husband would be only too happy to let you stay with us.'

'You are very generous,' Mireille had said.

They had talked of bringing Ffox-Webster down, but to no avail. 'My husband is a police officer,' Norah reminded them as the suggestions grew more and more outlandish. 'I can't possibly be part of anything illegal.'

She gazed out of the window as the train sped through the countryside. It should have looked peaceful, but the skies were filled with vapour trails. Clearly the Battle of Britain was still raging high above the clouds. The German she saw shot down over the sea wasn't the last to fall foul of the RAF. Someone had said that the Luftwaffe outnumbered RAF planes three to one but the boys in blue were certainly giving them a run for their money. Nonetheless, the situation was grave. This morning the papers were full of horrific tales of more than a hundred enemy bombers sighted over Essex. Seven were brought down but not before fourteen people had lost their lives. These were scary and uncertain times and everybody probably had more important things to think about than a persistent predator of young girls, no matter what he had got away with. Her mind drifted back to the night before and the beginning of a plan.

Her mother had come up with an idea that produced yet another bombshell. 'Where does your step-father live?'

'Just off Park Lane,' said Mireille. 'He has a house in South Audley Street.'

'And he has a daily woman?'

'Oh yes,' said Mireille, smiling fondly. 'Meeting her was the nicest thing about my life when we came to live in London. Sometimes she would bring her daughter along and I would play with her.'

'Does she still work for him?'

Mireille had shrugged. 'I suppose so. It's been ages since I was there and, quite frankly, I don't think I could bear to go back.'

'What was her name?'

'Mrs Scott,' said Mireille. 'Why do you ask?'

'I'm wondering if she's on my books,' said Elsie.

'My mother runs a domestic employment agency,' Norah explained.

Elsie rose to her feet. 'If Mrs Scott is one of my ladies, I might offer her a better post.'

'But that would leave him with no staff,' said Trixie.

'Precisely,' said Elsie, fetching a long box folder from the top of her dresser. 'If we can blackball him . . . I know it's not much, but it would be a terrible inconvenience for such a *great man* to have to clean his own house.' Her voice was full of sarcasm.

'And if no one will work for him,' Trixie remarked, 'what better way to start the tongues wagging?'

Elsie sat down again and began thumbing through the cards inside. 'Ah, here we are, Mrs Scott . . .' Her voice trailed and Norah noticed that her mother wore a puzzled expression.

'Mum?' she said. 'What is it?'

Elsie had looked up at Mireille. 'Was Mrs Scott's daughter called Vera?'

'Why yes,' said Mireille. 'She used to come to the house sometimes and we'd play together.'

'I think I might know her,' said Elsie vaguely. She frowned again and added, 'Though, funnily enough, she's not working at the moment and I haven't seen her around for a while.'

When Norah arrived home, the dogs ran at her with much wagging of tails and enthusiastic yelps. After such a jam-packed day yesterday, Norah felt like a limp rag and would have welcomed a quiet chair but it was obvious that Jim was bursting with excitement about something and she couldn't put a damper on his enthusiasm.

'Promotion,' she cried after he'd told her. 'Oh, darling, that's wonderful.'

'The best of it is,' he said, his eyes shining like buttons, 'because I have to be on call, they're going to give us a telephone.'

Norah gasped. 'A telephone!'

Jim nodded. 'That means you can get your mother to ring you whenever she likes. Obviously, you can't have long calls in case the station is trying to contact me, but in these uncertain times, it will make it a lot easier to keep in touch.'

Norah was delighted and to her surprise, Mrs Kirkwood had prepared the tea. All that was needed was a lighted taper under the saucepan. As she hung her coat in the hall, Norah wondered where her mother-in-law was. Jim walked past her and entered the sitting room.

'Oh, there you are,' said Mrs Kirkwood as Jim and Norah came through the door. 'You'd both better shut the door quickly. We've let the budgie have a little fly.' Norah realised then that her mother-in-law was sitting bolt upright in her chair with Joey happily chirruping on the top of her head. Ivan was tucked into the corner, between the wireless and the window. It wasn't on but he must have been listening to something before they came in because the yellow light still glowed.

Norah did as she was asked and closed the door. Jim flopped down into his armchair and shook out his *Daily Telegraph*.

'Did you have a nice time in London?' Mrs Kirkwood asked Norah as Joey flew towards the curtain rail.

'I think you'd better come back home now, young feller,' said Ivan. He stood to his feet and went to the window. Norah watched as he raised his hand towards the little bird. After cocking his head from side to side for a minute, Joey hopped onto Ivan's finger and the old man took him back to his cage. When the bird reached his perch, Ivan shut the cage door. Mrs Kirkwood clapped her hands. 'Well done, Joey,' she cried. 'You are a clever boy.'

Joey repeated what she had said in a voice exactly like hers. 'You are a clever boy.'

Jim pulled down the corner of his newspaper and blinked in surprise. Norah struggled not to let her mouth gape. She had never seen Mrs Kirkwood looking so relaxed and happy and this was the first time she'd ever heard her say anything remotely kind about the budgie.

'Jim's got a promotion,' said Norah.

'Another one?' Mrs Kirkwood said more surprised than critical. 'But you've only just had one.'

'Well done,' said Ivan with enthusiasm.

'Yes, well done, dear,' Mrs Kirkwood repeated meekly. 'What will you be now?'

Jim pulled his paper down again. 'Station Inspector, and in a few months' time, Chief Inspector!'

Ivan nodded, clearly impressed.

Mrs Kirkwood smiled. 'And did you have a nice time, dear?' she said, turning to Norah.

'Um . . . er . . . yes,' said Norah. Dear? Did she just call her 'dear'? She blinked uncertainly. Jim put his paper back up and Norah could see it was trembling. Her husband was clearly having a little giggle to himself behind the newsprint.

'Your mother all right?' said Mrs Kirkwood.

'Yes, thank you,' said Norah. 'She's fine.' Her mind was in a whirl. She wanted to talk about her meeting with Mireille but she had to tell Jim first. It wouldn't be fair to spring something on him without giving him a chance to express his point of view.

'I think I'll take a stroll around the garden,' Ivan suddenly announced. He stood to his feet. 'You coming, gal?'

Mrs Kirkwood looked from Ivan to Norah and back again before she rose to her feet. When they'd left the room, Jim muttered from behind his newspaper, 'Those two are as thick as thieves these days.'

'I think Ivan knew I wanted to tell you something.'

He put the paper down again. 'Not much in the paper anyway. Only got six pages now; that's half the size it was before the war.' He smiled at Norah. 'So, what did you want to tell me?'

Norah took a deep breath. 'While I was at Mum's I met Amy's sister.'

'Good God,' Jim gasped. 'How on earth did that happen? How is she? Did she tell you anything about Amy?'

'I don't mean Lillian,' said Norah. 'I met another sister. Her name is Mireille. She's Amy's older sister.'

Jim's paper slid to the floor. He was staring at her in bewildered astonishment. 'An older sister? We didn't know they had one, did we?'

Norah shook her head. 'Oh, Jim, it was awful. I found out that he'd abused her. He'd . . . he'd . . .' Suddenly overcome with the emotion of it all, her chin quivered and she fished up her sleeve for her handkerchief.

Jim got up and came to sit beside his wife on the arm of her chair. As he put a comforting arm around her shoulder, he murmured, 'Take your time, love. Take your time.'

She told him everything. She told him about the meeting in the café and how Mireille had come to her mother's house. She told him what had happened to the poor girl, the baby and how she was trying to make a new start in life.

'So, when is she coming here?' said Jim.

Norah's head went up and she stared at her husband.

'Oh come on, love,' he said quietly. 'I know you too well. I bet you said, "and what better place to make a completely new start than here in Worthing?"'

Norah screwed her handkerchief nervously. 'I admit I did offer,' she began, 'but on the way home, it suddenly dawned on me that with Ivan here, it's not very practical. After what happened to her, she won't want to walk through a man's bedroom to get to her own.'

Jim looked thoughtful. 'Hm,' he said, 'I see the problem.'

They could hear the dogs bouncing around the kitchen as they came back into the house with Mrs Kirkwood and Ivan.

'You'll have to tell Mother,' said Jim, getting up again. 'She was very fond of Amy.'

Their mealtime was a bit awkward. It was obvious that Norah had been crying but no one asked her why. Jim helped his mother with the dishing up and they all ate in comparative silence. As Mrs Kirkwood cleared away the plates, Norah said, 'Jim and I have decided we need to talk to you both.'

When she heard about Mireille, Mrs Kirkwood hung her head. 'I had a feeling that man was a rotter. Do you remember how terrified Amy was when he came in unannounced?'

'When we heard Mireille's story, we all thought that, too,' Norah admitted.

'Dirty dog,' Mrs Kirkwood snarled. No one noticed Max put his tail between his legs and head towards his blanket. 'He has to be stopped, Jim. How many more lives is he going to ruin before someone puts him behind bars?'

'You're right, Mother, but what can I do?'

'So you'll do nothing? Let him get away with it?' said Mrs Kirkwood in astonishment.

'If the girls won't talk . . .' Jim said with a shrug of his shoulders.

'How can they talk?' Mrs Kirkwood spat. 'If the bloke ends up in court for something like that, you can bet the *News of the World* will make sure the whole world will know who they are. What sort of a life will they have then?'

'It's the only way we can put a stop to it, Mother. We can't act without cast-iron proof. That's the law.'

'The law,' Mrs Kirkwood scoffed angrily, her neck and face becoming high in colour. 'Speak out and everybody labels you a tart because you "led him on", or stay quiet and you have to live with the knowledge that the blighter is free to do it to somebody else.' She rose to her feet and gathered her things before stomping out of the room.

As the door slammed, Jim turned to Norah with a helpless expression. 'I wish there was something I could do,' he said, shaking his head. 'It makes me sick to my stomach that those beautiful girls have been treated so shamefully but without proper testimony, my hands are tied. Mother's right, it *is* unfair, but that's the way it is.'

Norah looked away, her eyes smarting with unshed tears. Ivan leaned back in his chair with a long sigh.

CHAPTER 28

Norah

'Mrs Kirkwood,' Norah said at the breakfast table, 'I know you're upset about Amy but my mother thinks she has a way of getting our own back on Ffox-Webster.'

Her mother-in-law looked up from the cup of tea she was nursing. 'Oh?'

'It's nothing illegal but I'd still be grateful if you didn't tell Jim,' Norah went on. 'As you know, Mum runs a domestic agency and she actually placed the woman who works as his daily. Mum's going to offer her a much better paid job, which is closer to home, and Ffox-Webster will be blackballed so that he can't get anybody else.'

'Not much, is it?' said Mrs Kirkwood.

'No, but it's a start,' Norah said defensively. 'You know better than most that a bit of gossip can do the world of damage.'

Mrs Kirkwood nodded stiffly.

'And there's another thing,' Norah went on. 'His daily worked for him for years so she may be able to tell us something useful. Her name is Mrs Scott and apparently she has been ill. We're not sure what was wrong with her, but Mum is going to see her today.'

Mrs Kirkwood and Ivan exchanged a warm glance and then he raised an eyebrow in Norah's direction.

'I'm sorry for my outburst last night,' said Mrs Kirkwood.

Norah almost dropped her piece of toast but she managed to control her surprise long enough to mumble, 'That's all right.' She reached for the marmalade and added, 'I hope you don't mind, but I've invited Amy's older sister to come and stay. Like you said last night, it's hard to make a new start in a place where you're known, so I thought if she came here, we could help.'

'So you would like me to move out,' said Ivan.

'Oh, Ivan . . .' Norah began.

'That's fine,' he said quickly as he raised his hand to stop her saying more. 'I'm very grateful for what you've done for me. I'll start looking for new lodging right away.'

'But you can't turn the poor man out just like that,' Mrs Kirkwood exclaimed. 'It's not right.'

'And I'm not going to,' Norah protested. 'Look, I've talked it over with Jim and we have a proposal. Your room is quite large, Ivan, and Jim says if we get a builder to put up a false wall and create a small corridor at the side, Mireille could get to the room behind yours without having to go through your bedroom. What do you think?'

Ivan glanced at Mrs Kirkwood. 'I'd be quite happy with that.'

Mrs Kirkwood relaxed and smiled.

'In fact,' Ivan went on, 'I always was a dab hand at woodwork. I'll knock it up meself if you like. No charge.'

*

As it happened, it didn't take Ivan long to sort out the stud wall and while Norah and Jim were admiring his handiwork, he took the opportunity to mention starting up a market stall as well.

'I think it's a grand idea,' said Jim with a chuckle, 'but don't take on too much, will you? Setting up and putting down is hard work and you're not as young as you used to be.'

'Oh, I shan't be on me own,' said Ivan. 'Your ma is going to help me.'

Jim blinked in surprise. 'Er . . . oh, well, then go ahead,' he faltered. 'What do you think, Norah?'

Norah was just as stunned as he was. Mrs Kirkwood agreeing to help man a market stall? Unbelievable. 'Like Jim says,' she said sweetly, 'it sounds like a very good idea.'

It had been a while since Norah had popped over to Broadwater to see Penny and Victor, so she biked over one evening when Jim was doing a late shift and was pleased to find Penny looking very well. It was obvious from her chatty conversation that her friend was enjoying her work in the café and had made quite a few new friends. 'At first,' Penny explained, 'we catered for the British, but since that terrible business at Dunkirk, so many Canadians have arrived. They're busy helping to put up Worthing's sea defences.'

Norah hardly dared to ask the question burning on her lips as they sat in Penny's mum's sitting room while Victor played on a blanket on the floor. Eventually, though, she couldn't stop herself. 'Have you heard from Ted yet?'

'Well, yes and no,' said Penny. 'I had a telegram from the War Office to tell me he's a prisoner of war, but I haven't actually heard from him yet.'

'Oh, Penny, I'm so sorry,' said Norah, 'but I suppose it's something that you know he's alive.'

Penny nodded. 'You'd think so, wouldn't you, but that's only the beginning of my troubles. Mum and I have spent days trying to sort out his money. There was no time to go to the bank before he left and although there's money there for me, the bank won't let me have it because the account is in his name only.'

'How stupid!' Norah cried. 'What are you going to do?'

Penny sighed. 'I don't know. His army pay goes directly into the bank so I'm not eligible for any other money. That means because of red tape, Victor and I are left to bloody starve. Typical army cock-up.'

Victor rolled over onto his tummy and Norah reached for her handbag.

'No, no,' said Penny, her hand up in protest. 'I'm all right, really. Things are tight but I have the money I earn in the canteen and Mum has started giving piano lessons again. What with her widow's pension and all, we get by.'

'Are you sure?' said Norah. She had no wish to offend Penny but neither could she leave a friend in need.

Penny nodded. 'Thanks.'

'Well, tell your mum if she goes into Worthing on market day, we have a fruit and veg stall and we make sure everything is at affordable prices.'

Penny grinned. 'Thanks, Norah. You're a brick.'

Mireille came to Worthing the following week. Norah met her at the station and they walked in companionable silence back to the house. The dogs gave her a lively greeting and Norah showed her the room upstairs.

'You used to get to your room through this one,' she

256

explained, 'but Ivan has made a small corridor between them and he's put a bolt on the inside of your door so you'll feel quite safe.'

'Ivan?' Mireille said with a hint of suspicion in her voice.

'He lodges here, too,' said Norah, and noting that Mireille's face had paled, she quickly added, 'He's quite old, sixty, maybe more, so there's no need to worry.'

It was obvious that they were both feeling slightly uncomfortable but Mireille looked around the room. 'It's very nice,' she said quietly.

'Treat it as your home,' said Norah. 'If you don't like the pictures on the wall, feel free to take them down. I shan't be coming in here now. This is *your* room.'

Mireille's eyes had filled. 'Thank you.'

'I'll leave you to unpack,' said Norah. 'Come down when you're ready and we'll have a cup of tea.'

The next few days were busy. It was imperative that Mireille got a job if she was going to pay her way, so Jim arranged for her to go to the police canteen and meet Ma. Although they spent an amicable half-hour together, Mireille didn't commit herself as Norah had also arranged for her to meet Penny, though the only thing on offer in the café was part-time and not enough money. In the end, Mireille got herself a job in the telephone exchange in Goring-by-Sea, to start the following week.

'Well, you certainly didn't let the grass grow under your feet, did you?' Mrs Kirkwood remarked at the tea table.

She and Mireille got on well, and though it was perhaps not quite as close a relationship as Mrs Kirkwood had enjoyed with Amélie, there was a mutual respect between them. Mireille didn't speak much about her family or Ffox-Webster but somehow he was always lurking in the background like a bad smell.

To make it easier for her, Norah loaned Mireille the money to buy a bike. They found a clapped-out, ancient machine in the emporium on the corner of Lyndhurst Road. The chain needed a good oiling and it looked a bit like the one the teacher rode in the film *The Wizard of Oz*, but once Jim had performed his magic, it was a lot better. Sitting high and proud, Mireille set off for the telephone exchange at seven the following Monday morning.

Right from the word go, the market stall was a great success. Ivan got hold of a small pushcart and first thing on Wednesday mornings, he set off for Montague Street. They used the cart itself as a counter and put the money straight into their pouch pocket aprons, made by Mrs Kirkwood, which they wore around their waists. They did a roaring trade.

I've met this wonderful man. His name is Dan and he is one of the ground crew here at Ford. I can't wait for you to meet him. You'll like him, Norah. He's so tall that his mates call him Tree-top. He's got dark hair and brown eyes and he likes sailing and canoeing. Dan says he'll teach me to do it so that we can spend a few days in the peace and quiet on a canal somewhere. I can't wait.

I'm still very busy but loving it. We go to dances in a nearby village called Yapton and there are some lovely country walks nearby. If it weren't for the war, it would all be fantastic, but then if we hadn't had a war, I wouldn't have met Dan!

As she read her sister's letter, Norah smiled to herself. Rene was right. The war spoiled so much. It seemed that the drone of aircraft in the skies never stopped. There were dogfights and plane crashes all the time as the Luftwaffe did its best to pound the country into submission. At the end of June, after bombing Jersey and Guernsey harbours and killing a total of forty-four islanders, the Channel Islands fell to German occupation. Now the Nazis were on British soil and less than a hundred miles away. Terrible days and terrible things happening but on a much happier note, it seemed that Rene was in love!

Mireille settled in well, but she'd made it plain right from the start that she wanted to try and see her sisters. She asked Norah to go with her.

'I'm pretty sure I wouldn't be allowed to see them,' Norah said as she explained how cross Ffox-Webster had been after he'd heard that she and Jim had visited the girls. 'As soon as those matrons find out we're coming, they'll be sure to put up the shutters.'

'Then we won't tell them,' Mireille said. 'They can hardly refuse me. I'm their sister. Let's just turn up at the door and see what happens.'

They set out for Epsom one Saturday in August. Norah could tell that Mireille was both excited and nervous. She hadn't seen her sisters for more than four years. 'I'm wondering if Linnet will even remember me,' she remarked sadly.

They went to The Wells House first, the twenty-minute walk giving them both a chance to stretch their legs.

Once they had entered her office, Miss Reeves seemed very surprised to see them. 'Mrs Kirkwood, you were expressly asked not to call again,' she said frostily.

'I know,' said Norah, 'and I apologise but this lady is Lillian's older sister and she is desperate to see her.'

'I have brought proof of my identity,' said Mireille, reaching into her bag.

'I'm afraid it still won't be possible,' Miss Reeves said firmly.

'Please, Miss Reeves,' Norah insisted, 'I quite understand that you don't want me to see Lillian, but her sister has come a very long way.'

'Mrs Kirkwood,' Miss Reeve began again, 'you cannot see Lillian because she is no longer here.'

Norah's eyes widened. 'Then where is she?'

'I have no idea.'

Mireille frowned crossly. 'What do you mean you have no idea? Surely she must have left a forwarding address?'

Miss Reeve pinched her lips together and added haughtily, 'Your father removed her from the school soon after that previous upset.' She glared at Norah. 'Because of your interference, he simply cancelled our arrangement, and took her away.'

The two women were stunned. Mireille looked on the verge of tears.

'And he left no forwarding address?' said Norah.

'None.'

Norah rose to her feet. 'Then we need not detain you any longer, Miss Reeves,' she said. Helping Mireille to her feet, the two of them left.

'Why did he do that?' Mireille said as they walked back into Epsom.

'I'm not sure,' said Norah, 'but I'm guessing it must be my fault. He obviously thought that, given time, I'd want to go back there again and it seems he was right.'

'Nothing is your fault,' Mireille said brokenly.

Norah slipped her arm through hers. 'I hate to say this but I think you may have more bad news. It's quite possible that Amy has been moved as well.'

CHAPTER 29

Norah

Rene put her hand onto the top of her hip and stretched her aching back. She had been packing parachutes for nearly four hours and was desperate for a break. She glanced up at the clock on the wall. Only twenty minutes to go before lunch and it couldn't come soon enough. There was plenty of activity on the air strip but they were not nearly as busy as nearby Tangmere. Ford aerodrome still officially belonged to the Fleet Air Arm, whereas Tangmere was a fully-fledged RAF airfield. The only hotel in the area, along with several houses, had been flattened in order to enlarge it and with the Battle of Britain in full swing, things were moving on apace.

'Hello, freckle-face.'

The sound of his voice made her jump. As Rene turned around her heart was already beating wildly. 'Dan,' she exclaimed in a whisper, 'what are you doing in the parachute shed?'

'I came to see you, of course.'

'You'll get yourself shot,' she teased.

'It'll be worth it,' he said. 'I just wanted to ask you if you're coming to the dance tonight?'

Rene grinned. 'Try and stop me.'

'Wallace!' a voice bellowed by the door. 'What the hell are you doing in here?'

Dan leaned forward and gave her a quick peck on the cheek. 'See you outside the gates at seven,' he whispered and then calling out he added, 'Just checking the chute, sir.'

'Checking the chute?' the officer said incredulously. 'Why the hell do you need to check the chute?'

'Just being helpful, sir,' Dan said, giving Rene a wink before he headed towards the door.

'Come in here again and I'll put you on a charge,' the officer grumbled. 'You're here to fight a war, not to beef up your love life. And why the hell have you been sloshing blue paint everywhere?'

Their voices grew smaller but Rene could still hear them. ''Cos the Squadron Leader asked me to paint the underbelly of his Spit blue, sir.'

'Paint the under . . .' the officer began. He was clearly spitting feathers. 'This isn't a bloody nursery, Wallace!'

'He reckons the Germans can't see him in the clear skies if it's blue,' Dan went on, 'and he might be right, sir. He hasn't been shot down yet.'

Rene smiled and carried on with her work. She may be tired but now she had a newly found impetus. And something to look forward to.

After a small meal in The Copper Kettle restaurant, Norah and Mireille had taken a taxi up the hill to Dempster, the place where Amy was incarcerated. This time, when Mireille gave her name to the man on the gate, the taxi was allowed to drive up to the house. As was the case last time, Miss Short ushered them into her office. She had hardly changed since the last time Norah saw her. She was just as thin, although her hair was longer and she now wore it swept up at the sides with combs. As they sat in their chairs Miss Short pushed her thick pebble glasses up her nose.

'I remember telling you, Mrs er . . .'

'Kirkwood,' Norah prompted.

'Mrs Kirkwood,' Miss Short continued, 'not to come again.'

'I have only come to accompany Miss Ffox-Webster,' said Norah. 'This young lady is Amy's older sister.'

Miss Short looked Mireille up and down in a rather offensive way. 'And what proof do I have that what you say is true?'

Following Jim's advice, they had come prepared. Mireille not only produced her identity card but also a letter addressed to her when she got her telephonist job at the post office and a reference from her previous job in the factory. Miss Short scrutinised them carefully.

'Very well,' said Miss Short, 'but before I let you see your sister, I must ask you, have you come prepared to pay her outstanding fees?'

Mireille gave Norah a bewildered look.

'What fees?' Norah asked.

Miss Short stood up and went to a tall filing cabinet. Pulling out a buff-coloured folder, she came back to her seat and sat down. 'Amy's fees haven't been paid for the past four months,' she said, opening the folder. 'Your father has repeatedly been asked to settle his account. In fact, we sent out yet another reminder only last Monday.'

'I don't understand,' Norah said with a frown. 'When my husband and I came here before, you told us that Amy had been sent here by the courts with a predetermined sentence. Surely if that was the case, her fees would have been met by government.'

Miss Short gave an exaggerated sniff. 'This is a completely private establishment. As I'm sure I explained at the time, the girls who came here are unruly, disruptive and wilful.'

'My sister is none of those things!' cried Mireille, jerking forward in her seat.

Norah laid her hand gently on Mireille's arm to calm her. 'Miss Short,' she began again, 'if this is a completely private establishment, why did you tell us it was a court decision?'

Miss Short closed the folder. 'To put it bluntly, these girls are an embarrassment to their families. Rather than have them fall foul of the law, they are sent here, where we do our best to put them back onto the straight and narrow.'

'In other words, all this was decided by a kangaroo court,' Norah retorted.

'The people involved are barristers and judges in their own right,' Miss Short added haughtily. 'They decide what would have been done in a magistrate's or crown court and adjust their sentences accordingly. Over the years, we have brought many young girls back to their senses this way.'

'But that still doesn't make it right,' Mireille cried.

'And it's not legal,' Norah added.

Miss Short's expression soured. 'We are not here to discuss the rights and wrongs of what we do for these girls. What I want to know is, are you going to pay the fees owing?'

Mireille looked at her helplessly. 'How much is it?'

'At the moment it stands at fifty-four pounds, seven shillings and sixpence.'

Mireille took in her breath. 'I'm only a junior telephonist,' she said, lowering her eyes to her lap. 'I'd have to work a lifetime to get that kind of money.'

'Then I suggest that you contact your father before further steps are taken.'

'He's not my . . .' Mireille began angrily.

'We can't do that,' Norah interrupted, 'but we can do something much better.'

'Oh?' said Miss Short.

'It's obvious to me that you're not going to get paid,' said Norah. 'It looks like Mr Ffox-Webster has abandoned Amy to her fate and if you can't afford to keep the girl for free, why don't you release her into my care? You know my husband is a policeman and I am a person of good standing in my community. She would be with her own sister and I'll make sure she will do nothing to bring either the family or your school into disrepute.'

Miss Short gave Norah a stony stare. 'What about what I am owed?'

'You have a choice,' Norah said firmly. 'Cut your losses, or risk an even larger deficit.'

Miss Short rose to her feet and went back to the filing cabinet. As she slowly opened the drawer and put the folder inside, Norah guessed she was weighing up the pros and cons. Mireille went to say something but Norah indicated with her eyes that she should stay silent. Coming back to the desk, Miss Short picked up the bell and rang it. A few minutes later, a girl came into the office.

'Tell Amy Ffox-Webster to get her things together,' she said curtly. 'She's leaving.'

Norah held her breath.

The girl's face registered her surprise. 'Leaving?' She hesitated before adding, 'Yes, Miss Short. Right away, Miss Short.'

Amy was confused when Imelda Jordan came to her classroom and told her teacher that Miss Short wanted to see her. She racked her brains as to what she could have done wrong.

'Why does she want me?' Amy whispered when she and Imelda were alone in the corridor.

'You're leaving,' Imelda said.

Amy stood still, a wave of blind panic coursing through her veins. 'What?'

'Come on,' said Imelda. 'Get your bags packed before she changes her mind.'

Amy hurried after her. 'But where am I going?'

'I dunno.'

'Didn't she tell you anything more?'

They had reached the dormitory and taking a battered suitcase from the cupboard, Imelda hurried to Amy's locker. 'There's two women in the office,' she said as she began stuffing everything Amy owned into the case. 'A young one and an old one. Probably tarts,' she added ominously.

Amy gasped. She wasn't being sent to a brothel, was she? She felt sick. Imelda opened a cupboard. 'Which one is your coat?'

'I'm not going,' Amy said, sitting down on the bed.

'Don't be bloody daft,' said Imelda. 'Look, they're your ticket out of here. You don't have to stay with them. As soon as you get to the bloody gates, make a run for it. Nobody's going to send out a search party, are they?'

Amy stared at her helplessly.

'Come on,' Imelda urged.

By the time they reached the office door, Amy was trembling from head to toe. Imelda knocked once and Miss Short's cold voice said, 'Come.'

As the door opened Mireille stood up and with a cry of joy, Amy ran into her arms.

The twenty minutes they had just waited for Amy had been the longest of Norah's life. Miss Short had offered them tea, which they accepted although they had hardly touched it. Mireille was struggling not to cry and Norah was panic-stricken that at any minute the matron might have second thoughts and change her mind. She was asked to write down her home address and to sign a paper absolving Dempster of all responsibility for Amy's future actions. After that, Miss Short telephoned for another taxi for them.

'What's happening?' Amy whispered as the three of them headed towards the front door.

'We'll tell you later,' said Norah. Amy seemed bewildered as Norah hustled them both outside and into the waiting taxi. It was only as they reached the gate that she and the two girls could finally relax.

'Imelda told me I was leaving for good,' said Amy. 'Is that true?'

'Yes.' Mireille laughed aloud. 'Norah was amazing.'

'Oh, Auntie Norah,' Amy said brokenly as she and her sister hugged each other. 'Thank you, thank you.'

'Was it truly awful?' Mireille said.

Norah turned to glance nervously out of the back window for the third time since they'd left the home. As she sat back, she nudged Mireille and jerked her head towards the driver. 'Not now,' she said quietly.

*

'Belvedere Domestic Agency.' Elsie always used a cut-glass Oxford accent whenever she answered the telephone. Sometimes it would be a friend in need, or one of her daughters, and at other times it could be someone looking for work, but when it was a client looking for a domestic, she was glad that the callers couldn't see her surroundings. Few ordinary people had telephones so they always presumed that she was speaking from an office. Thank God they couldn't see her cluttered kitchen dresser or her sometimes flour-covered hands as she picked up the receiver. 'May I help you?'

'I hope so,' said a male voice. Unusual. Usually the women of the house dealt with domestic issues. 'My daily woman has just given her notice and I need a replacement,' he continued. 'A colleague of mine said your agency was very efficient so I thought I would give you a ring.'

'Yes, sir,' Elsie said, grabbing the notepad that had somehow ended up under the junk on the table. 'Always ready to help. Could I have some details?'

'I work chaotic hours in central London,' the man went on, 'so I need someone with impeccable references who is completely trustworthy because more often than not, she will have to let herself in.'

'All my girls are trustworthy, sir,' Elsie went on. 'We should have no problem with that.'

'I was thinking perhaps two or three times a week?'

Elsie scribbled it down on the pad. Her mind was racing ahead. Working in central London . . . that probably meant he was some kind of civil servant so he could easily pay top dollar. 'Perhaps you could give me your personal details?'

'Certainly,' he began. 'The name is Ffox-Webster.'

Elsie caught her breath. Lummy Charlie, it was him! She'd been trying to find Mrs Scott, his daily, but so far she hadn't had any luck. Her hand was already trembling and it took all she had to remain perfectly natural as she copied down the address.

'We require a down-payment of t . . .' She hesitated. Her normal fee was two pounds and five when the domestic took the post. She knew she wasn't going to get the second fee because he never would find a domestic, not from her anyway. She cleared her throat. 'Excuse me, sir. Our fee starts at three pounds with five pounds due if the girl suits. Will that be all right?'

'Bit steep,' he complained. 'Other agencies ask for thirty bob up front.'

'I'm sure they do, sir,' Elsie said stiffly, 'but they don't offer the better class of domestic.'

There was an ominous silence. He was waiting for her to lower the charge but she wasn't going to. She held her breath, hoping against hope that he wouldn't put the phone down.

'If I may confide in you,' Elsie said eventually. 'Our girls work for many titled people; people of class and breeding.'

'Like the chap who recommended you,' he said drily.

'So, would you like to go ahead, sir?'

He cleared his throat. 'I suppose so,' he said tetchily. 'I never realised how difficult it would be to find a bloody domestic.'

Only for you, chum, thought Elsie. 'A sign of the times we live in, I'm afraid, sir,' she said brightly. 'So many girls have joined up, you see.'

He made no comment.

'So as soon as I receive your remittance, I shall look for a suitable girl for the post.'

The telephone clicked. Elsie replaced her receiver and smiled to herself. The plan was beginning to work.

CHAPTER 30

Norah

It wasn't until they were safely back home at The Lilacs that Norah could truly relax. All the way home, she had been terrified that Miss Short would have changed her mind and sent somebody to chase them and demand that Amy go back. The girls said very little and remained huddled together for most of the journey.

'Would you still like us to call you by your French name, dear?' Norah asked as they finally sat on the Worthing train.

Amy looked up at her sister.

'I've decided I don't want anything that man gave me,' Mireille said acidly. 'And if I could change my surname, I would.'

Amy gave Norah a tired smile and nodded.

Norah leaned forward and said earnestly, 'It's wonderful to have you back, Amélie.'

As she sat opposite them in the railway carriage, Norah could see that Amélie was painfully thin; her face was gaunt and she had spots. What on earth had been going on in that terrible place? How could the lively pink-cheeked girl

271

she'd looked after the year before have ended up looking so unhealthy? Every time their eyes met, Norah could tell that Mireille was just as concerned as she was about her sister.

When they arrived at the house, the dogs gave Amélie an ecstatic welcome, which brought Mrs Kirkwood to the kitchen.

'Amélie!' she cried and when she held out her arms, Amélie went to her at once. As the two of them embraced, there were tears in the older lady's eyes.

Jim was happy to see Amélie again. After giving her a brief bear-hug, he glanced at Norah. 'This calls for a fish 'n' chips special, doesn't it?'

Later on, as they sat at the kitchen table, they were all dying to know what had happened to Amélie but the poor girl looked so done in that Norah said, 'We'll talk tomorrow.'

Ivan had been slightly concerned with yet another lodger in the house but there was no need. The two sisters were happy to share Mireille's room and the bed was large enough for the two of them. They didn't talk much and by ten thirty they were both asleep.

When they woke on Sunday, they talked about their shared experience with Ffox-Webster. 'I'd rather not talk about the sordid details,' Amélie said with an anxious frown, 'especially not to Auntie Norah and Uncle Jim.'

'He was vile,' said Mireille. 'The times I wished I could have taken a knife . . .'

'Don't,' Amélie said softly. 'I still have nightmares.'

'I'm so sorry,' said Mireille. 'Call me self-centred, if you like, but it never occurred to me that he would make a play for you once I'd gone.'

'You mustn't blame yourself,' said Amélie, sounding wiser than her years. She squeezed her sister's hand under the bed-clothes. 'I was jealous of you. The way he spoiled you and gave you things. I regret that now.'

'So shall we agree not to blame each other?' said Mireille. 'We couldn't have helped each other anyway.'

Amélie nodded. 'He took advantage of us. He knew how to keep us silent.'

When Mireille explained to the family that they'd rather not talk about Ffox-Webster in detail, Norah, Mrs Kirkwood and Jim respected the girls' wishes. Ivan had already made himself scarce, not because he wasn't interested, but because he had a gut feeling that as the girls didn't really know him, it might stop them from opening up.

Mireille told them that she was old enough to remember their mother and the circumstances leading up to her marriage to Ffox-Webster. After their father had died Ffox-Webster's smooth talk was enough to convince her that if she married him, she and the girls would be well looked after.

'I remember him bringing us to England when his best friend wanted to stand for Parliament,' Mireille told them. 'I thought we would be with *Maman* but he hired a nanny for us and left us in his friend's house. We stayed there for a few weeks. We played with his daughter, Vivien. Do you remember, Amélie?'

Her sister shook her head.

'Don't you remember the little summer house? And the fishpond? Vivien almost fell in.' Amélie gave her a blank look. 'Oh,' Mireille said, disappointed. 'It's a shame you don't remember. We had such fun there.'

'I remember Nanny,' Amélie said. 'She smacked me on the leg for tearing my frock on the rope swing.'

Norah gave her a sympathetic smile but Mireille just shrugged. 'Anyway, while he and *Maman* were abroad, she died, too.'

'How old were you then?' Norah asked.

'I must have been seven or eight,' said Amélie, looking to her sister for guidance.

'And I would have been almost ten when we went to the London house.' She dropped her gaze to the floor. 'For me, that's when it started.'

Mrs Kirkwood shifted awkwardly in her chair and everyone fell silent.

'I had a telephone call from my mother last night,' Norah said, desperately trying to lighten the mood. 'Your fath— Er, sorry, your step-father has applied to her agency for a domestic.'

Amélie frowned, clearly puzzled, so they explained their plan.

'I know is sounds very tame compared to what he's done to the both of you,' Norah added, glancing at Jim, 'and we have promised not to do anything illegal, but if there's enough gossip surrounding him, we think . . . no, we hope someone, somewhere, will ask questions.'

'I'm not sure I approve of all this,' Jim murmured. 'I think you may be playing a dangerous game around a dangerous man.'

'Our only hope is to get people talking,' said Norah. 'That man gets away with murder because everyone is too scared to say anything.'

It was a beautiful day and normally Norah would have suggested having their midday meal outside but despite being a Sunday, the drone of RAF activity in the skies above them was continuous. Every now and then, an aircraft would burst through the clouds followed by another and a terrifying dogfight would begin. The last thing anybody wanted was to have to dash to the Anderson Shelter and leave their meal to the gulls.

Since the meat rationing began in April, Norah hardly ever had a Sunday roast but today they were to enjoy a real luxury; pigeon pie, stuffed with home-grown onion, leek and carrots. For afters they were to have grated carrot and jam pudding with the last of the plum jam left over from 1939. What could be more fitting as a welcome home meal for a girl Norah had come to love?

Once they had eaten, Amélie went back to bed for a rest. Mireille and Mrs Kirkwood helped Norah clear up in the kitchen and then her mother-in-law joined Jim and Ivan as they listened to the wireless and dozed in the sitting room.

'Do you fancy a bike ride?' Norah asked Mireille. 'We could go and have a look at that German plane they shot down.'

The German Heinkel 111P had come down just north of the town between Cote Street and Honeysuckle Lane on High Salvington. Two of the five-man crew had been killed and the other three were captured, but as yet nobody had had the time to remove the wreckage. Jim had sent officers to the site to guard the plane from souvenir hunters but Norah couldn't resist the idea of having a look at it. They set off almost straight away.

At times like this it was so hard to believe that the country was at war. Norah took them along the Goring Road and they turned into Shaftesbury Avenue. The Canadians were building a hospital near the railway bridge but no one was working today as the two women headed up Durrington

Hill and across the main road. The climb to the top was steep and when they ran out of puff, they were forced to get off their bikes and walk. Norah had put a bottle of water in her saddle bag so they also had a quick drink.

The plane had come down almost intact and when they got there, a few police officers were posing in front of it while another policeman took photographs with a box Brownie. Riddled with bullet holes, the Heinkel was quite a sight.

The papers said the Germans had boasted that they had brought down thirty-three Spitfires. Norah tried to imagine the magnificent planes broken and shot up like this one. She shuddered. The thought of all those young men, at best injured, at worst, dead, was very sobering. War was truly ghastly and yet she knew they had no choice if they were going to stop Hitler. God only knew what life would be like if a monster like him ruled the world.

'We should have brought a camera,' said Mireille. 'I wish we could have a picture of us in front of that. It would be something for you and Jim to show your grandchildren.' She laughed, having no idea that her words were like a knife to Norah's heart.

'I'll take your picture, miss,' the policemen with the camera said, holding it up and giving Mireille a cheeky smile.

'Oooh, come on, Norah,' said Mireille, tugging at her sleeve. A couple of minutes later they were posing arm in arm beside the fuselage.

When he'd taken several snaps of them, the young policeman came over to Mireille. 'I shall have to take down your name and address if I'm to send you the photographs, miss,' he said with a suggestive leer.

Mireille stepped back and gave Norah an anxious glance.

'That's all right,' Norah said brightly. 'Next time you're at the station, you can give them to Inspector Kirkwood. He's my husband.'

His face paled and giving them a mock salute, the policeman backed off.

Norah and Mireille walked to the other side of the field and sat on the grass for a while in the early evening sun.

'I'm thinking of joining one of the services,' said Mireille.

'Good for you,' said Norah. 'If nothing else, this war is giving women opportunities people like my grandmother never had.' She leaned back on her hands with her face towards the sky. 'So what's it to be? Wrens, WAAFs or ATS?'

'Not sure.'

A man exercising his dog raised his hat as he walked past. 'Afternoon, ladies,' he called as he passed by. 'Lovely day.'

'It certainly is,' said Norah.

'Been to see the Jerry plane?'

Norah nodded.

'Good to see one of the buggers on the ground,' said the man, walking on.

They watched him for a minute or two then Norah lay back and closed her eyes. 'It's so peaceful up here,' she said. 'Sometimes it's hard to believe we're at war.'

Mireille, who was chewing a grass stalk, sighed contentedly. 'I can't thank you enough for what you've done for Amélie and me.'

'Think nothing of it,' said Norah. 'That's what friends are for.'

They heard a skylark singing but when they looked around they couldn't see it. 'You know . . .' Norah began hesitantly,

'I know you said you'd rather not, but you and your sister might find it helps to talk about what happened to you both.'

'Some things are better left unsaid,' said Mireille. 'I feel dirty and ashamed.'

'That's just the point,' said Norah, turning to look at her. 'You shouldn't feel like that. It wasn't your fault.'

'I had his child,' Mireille said bitterly.

'It wasn't your fault,' Norah repeated with emphasis.

Mireille looked away.

'I do respect your feelings, Mireille,' Norah said gently, 'but if you say nothing, it will lodge inside you like a canker. I know it's painful, but if you share the experience it might just lose some of its power over you. It will never go away, but this is one choice *you* can make.'

Mireille had her head down. 'It's disgusting. I hated it. Even though I spent ages in the bathroom, I forgot what it was like to feel clean. I still wish I could wash it from my mind.'

'Then talk to Jim and me,' said Norah. 'We already know, and we're not going to tell anybody else.'

In the silence that followed Norah was suddenly afraid that she'd said too much; been too pushy. 'Sorry, sorry.'

'I think Amélie has already said something to Mrs Kirkwood,' said Mireille. 'She likes Mrs Kirkwood.'

Norah took in a breath and nodded. 'I had a feeling there was a bond between them. My mother-in-law changed when your sister came to our house.'

Mireille pulled a dandelion clock from the grass and twirled it in her fingers.

'I shan't mention this again,' Norah promised, 'but if you ever want to talk, you know where to come.'

Mireille nodded and began to blow the dandelion seeds into the air.

'Still 'ere then?' The dog walker was back. His dog, a springer spaniel, bounded towards them, tongue lolling and stumpy tail wagging.

'Oh, he's lovely,' said Norah, sitting up to fondle the animal's ears. 'What's his name?'

'Chummy,' said the man. 'Careful, he sometimes gets over-excited.'

'Hello, Chummy,' Norah cooed. 'You're a lovely little fellow, aren't you?'

'Good job you came up here today,' said the man. 'They'll be taking the plane off the hill tomorrow. Damned thing. I don't suppose it'll be the last. Guided here, it was. I told that young copper but he wouldn't listen. What's the use of saying what you see if people don't listen?'

Norah frowned. 'What do you mean, guided here?'

'Well, it was the light, wasn't it? Plain as day.'

Norah stood to her feet. 'I'm sorry. What light? Where?'

The man pointed over the trees towards the east. 'Somebody over that way shines a light when the planes go over. I reported it to the town hall and they did nothing and I told that policeman, but he took no notice either.'

'But the Heinkel crashed on its way back from a bombing raid, didn't it?' said Mireille with a puzzled frown. 'That's what I heard.'

'It was damaged, granted,' said the man, becoming agitated, 'but somebody was guiding it back towards the French coast. You mark my words. There was a light in the sky the night it came down. I saw it with my own eyes!'

Norah pulled the corners of her mouth down.

'See,' the man said angrily. 'Nobody believes me.'

'No, no,' cried Norah, 'I do believe you. Look, my husband is a policeman. When we get home I'll tell him and he's sure to do something about it.'

But the man was already walking away. 'Come on, Chummy,' he said huffily. 'They'll all wish they'd believed me when the hill is covered in the bloody Hun coming down with parachutes.'

CHAPTER 31

Norah

As they biked back down the hill, Mireille said, 'I wish I could have taken a picture of that policeman's face when you told him that Inspector Kirkwood was your husband.'

They both laughed.

There was an anxious moment when a German plane flew overhead. Norah and Mireille dropped their bikes and looked for a place to shelter but instead of bullets they were showered with leaflets. Mireille picked one up. On one side was a skeletal head with an arm holding a lighted torch over London. She turned it over.

'*Massed, large-scale raids over London,*' she read aloud. '*These raids will be continued until a decisive military goal is reached.*'

Norah snatched it from her hand and screwed it up. 'Don't read that junk,' she said. 'It's only fit for lavatory paper.'

Back home, Mrs Kirkwood had laid the table for supper. While Norah put the bikes away, Mireille went to the outside toilet. 'Ha!' she cried as she came out, 'it looks like you weren't the only one to see the virtues of those leaflets, Norah. There's a whole pile of them by the seat!'

'You'd better take them out,' said Norah, laughing. 'They'll block the cistern.'

When Jim came into the kitchen she told him about the man on High Salvington.

'Did you get his name?'

Norah felt her face flush. 'Sorry, I just didn't think about it.'

Jim raised his eyebrows. 'So what did he look like?'

'Sixty or more, bald head and glasses. Oh, and he has a black springer spaniel called Chummy.'

'All right,' said Jim. 'Leave it with me.'

As they ate their supper, Norah suggested that Amélie should take a few days off to recover from her ordeal. 'Did you bring your ration book?'

Amélie looked horrified. 'I didn't think,' she blurted out.

'Don't worry,' Norah said. 'I can get it sorted. I'll write to Miss Short tonight to make sure she's notified the relevant authorities that you've gone.'

'And you'll have to get a job,' said Mireille.

'I'm sure Ma would have you back like a shot,' said Jim. 'She was very impressed with you.'

'But not yet,' Norah insisted. 'Let's give the girl a chance to recover first.'

Norah was very excited to get a letter to say that the General Post Office engineers would install the telephone sometime during the week. Not only would it help to have a more direct way of contacting her mother and Rene, but it would also help with the market garden. They'd had a bumper year as far as fruit and vegetables went, and the market

282

stall was doing a brisk trade even though they were often interrupted by air raid warnings. Carrots, tomatoes and potatoes were the most popular items, but there were still plenty of peas and other salad ingredients like lettuce and cucumber. Most days, she and Mrs Kirkwood were busy in the kitchen. Nothing was wasted as any damaged vegetable they couldn't sell went into relishes that could be added to stews to give them a bit of a kick in the winter. They pickled the shallots and beetroot and made anything from plum jam to marrow chutney. The pantry shelves, where it was cool and dark, groaned with produce.

'I remember helping you fill the sand box with potatoes last year,' Amélie said when she saw what they were doing. 'And I wrapped up the apples as well.'

'I'll be doing them shortly,' Mrs Kirkwood said with a smile. 'Only a few are ripe enough yet but as soon as they're ready you can help me again this year.'

'Shall I come and help you with the stall?' Amélie offered.

'Maybe next week,' Mrs Kirkwood said kindly. 'Norah is right. You need to get your strength back first.'

Amélie sighed. The dark circles under her eyes were fading but she was still easily tired. 'I was so miserable I couldn't be bothered to eat,' she confided. 'I just wanted to die.'

'You'll never guess what,' said Mrs Kirkwood when she returned home on Wednesday. 'There was a lady in the market selling some of those German leaflets as souvenirs in aid of the Red Cross. She reckoned they'll be worth a bit in years to come.'

Norah lowered herself onto the kitchen chair with a puzzled frown. At the weekend she had written a letter to Miss Short.

I know that now that she's turned sixteen, Amy's current

National Identity Card will be obsolete but it has all her details, including proof of her date of birth, which will make it easier to get the age 16–21 card, Norah had written. *I would also be grateful if you would pass on her ration book as well. You'll be pleased to know that Amy has settled very well and is enjoying being with her sister.*

Miss Short had indeed done what she'd requested but when Norah looked at the child ration card, the name was wrong. This card was made out to Amélie Osborne.

At first Norah tut-tutted angrily. The silly woman had sent the wrong cards, but on reflection, how many other girls in her school had a French name like Amélie? Miss Short called Amy Ffox-Webster when she and Jim went to Demspter. She thought back to when the girls first came to Worthing. Linnet had told her teacher their name was Osborne and their step-father had explained that he had insisted the girls take English-sounding first names when he had adopted them. Surely the card should have said Amy Ffox-Webster. How odd. She turned the card over. There was a piece of paper stuck on the back. *To be known as Amy Ffox-Webster.*

Norah frowned. She remembered that when they'd first arrived, Linnet had let slip that their surname was Osborne but it seemed slightly strange that their father, who was so pedantic about their names, hadn't bothered to change their identity cards.

Putting the card to one side, Norah took Miss Short's reply out of the envelope.

Dear Mrs Kirkwood
   I am so glad Amy has settled down in her new surroundings. It was never my wish to keep the girl against

284

her will. Whereas we may not actually be governed by the courts and the judicial system in this country, the people who send their children here are in places of high office. Amy came to me as a child completely out of control and in need of strict guidance and a firm hand. We at Dempster have done our best to carry out that edict.

I have enclosed Amy's ration book and her National Identity Card, as requested, and I had hoped that this will close the matter. However, I have to tell you that after I informed Mr Ffox-Webster of your visit he was thoroughly alarmed that you had removed his step-daughter. Since then, he has made an impromptu visit to the school and I am under strict instructions not to communicate with you any further. I have, however, decided that just this once and simply for expediency, I must send you this letter with the child's papers. Please do not contact me or the school again. As far as I am concerned, this matter is closed.

Yours sincerely Phyllis Short.

Norah held her breath. So if Ffox-Webster already knew the girls were back in Worthing, why hadn't he been in contact? She chewed her lip anxiously.

'Can I use the kitchen table?'

Mrs Kirkwood's interruption made Norah jump. 'Yes, of course. I was just looking at the post.'

'You look a bit worried,' said Mrs Kirkwood, putting a tray of apples onto the kitchen table. 'Anything I can do to help?'

Norah shook her head. 'No problem,' she said. 'I've got Amélie's ration book,' she added as she held it up.

'Well done,' said Mrs Kirkwood. 'She and I are going to wrap some apples for storage. Have we got any newspaper?'

'There's plenty under the stairs,' said Norah, stuffing the letter into the drawer in the dresser. 'I'm going to the garden in St Matthews Road for a bit.'

As soon as Norah had gone, Amélie was the one who fetched the pile of old newspapers because Mrs Kirkwood had complained that her 'poor old knees couldn't bend that far under the stairs to reach them'.

The two of them sorted through the fruit very carefully. According to Mrs Kirkwood, any bump or bruise, or damage to the skin or blemish on the apple could result in it going bad. 'And one bad apple can quickly make the others rotten,' she said.

As they worked their way through the tray and wrapped the perfect apples in newspaper, they made idle conversation.

'Are you going to marry Mr Steele?' Amélie asked.

'Heavens above, child,' cried Mrs Kirkwood, going a delicate shade of pink, 'whatever made you think that?'

Amélie smiled. 'He's very fond of you.'

Mrs Kirkwood took a deep breath. 'That's quite enough of that, my girl,' she said stiffly. 'I'll have you know I'm far too old for that sort of thing.'

Amélie was still smiling and as their eyes met, Mrs Kirkwood gave her a playful slap on her arm. 'Stop it.'

'Stop what?' said Mireille, coming into the room. She had finished her shift at the telephone exchange at two thirty.

'Nothing,' said Amélie. 'We were just having a bit of fun, that's all.'

'Anyone want a cup of tea?' Mireille asked as she filled the kettle with water.

'I thought you'd never ask,' Mrs Kirkwood joked.

286

Mireille lit the gas under the kettle then came to see what they were doing. 'They look good.'

'If you want one, you can have one of those,' said Mrs Kirkwood, pointing to some apples put to one side. 'You might have to cut out a bruise or look for a maggot inside but they can be eaten now. The ones wrapped in newspaper are all going back in the pantry on the stone floor and we can have them at Christmas.'

'What shall I do with the rest of the newspaper?' Amélie asked.

The kettle had boiled and Mireille made the tea.

'Well, I'm blowed,' she said as she put a cup and saucer in front of Mrs Kirkwood. 'That's his best friend.' She was pointing at a photograph in the ancient newspaper. It was of a tall man, a military type with small staring eyes and wearing a pinstripe suit. He sported a slightly Hitler style moustache.

'Whose friend?' Amélie asked.

Mrs Kirkwood leaned over to see.

'You remember I asked you if you remembered staying with Uncle Ernald and Auntie Cyn?' Mireille went on. 'That's them. We played with their daughter, Vivien.'

Amélie shrugged and shook her head. As she took the pile of newspapers back to the cupboard under the stairs, Ivan came in the door in his stockinged feet. 'I saw you biking up the path. Any chance of a cuppa?'

Mireille reached for another cup and saucer. 'Sit down,' she said, 'and I'll get you one.'

Not one of them had noticed how pale Mrs Kirkwood's face had become.

CHAPTER 32

Amélie

By the end of the week, Amélie was feeling a lot more relaxed and she was looking a lot better. She had begun taking the dogs for a walk every day and their walks grew longer and longer as she built up her strength. On Thursday, while Mireille was still in the bathroom, Amélie came to say goodnight to the others who were still sitting at the kitchen table.

'I've come to tell you I've got a job.'

'A job!' cried Norah.

'It's in the Stoke Abbott Road Clinic,' Amélie went on, 'and I start on Monday.'

'What sort of job?' Norah began. 'If it's cleaning . . .'

'No, it's not cleaning.' Amélie chuckled. 'I shall be a receptionist.'

'Well done you,' said Jim, his face wreathed in a smile.

'Yes, well done,' said Ivan.

The two older women were taken by surprise. 'A trainee receptionist,' Mrs Kirkwood said proudly.

Amélie shook her head. 'Not even that,' she said. 'I

suppose I've got one thing to be grateful for. Miss Short was hot on us girls learning shorthand and typing and she taught us how to create a decent filing system. The clinic was looking for a young girl to train up and I was the only one who already had the qualifications.'

'That's amazing, dear,' said Mrs Kirkwood. 'I'm so proud of you.'

Norah was still taken aback. 'Are you sure you're ready? I mean, you still don't look very strong.'

'Don't fuss, Norah,' said Jim. 'I'm sure the girl knows what she's doing.'

'I'll be fine,' Amélie insisted. 'And I want to pay my way.'

Mireille came out of the bathroom and the two girls said their goodnights.

'Night, loves,' said Jim.

As the girls left the room, Norah noticed Mrs Kirkwood's hand was trembling. 'Don't worry. Jim's right and I get the feeling she's going to be all right.'

'It's not that,' said Mrs Kirkwood. She gave them all an anxious look.

'Then what is it?' said Norah. Now she was worried.

'I've got something to show you. Wait here.'

A couple of minutes later she laid the pile of newspapers on the table and began shuffling through them. 'When Amélie was packing these up, Mireille noticed something.' Mrs Kirkwood came to one paper and pointed at a picture of a man with staring eyes. 'She said he was Ffox-Webster's best friend.'

The three of them leaned over the newspaper to look.

Norah took in her breath noisily.

'Good God!' cried Jim. 'Are you sure?'

Mrs Kirkwood nodded. 'She called him Uncle Ern but

she talked about Auntie Cyn and playing with their daughter Vivien.'

'Bloody hell,' Ivan spluttered. 'That's Oswald Mosley.'

Jago Ffox-Webster stood in front of the portrait and raised his glass in salute. As he sipped his drink he heard a footfall behind him and Hedges said, 'All gone to plan, sir?'

Jago spun round. Damn the man. He didn't like the way his chauffeur crept up behind him like that but once he'd gathered his wits he said, 'Capital, Hedges. In fact, you can join me in a small celebration.'

'Thank you very much, sir,' said Hedges, helping himself to a generous whiskey.

Jago lifted his glass again. 'To the cause.'

'To the cause,' Hedges repeated and they drank a toast.

'Eleven airfields,' said Ffox-Webster with a self-satisfied grin. 'Five here in the south and the rest up country. That should make the government sit up and take notice.'

'Very good, sir,' said Hedges, feeling the amber liquid slide down his gullet with a warm glow. This was the best whiskey he'd ever tasted. It must have cost an arm and a leg. Shame he wasn't likely to be able to sample it again.

His employer turned to the portrait on the wall and raised his glass once more.

'What now, sir?'

Ffox-Webster turned to face him. 'We lie low. We don't want to draw attention to ourselves, do we?'

'What about the other business, sir?'

'What other business?' Ffox-Webster snapped.

'You know. The girls.'

'Oh that,' said Ffox-Webster with a hollow laugh. 'I don't think Miss Short will make any waves. Not after our "little chat".' He drew quotation marks in the air. 'She's got her money, or at least as much as I intend to give her, and she knows if she crosses me again, I'll drop her in it.'

'But what if that copper starts sniffing around?' said Hedges.

His employer frowned, clearly irritated. 'Hedges, you forget I'm a powerful man. I have friends in high places.' He lowered himself into the leather chair and looking slightly more thoughtful added, 'But perhaps you have a point. Maybe I should have a little word with his superiors. Give him something else to worry about.'

The GPO had been in the street preparing for Norah and Jim's telephone. It hadn't been the easiest of jobs, because the engineers had to erect another telegraph pole outside their house, but at last the telephone was fully installed.

'Now that we've got something to celebrate,' Norah said as the last of the engineers were leaving, 'let's have a bit of a party.'

It was impromptu but several of their neighbours and some of the allotment people were happy to join in, too. Penny biked down from Broadwater and Norah manged to get hold of Miss Cummings, the teacher from Heene Road School. Everybody promised to contribute something so with an endless supply of tea, they feasted on fish paste sandwiches, rock buns and carrot cake. The evening was warm and sunny so they were able to spend most of the time outside. Jim and a couple of the men pushed the piano to the door nobody used and opened it. Norah and Mrs Kirkwood took turns to play so that, despite the ever-present worry that the Luftwaffe might suddenly reappear, for a few precious moments, a good time was had by all.

As they cleared up before the blackout, Jim leaned over

the chair he was carrying and gave Norah a kiss. 'That was a real tonic, love,' he said. 'You did us proud.'

'It was fun, wasn't it?' she said with a grin.

'Oh, by the way,' he continued. 'I keep forgetting to tell you. That dog walker on High Salvington and the light in the sky; the boys from MI5 are on to it.'

'I told him you'd get it sorted,' Norah said proudly. 'Mireille will be pleased.'

She found Mireille about ten minutes later. She was sitting on an upturned bucket on the edge of the nursery garden and she didn't look happy.

'What's wrong?' said Norah, placing her hand on her back.

Mireille sighed deeply. 'I can't stop thinking about Linnet,' she said. 'Tomorrow is her tenth birthday. We should all be together. Where could he have taken her? I was ten when he . . .' Her voice froze as a lone tear trickled down her face. 'I can't bear the thought that . . .'

They were interrupted by a small sound behind them and Mrs Kirkwood moved to slip her arm around Amélie's shoulders as she began to cry.

With a bit of persuasion, the two girls made their way to the sitting room. Amélie threw herself onto the sofa and Mireille sat beside her with her arm around her shoulder. Norah lowered herself onto one of the armchairs while Mrs Kirkwood shooed Ivan back out into the kitchen and closed the door behind them.

Norah waited for a few minutes and when Amélie's tears had subsided she said quietly, 'Shall we leave you to it? Do you want us to go?'

Mireille shook her head. 'You were right,' she said brokenly. 'This is eating us alive. We have to talk.'

'Can I get Jim?' Norah asked.

Mireille looked up sharply.

'I know you told me you didn't want the world to know what happened to you but Jim is a very experienced policeman.'

'This is a family affair,' Mireille said stoutly.

'With all due respect,' Norah said gently, 'you don't know that. Jim says men like Ffox-Webster seldom do something like this only once.'

Mireille hesitated.

Norah chewed her bottom lip before ploughing on. 'I've made Jim promise that he will never let your names be made public. All we want to do is stop Ffox-Webster from hurting anyone else.'

Amélie shuddered. 'Let them do it, Mireille.'

'You never know,' Norah said encouragingly, 'but you might even say something which could help us find Linnet. We know from my mother's investigations that there is no one else living at the London flat, so where is she?'

When Mireille nodded, albeit reluctantly, Norah rose to her feet. A couple of minutes later she came back into the room with Jim.

'I'm going to take some notes,' he said once he'd sat down. 'I promise I won't do anything with what you say unless you give me permission, but you might decide at some later date that you want to see your step-father in court. What you say now is still fresh in your mind and could be incredibly helpful later on.'

Norah's heart surged with love for this man. His voice was authoritative and yet quiet and very gentle; almost fatherly.

She swallowed hard. 'I think it will also help you both

to come to terms with what's happened to you,' she added. How her heart went out to these two beautiful girls. They looked as if they were in an agony of soul, and they probably were. They had both been robbed of so much, especially their innocence and their childhood.

In the silence that followed, they all became conscious of the ticking clock on the mantelpiece over the fireplace.

'For me, it started when I was ten,' said Mireille, staring down at her own hands in her lap. 'He asked me if I would like to have my room decorated.'

Amélie sat up straight and blew her nose. 'That's how it started for me, too.'

'Can I hear your stories one at a time?' Jim suggested.

Amélie nodded. 'Sorry.'

'No, no, it's fine,' said Jim. 'It just makes it a little easier, that's all.'

Mireille's story was difficult to listen to. What began with the joy of choosing wallpaper and new furniture led to a violation of the worst kind and ended sometime later in her pregnancy. 'He was so angry with me,' she said through her tears. 'He said it was all my fault. He called me a slut and a tart. I couldn't believe it and when I told him I never wanted to do it in the first place, he spat in my face.'

Norah pursed her lips to stop herself crying out in protest. How could any man do that? Mireille was still only fourteen at the time. What sort of a monster puts a child through that sort of trauma?

'Did you not have any female relatives you could talk to?' Jim asked.

Mireille shook her head.

Jim turned to Amélie. 'When my inspector first contacted your step-father about you and Linnet,' Jim said cautiously, 'he said he wasn't too worried because he thought you were staying with your aunt.'

Amelie frowned. 'What aunt? We don't have any relatives in this country.'

Jim turned back to Mireille. 'Earlier on you mentioned the daily woman,' he said, looking back at his notes. 'Did she know?'

Again, Mireille shook her head. 'He kept saying this was our special secret. He said if I told Mrs Scott he'd sack her and have me sent me away.'

'So, when he found out you were pregnant,' Jim continued, 'what did he do then?'

'He took me to a woman living in the country. I was to stay with her until the baby was due and then I was to go into a mother and baby home.'

Norah noticed that the two girls were holding hands very tightly.

'Wasn't it possible to run away?'

'Looking back,' said Mireille, with a sigh, 'I suppose I could have done, but where would I go? I didn't know anybody. I had nowhere to go and he'd already told the woman I was a bad girl. "*Out of control*", was what he said.'

'What about Mrs Scott?' said Jim. 'Did she know where you were?'

Mireille shook her head. 'When he left me there, he said if I so much as wrote to her, to anybody, he'd get me put in prison and I believed him.'

You and me both, Norah thought acidly.

There was a soft knock at the door and Mrs Kirkwood came in with a tray of tea. She didn't speak but Norah saw a heart-wrenching look pass between her and Amélie.

'All right?' Mrs Kirkwood mouthed and Amélie nodded.

'Do you want Mrs Kirkwood to stay?' Jim asked.

Amélie nodded again. Norah's eyebrows shot up. So that was why they had become so close. Amélie must have confided in her mother-in-law and far from being the unfeeling old bag Norah had always thought she was, Mrs Kirkwood had honoured that confidence. The two girls shifted up and Mrs Kirkwood wedged herself onto the sofa next to Amélie and grabbed her hand.

It was incredible how similar their stories were. The same room redecoration; the same days of fun choosing wallpaper and paint; Amélie talked of getting a new and bigger bed and then the terrifying moment when he came into her room for that first time.

'When I said I didn't like it, he told me it was my duty to take *Maman*'s place,' said Amélie. 'He said all little girls did this and this was how I should show him I loved him.' She took in a shuddering breath. 'But I didn't love him. I hated him then and I HATE him now!'

Mrs Kirkwood looked aghast. 'Oh my dear, you should have told me *everything*. If we had known what he was doing to you, we never would have let him take you away.'

And with that, Amélie burst into tears.

As she wept, Amélie tipped her head and leaned on Mrs Kirkwood's chest. 'Shh, shh. There, there,' the old woman soothed.

Jim listened impassively and wrote it all down. Mrs Kirkwood held Amélie close to her chest with a pained expression on her face. As she watched them through her own tears, Norah knew it was a moment she would never ever forget. Probably none of them would. Mrs Kirkwood had mellowed over the past few months and Norah realised that she had grown more comfortable in her company, but now, as she watched her comfort Amélie, she experienced a newfound respect. Another thought crossed her mind. When had Mrs Kirkwood stopped being bitter all the time? What had made her so super critical in the first place? Clearly Amélie's situation, even though none of them had known the half of it, had touched a chord in her mother-in-law, but it was more than that. Norah rose to her feet. She wasn't needed anymore. The girls were being comforted, Jim had finished his writing, and the dogs needed feeding.

As she left the room, Jim put his notepad to one side. 'You've both been very brave,' he told them as he stood to leave. 'One day; one day . . .' he added with a sympathetic smile and left the room.

The two girls blew their noses and wiped their eyes. Amélie looked up at Mrs Kirkwood. 'Thank you, *grand-mère*,' she whispered. 'You gave me the courage.'

'Not at all, my dear,' said Mrs Kirkwood. 'You did that all by yourself.'

'Jim and Norah are so kind,' Mireille remarked. 'No one else has ever done for us what they have done.'

Mrs Kirkwood smiled.

'It's almost as if they know exactly how we feel,' said Amélie.

'Perhaps they do – in part.' They both turned to Mrs Kirkwood. 'My son and daughter-in-law have their own heartache,' she began with a sigh.

'Oh?'

Mrs Kirkwood glanced at the door to make sure that Jim was out of earshot. 'They want to adopt a baby,' she said confidentially. 'In fact, they had one all lined up, but then, because Norah went to see you, Amélie, in the Home, and then wrote to you, someone, who shall remain nameless, reported them to the agency as unsuitable parents.'

Amélie took in her breath. 'What happened?'

Mrs Kirkwood shrugged. 'Their baby was adopted by somebody else.'

Amélie looked at her in horror.

'*Mon Dieu!*' cried Mireille.

CHAPTER 33

Norah

Sunday was such a lovely afternoon that the people in Clifton Road stood by their gates chatting to their neighbours. As soon as the air raid warning came, everyone scattered, leaving the road empty except for part-time firemen, wardens, special police officers and ambulance men in steel hats as they ran or biked to their various rendezvous places.

Everybody was already tired. After a hard day's work, spending half the night fire-watching, attending drill practice or first aid classes was beginning to take its toll on the volunteers. At times, Jim was snappy and bad-tempered. He was always quick to apologise but a show of temper was uncharacteristic of him.

Things were becoming more and more desperate. Norah had reached the point where she busied herself in the kitchen rather than listen to the news on the wireless but there was no getting away from it.

This time, when the siren went off, it didn't take long before they heard the distant thud, thud of explosions. Vibrations shook the windowpanes as they made a dash for cover. Nobody voiced it but they were all thinking the same thing. Last week Lancing had been bombed. Maybe today it would be Worthing's turn.

'This is the seventeenth air raid warning,' Mrs Kirkwood complained as they all scrambled into the Anderson Shelter.

'Sounds like some poor devil is getting a pasting this time,' Ivan remarked.

'And not too far away,' Mireille said darkly.

'I hope Rene's all right,' Norah said anxiously.

As she walked back to her hangar after lunch, Rene looked up at the sky. It was a beautiful day. It was such a shame that she couldn't have had the day off but things were getting pretty desperate now. Although people had become used to the drone of aircraft high above them, everything had moved up another gear since July. The Battle of Britain was fully under way.

Although the WAAFs were not allowed to mix socially while on duty, Rene had managed to sit near Dan and they'd shared a little conversation across the gangway between their tables. Every time she saw him her heart would skip a beat and she wondered if she could be in love. Was this how it felt? She had been out with men before but Dan was the only one who made her feel this way. Next time she got leave, she would take him to meet Norah and her parents. Perhaps she should write to Norah tonight and ask her to set it up. It seemed foolhardy to wait; you never knew what was just around the corner. After the bombing of the airfield at Tangmere just up the road a couple of days ago, she was worried that Ford might suffer the same fate.

Dan did his best to put her mind at rest. 'No need to

worry, freckle-face,' he'd said as they'd cuddled together in the darkness behind her billet the night before. 'Tangmere is a proper airfield. We're only a training base. Any German worth his salt would know that. They're out to damage as many aircraft on the ground as they can. They won't be bothered with the likes of us.'

Of the hundreds of Stuka dive bombers that crossed the Channel that day, seventy or more had made for Tangmere. When the dust finally settled twenty minutes later, fourteen ground crew and six civilians had been killed but the aircraft the Jerries were aiming for had remained intact. The reason was simple. Of the thirty-six Hurricanes on the base, only seven had been on the ground. The rest were already in the skies, doing their best to head off the attack.

Dan had kissed her again and again until their mouths were dry. 'Oh, Rene, you're so lovely I could eat you.' She'd laughed. Dan always made her laugh.

She spotted him walking across the field, back to the gun position on the edge of the perimeter, and willed him to turn and wave but he didn't. Never mind. They were meeting up tonight for a drink in the local pub. Only six hours to go. She could hardly wait.

Jim was on duty, which made one less to squeeze in, but still the shelter at The Lilacs was cramped with everybody including the terrified dogs inside. Once Norah had closed the door, Amélie read aloud from a book called *The World's Greatest Detective Stories* to take their minds off things. By the time the all clear came at half past two, they were partway through Dorothy L. Sayers *The Inspiration of Mr Budd*.

'You should be on the wireless,' Norah remarked as they

emerged into the sparkling sunlight. 'You've got a lovely speaking voice.'

Rene was partway across the field when she heard them coming. The hum of approaching engines became a scream as the JU 87B dive bombers hurtled out of the clear blue sky. The sirens began to wail and someone shouted, 'Take cover, take cover.' They were heading straight towards her. Rene knew she was too far from the hangar to get there but she had just passed a shallow dugout where the men kept stores. She ran back towards the straw bales and camouflage netting which protected it. Already the ground beneath her feet was shaking as the bombs rained down. Only blind panic drove her on. Oh God, I don't want to die. Don't let me die . . .

As she flung herself behind the bales, she landed breathlessly into the arms of a man who pulled her further into the dugout. They lay there staring up through the camouflage netting, not daring to speak, the only sound being their ragged, panic-stricken breath. Rene was trembling like a leaf. Then she heard him say, 'Bloody hell. They're coming back,' and she saw the machine gun bullets ripping a path along the grass towards them.

Lunch at The Lilacs had been ruined. The bit of brisket Norah put in the oven was burnt to a crisp and the potatoes had boiled dry and stuck to the pan in a mushy mess. Fortunately, the shilling had run out in the gas meter before the pan caught fire, so apart from burn on the bottom of the saucepan, no lasting damage was done.

'At least I didn't burn the house down,' Norah remarked stoically.

There was no other meat available so their Sunday lunch became a vegetable only affair, but funnily enough, nobody minded. They finished eating at about four o'clock and after doing the washing-up, Norah suggested going for a walk. Mrs Kirkwood and Ivan preferred to rest but Mireille and Amélie were up for it.

'Are you feeling any better?' Norah asked Amélie as they headed down Heene Road towards the sea.

'Yes and no,' said Amélie. 'I'm glad you persuaded us to talk but I still have nightmares and the thought of what he did makes my stomach turn.'

'Well, I refuse to let him carry on ruining my life,' said Mireille. 'Norah, I think I want to take Jim up on his suggestion. I don't think I could ever bring myself to stand up in court, but let's put on record what he did to us . . .' She faltered and then corrected herself. '. . . what he did to me.'

Amélie glanced at her sister. 'No one will believe it,' she said cautiously.

'Maybe not,' said Mireille, 'but I won't be made to feel ashamed anymore. Norah is right. I am not to blame. I was a child. More than that, I was a child grieving for her mother. He took advantage of me. The guilt rests on his shoulders, not mine.' Her voice had risen. 'And you must stop thinking you're to blame for what happened to you. It wasn't your fault either!'

'You've made me feel awful now,' said Amélie.

'Oh, no, darling, no,' Mireille cried. 'I never intended that. It's just that now that all this is finally out in the open, we need to take control. I'm doing this for myself. You must do what you think is right for you. Whatever you decide, no one will think any the less of you.' She slipped her arm

303

through her sister's and hugged her close. 'Thank you, Norah.'

'Why thank me?' Norah said with a puzzled expression.

Mireille pushed her arm through Norah's as well. 'We never would have got this far without you. You've given us our lives back. From now on it's up to us what we do with them, isn't it?'

There were very few people out and about but the three of them were glad to see the sea, even if the beach was covered in barbed wire. Further along, they spotted a gull that had somehow got its wing snagged in the wire. It was hanging upside down, quite dead.

'Poor thing,' Mireille said sadly. 'How absolutely bloody awful. Oh, where will it all end?'

'When I was at school,' Norah began, 'we had to find a poet and learn some of his verses. I chose Mother Julian of Norwich. "*It was necessary that there should be sin; but all shall be well, and all shall be well, and all manner of thing shall be well*,"' she quoted. The girls stared at her for a second. Norah smiled. 'There will be a brighter tomorrow. Promise.'

They walked in silence for a while then Norah said, 'Can I ask you something?' The girls nodded. 'When you were wrapping apples, you recognised someone in the newspaper. Your Uncle Ernald.'

'Yes,' said Mireille. 'Our step-father really admired him. They were the best of friends. He said he would be Prime Minister one day.'

'What else do you remember about him?' Norah asked.

'I remember him shouting at me once, when he caught me in my step-father's study in the London house,' said Mireille.

Amélie caught her breath. 'We were never allowed in there.'

304

'I know,' said Mireille, 'but there was this beautiful ballerina statue by the drinks cabinet. I wanted to pick it up; just to look at it, that's all. I went to grab hold of it and all hell broke loose. He could be quite scary when he was angry.'

Amélie smiled. 'It was funny seeing him in the paper after all this time.'

'I didn't actually read the article,' Mireille said.

'He was being arrested,' said Norah.

The sisters gasped. 'Arrested?' said Mireille. 'What for?'

'I don't think you realise that your "uncle" is Oswald Mosley,' said Norah, 'the leader of the British Union of Fascists.'

The two girls looked completely blank.

'He's a friend of Adolf Hitler,' Norah said carefully. 'At one time he was very popular but these days he's considered a danger to the whole country. He wants us to capitulate.'

'And you're suggesting that our step-father might feel the same?' said Mireille.

'Probably,' said Norah with a slight shrug. 'You did say he was Mosley's best friend.'

Now that the planes had gone, the field at Ford was a frenzy of activity. The air was filled with an acrid smell of cordite, smoke and burning. An ambulance raced towards the perimeter and the gun placement but as the smoke cleared, the crew realised to their horror it wasn't there anymore.

'No sign of the gunner,' the driver said, staring at the huge crater.

'Blown to bloody bits,' said his companion. There was a moment of silence, then he added, 'Sill, he wouldn't have felt a thing.'

*

305

Norah and the girls arrived back home a couple of hours later. They'd stopped off to chat with a few neighbours and then old Mrs Drake had offered them a cup of tea. As they walked through the back door, Mrs Kirkwood waved a telegram at Norah. 'I'm sorry,' she said, 'but the post boy said Mrs Kirkwood so I took it but as soon as I read it, I realised that it was meant for you.'

Norah frowned anxiously. 'Oh God, is it my mother?'

Mrs Kirkwood shook her head.

Norah looked down at the words and her blood ran cold.

Ford airfield bombed stop Several killed and many injuries stop Irene Carson in Arundel Hospital.

CHAPTER 34

Norah

The scramble to get to Arundel Cottage Hospital as quickly as possible was desperate. Norah was running down the road towards the station within minutes of getting the telegram.

'Telephone my parents,' she called over her shoulder to Mrs Kirkwood who stood by the gate. 'Tell them I'll ring this evening.'

Fortunately, a woman on the train, who had noticed that Norah was visibly upset, offered her a lift when they both stepped onto the platform at Ford.

The hospital was just off the main road, behind a bank of trees. Built less than ten years before on land gifted by the Duke of Norfolk who owned Arundel Castle, it was modern and up to date.

When she got inside the receptionist asked her to wait. Several visitors were waiting for the wards to open and about ten minutes later, a ward sister came into the corridor to usher them in. Norah was left anxiously fidgeting with her handbag and watching the clock. After a few minutes she leaned back and closed her eyes in prayer.

'Miss Carson?' said a voice.

Norah opened her eyes to see a doctor in a white coat, a stethoscope around his neck, standing in front of her. He looked tired. There were dark circles under his eyes. 'Mrs Kirkwood,' Norah corrected. 'I was Carson, but I'm married now.'

'I beg your pardon,' said the doctor. 'I was told Miss Carson's sister was waiting and I naturally assumed . . .' His voice trailed.

'How is she?' Norah blurted out. 'How is Rene?'

As soon as he lowered himself wearily onto the seat next to her, Norah feared the worst. Her heart was already beating much too fast and her mouth was dry.

'She's fine,' he began cautiously. 'She's had an operation, which was successful, but there has been a lot of muscle damage to her foot. She will have to undertake special exercises for some time, but even then I'm afraid she will most likely walk with a limp.'

Norah's hand trembled over her mouth. Oh, poor Rene, and she so loved dancing. 'What happened?'

'From what I can gather, she was sheltering in a dugout when she was hit by shrapnel. It entered her foot here.' He indicated the area on his own foot with the aid of his fountain pen. 'It's a tricky place. So close to the ankle bones, you see.'

Norah nodded dully. 'Can I see her?'

'I don't see why not,' said the doctor, 'seeing as how you've come so quickly.' He rose to his feet. 'I'll clear it with the nurses, but I don't think you'll get much sense out of your sister. She's not long been out of theatre and is still a bit woozy.'

'Thank you, doctor,' Norah said gratefully, and they shook

hands. 'My telegram said there were other injured people,' she added.

The doctor nodded. 'Twenty-eight killed,' he said grimly, 'and many more injured. That's why she's here. After the raid on Tangmere, the Chichester and Littlehampton hospitals are overrun with casualties.' He hesitated. 'I . . . I'm sorry. I shouldn't have told you all that. Just be grateful your sister will be all right eventually.'

Norah gave him a smile. 'I am,' she said, 'and thank you for all you've done.'

He nodded briefly and walked away.

She didn't have to wait long before the efficient-looking ward sister came towards her. 'Mrs Kirkwood?' she said brusquely. 'If you would like to come this way. Your sister is awake, but she hasn't fully come round yet. I would be grateful if you wouldn't say anything to her about her injury. I don't want her unduly upset.'

Rene was in a side room. She looked so small and vulnerable under the white sheet and cover. There was a large cage over her legs. She moaned slightly as Norah came towards her.

'Hello, darling.'

Rene did her best to focus her eyes and as she did, they filled with tears.

'Oh, Norah . . .' she began.

'Don't worry,' Norah said quickly. 'The doctor's just told me. It won't be long before you're as right as ninepence.'

Rene turned her head away from her. 'I wish I was dead.'

'No, no,' Norah said, alarmed. 'I promise. They've said you'll be absolutely fine.'

'You don't understand,' said Rene, her voice breaking. 'I

don't want to be all right. Not without him. Not without Dan. Norah, my Dan is dead.'

Back home, after she'd told everybody about Rene, Norah and Jim went outside to be alone. She sank into Jim's arms and silently wept. It was a relief to know that Rene would survive and that her injuries, although serious, were not life threatening, but it was terrible to hear her wishing herself dead. Norah hadn't mentioned that to the others but she told Jim.

Her husband was concerned and understanding. 'It's only the shock making her talk like that,' Jim said into Norah's hair. He kissed the top of her head and tightened his arms around her. 'As soon as she's well enough, we'll have her here. I'm sure a bit of your home cooking and the distraction of the dogs will help to get her thinking straight again.'

Norah leaned back and blew her nose. 'If that wasn't bad enough, when I left the ward the sister called me to her desk and tore me off a strip. She'd seen Rene crying and she thought I'd told Rene something bad about her foot.'

Jim stroked her hair. 'Oh dear,' he said, but at the same time, he had just the ghost of a smile on his lips.

'It's all right for you,' Norah complained petulantly. There was a moment's silence as they looked at each other and then they both laughed.

Jim kissed his wife's cheek. 'We heard about the bombing raid on the six o'clock news on the wireless. They didn't name the airfield, of course, they only said "somewhere on the South Coast", but you'd better ring your mother with an update before she goes out of her mind with worry.'

*

310

A couple of days later, Rene lay on her back staring at the ceiling. A nurse with a bedpan came through the doors and went to a patient further down the room, drawing the squeaky wheeled screens around the bed, but otherwise it was quiet on the ward. She could hear low whispers as the nurse helped the patient onto the bedpan. Rene's mind drifted back to the day before . . . or was it the day before that? What day was it now? How long had she been here? She sighed. The terrible moment when she'd been so sure she was going to die she'd been saved by that ground-crew man who had rolled on top of her. She'd have to make sure she sought him out and thanked him.

A ghastly feeling of loss washed over her again, as if someone had ripped her heart from her chest. Norah kept telling her everything was going to be all right but she didn't want to hear it. Dan, her handsome, witty, fun-loving Dan, was dead.

There were visitors waiting on the other side of the swing doors and Rene caught a glimpse of Norah with a bunch of flowers. She closed her eyes with a sigh. It was nice of her to come all this way but she didn't really want to talk.

The visiting hour always seemed endless. Norah chatted about the girls, Jim and his promotion, Mrs Cow-bags and Ivan, anything and everything, but Rene couldn't care less about any of it. Why should Mrs Cow-bags have a man friend when Dan was dead? Love belonged to the young not the old and decrepit. Rene knew she was being cruel and unreasonable but she couldn't help it.

It was a great relief to them both when the ward sister came in with the hand bell and everyone had to leave.

'I'll come again tomorrow, darling,' said Norah helplessly as she bent to give her sister a peck on the cheek.

Rene nodded dully and turned her face to the wall.

As Norah went through the big double doors, she crashed against a tall man on crutches. 'Oh, sorry, sorry,' she said as he wobbled.

'Is the visiting time over?' he asked breathlessly. His head was bandaged and his face was covered in scratches and blast marks.

'I'm afraid so,' said Norah.

'Bugger it,' he cursed.

Norah had seen the ward sister going into the sluice room so she said, 'You could chance it. Nobody's looking.'

The man nodded with a conspiratorial grin and Norah held the door as he blundered on. To her surprise he headed towards Rene's bed.

'Hello, freckle-face,' she heard him say.

Rene didn't move but Norah noticed she'd dropped her scarf on the floor. She went back to pick it up.

'How are you?' The man's crutch clattered to the floor as he pulled the chair around to sit on it. 'I was so scared. I thought I'd lost you.'

Norah reached for her scarf and hesitated. Could this be . . .? No, it couldn't be, could it? Rene said Dan was dead . . . but on the other hand, he was very tall. Didn't she once say they called him Tree-top?

'You do know that dugout you dived into was an arms dump?' he went on. 'One bit of shrapnel, one bullet in that lot and you'd have gone up like a bloody rocket.'

Rene turned over and Norah heard her gasp. 'Dan! Is it really you? I'm not imagining it.'

'No, freckle-face.' He chuckled. 'You're not. It's me all right. You don't think Jerry could get ol' Dan, do you?'

'But how?' she blurted out.

Yes, how, thought Norah.

312

'They came before I had time to get into position,' he said. 'Ray Lucardo and me, we rolled into the perimeter ditch. For that split second, nobody was on the gun.'

Norah pushed her scarf into her pocket. A nurse came up behind them. 'Visiting time is over.' Norah turned to leave.

'Aw, go on, nurse,' said Dan, grabbing his fallen crutch. 'Give a wounded man a break.'

The nurse looked around cautiously. 'Five minutes,' she whispered. 'Your wife needs to sleep.'

Norah caught her breath.

'Thanks, nurse,' said Dan, lowering himself back down onto the chair. He and Rene held hands. 'Your wife?' Rene said teasingly.

'Soon will be, I hope,' he said.

Norah, her hand on the door, stopped and smiled.

'I don't know about that,' Rene teased. 'I'd need to be asked first.'

She saw Dan glance around then lean forward. 'Rene Carson, will you marry me?'

'Well . . .' Rene teased.

'You'll have to be quick,' he said. 'Everybody's out to get me. If it isn't Hitler, it's some crazy yellow peril almost knocking me off my feet by the ward doors.'

Norah froze.

'What d'you mean?' Rene said incredulously.

'I'm not used to hopping around on one leg,' Dan explained, 'and this woman in a yellow flowery dress burst through the door and I almost went over.'

Rene looked up and saw Norah in the doorway. 'Sorry,' Norah mouthed.

Rene laughed aloud. 'You'll have to get used to her and all,' she said with a big grin. 'That was my sister.'

CHAPTER 35

Norah

As Norah walked back into the house the telephone was ringing. 'I'll get it.'

She reached for the receiver convinced it must be her mother. 'Hello, Mum.'

A man's voice answered. 'Mrs Kirkwood?'

'Yes.' His voice was vaguely familiar but Norah couldn't quite place it.

'Mrs Norah Kirkwood?'

'Yes,' she said tetchily. 'Who is this? What do you want?' A sudden thought crossed her mind and she added, 'Oh Lord. Is this the hospital? Has something happened to my sister?'

'I thought I made it quite clear that I didn't want you interfering in my family affairs again,' he hissed.

Norah caught her breath. Now she knew who it was. Ffox-Webster! She felt herself going weak at the knees.

'You went to Dempster,' he continued, 'even though I expressly told you not to. You deliberately took Amy out of the school.'

314

Norah bristled. He was talking to her as if she was a two-year-old.

'You had no right to do that, you mad witch.'

What did he say? What did he call her? 'How did you get hold of this number?' Norah said breathlessly.

'Oh, I can do a lot of things, Mrs Kirkwood.' He sounded menacing. 'Did you ever manage to adopt that baby?'

Norah's throat seized up. 'What's it to do with you?'

She heard him chuckle. 'I shall tell you in words of one syllable. Do. Not. Cross. Me. Again.' He spoke with emphasis, as if she were a naughty child. 'When I tell you to stay away, you do as I say. Do I make myself clear?'

Norah was trembling. 'Are you threatening me?' she said, willing her voice to sound strong and in control.

'And don't believe a word those lying bitches tell you.'

Norah's jaw dropped. That he should talk this way about his own daughters was unbelievable.

'And if I find out that you are still trying to find my youngest daughter . . . well, your dear husband can kiss his promotion goodbye, for a start.'

Norah almost dropped the phone. 'You can't talk to me like that,' she said indignantly. 'How dare you.'

'Who's that?' said Jim, coming up behind her.

'Oh I think I can, Mrs Kirkwood,' Ffox-Webster continued. 'Just remember this; stay away from Lillian.'

Jim snatched the phone from her hand. 'Ffox-Webster?' he began, but at the sound of his voice, the phone went dead.

Jim turned to Norah and he watched the blood draining from her face. 'What did he say? Was he threatening you?'

'He told me not to look for Lillian,' she said. 'He was annoyed that we've got Amélie. He didn't mention Mireille by name but he knows she's here, too.'

315

'I don't understand,' Jim said with a frown. 'How did he get this number?'

'Oh, Jim, he said you could kiss your promotion goodbye.'

Jim gave a hollow laugh. 'He's just trying to cover his tracks. He thinks that by threatening us he can stop the truth coming out.'

'But the girls haven't said anything,' said Norah.

'Yes, but he doesn't know that, does he?' Jim said sourly. 'I wish they would speak up and then we can put the blighter where he belongs.'

'Oh, darling,' Norah cried, 'what girl in this day and age is going to risk her reputation in a court of law? Even if he was convicted, she'd be ruined.'

Jim shook his head. 'You're right but it's damned frustrating.' He slipped his arm around Norah's waist. 'Are you all right now? You were as white as a sheet when I came in.'

She snuggled into him. 'Yes. It was just a shock, that's all.'

'Well, if he rings again, tell me,' Jim said firmly. 'Plummy bastard.'

Norah pulled back. 'I will, and now I'd better ring Mum.'

Elsie was relieved when Norah telephoned and updated her on Rene's progress. She had hoped for the best and dreaded the worst.

'I don't think she understands how badly injured she is,' said Norah.

'Any idea when she's coming out of hospital?' Elsie asked.

'Not sure, Mum. I would think they'd keep her in for another week at least.'

'Shall I come down on the train?'

'It's up to you, Mum. I can put you up in the alcove we used when we had Granny's funeral. All the other rooms are filled.'

'Perhaps we'll leave it until she comes out then,' said Elsie. 'Dad and I could come for the day.'

'I think that would be a better idea,' Norah agreed. She was sorely tempted to tell her mother about Dan but decided that was Rene's news. 'How are you both? Have you had any trouble with the bombings?'

'There's been a few explosions but you seem to be getting the worst of it down on the South Coast at the moment,' said Elsie. 'By the way, I've managed to track down the girls' old daily woman. Mrs Scott. She's in prison.'

'Prison!' Norah gasped. 'Whatever for?'

'It seems she was convicted of soliciting,' said Elsie.

'You're kidding,' Norah cried. 'Are you sure? I would have thought she was a bit old for that sort of thing. Amélie used to play with her daughter.'

There was a silence and then her mother said, 'I was going to tell you to forget all about it but now you've made me think there may be more to it. Tell you what, I'll go and see her when she gets out in a couple of days, but I won't say anything about the girls. If I can get her to open up, we might learn something.'

'Okay, Mum,' said Norah, 'but be careful. Get her to meet you in a public place and don't, whatever you do, tell her where you live.'

'I'd planned to do that anyway,' said Elsie, 'but don't breathe a word to the girls until I get back to you.'

'Mum's the word, Mum.' Norah chuckled. Her mother hung up but just before Norah put the receiver down, she thought she heard a strange click. That's funny, she thought.

She shrugged. The telephone was new. Probably just teething troubles.

'Norah, I may be working tonight,' Jim had told her on the train coming back home after another visit to Rene. Her sister was doing well and there was talk of her being discharged in the coming days. 'I can't say what it's about,' Jim continued, 'but they want a senior police officer to take part in a special operation.'

Norah looked up at him anxiously. 'It's not dangerous, is it?'

Jim chuckled. 'I shan't be risking life and limb, if that's what you mean, but I can't tell you anything else.'

The train pulled into Goring-by-Sea Station and Norah slipped her arm through his.

'Don't worry about it, will you?' he said.

'I won't,' she quipped. 'Just remember to give me a ring when you're on your way back so I can get rid of my new boyfriend.'

Rene came back to The Lilacs a couple of days later. Norah had borrowed a bed from a neighbour and Jim rigged up an area in the alcove by the front door they never used. A screen hid her from prying eyes and although Norah apologised that she had to be there, Rene didn't seem to mind. The budgie was now in a corner of the sitting room and the piano had been pushed right under the stairs. You could just about squeeze in a chair for the pianist but that was about all.

Rene still had a problem walking but she was a lot happier, especially now that she sported an engagement ring. Norah and Jim had been properly introduced to Dan and they both liked him a lot. It was obvious that he and Rene were deeply in love. He was about to start work again, this time in Tangmere, which had become fully operational once again just ten days after the bombing raid.

The next day being Saturday, Elsie and Pete came down on the London train to see their daughters. Norah had given her mother regular updates on Rene's progress and Rene herself had written to them but Elsie said she couldn't rest until she'd seen Rene for herself. Of course Rene was thrilled to see her mother and father, and she wasted no time in showing them her engagement ring.

'How did you get on with Mrs Scott?' Norah had asked Elsie as they strolled around the market garden later that afternoon. Nobody else was around.

'I met her in the corner café by Victoria Station,' said Elsie. 'I remembered her as a smart little woman but when I saw her, I was shocked. She looked . . . broken. That girl Amélie used to play with . . . she's dead.'

Norah had nearly choked. 'Dead? But she couldn't have been very old. What happened, Mum?'

'I wouldn't mention it to them if I was you,' Elsie cautioned, 'but she jumped off a bridge, into the Thames.'

Norah put her hand to her mouth as she gasped. 'Dear Lord. How awful.'

'And if that wasn't bad enough,' her mother continued, 'when they did a postmortem, they found out she was pregnant. Mrs Scott had no idea.'

Norah sighed. 'The poor woman.'

'She blames Ffox-Webster.'

'What?'

'She says when the girls ran off, he was so upset, so she did extra hours to help him out and brought Vera along with her. Apparently, he took to spoiling the girl. She didn't mind. Vera enjoyed the attention and Mrs Scott thought it was an opportunity for her daughter to see a bit of the world. He'd take her to posh restaurants for afternoon tea, or for a drive to the beach or to the country. One day they went to Brighton.'

'Oh no . . .' Norah groaned. 'That's when he probably . . .'

'Yes,' her mother said, 'he must have done. Of course her mother had no idea what was wrong, but the girl suddenly refused to come with her to the house anymore and she became withdrawn and sullen. Then, a couple of months later, she threw herself off the bridge.'

'I suppose when Mrs Scott found out about the baby,' said Norah, 'she realised what had happened and that there was no doubt that Ffox-Webster was the father.'

Norah heard her mother take in a breath. 'That's about the sum of it.'

'So how come she was the one who ended up in prison?'

'Like I said, she didn't know her daughter was pregnant until after the inquest. She was so angry she went round to the house to have it out with him. He wouldn't open the door no matter how loud she knocked and she refused to go away. In the end the police turned up and she ended up in court.'

'Oh, Mum, that's awful,' said Norah, remembering Ffox-Webster's threats on the telephone. 'How does he get away with it?'

'Because he's got the money and the influence I suppose,' said Elsie.

'*Your husband can kiss his promotion goodbye.*' Ffox-Webster's smarmy voice drifted through Norah's mind and she shuddered involuntarily.

'You're shivering,' said her mother. 'It is getting a bit

chilly. We should have brought cardigans. Shall we go indoors?' They turned back. When they reached the back door of The Lilacs, Elsie paused for a moment. 'Do you think the girls would want to see Mrs Scott?'

Norah sighed. 'The truth is, Mum, I really don't know. Can you leave it with me for a bit and I'll talk to Jim and Mrs Kirkwood first?'

'Why do you need to tell the old bag?' Elsie asked.

'She's very close to Amélie, Mum,' Norah had said. 'In fact, I think Amélie told her a little bit of what was going on long before she trusted Jim and me.'

Elsie gasped. 'Well, blow me down with a feather . . .'

'I thought you might like a cup of tea,' a voice said softly.

Rene opened a bleary eye and pulled herself up the bed. 'Sorry if I woke you.'

Mireille was standing at the foot of the bed holding a steaming cup.

'You didn't,' said Rene. 'Not really.' She reached for her bed jacket. Although it was summer, the hallway had a distinct draught. She took the cup and saucer gratefully. 'Thanks.'

Rene had come back to The Lilacs and everyone fell over one another to look after her. Rene didn't mind. It was nice being spoiled for a change.

Mireille had just returned home after an early shift at the telephone exchange. 'How are you feeling?'

'So-so,' said Rene.

'What's it like?' asked Mireille.

'My foot hurts like Billy-o but I'm getting there.'

'No, I meant the WAAFs,' said Mireille. 'Only I'm thinking of joining up and I can't decide which service to go for.'

'Well I don't regret joining the WAAFs,' said Rene. 'Best thing I ever did.'

'Is that because of Dan?'

'I won't deny meeting Dan has been the most wonderful thing that's ever happened to me, but I was loving the WAAFs long before I met him.'

'Tell me about it,' said Mireille.

Rene patted the edge of her bed and Mireille sat down.

The midweek *Worthing Herald* had a front-page scoop: *Worthing spy arrested*. Jim hadn't said anything about his 'night' shift, and Norah knew better than to ask, but the article underneath the headline said it all. A man had been arrested for showing a light from his attic window. His wife had told the reporter that the light must have been accidentally left on after her husband had been looking for something in the attic that afternoon, but the editorial in the paper was unequivocal in its condemnation. Accident or not, the man had endangered lives and his carelessness had aided the enemy.

'Let's hope the dog walker feels vindicated,' said Mireille when Norah showed her the article.

Everyone was hoping that the Luftwaffe who, despite bombing just about every airfield in the country, had been given a bloody nose, would pack up and go home. The papers were full of RAF bombings of the Black Forest and the widespread wildfires it caused. There were amusing cartoons in the papers of a furious Adolf Hitler stamping his feet as the fires raged around him and people at the market stall told Mrs Kirkwood they thought it jolly well served him right.

Rene was making slow progress and Dan came as often

as he could to see her. Norah had really taken to him. He was kind and funny and totally besotted with her sister. When she overheard them talking about weddings, rooms to let and babies, she was happy for Rene but it rekindled her own disappointment as far as having children was concerned. She and Jim had kept in contact with the adoption agency and although Miss Bundy was sympathetic, it seemed that the people higher up the pecking order were being ultra-cautious. In her frustration, Norah had contacted other agencies but it seemed that the word had got around. No one was keen to have their names on their books.

It was all very upsetting.

CHAPTER 36

Norah

Jim had been called to Chief Inspector Reece's office. When he walked in there were two other men in plain clothes in the room. Jim stood to attention in front of the desk.

'These men are from MI5,' said CI Reece. 'I'm afraid I'm going to have to ask you for your warrant card, Jim.'

Jim's first reaction was one of profound shock. Glancing towards the two men he frowned. 'Am I under arrest?'

'No,' said Reece, 'but certain allegations have been made and these men have been sent down from London to investigate.'

'Certain allegations,' Jim repeated angrily. 'Allegations about what?'

CI Reece held out his hand. 'Your warrant card, please, Jim.'

Norah was preparing the cold frames, ready for the lettuce seedlings that would overwinter before she planted them out in the spring. The last of the runner beans had been picked and she was ready to harvest the rest for bean seeds

324

before pulling the dying climbers off the canes. When she heard the dogs barking she looked up and was surprised to see Jim home so early.

'Hello,' she called. 'Is everything all right? You're not ill, are you?'

He shook his head and went indoors. Norah knew at once that something was wrong. Jim usually joined her when she was in the garden, sometimes getting in the way but showing an interest in what she was doing. The round-shouldered man who shuffled through the kitchen door had something on his mind. She pulled her gloves off and followed him into the kitchen.

'Where are Mother and Ivan?' he said gruffly.

'Gone for a bus ride,' she said, washing her hands at the sink. 'Not far. Littlehampton, I think. Tea?'

He nodded. He threw himself into a chair by the kitchen table, a glum expression on his face.

She filled the kettle with water. 'What's wrong?'

'I've been suspended,' he said bitterly, 'and I've just spent the last hour and a half answering damned foolish questions.'

Norah's heart sank. Suspended? That sort of thing didn't happen unless it was something very serious. She sucked in her lips and lowered herself into the chair next to him. She wanted to fling her arms around him and tell him it was going to be all right, say that she loved him to the moon and back, but she knew Jim well enough to know he wouldn't want any of that at the moment. So, hard as it was, she waited for him to take the initiative.

The tea was in front of him before he spoke again. 'I was called to Reece's office and told to surrender my warrant card,' he said indignantly. 'Then I had to go to the interview room and talk to some boffins from MI5. It turns out that they've had an anonymous tip-off accusing me of failing to report enemy activity. Now the finger of suspicion is on me.'

Her first thought was Ffox-Webster but Norah bit her tongue and stayed silent.

'Apparently, they have evidence that I was aware of that man shining his attic light to aid enemy aircraft long before I reported it,' he went on. 'And I'm supposed to have seen some sort of exchange between two agents and kept it to myself. Goddammit, Norah. As if I would do such a thing! I've always worked by the book.'

Once again Ffox-Webster's threat floated back into Norah's thoughts. '*Your dear husband can kiss his promotion goodbye.*' She just wanted to shut the sound of that man's evil voice out of her thoughts. It was bad enough to know that he was probably the reason why the adoption had been stopped but now that Jim had been suspended . . . She should have said something before. If she said something now it would sound preposterous. What a fool she had been. She gripped his hand.

They sat together at the table for some time. The one consolation, Jim told her, was that Reece was fully supportive of him, but when she eventually suggested that Ffox-Webster might have something to do with all this, Jim waved the idea away. 'Nobody has that kind of power in this country,' he said. 'And besides, what would he gain from it? The deed is done. The girls are here. He didn't want them anyway.'

But perhaps he wanted to get back at you for the satisfaction of his own black heart, she thought helplessly.

They decided to tell the family Jim was on leave. He hadn't had a break for some while so it sounded quite feasible. 'I'm not allowed to travel outside the county,' he said with a tired smile, 'so I might do a spot of fishing over Arundel way.'

Norah hugged him and suggested he got his fishing gear out of the shed. 'It's a while since you used it. There may be repairs needed.'

Back out in the garden after lunch, Norah's brain was working overtime. Jim was all for leaving well alone and letting the official methods take their course, but Norah knew she couldn't let it rest there. To her way of thinking, Ffox-Webster had to be the cause of all this and yes, no matter what Jim said, it seemed he really did have that kind of power. He was charm itself to your face but a totally different kind of animal when roused. Yet they say everyone has a redeeming feature, don't they? Even if he was as awful as she thought; if she promised to make sure the girls never spoke about what he'd done, he would take her word for it, wouldn't he? He had no idea they didn't actually *want* to talk about it. He didn't have to explain anything, just call the dogs off. Jim was such a wonderful man. She couldn't bear to see him so worried. And if he was dismissed from the police force, it would break his heart. By the end of the day, Norah had a plan. As soon as Jim went fishing she would go up to London and try appealing to that dreadful man face to face.

Two days later, she was on the train. Some of Jim's fishing gear had indeed needed replacing and he had to buy a new net, all of which had taken a couple of days to arrange. With no word from CI Reece, he'd set off early in the morning, which gave Norah plenty of time to catch the train. As luck would have it, it was Wednesday, so Mrs

Kirkwood and Ivan were doing the market stall and the girls were at work. Norah had let Rene in on the secret and she was coming with her.

'I can stay a couple of days with Mum before I go back on duty,' said Rene. 'By that time, I should be able to manage the train on my own.'

'I'll make sure you get to Mum's first,' Norah said, 'and then I'll head off to South Audley Street.'

'Is that where he lives then?' Rene asked.

'He wrote once so I knew it was W1,' said Norah, 'and then I remembered that when she first came here, Linnet let it slip. I heard her asking one of the other girls how to spell Audley and she'd already written "South" on the envelope. When she saw me looking she rubbed it out but when I held the envelope up, I could see what she'd written. I gave her letters to her father when he came and forgot all about it.'

'Posh place,' said Rene. 'Off Park Lane, isn't it?'

'Never been there,' Norah confessed.

Rene gave her directions. 'Are you sure you don't want me to come with you?'

Norah shook her head. 'I'll be fine,' she said. 'What could he possibly do in the street in broad daylight?'

When they reached 72 Hugh Street, Elsie was waiting for them. Rene limped up to her mother and Elsie enfolded her in her arms.

'Good to see you, love,' she said. 'How's the foot?'

'Not too bad,' said Rene, although Norah knew that despite being on crutches, it was killing her. They'd said Rene was lucky. She'd been hit on the side of her foot by a ricocheting piece of shrapnel. Half an inch over and her ankle would have been shattered, which might have meant she'd have lost her whole foot.

Elsie turned to Norah and it was her turn for a hug. There was nothing like the warmth of her mother's embrace and although she couldn't tell her why, Norah desperately needed that reassurance right now. 'It's lovely to see you,' her mother said. 'Can you stay a while?'

'I have to get back, Mum,' Norah explained, 'but I'll wait until the six o'clock train.'

'That's nice,' said Elsie, turning to go back indoors. 'At least we'll have most of the day.'

The two sisters glanced at each other. 'Norah's got to see somebody first, Mum,' said Rene.

'What now?' said Elsie, clearly disappointed.

'It's important, Mum.'

Norah was all for heading off straight away but her mother insisted she come in first. 'There's someone here I want you both to meet.'

It was lovely walking into her mother's neat and tidy kitchen. One whiff of the smell of home-made cake and seeing the best Willow pattern china tea cups and saucers on the kitchen table and Norah was transported back to her childhood. The hours and hours she'd spent at that table, painting and drawing, doing her homework, learning how to sew, playing parlour games and doing jigsaws . . . The years just rolled back. Theirs was the cleanest house in the terrace and it was always full of warmth and love, something Norah had been determined to replicate when she'd married.

A woman who was sitting at the table looked up as the girls came in with Elsie. Her mother had an open-door policy so it was no surprise to find someone sitting there. They all beat a path to Elsie's door when they were in trouble or simply wanted a bit of company and a natter.

Norah knew most of her neighbours but she'd never seen this one before. Plump, with greying hair peeping from under a tired-looking felt hat, her face was pale and she wore a troubled expression.

'Norah, love,' said Elsie. 'This is Mrs Scott. She used to work for Mr Ffox-Webster.'

Mrs Scott's story had been difficult to listen to and even more difficult for her to tell. Norah knew most of the facts already but listening to this bereft woman going over and over her painful memories was traumatic. Elsie poured the tea and kept her supplied with clean handkerchiefs while Norah listened. After a while, Rene put her foot onto a cushion on another chair while her mother gave her two aspirins and a glass of water.

'A prostitute!' Mrs Scott said bitterly. 'That's what he told the police. Me, what never so much as looked at another man since my poor Arthur died. I shall never be able to lift my head up again.' She blew her nose into a second handkerchief Elsie had given her. 'He's ruined my life and he's ruined those poor girls' as well.'

Norah took a deep breath. 'Mrs Scott, can I ask you some questions? There are a few things which puzzle me.'

Mrs Scott looked up at her with a blotchy face and red-rimmed eyes. 'I'll try and help, dear.'

'The girls want to find their sister,' she said. 'Do you know where Lillian is?'

Mrs Scott shook her head.

Norah looked thoughtful. 'When did you start working for him?'

'Must have been 1933.' She paused and looking thoughtful added, 'No, it was the end of 1932. Being a widow with a small child I had to get work, see? Poor Mrs Ffox-Webster's first husband died of TB, you know.'

'She got it as well, didn't she, so he took her to Switzerland, I believe,' said Norah.

Mrs Scott frowned. 'They went to Switzerland on a little honeymoon,' she said. 'But then, sad to say, she had that awful accident.'

Norah caught her breath. 'Accident, what accident? I thought she died of TB.'

'Oh, no, dear,' said Mrs Scott. 'She fell over the balcony of her hotel room.'

The room had suddenly gone quiet as all three of them stared at Mrs Scott. 'Of course, we told the girls their mummy was too ill and that's why she didn't come back. Mr Ffox-Webster was distraught. He blamed himself. He said he'd only left her for a few minutes to go down to the foyer to meet someone and when he got back . . .' She shrugged helplessly. 'Well, there it is.'

'Mrs Scott,' Norah began again after a few minutes. 'I've just got Amélie's ration book and there's a different name on it. I was wondering—'

'Amélie?' Mrs Scott interrupted.

'Oh, sorry,' said Norah. 'The girls wanted to use their French names so we've agreed to call them Amélie and Mireille. The names are quite pretty, don't you think? But when I got Amélie's ration book, it says Amy Osborne.'

'That's right,' Mrs Scott nodded. 'Osborne was her mother's name.'

'But she married Ffox-Webster, didn't she?'

'As far as I know, she did,' said Mrs Scott. She looked thoughtful. 'It was all very quick. They hadn't long been married when I came, and come to think of it, I do remember wedding photographs on the grand piano.' She sighed. 'Poor Mrs Ffox-Webster.'

Norah could hardly dare ask the next question but she had to. 'Did he adopt the girls after their mother died?'

'Adopt?' said Mrs Scott. She shook her head. 'I don't think so. As a matter of fact, he didn't have a lot to do with them. He was a busy man.'

Norah sat back in her chair. Well, that was a bit of a bombshell. Could it be true? Could it be that their mother's husband never legally became their step-father? She'd have to try and find out without the girls knowing, just in case it all led nowhere, but she may have stumbled on the best bit of news ever.

CHAPTER 37

Norah

Norah refused lunch. Her mother wanted her to eat a sandwich before she headed off to Ffox-Webster's place but it was already gone one o'clock and she didn't have a lot of time if she was to get back to Worthing on the six o'clock train. Her mother and Mrs Scott had been uneasy when she'd told them the real reason why she was in London.

'Oh, darling, do be careful,' said Elsie.

'But don't you see?' said Norah. 'I must try and talk to him. I have to, for Jim's sake.'

'I wouldn't if I were you, dear,' Mrs Scott had cautioned. 'That's what I did and look where it got me. I tell you, if I ever saw him again I'd stick a knife in him.'

'And they'd hang you for that,' Elsie had said.

'And it would be worth it,' Mrs Scott said bitterly. She dabbed her eyes with her handkerchief.

Elsie turned to Norah. 'Let me come with you.'

'No, Mum,' said Norah. 'This is between him and me. It's me he's trying to hurt. I don't care what happens to me but I can't let him do this to Jim.'

She got off the bus at Marble Arch and walked from there. Rene's directions were excellent and Norah found South Audley Street quite quickly. All she had to do now was find the number. Near the church, with black railings around the steps, Mrs Scott had said.

Norah was so wound up and nervous that a couple of times she had this ridiculous feeling that someone was following her but, of course, when she spun around there was no one there. Pull yourself together, she told herself crossly, and calm down, or you're going to make a muck of it.

There was a black car parked outside the house and a policeman was standing near the steps. Norah was just about to walk up to the door when it burst open and a man wearing an army raincoat and a trilby hat came out. He stood at the top of the steps. Two other men followed him, one of them Ffox-Webster.

'Excuse me, sir,' Norah called. He didn't answer and it took her a couple of seconds to register that Ffox-Webster was handcuffed to the man next to him. As they came down the steps, the policeman positioned himself between the three men and Norah. At the same time someone in the black car swung the back passenger door open.

When he reached the pavement, Ffox-Webster saw Norah for the first time.

'You!' he cried. He began to struggle. 'What's she been saying, the witch? What's she been telling you?'

Norah was frozen to the spot. There was a massive scuffle as the two men manhandled him towards the car, still shouting. 'You interfering cow. You're responsible for all this! I should have got you black-listed long ago.'

Embarrassed by his outburst, Norah became aware that

passers-by were stopping in the street to watch the spectacle. She kept her head down and turned her face away but not before she saw the men finally push Ffox-Webster onto the back seat of the car and the man he was handcuffed to climbed in after him. The policeman then slammed the door. She was expecting the car to drive off but the man with the trilby hat pulled the policeman to one side and they walked towards the wall of the building, deep in conversation.

Norah took a step backwards. She felt hot and flustered. She was also upset. She'd come all this way and for what? Where were they taking him? What was she going to do if she couldn't even speak to Ffox-Webster? Poor Jim, oh poor Jim.

The driver of the black car revved the engine and the man in the trilby walked around to the passenger side and got in the front. Seconds later, the car drove off and the small crowd of bystanders began to disperse.

As she turned to leave, the policeman stepped in front of her. 'Just a minute, miss,' he said. 'May I have your name?'

Norah was slightly surprised but she said, 'Norah Kirkwood, Mrs.'

The policeman puffed his chest up. 'Norah Kirkwood, you are under arrest on suspicion of aiding and abetting the enemy.'

Norah gasped. 'What?'

'You do not have to say anything . . .' As the policeman droned on, someone passing by spat in her face. Norah stood trembling in bewilderment. The policeman let her take her handkerchief from her pocket to wipe her face and then she was frog-marched along the street in the direction of the nearest police station.

*

Jim was really chuffed. When he got off the bus from Arundel, he felt relaxed, sun-kissed and he was carrying three good-sized mullet in his bag. A day by the riverbank was just what he had needed, and it had given him plenty of time to think. The weather had been perfect. In fact, it had been so long since he'd had time to himself, he'd almost forgotten how pleasant it was to hold a rod in his hand. The obvious places to go would have been Worthing Pier or Goring-by-Sea, but as he'd planned his outing, he'd decided it would be better to be in a place where he was less well known.

The river Arun had been a first-class choice. The scenery was lovely. He'd had the castle and the town behind him and the low-lying meadows in front of him. This part of the river was tidal but it began its journey from its source to the east of Horsham and passed through some of the most picturesque villages in Sussex. Someday, Jim told himself, he would get on his bike and trace its journey through places like Wisborough Green, Adversane, Burpham, Ford, and finally on to Littlehampton and the English Channel.

As he walked home, he was tired but happy. He couldn't wait to show Norah his catch and then put his feet up. The house was a hive of activity as he walked in through the kitchen door. Mrs Kirkwood was laying the table, Mireille was stirring something on the stove, and Amélie was taking a pie out of the oven.

Jim looked around. 'Where's Norah?'

His mother shrugged. 'I'm guessing she's taken Rene back to her mother's as all her things are gone from the alcove. There's a note on the kitchen dresser for you.'

Jim produced his catch and enjoyed everybody's admiration before putting the fish on a plate in the cool pantry.

As tea was almost ready, he washed up and changed. He was glad to be in a sweater and shirt that didn't smell of the outdoors and fish! Comfortable at last, he sat at the table and opened Norah's letter.

'Good God!' he exclaimed. 'She's gone to London all right, but she's gone to see Ffox-Webster!'

Elsie Carter was peeling potatoes when she heard the frantic banging on her front door. It took a minute or two to grab a towel to dry her hands before she hurried to answer it. Rene had hopped into the hallway from the sitting room where she'd been resting with her foot up.

'It's all right, love,' said Elsie, undoing her apron. 'I'll get it.'

As the door swung open, Mrs Scott almost fell over the threshold. Her face was scarlet and she'd clearly been running. 'They've taken him away,' she blurted out, 'and the bugger's only gone and got your Norah arrested, too!'

Norah sat at the table in a small room at the police station with her head in her hands. She was willing herself not to cry. If they saw her shedding tears, they would be bound to think she'd done something wrong.

After she'd been arrested, she'd tried to tell the policeman there had been a terrible mistake but he wouldn't listen. He wouldn't even talk to her. He just held her arm in a vice-like grip as he propelled her along the street. Once in the station, the sergeant at the desk had taken down her particulars.

'Name?'

'Norah Kirkwood.'

'Miss or Mrs?'

'Mrs. My husband is a police inspector in Worthing.'

'Yeah? And my wife's the Queen of Sheba. Address?'

It was hopeless. After she'd given them the bare facts, she was escorted to the cells but not before they had taken her bag and the belt of her dress. After that she was locked into a tiny room with white-washed walls. There was a bed (which was about as cosy as a park bench), a black and white twill pillow (no pillowcase), and a dark grey blanket folded on the end of the skinny apology for a mattress. In the corner there was a toilet (no seat and no toilet paper). The window was high up and covered in grime. After some while, the police matron brought her a cup of tea. Norah accepted it gratefully.

'How long am I to be kept here?'

'Sorry, dear,' said the woman. 'They don't tell me the details.'

After she'd gone, it seemed like a lifetime before someone came back to the cell. The sudden sound of the key in the lock made Norah jump and she rose to her feet.

'This way, miss.'

The policeman standing in the doorway was huge. Norah followed him like a lamb. He took her to a room with a small table in the middle and a canvas and tubular steel chair at either end. After a minute or two, the man in the trilby hat came in. He was now bareheaded and he carried a folder under his arm. Pulling the chair out, he slapped the folder onto the table and sat down. Norah shivered.

'I don't understand why I'm here,' she protested. 'Why did you arrest me?'

The man leaned back and stared at her with a cold expression.

'I haven't done anything wrong,' Norah went on. 'There must be some mistake.'

'Your accomplice has dropped you right in it, lovey,' the man said mockingly.

Norah's heart sank. What accomplice? Then her stomach fell away as she realised he must mean Ffox-Webster. 'He is not my accomplice,' she protested. 'I looked after his children when they were evacuated, that's all.'

The man raised his eyebrows. It was obvious that he didn't believe her.

'Anyway,' Norah went on. 'Shouldn't you have told me who you are?'

'You know a bit about police procedure then,' he said sarcastically.

'Only because my husband is a policeman,' she snapped.

He sat up straight. 'Is he now?'

'Yes, he is,' Norah said emphatically.

'My name is Detective Inspector Havelock,' he said, opening the folder. 'The man we have just arrested, Jago Ffox-Webster, has made a statement implicating you in a plot to overthrow His Majesty's government. I am here to collect your statement and then it will be passed to the appropriate authorities. Do you understand?'

Norah blinked in disbelief. A plot to overthrow the government? What was he talking about? The man was mad. Her heartbeat quickened. What should she say?

'*Do you understand?*' Havelock repeated with emphasis.

'I understand what you're saying,' said Norah, 'but it's complete nonsense. I am a market gardener and housewife from Worthing. I'm not the enemy. Do I look like a traitor?'

'I wouldn't be at all surprised,' said Havelock. 'Traitors and spies come in all sorts of guises.'

Norah glared angrily. 'This is ridiculous. You're scaring me.'

'Oh, you'd better be scared,' he said, clearly enjoying this. 'In this country we still hang traitors.' He opened his folder and shuffled some papers. 'What's your address?'

'The Lilacs, Clifton Road, Worthing,' Norah snapped. 'That's in Sussex. On the South Coast.'

'Don't get lippy with me,' he said, looking up with hooded eyes.

Norah leaned back in her chair. Taking a deep breath, she made herself calm down. She felt sick and she felt scared but if she was to get out of this place, she mustn't antagonise this dreadful man any further.

'So,' he began again. 'I want to know all about you and your husband. Start by telling me why he's suspended from duty.'

CHAPTER 38

Norah

Jim was beside himself with worry. He had telephoned his mother-in-law soon after he'd read Norah's letter. When she'd answered the phone he'd never heard her in such a state. 'Calm down, Elsie. Calm down. I can't understand a word you're saying.'

'Norah went to see Ffox-Webster,' said Elsie, taking a gulp of air. 'Mrs Scott followed her.'

'Who's Mrs Scott?'

'Ffox-Webster's old housekeeper. She was worried about our Norah and it seems she was right. When she got to the house, the police were taking him away and when he saw Norah in the street, he shouted something and then the police arrested her as well.'

'Arrested her?' Jim gasped. 'On what grounds?'

'I've no idea,' an exasperated Elsie cried.

'Why were the police arresting Ffox-Webster?'

'I don't know,' Elsie cried again. 'Jim, you must come. You've got to do something. She's all alone.'

341

'I can't,' said Jim helplessly. 'I'm not allowed to leave the county. Where did they take her?'

'I don't know,' cried Elsie. 'Mrs Scott didn't see. She came straight back here to tell me. What do you mean you can't leave the county?'

Jim could hear someone in the background crying. 'Why didn't you stop her?' he shouted angrily. 'What the hell was Norah thinking?'

There was a pause then Elsie said, 'You. She was thinking about you, Jim. Norah was trying to help *you*.'

'What do you mean, help me? How is this going to help me?'

'Oh, Jim, don't be like this. She wanted to plead with that awful man to call the dogs off. She was convinced he'd told the police some lie about you. She was only trying to help you.'

Jim closed his eyes. 'Yes, yes, I understand,' he said, suddenly subdued. 'I'll do what I can. Let me know if you get any more news.'

'What's happened?' said Mrs Kirkwood as Jim put the receiver on its rest. Ivan and the two girls were hovering in the doorway.

'Norah's been arrested,' said Jim.

Mrs Kirkwood clutched her throat and Amélie began to cry. Jim quickly told them all that he knew.

'Well, you'll have to go up there,' said Mrs Kirkwood.

'I can't,' Jim said helplessly. 'I'm not allowed to travel.'

'What about your chief, lad?' said Ivan. 'He'd help her, wouldn't he?'

Jim picked up the phone again and this time he dialled Worthing Police Station.

*

Ivan had pulled Mrs Kirkwood into the tool shed. She'd just gone outside to bring in the last of the washing and as she came in, he closed the door.

'What?' she said when she saw his anxious expression.

'We'll have to tell him,' said Ivan. 'About that chauffeur of his. A leopard don't change its spots and I've got an awful feeling that this is something to do with them bloody black shirts again.'

'Don't be daft,' said Mrs Kirkwood. 'Mosley's been put away. It was one of the first things Mr Churchill did when he became Prime Minister and if you ask me, he was quite right to!'

'He may be behind bars but he wasn't the only one wanting us to give in to Hitler. What if that chauffeur is still one of them? We know he was a black shirt. What if Norah's arrest is Ffox-Webster's doing?'

'But he was arrested himself.'

'He could have said something to implicate her.'

Mrs Kirkwood gasped as she stared at him. 'But why? Norah is a wonderful girl. Why on earth would he bother with small fry like her?'

'Because she crossed him,' Ivan said emphatically. 'Why did that sod hit poor old Mrs Hodgkiss with his swagger stick? Only because he was angry and she couldn't fight back. It's all about power, Christine. They're drunk on it.'

Mrs Kirkwood lowered herself onto an upturned bucket. 'So, what do we do?'

'We've got to tell Jim,' Ivan insisted. 'There may be a connection. A leopard doesn't change its spots.'

'Then what?' Mrs Kirkwood began cautiously. 'You heard what he said. Jim can't go to London to sort it out.'

'Then I'll go meself,' Ivan said stoutly.

She gave him an unsteady smile. 'That's kind of you, and I'd gladly come with you, but we don't know where she is.'

'There must be a way to find out,' said Ivan, pulling open the shed door.

Back in the kitchen there was another argument taking place. Mireille had her best coat on.

'I know you both want to help,' Jim was saying. 'But in my opinion Amélie is far too young and even with the best will in the world, Mireille, you can't do anything about it.'

'Perhaps not,' said Mireille, 'but it's not just about Norah.'

'What's going on?' Mrs Kirkwood demanded.

'She wants to go up to London and talk to the police,' said Jim, throwing his hands in the air in exasperation.

'I think that's a good idea,' said Mrs Kirkwood and when Jim glared at her she retorted, 'Well, somebody's got to do it!'

'But I've already spoken to the Super,' said Jim, calming down. 'When it comes to these things, it's always better to go through the official channels. He'll sort it out for us.'

'I'm still going,' said Mireille. 'Like I said, it's not just about Norah.'

'Then what's it about?'

'I'm going to the house in South Audley Street,' said Mireille. 'If he's been arrested, he won't be there and it gives me a chance to look through his desk. There must be something in there which will tell us where Linnet is.'

'Don't you see?' cried Amélie. 'We have to find our sister. This is our one and only chance!'

Everybody froze.

'But how will you get in?' said Mrs Kirkwood. 'Surely you don't have a key. Not after all this time?'

'I know how to get in round the back,' said Mireille.

'There's a garage in the mews. He keeps a spare key hidden nearby.'

'What about the chauffeur?' said Mrs Kirkwood.

'I doubt he'll be there. He's only part time,' said Mireille. 'My step-father is too stingy to employ anyone full time.'

Jim ran his hand through his hair. 'I suppose I can't stop you but you're putting yourself in danger. It's light now but by the time you get up there it will be dark and the thought of a young girl walking about the streets of London on her own . . .' His voice faded. 'It doesn't bear thinking about.'

'She won't be on her own though, will she?' Everyone turned towards Ivan standing near the door. 'I'm going with her.'

Mireille put her hand up in protest.

'Ivan . . .' Jim began.

'There's no more to be said,' Ivan insisted. 'And besides,' he added, with a twinkle in his eye, 'if we get stopped, what could be more natural than a loving granddaughter walking her old grandad home?'

By the time they arrived in London at nine forty-five, it was dark. Mireille slipped her arm through Ivan's when they got off the bus at Marble Arch. For someone used to a country mile, it wasn't far to go and because of the blackout the streets were deserted. They were both glad that Ivan had thought to bring his shaded torch. It was handy in the dark streets. In the mews behind the house, Mireille found the key and let them in through the garage. Just to be on the safe side, they didn't flood the house with light.

'His office is up there,' Mireille whispered, pointing to the top of sweeping, circular staircase.

*

A mile away, on the top of Selfridges department store, two fire-watchers stared out over the city. They were mismatched socially, but both treated their responsibilities very seriously. Young John Kitchen, a trainee porter, was keen to impress his superiors who had entrusted him to keep watch. This was his first job and he was aiming high. He could see that Selfridges gave their employees every opportunity of advancement and John was keen to work his way up the ladder. Who knows, in a few years' time he could be a warehouseman or, better still, in management. On the other hand, Stan Loftus had worked in the customer lift for twenty years. His main concern was trying to avoid management's recent staff changes and reallocation. Since the call-up began, some had been asked to move to other departments but Stan didn't want to go anywhere else. He liked being in the lift. He got on well with the customers, so much so that at Christmas time some of them gave him a small Christmas 'box'; five bob here and two bob there, all slipped discreetly into his pocket to save embarrassment. He hated being up here. Even with the search lights scanning the night sky and the drone of aircraft high above them, it was dark, cold and boring. Stan would have much preferred to be in his warm bed beside Maisie, his wife of thirty-four years.

John stepped down to where Stan was pouring some tea out of his flask. Better not drink too much. He'd be wanting a pee before long and it was a long trek to the toilets from this height. 'Anything doing?' he asked John.

'There's a strange light over Park Lane way,' said John. 'It keeps getting bigger and then going dim again.'

With a weary heart, Stan rose to his feet and followed the boy to the edge of the parapet. 'Look,' said John, pointing. 'Over there.'

Stan peered into the gloom and all at once he saw it. Yes, he had to agree, it was odd, but more importantly, it shouldn't be there. 'Better get onto the telephone and report it, lad,' he said. 'Tell the supervisor to get over there.'

John took off and Stan could hear his footsteps clattering on the fire escape until the door slammed. He peered at the light again. Yes, it was still there. Still moving.

'Dash dot dot, dash dot . . .'

Stan took in his breath noisily. Bloody hell – it was Morse code! Some bugger was helping the Germans right under their very noses!

With their only light the beam from her shaded torch, Mireille and Ivan crept silently up the stairs to the top of the house. Although it was obviously deserted, Mireille's heart was in her mouth. She felt hot and shaky. The memories of what had happened under this roof clambered for attention in her brain but she deliberately pushed the thoughts away. She knew if she dwelt on them in this moment her legs would freeze so she had to keep moving. Passing what had once been her bedroom door was the most difficult. She thought of the little girl who once lay behind the door, dreading the sound of footsteps on the stairs. *Don't think of it, she told herself. Shut it out.* She didn't want to cry. She didn't want to remember. She forced herself to think only of Amélie and Linnet. They were the reason she was here. She owed it to both her sisters to get to his study and do what was required. This was no time for self-pity. She only had this moment to find Linnet's address. This was most likely their last chance.

Her step-father's office was at the end of the sweeping corridor. She pushed the door open and Ivan stayed in the doorway. Mireille took a deep breath. The desk. The most logical place would be on the top of or inside one of the drawers. She motioned to Ivan and tiptoed across the room. There was nothing on the top of the desk except a pen tray, a blotting pad and ink.

Mireille opened each drawer in turn and moved the papers she found inside. Nothing. Swinging the torch round she glanced at the shelves of books. Everything was neat and tidy. In the corner there was a small table with a newspaper on the top. She went over to it and picked up the newspaper. Nothing underneath. Disappointment rose within her and made her eyes sting with unshed tears. Outside in the street they heard speeding cars and the squeal of brakes. Wide-eyed, Mireille glanced at Ivan.

'We'd better get a move on,' he said in a low whisper.

She nodded and took one more look around the room. That's when she saw it. The ballerina statue that had got her into so much trouble all those years ago. It still looked so beautiful. Mireille couldn't help but walk to the other side of the room to take one more look at it. She ran her fingers down the bronze, feeling the slightly raised muscles in the ballerina's leg, the daintiness of her tutu. She went to pick it up but it wouldn't move.

'Come on, love,' Ivan whispered urgently. 'We'd better get out of here before somebody comes in.'

As her hand let go of the statue Mireille accidentally pushed it. They heard a click, which was followed by a low rumble, and the light from another room flooded all around them. It was debatable as to who was the most shocked and surprised, Mireille and Ivan . . . or the man in the hidden enclosure that had just been revealed.

CHAPTER 39

The room beyond the door struck her as masculine. The walls were lined with books and the decor was predominately brown. An electric fire glowed in the hearth and a large picture of Adolf Hitler draped with the British Union of Fascist flag hung over the mantelpiece. There was a small receiver on the table beside the occupant which, although silent, flickered with life. Dressed in what looked like a Nazi uniform, the man inside had been reclining in a large leather armchair with headphones over his ears. He held a whiskey glass in his hand and as he saw her, he kicked out with his foot and knocked over a large Aldis signalling lamp. Mireille recognised him at once and as soon as he caught a glimpse of the livid raspberry birthmark on his face, so did Ivan. It was Hedges, Ffox-Webster's chauffeur.

'Good God!' Ivan cried. 'He's one of Mosley's Biff boys. That's the bugger what bit off my ear!'

Suddenly shocked into action, Mireille pushed the ballerina again and with a rumble the door began to close. The man in the room jumped to his feet and as he tore off his headphones, the glass of whiskey tumbled to the floor. Now they could hear the guttural sounds of the German language coming from the headset. As the door finally closed, Mireille glimpsed Hedges reach into a drawer and pull out a gun.

Downstairs they could hear someone's frantic banging on the front door. 'Open up. This is the police. Open the door.'

'Come on,' Ivan hissed.

Mireille ran towards him but where could they go? They had a man with a gun behind them and some angry-sounding policemen at the front door. As they raced towards the stairs, they heard breaking glass and a policeman's leg appeared over the windowsill in the hallway. Seconds later, he had the front door open and several more officers tumbled into the hallway. The hall was suddenly flooded with light and someone cried, 'Watch the blackout you fool!'

Mireille and Ivan froze.

'Stay where you are,' another voice barked.

Mireille glanced behind her just in time to see the man in the Nazi uniform appear in the doorway then dart back into her step-father's study. Even with a gun in his hand, he knew he was outnumbered.

Three policemen bounded up the stairs. At the top, Ivan cried out as one grabbed his arm and spun him round to handcuff his hands behind his back. 'You're under arrest for breaking and entering, sunshine.'

A second policeman made a grab for Mireille but she stepped back, snatching her arm away from him. 'How dare you!' she cried in ringing tones. 'Why should you arrest me for being in my own home?'

The policeman faltered and with a confused expression on his face turned to his superior who was coming up behind him.

The inspector bringing up the rear seemed unconvinced. 'We happen to know the gent who lives here, a Mr Ffox-Webster, and he lives alone.'

'He's my step-father,' said Mireille, maintaining her superior stance.

'Your identification papers, please,' said the inspector, holding out his hand.

Mireille had no handbag, but she reached into the inside pocket of her coat and gave him her identity card. He scrutinised the folder and handed it back to her. 'Beg pardon, Miss Ffox-Webster.' His tone was far less strident but still not exactly acquiescent. 'But we're not finished yet. We've had a report of someone signalling to German planes from this address.'

'That doesn't surprise me,' said Mireille, still superior. She jerked her head towards the door. 'I think you'll find the culprit in my step-father's office.'

The inspector gave his younger colleague a nod and he made his way into the study. A second later he was back out on the landing. 'Room's empty, sir.'

'Very clever,' the inspector said contemptuously. 'Come along, you two. You've got some explaining to do.'

'He's in the secret room,' Mireille protested.

'Followed a white rabbit, did he?' the inspector said drily. He pulled Mireille's arm to encourage her down the stairs.

'Listen,' Mireille cried as she jerked her arm away, 'if you leave now you'll let him get away with it. He's behind the wall. There's a secret room . . .' Her protestations stopped as they all heard the muffled sound of a gun coming from the direction of the study. The younger policeman ran back into the room only to come back out again. 'There's still no one there, sir.'

'I'll show you,' cried Mireille as she pushed past.

They followed her reluctantly and once again Mireille slid the bronze ballerina along the desk. As the door rumbled open once again everyone gasped. The man dressed in a German officer's uniform was slumped over the side of the big armchair. Blood trickled across the livid birthmark on his face and down the sleeve of his jacket from a self-inflicted bullet wound in his head.

When Norah heard footsteps coming along the corridor outside her cell, her heart sank. What now? She had no clock but when she woke it was almost light. Given the time of year, she guessed it must be somewhere around five fifteen. The cell was cold and although she was exhausted, Norah knew she wouldn't sleep any more so she sat up on the hard bed and wrapped the thin blanket around her shoulders. Leaning against the cold brick wall, she went over and over the events of the previous day. How many times had she told them her story? It must have been four or five times. They always asked the same things. How had she met Ffox-Webster; did she know what he did; why had she come to London; what was she going to talk to him about; why was Jim's promotion on hold; what did she do in Worthing? On and on and on they went until her mind was in a whirl. Then they'd all leave the room but only for a few minutes. After that, they'd either all troop back in and it would start all over again, or one man would come back on his own and try to persuade her that if she told him everything, he'd make sure nobody else bothered her. Eventually, Norah was so weak with tiredness and the strain of it all, she could hardly speak. The trouble was, when they finally took her back to the cell, she couldn't sleep either. She lay on her back staring at the cobwebby ceiling, waiting for them to put the light out, only they never did. It was on all night until it went off at dawn. She was exhausted but all she could do was stare at the sky through the dirty window. Now she fixed her eyes on the door.

Chains and keys rattled and she heard the clunk as the door unlocked. A policeman pushed it open and the matron came into the room with a bowl of water in her hands and a towel over her forearm.

'Here we are, dear,' she said cheerfully. 'Thought you'd like a nice wash.'

She'd also brought soap, a flannel and a comb. The matron left and they closed the door behind her so Norah was able to have a strip wash. The soap was hardly Yardley's – more like carbolic – and it upset her when she realised that the HMP on the threadbare towel stood for His Majesty's Prison, but that wash had never felt so good. Norah was ridiculously grateful but she was frustrated that she had to put on the same stale clothing.

They came back about twenty minutes later, not with the early morning cup of tea she was expecting but to tell her she was on the move again. Although light-headed from lack of food, she knew it would be useless to argue. She could only suppose that they thought a little more deprivation would yield better results.

She followed the policeman through a maze of corridors until he showed her into another bare room with only a table and two chairs.

'Could I have a drink of water, please?' asked Norah, but he was already shutting the door.

She sank onto a chair and waited. After a few minutes the door opened again but Norah didn't bother to look up.

She was sick of them. Sick to her stomach. She'd always admired the British way of doing things but this bordered on . . . would torture be too strong a word? It was certainly excessive bullying, if nothing else.

Someone put a tray of tea onto the table in front of her. Norah started, unbelieving. Not enamel mugs but a tray of matching green tea cups and saucers. And was that a sandwich as well? She frowned. Were they only going to let her have this if she 'co-operated'?

A policeman had entered the room. She could see the blue serge of his uniform but she still didn't look up. 'Can I eat that?' she asked quietly.

'Of course you can, darling.'

Norah's head shot up. 'Jim,' she cried. Jumping to her feet, she flung her arms around her husband's neck. 'Oh, Jim, thank God you've come!'

'Here you are, love. I've made you a nice cup of tea.'

Mireille opened her eyes to see Ivan putting a cup on the little cabinet beside her bed. 'Thank you,' she said, stifling a yawn.

'As soon as you're ready,' he continued, 'there's some breakfast downstairs. Bacon and eggs.'

Mireille pulled herself up the bed. She had no nightie; she'd slept in her petticoat. She would have dismissed his promise of a cooked breakfast as a ruse to make her get up if it hadn't been for the delicious smell of cooking bacon that wafted through the door.

'You won't believe the stuff he's got in that larder,' Ivan called out as he left the room. 'All black market, I suppose, but he won't be needing it, will he? Shame to waste good food.'

Mireille yawned and took a sip of the tea; it was the colour of paint stripper and very strong, but it was none the less very welcome. She hadn't slept well. The police had stayed at the house for some time. They had examined the secret room very thoroughly and taken loads of pictures before Hedges's body was removed in the small hours. Because the window was broken, they had left a policeman on guard outside the front door.

Both Mireille and Ivan had been questioned at length by some men from MI5 before everybody was completely satisfied that they knew nothing of what Hedges and Ffox-Webster had been up to.

'Is my step-father likely to come home tonight?' Mireille asked anxiously as the last of them left the house.

'I'm afraid your step-father won't be going anywhere for some time, miss,' said the inspector. 'He has some serious questions to answer about where his sympathies lie.' He shook his head. 'I'm sorry.'

'Oh, please don't apologise,' Mireille said scornfully. 'I'm glad to see the back of him. I hate him.'

Mireille had decided that she and Ivan would have to stay the night as it was already gone two in the morning and neither of them fancied sleeping on the platform in Victoria Station until the milk train set off. She put Ivan in the guest room but she couldn't face sleeping in her old bedroom. Even though she knew Ffox-Webster wouldn't be coming back, Mireille knew she would be listening for those dreaded footsteps on the stone staircase if she went in there. In the end, she made up the bed in the room behind the kitchen. In the days when her father was alive, they'd had a live-in cook and this had been her room. Mrs Scott had slept in here, too, on occasion.

Her stomach rumbled. 'What's the time?' she called out.

'Nine thirty.'

Washed and dressed, Mireille and Ivan sat down to a luxurious meal. For people used to an allowance of one egg and two ounces of bacon a week, they stuffed themselves on two eggs each and four rashers of bacon between them. Ivan wasn't a bad cook.

'What now, love?' he asked.

'I want to go over the house in daylight,' she said. 'I know I've already looked but now that we know he's not coming back, I can be more thorough.'

Ivan nodded.

'If you want to go back home . . .' she began.

'I'm staying here with you,' said Ivan. 'Just give me a minute or two to clear up the kitchen, then I'll give you a hand.'

Mireille gave him a tired smile. 'Thank you, Ivan. You've been wonderful.'

He waved her compliment away and took the plates to the sink.

As Mireille rose to her feet the doorbell rang. The two of them looked at each other in alarm.

'The coppers didn't say they was coming back, did they?' Ivan asked anxiously.

Mireille shook her head. The doorbell rang again, longer this time. Mireille headed for the hallway.

'Hang on,' said Ivan, grabbing the rolling pin. 'I'm coming with you.'

They were both standing in the hall when the bell rang a third time. Then the letter box was lifted from the outside and a voice called, 'Mireille. Are you there? It's Norah and Jim.'

CHAPTER 40

Norah

At twelve o'clock they sent Jim out to look for something to eat but it wasn't easy to find anything in that part of London. It was very frustrating.

Mireille and Ivan had been horrified to hear that Norah had spent the night in a police cell. It was only when Jim contacted his superiors that everybody began to put two and two together. Jim was supposed to have passed secrets to another party on Worthing seafront on the day he had been in Lewes crown court giving evidence against the women stealing handbags from the ladies toilets in the town. It didn't take a Sherlock Holmes to work out that the accusations made against Norah had come from the same person. Luckily for Jim, Inspector Reece had friends in high places and once the ball got rolling, it didn't take long to convince them that all the accusations against him and his wife were both malicious and groundless.

'It's a good job I've kept a detailed log of everything that's happened,' said Jim.

Mireille's face paled. 'You didn't . . .'

Jim touched the top of her arm. 'No,' he said kindly. 'I promised I would get your permission before I told anyone about that.'

Norah, Mireille and Ivan had scoured the whole house but there was still no sign of Linnet's address, nor anything connected with her. Norah had been the one to search the room which had once been Mireille's, then Amélie's and most likely would eventually have been Linnet's, should she have come home. Amélie had described pink rosebuds on the wallpaper whereas Mireille remembered her paper having Mabel Lucie Attwell's chubby babies all over it. She stood outside the door when Norah went inside and listened to her opening drawers, the wardrobe, and the tall cupboard in the corner of the room.

'I can't find anything,' Norah told her. 'All the drawers are empty. I think it's only just been redecorated.'

The door creaked open and Mireille's curiosity got the better of her. She pushed it right back against the wall, but she didn't go inside. The wallpaper was very pretty; blue and yellow butterflies with a trail of white ribbon surrounding them. Here and there she saw a small yellow daisy-like flower. She began to tremble. Oh God. They had to find Linnet. He was already planning to do it all over again.

Norah saw her trembling and came out onto the landing. Putting her arm around Mireille's shoulders she said, 'Jim assures me they're going to charge him with aiding and abetting the enemy. It'll go to trial. They've got enough evidence to convict him and he'll go to prison. Whatever happens, he's not coming back.'

Mireille nodded. 'But he's clever,' she said. 'He's got away with this for so long, what's to say he won't talk himself out of it again?'

Norah shook her head. 'Apparently they've been watching him for some time,' she said. 'They have proof, letters.'

Mireille shook her head. 'He'll say it was nothing to do with him; Hedges was doing it.'

Norah sighed. There was some truth in what Mireille feared but she wasn't about to agree with her. The poor girl was distraught enough.

'Pie and chips are here,' Jim called up the stairs.

They had already telephoned Norah's mum and then they'd called Mrs Kirkwood. Everyone was relieved that they were all right but their pleasure was tinged with disappointment because there was still no sign of Linnet's whereabouts. Jim said they should all leave for Worthing by two thirty and it was with a heavy heart that Mireille began one last look around the house. She was now ferreting around the daftest places; in the toilet, at the back of wardrobes in rooms obviously never used, in the tea caddy, the pantry, the garage.

Just before two, the doorbell rang. It was Mrs Scott. She and Mireille were delighted to see each other and Norah and Jim left them alone in the sitting room to weep over their shared grief for Mrs Scott's daughter, Vera.

'Mrs Carson has told me about that wicked man,' Mrs Scott said brokenly. 'I'm so sorry for what happened to you, my dear. I honestly never knew.'

'Perhaps I should apologise to you for not telling you,' said Mireille. 'Maybe if I'd said something earlier poor Vera would still be alive today.'

Mrs Scott gave her a sad smile. 'We mustn't blame ourselves,' she said, grasping Mireille's hands tightly. 'It's easy to be wise after the event.'

'He told me I could go to prison,' said Mireille, her eyes

filling again, 'and I – like a stupid, stupid idiot – I believed him.'

'My dear,' said Mrs Scott, 'try not to be so hard on yourself. You were a child. Only a little girl.'

'When all this is over, you must come to Worthing to see us,' said Norah as Mrs Scott took her leave. 'Hopefully by then all the girls will be together.'

'I should like that,' said Mrs Scott.

'Keep in touch,' said Norah as they shook hands.

As everyone enjoyed a last cup of tea together, Jim got the map out to plan the route home. 'I got stuck at a road-block just north of Box Hill,' he said. 'A plane had crashed on the bank and they had to close the main route to clear it. I think it best to avoid going that way if we can.'

As Norah watched him carefully pencilling in a new route a thought suddenly crossed her mind. Without a word she suddenly jumped to her feet and opened the kitchen door, which led to the garage.

'What?' cried Mireille. 'What is it?'

Norah was desperately trying to open the car door. 'How do you get into this thing?' she cried. 'Where's the key?'

At the same moment Jim, Mireille, and Ivan had the same thought. Could the chauffeur have marked his map in the same way that Jim was doing, and if so, was Linnet's address there? They began a frantic search for the keys to the Bentley as they weren't in the garage.

Mireille legged it up the stairs two at a time and burst into Hedges's room at the opposite end of the corridor. Her sudden whoop of delight had everybody holding their breath. Two minutes later, she had the car door open. Norah was the one who found Hedges's road map. It was in the boot.

She opened it to the page that contained the map to Worthing. There it was; a pencil guide which led straight to Clifton Road.

All that remained was to find a route which could lead to Linnet. They found the page for Epsom. The roads to the Wells Estate and Dempster were pencilled in as was the address of Charles Bentinck Budd, Worthing's (indeed the country's) only Fascist councillor. It didn't take long to realise that several other notable names were marked on the pages, but which address was Linnet's?

Mireille groaned. 'There are too many. How can we tell which one it is?'

Jim glanced at his watch. 'Bring it with us,' he said. 'We've got to go.'

They set off soon after in the car CI Reece had loaned him by way of an apology for his wrongful suspension. Mireille sat in the front with Jim. He had given her the job of navigator at Norah's suggestion. It would keep her occupied and perhaps make the journey back home less painful. Norah sat with Hedges's map on her lap on the back seat. Ivan dozed.

By the time they reached the outskirts of Horsham, Norah had a splitting headache. She'd gone through every single page but short of following the routes in person, it was still unclear as to whether or not she had a find. She closed the book and leaned her head back on the seat.

She woke up with a start as Jim motored along the Findon Road. She couldn't wait to get home and have a cup of tea. Her head still ached and she was dog-tired. The map book had fallen to the floor. As she bent to pick it up, she grabbed it by the back page. In the middle of a group of smaller maps advertising other books in the series, she saw a list of addresses pencilled in. 'Sunny Vale Mother and Baby Home; The Lilacs, Clifton Road Worthing; Dempster Approved School for Girls; The Wells House, The Wells Estate, Epsom; and The Mouse House School, St Margaret's Hill, Wimborne.

'I think I've found it,' said Norah, at first quietly, then much louder. 'I've found Linnet's address!'

Back home, Norah was hardly through the door before she was on the telephone. 'Operator, give me the telephone number of The Mouse House School, Wimborne, please.'

Mireille and Amélie sat together in their room while Ivan and Mrs Kirkwood sat together in the kitchen. She listened quietly as Jim told her what had happened in London. Afterwards, Mrs Kirkwood made them all a pot of tea and Jim took his and Norah's on a tray into the sitting room.

Alone again, Ivan frowned as she pushed the cup and saucer in front of him. 'Something's bothering you.'

'It's nothing,' she said, getting up from her seat for the sugar.

'Come on,' he said doggedly. 'I should have mentioned it then but I noticed you were out of sorts even before I left for London.'

Mrs Kirkwood got up and closed the kitchen door. 'I've had a letter,' she said, coming back to the table. 'The government don't want my house anymore. Now that the Canadians have come over here, they've requisitioned some much bigger houses in Broadwater.' She sighed. 'I feel awful that Rene had to sleep in a bed in the alcove.'

'She didn't mind.'

'But she's Norah's sister,' Mrs Kirkwood protested. 'She should have had a room to herself. I ought to say something.

362

I should tell Norah about the house but I don't want to leave. I enjoy the company.'

Ivan nodded and reached across the table to grasp her hand. 'I can tell you, gal, I'd be gutted if you wasn't here.'

Mrs Kirkwood chewed her bottom lip. 'Look, I know it's not the done thing for a woman to propose,' she began, 'and I know you would never ask me yourself, but what if we . . . I mean there's no reason why we couldn't . . . just for company, you understand. I'm not asking for any of that other nonsense.'

'Maybe I haven't asked you because I've nothing to offer,' said Ivan.

'But you have,' said Mrs Kirkwood. He grinned and she could feel her face going red. 'I enjoy our outings and I enjoy being with you. You make me feel . . . safe.' She wasn't brave enough to say what was really in her heart.

'Safe, is it?' he teased. 'Is that all?'

She looked away and he took her hand in his. She left it there for a moment or two before snatching it away.

'I suppose if we was wed, we could share the same room,' he said casually. 'Rene could have slept in my room.'

Mrs Kirkwood nodded.

He pretended to ponder the suggestion. 'Just for company, you say?'

She nodded again.

He raised his eyebrows. 'And none of that other nonsense?'

She took a deep breath. 'Well . . .'

The corners of his mouth went down and he hung his head with a sigh. 'A man likes a little comfort . . .'

Mrs Kirkwood seemed embarrassed.

'What if I promise I'd . . .' he began and they both finished the sentence together '. . . put my teeth in.'

She gave him a playful nudge and the sound of their laughter filled the room. Ivan kissed her fingers. As their eyes met, to her absolute delight, he moved forward and kissed her gently on the lips. His lips tasted of tea but Mrs Kirkwood's heart melted. It had been years – almost two decades – since someone had kissed her so tenderly. James gave her the odd perfunctory kiss on the cheek but this was nowhere near the same.

'It won't be the same as it was with me and Ada,' he said quietly. 'Nor, I suppose, how it once was with you and your Cecil. We was all a lot younger then.'

'I know,' she whispered.

'But I thinks an awful lot of you, Christine,' he said, leaning back, 'and I reckon we could have a good few years together.'

She smiled. It wasn't quite what she wanted to hear but he was still offering her companionship and kindness. Love was for the young. She mustn't expect too much.

'There's just one small thing . . .'

She held her breath. Then, to her amazement, she saw Ivan reach into his waistcoat pocket and draw out a small box. 'It may be a leap year,' he said teasingly, 'and you may have jumped the gun, but I likes to do things proper like. So, Christine Kirkwood, would you do me the honour of being my wife?'

He flipped the lid open and there was a pretty diamond-shaped engagement ring with a small ruby in the middle. Mrs Kirkwood blinked in surprise and her mouth fell open.

She gasped. 'You already planned . . .?'

He grinned. 'It didn't quite work out the way I planned,' he confessed with a raise of his eyebrow, 'but now I knows that the lady I love, loves me, too.'

She cuffed him on the sleeve playfully. 'Ivan Steele, you'll be the death of me.'

'Ouch,' he said, covering his arm and pretending to feel pain. 'Oh Lor, she's knocking me about now. What have I let myself in for?'

Mrs Kirkwood held out her left hand and he slipped the ring onto her finger. It was so pretty. She loved it. Ivan kissed her again.

The kitchen door burst open and they sprang apart as Norah came in. Mrs Kirkwood was about to tell her that she and Ivan had decided to marry but it was obvious that she'd been crying.

'What's up, love?' said Ivan.

Mrs Kirkwood pulled out a chair for her to sit down. 'I was so sure,' Norah said tearfully. 'So sure I'd found Linnet. I rang The Mouse House School. Such a lovely name, isn't it?' Her breath was ragged. 'But I've just had to tell those poor girls, she's not there. He's moved her on again and nobody knows where she is.'

CHAPTER 41

The door of his prison cell opened and three men came in.
Jago Ffox-Webster, who was lying on his bed reading a
book, recognised one as Sir Humphry Wilson, an acquaint-
ance from his army days in the First World War. Sir Humphry
was a mere second lieutenant back then, but now his three
stars under a crown told Jago that he was no less than a
brigadier. The other two men were strangers to him.

'Please stand,' said Sir Humphry.

Taking his time, Jago rose to his feet.

One of the other men, the taller of the two, opened a
buff-coloured folder and began to read.

'Jago Aloysius Ffox-Webster, you are charged with the
following: that, contrary to the Treachery Act of 1940, you,
believing another person was engaged in assisting the enemy
– that is, Germany – gave to that person a detailed map of
the defences along the south coast of England. You are also
charged with handing over to German Intelligence details
of the British merchant fleet transports and aiding and abetting the enemy. Furthermore, you are charged with being

part of a conspiracy to launch a Fascist revolution, for which you have been found to be in possession of a large stock of inner pages of British passports and a Foreign Office embossing stamp.'

Sir Humphry nodded to the men as they left the cell and then took off his hat. Tucking it under his arm, he closed the door behind them. 'Well, well, Jago,' he said, peeling off his gloves, 'this is a sorry state of affairs, I must say.'

'Nice to see you too, Humphry,' Jago said sarcastically.

'It's a pity we didn't intern you along with Mosley,' Sir Humphry said. 'You might not be in this mess if we had.'

'I'll take my chances,' said Jago, sitting down again. 'What will happen now? By the way, there's not a word of truth in those allegations.'

'That will be for the court to decide,' said Sir Humphry.

'I'm a popular man,' Jago said smoothly as he looked down at his manicured nails. 'The press will crucify you when this gets out.'

'As these charges have been brought against you for high treason,' Sir Humphry said drily, 'the case will be heard *in camera*. We shall all be in a locked courtroom with the windows covered.'

'Then I'll put my faith in twelve good men and true,' Jago retorted.

Sir Humphrey shook his head. 'No jury, I'm afraid.'

Jago Ffox-Webster's head jerked up. 'What?'

'There will be no press, no reporting and you will be sentenced the same day.'

Jago frowned. 'But that's nothing short of a Star Chamber.'

The brigadier shrugged. 'That's the way it is in times of war, old man,' he said.

'You can't do that!' cried Jago. 'It's a bloody farce.'

'Come, come, old man. I'm quite sure that your cohorts in Germany wouldn't even be bothered to give me a trial should the situation be reversed,' said the brigadier, putting on his hat. 'Pity you were so careless when you went to Worthing to collect your girls. The man who took those papers from you outside The Lilacs was one of ours.'

'Then why didn't you arrest me back then?' Jago retorted.

'What and let Hedges go free?' said the brigadier. 'No, no, old man, we wanted the pair of you. It's a pity but he's avoided British justice. Hedges shot himself.'

Ffox-Webster's face paled. He glared at Wilson's smug expression and wished with all of his heart that he could punch him.

'You won't be seeing your lovely girls for a long, long time,' the brigadier remarked smugly. 'I remember your wife. Such a tragedy when she died. So young. So beautiful, too. Remind me, Jago, how did she die?'

'You know perfectly well that she fell from a hotel balcony,' Ffox-Webster mumbled.

'Hmm,' said the brigadier. 'She was quite a wealthy woman in her own right, wasn't she?' He leaned into Ffox-Webster's face. 'I've always wondered; did she fall, or was she pushed?'

There was a smirk on Ffox-Webster's face as he said, 'You can't prove anything.'

Sir Humphrey's lip curled. 'You bloody sod.'

Ffox-Webster picked up his book and sat back on the bed in a relaxed fashion.

The brigadier could hardly contain his rage. 'I also have to tell you that you shall be tried by Mr Justice Merriman the day after tomorrow,' he continued. He tapped the cell door with his baton and it swung open.

'The day after tomorrow?' Ffox-Webster squeaked.

The brigadier smiled sardonically. 'The day after tomorrow, Jago. See you in court.'

Gradually, Mireille and Amélie came to terms with the fact that they might never see Linnet again, but the long hours they had held each other and cried filled them both with a new resolve.

'I'm not going to forget her,' Amélie said stoutly. 'If the opportunity ever comes to find her, I shall seize it with both hands.'

'So will I,' said Mireille. 'Norah is right. We have to think about other things now. If we don't, it's going to eat us alive.'

'So, what happens now?'

Mireille thought for a moment then said, 'I've talked it over with Rene and I want to join the WAAFs as soon as possible. What about you?'

Amélie said she rather fancied training to be a nurse. 'You may be old enough to apply to the WAAFs but I shall have to wait at least another year. When I'm seventeen I can be taken on as a ward orderly until I'm old enough to apply. In the meantime, I'm quite happy to stay in the Stoke Abbot Road Clinic.'

'And we shall keep in touch,' said Mireille.

'Of course we will,' cried Amélie. 'You're my sister!'

'I should like to ask you and Jim something,' Mireille said cautiously as she walked into the sitting room a couple of nights later.

Everyone was relaxing after their evening meal. Jim was reading his paper, Norah was knitting a cardigan, and Amélie was leafing through a *Picturegoer* magazine someone had left in the waiting room at the clinic. The radio was on and Bud Flanagan and Chesney Allen of the Crazy Gang were singing a silly song, saying, 'Run rabbit, run rabbit, run, run, run'. Mrs Kirkwood tapped the arm of her chair in time to the music while Ivan softly sang the words. 'Is it private?' she asked. 'Would you like Ivan and me to go into the kitchen?'

'No, it's fine,' said Mireille.

Jim pulled down his paper. 'Fire away.'

'I hate my surname,' said Mireille. 'I don't want to be reminded of my step-father for the rest of my life. A friend has told me I could change it by deed poll. I intend to find out about it but what I really want to know is, would you mind if I took your surname?'

Norah and Jim glanced at each other. 'We'd be delighted,' said Jim.

'And honoured,' Norah added.

Mireille smiled, relieved. 'I'd also like to name you both as next of kin when I join the WAAFs.' She hesitated. 'Until I get married, of course.'

Norah's eyes grew wide.

'And have you someone in mind?' said Jim. 'To marry, I mean?'

'Oh no,' said Mireille. 'I was just thinking that I should get everything shipshape before I join up, that's all.'

'That's fine by us,' said Jim. 'You go ahead, love.'

Mireille opened her mouth to continue but after glancing at Mrs Kirkwood, Norah interrupted. 'I think this is the moment when I should tell you girls something else.'

Mrs Kirkwood turned the radio off.

Mireille sat on the pouffe.

'When I sent for Amélie's ration card,' Norah continued, 'I noticed that your surname was different. You are registered as Amélie Osborne,' she said, turning to Amélie. 'I talked it over with Mrs Kirkwood and we were both confused because Mireille's ration card has your step-father's name on it. It's taken me a while to find out whether it was a mistake or not.'

'He adopted us when my mother died,' said Mireille.

Norah chewed her bottom lip. 'I'm not so sure he did,' she said. 'With Miss Bundy's help, I've been in touch with Somerset House but I'm afraid these things take forever these days. They keep telling me to be patient, there's a war on, but the gist of it is, they can't find any records of an adoption. As far as I can see, your names are as they were at your birth; Mireille and Amélie Osborne.'

Amélie was obviously delighted, but Mireille seemed puzzled.

'I haven't mentioned it before,' said Norah, feeling slightly awkward, 'because I didn't want to get your hopes up. I have to wait for one more letter before it's completely settled, but so far it looks as if both of you still have your father's name. We're still looking into whether Ffox-Webster adopted Linnet or not.'

'So how come Mireille has Ffox-Webster on her identity card?' Amélie asked.

'That must be my fault,' said Mireille. 'When I applied for it I just presumed my name was Ffox-Webster.'

'If it turns out that he didn't give you his name,' said Jim, 'there's no need to change your name to ours . . . unless you really want to, of course. You could stick with your father's name.'

As the two girls looked at each other, Mrs Kirkwood

371

thought she saw a glimmer of disappointment on Amélie's face. And why not, she thought to herself. They had probably spent hours going over all the options before they asked if they could take Jim's name.

'You could always adopt them,' she suddenly said. Everyone was stunned into silence. 'Well, why not?' she continued. 'That way they get your name and you're next of kin all rolled into one.'

'Mireille is twenty, Mother,' said Jim.

'In the eyes of the law, both girls are minors until they're twenty-one,' Mrs Kirkwood insisted.

Norah was watching Mireille's face. What was the girl thinking? Her cheeks were flushed. Was that embarrassment? 'I think the girls would prefer to keep their mother's name,' she said.

'Norah . . .' Mireille began apologetically.

'It's fine,' said Norah. 'We understand. All you wanted to do was to sever your connection with that man. Well, you don't have to change anything. You can simply be the person you always were.'

'You won't be upset?' Amélie asked.

Norah's eyes filled with tears. 'Oh my dears . . . of course not.'

'Could we still name you as next of kin?' asked Mireille.

Jim suddenly beamed from ear to ear. 'Well, what do you think, Norah?' he exclaimed. 'I think that would be a capital idea!'

It was smiles and hugs all round.

'You've made us both very happy,' said Norah. 'We could all do with a bit of good news.'

'Then I'd like to share a bit more,' said Mrs Kirkwood. She glanced shyly at Ivan, then held out her left hand. 'Ivan

372

has applied for a special licence and Reverend Puckle had agreed to marry us in two weeks' time.'

The next few days were filled with excitement. Norah was determined to make this wedding something special. People in Clifton Road gave her some of their sugar rations for cakes and she managed to hire the church hall for the first Friday in September. Mrs Kirkwood's two up two down terraced house would be vacated the following week so, for the time being, the happy couple would stay at The Lilacs after the wedding although Ivan would move downstairs into Mrs Kirkwood's room.

It promised to be a joyful occasion. Rene and her Dan came. Her sick leave was almost up so it was easy to stay with Norah before reporting for duty at 1800 hours on Sunday. She was thrilled to hear that Mireille had applied to join the WAAFs and was waiting for her start date.

'You never know,' she said, 'we might meet up somewhere in the near future.'

But of course they both knew Rene probably wouldn't be in the service that long. She and Dan were saving hard to get married.

The wedding day itself was cool but thankfully dry. They all walked to St Matthew's and well-wishers called out their good wishes as they went past. Mrs Kirkwood was wearing a lilac silk dress and matching jacket. Norah had pinned a yellow corsage on her mother-in-law's right lapel and she also had a matching spray on her clutch-bag. Ivan, looking very smart in a dark suit, wore a buttonhole of the same-coloured flowers and Jim was his best man.

Norah wore her best dress; pale yellow with a small white belt, it was the one she wore when she went to find Amélie.

Both the girls looked as pretty as a picture; Amélie in a taffeta dress with a pleated neckline and cap sleeves she had borrowed from one of the nurses in the clinic. A delicate shade of blue, the dress had a drop waistline and a softly pleated skirt. Mireille wore ruby red, her only smart dress, which had a print pattern of white birds in flight. It was slightly fitted with a draped neckline and a narrow, folded collar, and showed off her trim figure.

The wedding breakfast with thirty guests was relaxed and happy and Jim's speech had everyone rocking with laughter. Norah had never seen Mrs Kirkwood – now Mrs Steele – looking so happy. There was no honeymoon. Instead, the happy couple went to the pictures in the early evening and then on to the Richard Cobden pub at the other end of Clifton Road. They didn't buy a drink all evening as the regulars treated them, and to round off a lovely day, they all had a sing-song around the piano.

That same Saturday afternoon, nine hundred German bombers flew over London in the biggest daylight raid the country had ever seen. It lasted for eight long hours and by the time they turned back, a large portion of the East End dockland area was ablaze. The family spent Sunday glued to the radio to hear Alvar Liddell reading the news. Norah had tried to telephone several times but there had been no contact with her parents. She and Rene were frantic with worry. The worst of it was, on the six o'clock news they heard that the Germans were back and once again London was ablaze. Norah was all for going up to London on the train but Jim was against it. It would have been impossible anyway, as all trains were cancelled.

'I have to persuade Mum and Dad to leave London,' Norah said helplessly. 'They've just got to.'

'You're batting a sticky wicket there, love,' said Jim. 'You know your dad won't walk out on his job and your mum won't leave your dad.'

He was right, of course.

As it turned out, Norah's parents came to Worthing at the end of the week. They had been left with no choice. When they'd emerged from their air raid shelter first thing on Monday morning, all the odd numbers on one side of Hugh Street had broken windows and blown-out doors. On the other side of the street, all the even numbers, including number 72, were completely gone. There was nothing left but a pile of rubble.

CHAPTER 42

Norah

Before the newly-weds could go back to what had been Mrs Kirkwood's old house, it had to have a thorough clean. The men who had been billeted there had shown little respect towards what was, after all, somebody's home. A stack of empty beer bottles lay outside the back door, the kitchen sink was full of dirty crockery, and everywhere was covered in dust and grime. Ivan had told them that Christine, as the new Mrs Steele now asked everyone to call her, almost wept, and when Norah saw the state of the place she could understand why. Rene had gone back to work, but Norah's mum, Amélie, and Mireille all joined forces to help clean the place up the following Saturday.

Everybody worked very hard and by the end of the morning it was almost back to normal.

'Christine doesn't seem all that happy to be coming back here,' Elsie remarked as she and Norah happened to meet up in the kitchen. Norah was wiping out the kitchen cupboards and Elsie, who had been washing the hall floor, needed to empty her third bucket of dirty water. The two girls were upstairs doing the bedrooms and Christine herself was in the garden with Ivan sweeping up cigarette ends, stacking beer bottles, and generally tidying everything up.

'I noticed that,' said Norah, standing up to stretch her back. 'She told Amélie she would miss the company at The Lilacs. If I didn't know better, I would think she doesn't want to come back here.'

Elsie sighed and her eyes filled with tears. 'What I wouldn't give for a lovely little place like this.'

'Oh, Mum,' Norah said sympathetically, 'I'm sure you'll find something before long.' Her mother had put on a brave face since she'd arrived in Worthing but Norah knew that inside she was all broken up. And who wouldn't be? Her home and everything that was precious to her – indeed everything she owned – had gone up in smoke along with twelve other houses in her street. Thankfully, friends and neighbours in Clifton Road had rallied round with clothing and other necessities and encouraged her to look forward to a better day. 'Things are just things,' they told her. 'They can be replaced.' It was true, of course, but Elsie shed most of her tears over the things which were irreplaceable, like her photographs.

Elsie shook her head. 'I'm afraid a new house will be a long time coming,' she said. 'The raids don't stop and already they're saying hundreds and hundreds of people are being made homeless. You can't conjure up new homes, can you?'

The front door burst open and Jim called out, 'Get the plates warmed up. Fish and chips all round.'

Everyone had worked up an appetite so fish and chips had never tasted so good. 'There's a big cobweb up there,' Norah remarked as she looked up at the corner of the ceiling.

'Slave-driver,' Jim quipped.

While Elsie made a cup of tea, Christine popped back outside to fetch her long-handled brush to reach it.

'So, you've come back, have you,' they heard a harsh voice saying. Norah stretched her neck to see her mother-in-law's neighbour looking over the fence. Mrs Hill was a sour-faced woman at the best of times. She was dressed in her usual turban and floral cross-over apron. In fact, Norah couldn't remember ever seeing her looking any different, not even when she went to the church bazaar before the war.

Ignoring her, Christine picked up the broom, which had somehow got itself tangled in a bit of spare washing line.

'You know it was the best day of my life when you left and they billeted them soldiers in here,' Mrs Hill hissed.

Shocked to the core, Norah's eyes grew wide. She knew Christine's neighbour wasn't very nice but how dare she say such a cruel thing? She jumped up and started for the door but Jim tugged at her arm to hold her back. Ivan had also stood. Jim put his hand up and said very quietly, 'Hang on, will you, mate.'

Ivan gave him a quizzical look.

'I've often wondered if that old witch was still upsetting Mother,' he whispered, 'but she would never say. Let's wait a minute.'

'What for?' Ivan demanded.

'Evidence,' said Jim.

'I enjoyed having some *real* men living next door to me,' Mrs Hill's shrill voice went on. 'It's better than living next door to the wife of a lily-livered runaway.'

Christine looked up. 'Oh, Mrs Hill,' she said quietly, 'all that was years ago. Cecil paid the price for what he did. He couldn't help it.'

378

'Couldn't help it?' Mrs Hill scoffed. 'Running off like a rabbit and leaving all of his pals to their fate. Couldn't help it, my eye. He was a dirty rotten coward, and you know it.' She spat onto the flower bed. 'Trust you to still be sticking up for him. You're as bad as he was. No wonder everybody steers clear of you. Living next door to the likes of you has been the bane of my life.'

Ivan could bear it no longer. Pushing past Jim he strode through the door and into the garden.

'Don't you dare speak to my wife like that,' he snapped. 'You should be ashamed of yourself, Mrs Hill!'

'Oh, here he comes,' cried Mrs Hill. 'I heard you two had wed. Well, I must say you make a fine pair. The thicko who can't read and the wife of a coward.'

Christine shook her head and tried to pull her husband indoors. 'It's all right, Ivan. Leave it.'

'No, I won't leave it,' Ivan cried angrily. 'What right has she got to talk to you like that?'

'I heard they got rid of you at the school. Why was that, I wonder? Touching the little kiddies, were you?'

Now Jim was in the garden. 'It's a good job I'm not in uniform, Mrs Hill,' he said in a measured tone. 'If I was, I would arrest you here and now for slander.'

Mrs Hill's face paled. 'I'm only saying what everybody else thinks,' she said huffily.

'You've been saying stuff like that ever since I was a lad,' Jim said. 'Only it isn't what everybody else thinks, is it, Mrs Hill? It's what *you* think. Furthermore, as you very well know, there's not a word of truth in any of it.'

Mrs Hill's face was pink. 'She never told you, did she?' she cried, her voice full of sarcasm. 'Your father wasn't a hero. He was shot for cowardice!'

'Sorry to disappoint you, Mrs Hill,' said Jim, putting his arm around his mother's shoulders, 'but we have no secrets. I know what happened to my father and just for your information he had war neurosis. The army is wiser now and so are the police.' He turned and waved his hand at the anxious-looking faces at the kitchen window and in the doorway. 'These people are all witnesses. They've heard your lies, your harassment, and your slander, so let's hear your apology and a promise not to repeat these bare-faced lies.'

Mrs Hill turned to go into her house.

'An apology, Mrs Hill, or I shall come back with my officers.'

'Sorry,' Mrs Hill said grudgingly.

'And if ever you make disparaging remarks like that again,' Jim called after her, 'I shall be down here like a shot.'

As she went into her house, Mrs Hill's back door slammed so hard it rattled her windows.

Ivan put his arm around Christine's shoulder and brought her back into the kitchen. She was visibly upset.

'How long has that been going on, Mother?' said Jim.

'All my life,' Christine said miserably. 'She never stops.'

'But that's awful,' said Amélie, squeezing Christine's hands.

Norah pushed a cup of tea in front of her. 'Here, drink this. It'll do you good. I found a drop of brandy in the cupboard,' she said kindly, adding, 'Listen, you don't have to come back here if you don't want to. You can stay with us. We'll manage.'

Christine looked up and gave her a watery smile. 'Thanks, love, but your mum and dad are here. You'll be wanting the space for your family.'

'Don't worry about us,' said Elsie. 'Pete and me'll be moving on just as soon as we can find a place of our own.'

Christine looked up at her new husband and saw the slight nod of his head. 'You can come here, if you like,' she said. 'Next door won't bother you like she did me.'

'I'd like to see her try,' Elsie said with a snort. She paused as if digesting what Christine was saying. 'Do you really mean it, love? Could me and Pete really live here?'

'I don't see why not,' said Ivan. 'If it's all right with Norah, the missus and me, well, we likes being at The Lilacs. We've made friends round there. We'd miss the company.'

'We'll pay rent, of course,' said Elsie, looking around the kitchen with new eyes.

'Seven and six a week,' said Christine.

'Is that what you pay Norah?'

Christine looked a tad uncomfortable.

'They pay me twelve bob, Mum.'

'Yes, but that's with board and lodging,' Christine protested.

'Ten bob,' said Elsie, waving her hand as Ivan went to protest. 'We'll pay you ten bob for the rent and . . .' Her voice trailed.

'And?' said Christine.

'No offence, mind,' Elsie said cautiously, 'but can we redecorate?'

Christine's face broke into a smile. ''Course you can, love.'

Some weeks later, Norah was washing out some old flower-pots in the garden. She was alone in the house as Christine and Ivan had caught the bus to Brighton to do a little shopping. The weather was turning colder and it wouldn't be long before the nights were drawing in. She planned to make a Christmas cake at the weekend but it wouldn't be the same. Food shortages were beginning to bite although, thankfully, she and the family wouldn't go without the basics.

'We've done very well this year,' she'd told them, 'and we're well placed for winter. Our larder is full and we still have enough root vegetables in the ground to see us through.'

Although they'd given up the Wednesday stall in the market, her mother-in-law hadn't been idle. Already she'd booked a stall in the assembly rooms for the Christmas sale and she was hard at work making woolly toys, jumpers and aprons, which would make ideal presents. Norah planned to make a few things herself but just lately she'd spent a lot of time with Miss Bundy trying to get Mireille and Amélie's identity papers sorted out.

In a fortnight's time, Mireille was coming home on leave from No.2 WAAF Depot in Gloucester, the first part of her training having been completed. Amélie was still at the clinic but she would be starting as a ward orderly at Worthing Hospital in January. The war, which they'd all hoped would be over by Christmas 1939, was still raging. The raids in London, which had driven Norah's mother and father to Worthing, were still ongoing although the Germans had switched from daylight raids to night-time bombing. London wasn't the only place getting a pasting. Other big cities were having their share of bombing; Bristol, Cardiff and Portsmouth, and in the north, industrial cities like Birmingham and Coventry. Obviously, the plan was to break British morale, but to Hitler's frustration, it was having the opposite effect.

Norah heard a car drawing up outside and a second later the doors slammed and the dogs rushed to the gate, barking. She stood up to stretch her back and saw two men walking towards the house. One looked horribly familiar but she couldn't remember his name.

'Mrs Kirkwood?' he said.

'Yes.'

'Detective Inspector Havelock,' he went on. 'You may remember me.'

Norah's blood ran cold. Of course she remembered him. He was the policeman who had interrogated her in London. What on earth was he doing here? Surely he hadn't come to arrest her again? She felt herself stagger and he reached out to grasp her arm to steady her.

'It's all right,' he said gently. 'You're not in trouble. This man is Rupert Bromley from MI5 and we just want to talk to you.'

Norah stared at them blankly.

'Could we perhaps go inside?' asked Bromley.

Norah nodded and led the way. Inside the kitchen she motioned them to the table while she washed her hands in the sink. 'Can I get you some tea?'

Rupert Bromley nodded. 'That would be absolutely splendid,' he said in a plummy voice.

She busied herself and when it was ready, sat at the table with them.

'We've come to close a chapter, if you like,' said Havelock matter-of-factly. 'Jago Ffox-Webster is dead.'

Norah took in her breath. 'Dead?'

'He was executed for high treason at eight o'clock yesterday morning. Hanged.'

Norah's heartbeat quickened. Much as she loathed the man, it came as a shock to hear of his fate. At least he would never hurt little girls again. She stared down at the tablecloth as a wave of relief flooded through her. Havelock was still talking but other thoughts crowded into her mind and for a moment they blotted out the sound of his voice. How was she going to tell the girls? What would their reaction be? And what of Linnet? How on earth were they ever going to find her now? The girls might never know what happened to her. It was heart-breaking.

'Mrs Kirkwood . . . Mrs Kirkwood.'

Norah put her hand to her mouth as she looked up at Havelock.

'Are you all right?'

She nodded.

'We cannot tell you what he did,' said Bromley, 'but suffice to say, his death has averted a plot to endanger this country. We are grateful for your help.'

'I knew nothing of his intent,' Norah said in a flat and exhausted tone.

'Nevertheless,' Bromley insisted. He gave her a thin smile.

'He left a few personal effects,' said Havelock. 'And he wrote you a letter.'

Norah frowned. 'A letter? For me?'

Havelock nodded.

'Not his children?'

Bromley reached into his inside breast pocket and pulled out a padded envelope. 'For security reasons we've had to open it,' he continued, 'and you will find some parts of the letter have been censored.'

Norah took it from him. 'You want me to read it now?'

'No,' he said. 'We'll leave it with you. Read it in your own time.' He drained his cup. 'Thank you for the tea, Mrs Kirkwood. We'll bid you a good afternoon.'

They all stood up. 'You've come all the way from London just to give me this?' said Norah.

'And to thank you,' said Bromley, '. . . personally.'

Norah was slightly bewildered as she shook their hands. 'You do know the man was a monster,' she said bitterly. 'What he did to his children—'

'The man is dead, Mrs Kirkwood,' Havelock said quickly. 'What he did is neither here nor there now.'

Norah was shaking with rage. 'You knew, didn't you?' she spat at him angrily. 'You sacrificed those children. You knew what he was up to and you did nothing about it.'

'Sometimes we have to turn a blind eye for the greater good,' Havelock said pompously.

'Well, I hope you can live with yourself, sir,' Norah retorted. 'And I hope nobody ever thinks it would be all right for *your* children to be molested "for the greater good". Now I'll thank you to get out of my house!'

CHAPTER 43

Norah

The wind was chilly off the sea so Norah wrapped her coat tightly around her body. She wouldn't stay here long. She needed to get back home before anyone missed her and asked questions she didn't want to answer.

She had kept Ffox-Webster's letter for three days without reading it. No one knew of her visit from Havelock and Bromley but she'd have to tell them sooner or later. In her experience, if you didn't grasp the nettle, secrets had a way of slipping out when you least expected them, causing unnecessary havoc. Sitting on a bench opposite Heene Terrace it wasn't very pleasant, and the wind-swept beaches covered in barbed wire and anti-tank blocks all along the shore made it a forbidding place, especially at this time of year.

Norah took the envelope out of her pocket and stared at it. Why would Ffox-Webster write to her? Why not send a letter to the girls? She had a horrible feeling that whatever he wanted to tell her, it wouldn't be pretty. She chewed her bottom lip anxiously. The authorities had opened it and read it; they'd told her that much, so surely if the letter was filled only with vitriol and nastiness, they wouldn't have given it to her in the first place. Would they? There must be something within its pages that was important. With trembling hands she lifted the envelope flap and pulled it out.

Wormwood Scrubs

Dear Mrs Kirkwood

By the time you read this I shall be dead. I have no regrets for what I have done. I sincerely believe that – and here the words were heavily censored with black ink – When I married Natalie Osborne it was for one reason and one reason only. The cause. **More censored words.** *Her money and her position helped the cause but she was expendable. The girls were charming. I enjoyed my time with them very much and I have some delicious memories. You meant well, I can see that now, but I shall not allow you to have my little Lillian. You can rest assured that she is perfectly safe but far out of your reach. I give you no forwarding address. Lillian is an obedient child so she will not be contacting you or her sisters. She has been told they both died in an air raid in London. I think it better if she has a clean break and a completely new start in life.*

The last of the censored words.

Jago Ffox-Webster.

Norah put her hand over her eyes and wept.

With no contact address, there was little hope of Mireille and Amélie ever finding their sister and so their agony went on. How cruel. Of course, she knew it was Ffox-Webster's intention to cause as much heartache and pain as possible.

This was his way of retaining his power over them, even in death. Dear God, what a despicable man.

She put the letter back in the envelope but something prevented it sliding in. She tipped it up to find two rings; a delightful opal and diamond ring and a plain wedding band. She had no way of knowing for sure but Norah guessed they must have once belonged to the girls' mother. Normally these would have been a keepsake; but coming from Jago Ffox-Webster they felt more like a trophy. She could almost imagine him saying, '*She was mine and they shall never have her.*'

It took Norah a few minutes to recover from the shock, but she ultimately decided that she would give the girls the rings. They might not see things the way she did.

It was as she put them back that she found the newspaper cutting.

Parents. Are you worried about the safety of your children? Why not consider sending them to the safety of the British dominions, with guaranteed safe passage to Canada, South Africa, and Australia, and escorts arranged for the voyage. Once there, your child will be placed in a respectable family with impeccable references. With the chance to be educated in the very best schools this is an opportunity not to be missed.

Norah gasped. He'd sent Linnet abroad! But where? Which country? Oh, did it even matter? Canada, South Africa or Australia were all equally out of reach. Her hand was shaking. They'd never get her back while the country was at war. It would cost a fortune and besides, it wouldn't be safe. But when the war was over . . .? She closed her

388

eyes. How was she going to tell Amélie and Mireille? And, more importantly, *what* should she tell them?

Norah glanced down at the cutting again. It was in pristine condition. Neatly cut. Ffox-Webster didn't send this! He would never have been allowed scissors in the death cell. No, that Bromley bloke must have put it in the envelope and by doing so he'd more or less told her that Linnet was safe.

All at once, Norah knew what she was going to do. Slipping the newspaper cutting and the letter into her coat pocket she put the rings back in the envelope. She would give Mireille and Amélie their mother's rings when she told them that Ffox-Webster was dead but she would hide the newspaper cutting until after the war. They would probably be angry with her for not telling them sooner, but why let them carry the burden of wondering which country Linnet was in until they could do something about it? Better that they thought she was somewhere close by for the time being. As for the letter itself, she wouldn't destroy it but if she ever showed them, the girls would be much older and more able to cope with the cruelty of his words.

Was it the right thing to do? Norah wasn't sure, but she wanted more than anything to protect the girls from any more heartache than that which was absolutely necessary. Mireille and Amélie had shed enough tears for the time being.

She stood for a while gazing out across the water. A sea mist was rolling in and the temperature had dropped. It was time to go home.

As she reached the back door, she heard Jim come through the gate and waited for him. She could hear voices in the kitchen and a glance through the window showed Amélie and Christine poring over the application papers for her nursing career. The table was laid for tea but Norah's mother and father were looking at paint charts. These days there wasn't a lot of choice and you'd have to wait ages for it to come into the shops, but they were obviously enjoying the act of making a new start. Ivan sat fondling Max's ear and the smell of cooking wafted through the open window. Sausage gave her a little yip when he noticed her and Norah smiled to herself. How she loved these people. What did the future hold for them all? She had no idea but every moment they had together was precious.

Jim leaned his bike against the wall.

'Is that you, Norah?' Mireille called from inside. 'We're just about to dish up.'

'Coming,' Norah cried, but Jim countermanded her, saying, 'Be in in a minute, love.'

Then, slipping his arm around her waist, he pulled Norah closer and whispered, 'I'm just taking my wife into custody first.'

And his mouth tenderly closed over hers.

Acknowledgements

It's always hard to find superlatives which do justice to the people who have helped me on my way with this book. For the team at Avon I have to express my admiration and heartfelt thanks for all the help and support you've given me. I am eternally grateful for your eagle eyes which pick up my mistakes. My special thanks goes to my editor Cara Chimirri whose skill and enthusiasm is such a joy. I also want to thank my agent Juliet Burton for her tireless encouragement over many years. It's absolutely true to say I couldn't have done it without you! Finally I want to thank you, dear reader, for risking an hour or two of your life to read these pages. I hope you will have enjoyed the story as much as I have enjoyed writing it.

Read on for an exclusive short story by Pam Weaver...

Windfall

'Will you be all right out there on your own, Mum?'

'I'm not setting out for the Himalayas,' Gloria chided good naturedly.

Her daughter Maureen meant well but she wasn't ill. Just old.

It was grand being back in her old garden with some of the family for Maureen's fiftieth birthday. There would be a proper celebration at the weekend but today was the actual day. Gloria would have liked to end her days in this house but it wasn't to be. Although she had lived here for most of her life, Knossington belonged to her granddaughter, Sally, now.

Gloria had come to Knossington in 1944 as a blushing bride, eighteen years old. She and Bob had raised their family and when the children left home and Bob died she'd stayed on, rattling around in the great barn of a place until it became too much. It took some courage to move out two years ago but she'd been luckier than most. She'd found a nice little bungalow and she already had some wonderful friends and neighbours.

The sun filtered through the blossom of the apple tree, making pretty dappled shadows on the grass. But for the first time she knew she wouldn't want to be back here now. All that worry about finding a decent window cleaner who didn't charge the earth and wondering how she would manage to mow the huge lawn with her dodgy hip . . . no thanks. All the same, when Maureen had asked her if she would like to join her and Sally with baby Chloe for tea in the garden, she'd jumped at the chance. Four generations of the Barrington girls in one place at the same time? That had to be quite an achievement.

There was a small sound and Gloria suddenly glanced over her shoulder. What was that? She had the strangest feeling that she wasn't alone but there was no one there. Settling in her chair, she relaxed again.

The outside of the house looked fresher from the new coat of paint. Cornish cream. A warm yet lively and light colour, and Sally's husband had got rid of the old broken fence too. But it was the work they'd done in the garden that impressed her the most. It had become what she'd always hoped it would be. Tulips and narcissi nodded in the patch where the dilapidated shed used to be and there was a new one further down the garden. Sally had planted rose bushes, too. Gloria suddenly got up to wander around and look at the labels. Darcey Bussell; that was a rose with cherry red rosettes and a fruity fragrance. Claire Austin; wasn't that the one with creamy-white blooms and a delicate vanilla perfume? Yes the picture confirmed it. And Wild Edric; that was a scented rose with large blooms. Of course, they weren't out yet but already there were healthy signs of growth. She sighed contentedly. It was very different from the garden Bob had come back to in 1953 after The Korean War, and a world away from the wilderness she'd left behind when Sally moved in.

Sally and her husband were starting on the kitchen next week. Everything would be ripped out and a brand new state-of-the-art kitchen would be left in its place. Things Gloria had never even heard of like fold back doors and kitchen islands.

She felt a movement in the air and glanced around again. There was something about this place today. She wasn't scared but there it was again; a sort of presence . . .

Maureen came out of the house. 'You're not getting cold are you, Mum?'

'I'm as warm as toast, love,' Gloria said with a smile.

Her daughter began wheeling a trolley along the gravel path, the cups rattling furiously. Sally followed close behind, little Chloe looking around with curious eyes, in her arms.

Gloria helped Maureen lift the trolley onto the lawn and went back to her chair. Chloe was placed in the travel cot beside it as Maureen organised the cups and saucers and poured the tea.

Sally handed her grandmother a plate, planting a kiss on her cheek at the same time. 'We thought you'd like tea in the garden the old fashioned way, Gran.'

'Lovely idea,' said Gloria, helping herself to an egg sandwich.

They munched on their sandwiches while Maureen handed round the tea.

'Actually I've got a bit of a surprise for you, Gran,' Sally said. 'I found an old diary and I'm sure it's all about you.'

Gloria was agog. 'All about me? But I've never kept a diary.'

'It seems that someone you know kept a diary all through the war,' Sally went on.

'Lots of people did,' said Maureen. 'Mass Observation they called it.'

'Yes but this person carried on writing until well after the war, Mum,' Sally went on. She held up a rather battered looking book. 'It's dated from September 1942 to July 1961.'

'Where on earth did you find it?'

'Charity shop.'

'I don't understand,' Gloria began again. 'Who on earth would write about me?'

'Come on then,' said Maureen settling into her seat with a tuna sandwich. 'Let's be hearing it.'

Sally opened the battered book. 'I'll read the bit dated August 23rd 1953.'

'That's the day before Bob came back from Korea,' Gloria said with a frown.

'Dear old Dad,' said Maureen. 'How could I ever forget that day?'

Sally cleared her throat. '*She struggled a bit pushing the big pram up the hill.*'

'Does it say who wrote it?' Gloria interrupted.

Sally shook her head. 'Whoever it was used a pen name.'

'Go on, dear,' said Maureen.

'Let me read the bit where I felt sure it was about you Gran,' said Sally beginning again. '*The pram was full of stuff from the allotment. The twins, six-year-old Maureen,*' Sally paused and looked directly at her mother, '*and her sister Susan were walking on either side holding onto the handle. Their mum was holding little Brian's hand and bringing up the rear was eight-year-old James, dragging his feet as usual.'*

'That must have been about a year before poor Susan died,' Maureen murmured quietly.

'*The butcher had saved her some sausages,*' Sally read on. '*It's not right, making favourites of people, even if they have been in another war. Everybody should have the same rationing. I think I should complain about it.*'

'The spiteful old biddy,' Maureen snapped. 'Any idea who it was Mum?'

Gloria shook her head. 'Times were hard,' she said more generously.

'I thought rationing stopped in 1945,' Sally remarked.

'It went on for some time afterwards,' said Gloria. 'In fact I think meat was rationed until 1954.'

'I remember Susan and I made Dad a card each,' said Maureen. 'And James saved all the pocket money Grandad gave him to buy Dad a packet of fags.'

Chloe squealed and almost rolled over. Everyone's attention shifted towards her as they encouraged her to do it again. She enjoyed the attention but remained firmly on her tummy, her little fat arms waving like a swimmer.

Settled back in their chairs once more, Maureen passed around the cake. 'Dad was gone for a long time,' she said, 'but Mum kept his memory alive for us. Do you remember what you used to say to us every night, Mum? "*Kiss your Dad goodnight*".'

Sally frowned, clearly puzzled.

'His picture was in a silver frame in our bedroom,' Maureen explained, 'and we'd kiss it one by one.'

'I wanted to keep his memory alive,' said Gloria.

'James remembered him,' Maureen continued, 'but Susan

and I couldn't really. We were barely three when he left and of course Brian was born after he'd gone.'

Maureen poured more tea, while Sally plastered some butter onto a scone. Gloria had her eyes closed and her head back on the chair.

'Shall I read some more of the diary?' Sally asked eventually.

'Go for it, dear,' Maureen said absentmindedly.

'The girls complained bitterly when the saw their brother running down the road to meet their father. She made them stay by the gate. Mrs Barrington stood in the doorway, wiping her hands on her apron. When James got to the corner, by the post box, he and Mr Barrington shook hands.'

'Why didn't he give him a hug?' Sally cried.

'People didn't do that sort of thing back then,' said Maureen. 'Men didn't show their emotions.'

Gloria smiled, remembering her own greeting. That was hardly the stuff of a romantic Hollywood film either.

'Were things difficult for you, Glor?'

'Not too bad. How about you?'

'Not too bad.'

'You'd better come in, then.'

'James swung the kit bag over his shoulder, almost losing his footing,' Sally read on. *'It was obviously very heavy but Mr Barrington's son was very determined to carry it home for his father.'*

'He hasn't changed much has he,' Gloria said with smile. Her son, once a big strapping rugby player, now had a career as a care-worker and was a very good one by all accounts. 'He always did want to help other people.'

'As they crossed the road,' Sally continued with a

sympathetic smile towards her mother, '*Maureen couldn't contain her excitement any longer. She ran along the pavement to meet her Daddy but Susan walked back indoors.*'

'I tried to encourage her not be scared,' said Gloria, remembering how pretty Susan had looked in that red gingham dress she'd made for her especially for the occasion.

'Susan never was one to show her feelings,' said Maureen flatly. She sighed. 'Even after all this time, I still miss her, Mum.'

Gloria leaned over and squeezed her arm affectionately. 'Me too, love.'

Sally read on. '*I accidentally let the curtain drop but Mrs Barrington saw me.*'

'Olive Barlow!' Gloria gasped. 'It must have been Olive Barlow who wrote that diary.'

'I remember her,' said Maureen. 'She used to bang on the window every time we played outside.'

'What happened to Olive Barlow?' asked Sally.

Gloria shrugged. 'She moved away.'

'Soon after Susan died,' said Maureen coldly.

'Auntie Susan died of polio, didn't she?' said Sally. 'What did she look like?'

'Well she and your mother weren't identical twins,' Gloria said, 'but they did look a bit alike.' She sighed. 'I don't have a picture of Susan.'

'What?' gasped Sally.

'We didn't have a camera in those days,' said Gloria. 'Couldn't afford one.'

'Olive Barlow had a box Brownie,' said Maureen, 'but she wasn't the type of person you could ask, was she, Mum?'

Gloria shook her head and blinked.

Sensing they had brought back a painful memory, Sally closed the book. 'Perhaps I should let you read the rest by yourself, Gran.'

Gloria smiled at her gratefully. It pained her to talk about Susan and she didn't want her sad memories to spoil this lovely afternoon. Sally handed Gloria the diary and the conversation moved on to something else.

'There's an apple on that tree,' said Sally looking up.

'S'funny,' said Maureen. 'It's the wrong time of year for apples and yet it doesn't look as if its been there all winter, does it.'

'I quite fancy an apple,' Gloria mused.

They sat and dozed for a while until Sally's mobile phone rang. She'd left it indoors so she went in to answer it. Maureen got up to go to the loo.

'Keep an eye on Chloe, Mum,' she called.

The sound of her voice woke Chloe, who started, and suddenly swung her arm, not understanding that she was still holding her rattle. She hit herself in the face. The blow startled her more than it hurt but she cried. Gloria leaned over the travel cot to stroke her face and speak to her in a soothing tone. 'There, there, my lovely. Fancy that naughty old rattle hitting you like that . . .'

As she straightened up again to sit back, Gloria thought she saw something red out of the corner of her eye. She turned her head too late to spot what it was but the baby giggled, all smiles. Gloria settled back and closed her eyes remembering...

Even though he'd seen some terrible things in Korea, Bob hadn't lost his gentle ways. He'd loved the presents they'd given him and the children were delighted by his hearty, 'Cor! Look at that!' when he saw the Christmas decorations they'd put up even though it was way past Christmas and already springtime.

As they all ate their first meal together in two years, she and Bob eyed each other across the table while their children chattered. Not Christmas dinner of course, but the fresh new potatoes, spring greens and sausages had never tasted so good. She remembered how her heart had surged with love for him despite the strangeness of it all. When it came to bedtime, although she could see he was exhausted, Bob had insisted on helping her put the children to bed. Back downstairs, he flopped into his old armchair. 'Family life is going to take a bit of getting used to,' he said.

'We've got the rest of our lives, Bob.'

He frowned sadly and shook his head. 'Susan . . .'

Gloria knew what he was thinking. Brian had proudly showed him his Meccano that he'd been working on. Little John and Maureen had played with their father as he'd put them into bed but Susan would have nothing to do with him.

'She's feeling shy, that's all,' Gloria said running her fingers through Bob's hair. Was that grey on his temples? 'Give her time, love.'

A little later, they heard kitchen door creaking open. It was Susan. Bob went to say something but Gloria gave him a hefty dig in the ribs to shut him up. They watched as their little girl walked to her hidey-hole at the back of the big kitchen cupboard. A moment later, they saw her take something out. Gloria felt her eyes smarting as she remembered. It was a little doll made out of scraps of red gingham.

'I made this for you,' Susan blurted out as she held it towards her father.

The garden was suddenly filled was a rustling sound and something heavy fell into her lap. Gloria opened her eyes with a start.

*

She was very tired when she got back to home to the bungalow. As soon as Maureen had gone, Gloria flopped into her chair.

Maureen and Sally had thought she had given leave of her senses when she insisted they all go back into the kitchen.

Sally was amazed when Gloria showed them Susan's secret place. 'We had no idea that little shelf was there!'

And right at the back, they found a small gift, wrapped in newspaper, yellowing with age.

'However long has that been there?' gasped Maureen.

'Susan died in 1956,' said Gloria. 'This was her hidey-hole. I'd forgotten all about it until today.'

'Good job you remembered, Gran,' said Sally. 'The kitchen people have just phoned to say they've had a cancellation. They'll be here first thing tomorrow morning.'

Unwrapping the gift they found a photograph of Susan in a hand-made frame. She was standing in Olive Barlow's garden.

'Good Lord!' Gloria gasped. 'Olive must have taken the picture with her box Brownie.'

'Oh Mum, it's lovely,' cried Maureen. 'I remember that dress she's wearing. Red wasn't it?'

Gloria hesitated, a thought running through her mind. 'Red gingham.'

Maureen smoothed the glass in the frame with her palm. 'You should put it on your dressing table, Mum.'

'It's not for me, Maureen, love,' said Gloria. 'Today is

your special birthday. I think Susan meant for you to have it.'

Of course, there were lots of tears, but Gloria absolutely knew she'd done the right thing.

Besides, she had the apple. Funny that it had fallen into her lap like that. And, come to think of it, she wasn't even sitting directly under the tree.

**Can she be brave enough
to follow her heart?**

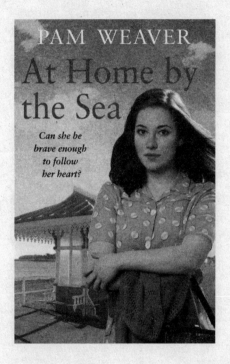

Can a second chance heal their broken family?

Can love find a way to
overcome hate?

A moving, thought-provoking story, perfect for
fans of Katie Flynn and Maureen Lee.

**An unexpected letter will change
her life forever . . .**

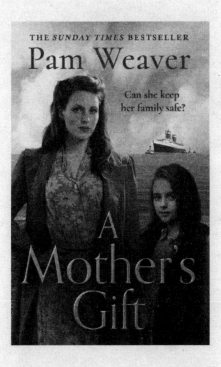

A dramatic story filled with family, scandal and
friendships that bring hope in the darkness.